# Benediction

# Benediction

*The love, honour, and
betrayal of Richard III*

Virginia Cross

Cover art: Heidi G. Yoder
Cover design: Stephanie Barr
Editing, interior design, and production: Deborah Robson
Proofreading: Meg Weglarz
Maps: Stephanie Barr and Deborah Robson
Base maps copyright © FreeVectorMaps.com

First published in the United States of America in 2017 by the Virginia Cross
Estate, Fort Collins, Colorado.
ISBN 978-0-9985810-0-2 (U.S. paperback)
ISBN 978-0-9985810-1-9 (ePub)
ISBN 978-0-9985810-2-6 (Kindle)

This edition first published in the United Kingdom in 2017 by The Choir
Press, 132 Bristol Road, Gloucester, England, GL1 5SR.
ISBN 978-1-911589-06-8

Website: VirginiaCross.net

## Colophon

The text is set in LTC Italian Oldstyle, based on the work of fifteenth-century
type designer Nicolas Jenson (Frederic Goudy, Lanston Type Company/P22).
Additional type includes Luminari (Philip Bouwsma, Canada Type) and
Bowen (Andrew Ashton).

# Overview

# Places

- Edinburgh ◇
- **Scotland**
- ◇ Berwick-upon-Tweed
- Dryhope ◇ Roxburgh ◇
- Liddesdale ◇
- ◇ Alnwick
- Dumfries ◇
- Durham ◇
- Barnard Castle ✠
- ✠ Middleham
- † Jervaulx Abbey
- *Yorkshire* ◇ Sheriff Hutton
- Towton ◇ ✠ **York**
- Wakefield ◇◇ Pontefract Castle ◇
- Bolton ◇
- Sandal Castle ◇ ◇ Doncaster
- **England**
- Nottingham Castle ✠
- Market Bosworth ◇ ◇ Leicester
- Ludlow ◇ Coventry ◇ ✠ Fotheringhay Castle
- Cambridge ◇
- Tewkesbury ◇ *Oxfordshire* Stony Stratford
- **Wales**
- Gloucester ◇
- Minster Lovell ◇ Barnet ◇
- Milford Haven ◇
- Sodbury Hill ◇ **London** ◇✠ Epping Forest ◇
- Calais ◇
- Bruges ◇
- Beaulieu Abbey †
- **Burgundy**
- Weymouth ◇
- ◇ Agincourt
- ◇ Crécy
- Picquigny ◇ ◇ Amiens ◇ Péronne
- **France**

6

# *Notes*

*Historical context* by Virginia Cross

*Benediction* is the story of Richard Plantagenet, later Richard III, king of England. Richard reigned in the last few years of the Wars of the Roses, the hundred-year internecine struggle for the crown that periodically threw England into chaos and bloodshed.

In principle, England's rule of succession was simple. The kingship passed from eldest son to eldest son, and the system was seen as part of the cosmic order: anointed kings ruled by divine appointment. As with marriages, however, unions between kings and kingdoms may be made in heaven, but they are lived out on earth. In addition to the God-given right to rule, a king needed adequate chronological and mental maturity, the backing of powerful lords, and a quality of leadership. If any one of these was lacking, any number of other potential kings could step forward with a reasonable hope of pressing their claims to the throne.

The seeds of conflict that came to fruition in Richard's life were sown five generations earlier in the reign of his great-great-grandfather, King Edward III. Edward had five sons, the eldest of whom, called the Black Prince, predeceased his father. The prince's heir was his nine-year-old son, who assumed the crown at the age of ten as Richard II. Richard's minority rule was corrupted by the greed of his advisors, but even as an adult he did not have the temperament to rule. He was deposed by a cousin, Henry IV, also a grandson of Edward III, and died childless in prison. The specific cause of death is unknown, but he almost certainly was either murdered or starved to death: deposed kings could not expect long lives.

Henry IV was a competent if unpopular king. He sired one son, also named Henry, who promised to be the charismatic leader for whom the kingdom had been waiting. Henry V, known in his lifetime as Harry of Monmouth, for his place of birth, won a great upset victory over the French at Agincourt, regaining land that England had long claimed as her own. Henry subsequently styled himself King of England and of France and married a French princess, Catherine of Valois.

Against all expectations, the virile warrior Henry V died young while campaigning in France. The son he left to inherit the throne was only nine months old. In addition to a long minority, the unfortunate Henry VI suffered another, more severe disadvantage: the Valois family had a history of madness, which appeared in the adult Henry in the form of melancholia and confusion.

Henry VI married Margaret of Anjou (a French province) in yet another attempt to bind England and France with domestic chains, but it was a marriage of milk and vinegar: the mild, bewildered king was no match for his headstrong wife. Margaret created bitter factions at court with her favoritism and hot temper. She bore one son, Edward of Lancaster, but it was widely rumored that the father was, instead of the king, Margaret's pet nobleman, the Duke of Somerset. As Henry's sanity waned, Margaret's resolve to see her son on the throne hardened. The great nobles of England split between those who wished to see Lancaster reach the throne unimpeded and those who believed the time had come to rid England of Margaret's influence. The field thus was opened for all the male descendants of the sons of Edward III to make their claim to the throne.

Meanwhile, another drama was unfolding offstage, so to speak. After the death of her husband Henry V, Catherine of Valois secretly married a servant of the late king, the Welshman Owen Tudor, by whom she bore a son, Edmund. Catherine died young, and Tudor was eventually executed for the liaison, but their descendants would prove to be important to a degree no one would have believed possible at the time.

The field was now open for all the heirs of the other four sons of Edward III, and there were many. *Benediction* begins in the reign of Henry VI, in perhaps the greatest flowering of contenders for the throne, about halfway through the fifty-year span of the internecine struggle now know as the Wars of the Roses.

In the fifteenth century, France and England were the great powers of the Western world. War was almost always a threat between them, primarily because England persisted in claiming parts of France. (The land that Henry V had recovered at the Battle of Agincourt reverted to France during the reign of Henry VI.) As a result of this rivalry, smaller principalities such as Scotland and Burgundy were often treated as pawns in the power struggle between the two greater nations. By the late 1400s, England was thoroughly weary of the constant threat of war, of child-kings, and of the disrupted society that disputed successions brought about. This was the world into which Richard III, the last Plantagenet King of England, was born.

## *From the author* by Virginia Cross

I have made some minor logistical departures from history in order to simplify an extremely complex tale. First is the matter of names. It seems that nearly every male of the period was named Richard, Edward, or Henry, while the women were Anne, Elizabeth, or Margaret. I have tried to separate the Edwards by consistently substituting a diminutive, like Ned, or a man's title, such as Lancaster, for the given name. I renamed two Annes, calling the mother of Anne Neville *Alice* and Francis Lovell's wife *Anna*. I collapsed two characters, Thomas and William Stanley, into one, here called Thomas.

Most of the characters are named in historical records. History has often left little or ambiguous evidence of their personalities, however, and I have freely invented those when evidence is sparse or conflicting. Likewise, while I have tried to be faithful to recorded events such as battles and terms of office, domestic events and conversations are imagined.

*From the editor* by Deborah Robson

It has been an honor to prepare *Benediction* for a readership wider
than my friend's family and a small group of fellow writers. When
Ginny died in August 2013, we knew this book should not remain
hidden in computer files and boxes of printout.

My task has been to bring it to the current form while intuiting
Ginny's intent in several ways, a responsibility made easier by having
known and talked with her about the book's progress for, literally,
decades, and more challenging by the depth and intensity of her work:
I didn't want to "break" anything! Her writing for this project was
strong twenty-plus years ago, when I first encountered it, and has
become even stronger since. *Benediction* should have seen publication
and acclaim while she was alive, but she was always convinced it
could be better.

I've changed as little as possible editorially, while doing my best to
recognize what Ginny and the staff at a publishing house would have
done if they had worked together while turning her refined manuscript into a finished book. In the final manuscript files, it was not
clear where Book 3 began or what its title was; digging through drafts
and notes, I located both its location and its name. I added six words
to chapter 4: "the fairest sight he could imagine," which links to other
images in the manuscript and makes sense of the chapter title. After
I did this, I found an indication in one of Ginny's older drafts that
this aligned with her intention. So grateful that she left clues! Beyond
that, I endeavored to be sure that the names of castles, towns, and
people match currently accepted historical forms (although contem-
poraneous spelling was not standardized) and adjusted dates where
typographical errors had crept in over the long years of development
or where they were missing. I consulted multiple sources, and became acutely aware that for crucial events the historical record is not
clear: one example concerns the month and location of the marriage
of Richard and Anne, and another the year of their son's birth, either
1473 or 1476. Where I discovered doubt, I followed Ginny's lead; the
number of books she consulted on the period would have satisfied any
specialist.

There is one sentence that the editor in me wanted to change
slightly but the fiction writer in me could not. It's in a dream sequence within chapter 17, "Unwritten Letters, Unspoken Words," and
it reads: "The rider guided the horse down the slope, on a narrow

path through frieze and bracken. . . ." I've been unable to discover an appropriate plant by the name of *frieze* (an architectural term, for the most part), but removing the word would have affected the sentence structure, sound, and texture of the prose, which above all else I did not want to do. I remain open to suggestions from British medievalists or naturalists for a word with similar sounds and pacing.

*Benediction:* It is my pleasure to bring this work into a form where others can read it. Thanks, Ginny. *Benediction* is worth everything you invested in it.

# Principal characters

## Kings of England and their families

Henry VI, reigned 1422–1461 and 1470–1471 (1421–1471)
Margaret of Anjou, *his wife* (1430–1482)
Edward, Duke of Lancaster, *their son* (1453–1471)

Edward IV, reigned 1461–1470 and 1471–1483 (1442–1483)
Elizabeth Woodville, *his wife* (c. 1437–1492)
Elizabeth, *their daughter (called here "Bess")* (1466–1503)
Edward, *their son (called here "young Edward")* (c. 1471–1483)
Richard, *their son (called here "Dickon")* (c. 1473–1483)
Other daughters

Edward V, reigned April–June, 1483

Richard III, reigned 1483–1485 (1452–1485)
Anne Neville, *his wife* (1456–1485)
Edward, *their son (called here "Ned")* (c. 1473–1484)
Katherine, *Richard's illegitimate daughter*
John of Gloucester, *Richard's illegitimate son*

## Plantagenets

Richard, Duke of York (1411–1460)
Cecily Neville, *his wife* (1415–1495)
        *a total of thirteen children including:*
Edward, Earl of March, *their son, later King Edward IV* (1442–1483)
Edmund, Earl of Rutland, *their son* (1443–1460)
Elizabeth, *their daughter* (1444–1503)
Margaret, later Duchess of Burgundy, *their daughter*
        *(called here "Meg")* (1446–1503)
George, Duke of Clarence, *their son* (1449–1478)
Richard, Duke of Gloucester, *their son,*
        *later King Richard III* (1452–1485)

## Nevilles

Richard Neville, Earl of Warwick (1428–1471)
Anne Neville, his wife (*called here "Alice"*) (1426–1492)
Isabel, *their daughter, wife of George, Duke of Clarence* (1451–1478)
Anne, *their daughter, wife of Richard III* (1456–1485)

John Neville, Lord Montagu, *Warwick's brother*
  (*called here "Jack"*)

## Other principal characters

William Hobbes, *court physician*
Thomas Stanley, *noble*
Margaret Beaufort, *wife of Thomas Stanley*
Henry Tudor, *son of Margaret Beaufort* (*later King Henry VII*)
Francis Lovell, *noble*
John Howard, Duke of Norfolk, *noble*
James Tyrrell, *knight*
Robert Percy, *knight* (*called here "Rob," cousin to Henry Percy*)
Henry Percy, Earl of Northumberland, *noble*
  (*cousin to Robert Percy*)
William Hastings, *friend and Lord Chamberlain to Edward IV*
  (*called here "Will"*)
Anthony Woodville, *brother to Elizabeth Woodville*
  (*wife of Edward IV*)
Philip, Duke of Burgundy, r. 1419–1467
Charles, Duke of Burgundy, r. 1465–1477
  (*overlap with his father, Philip*)

## Fictitious characters

Roger, *squire*
Agnes, *nursemaid*
Jeremy, *squire*
Brother Simon, *Cistercian monk*
John Parr, *squire*
Bennett, *tutor*

# Family relationships

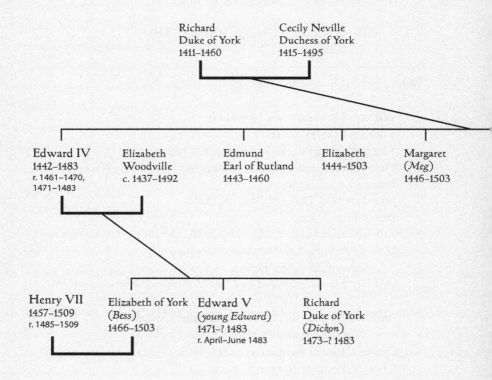

Richard
Duke of York
1411–1460

Cecily Neville
Duchess of York
1415–1495

Edward IV
1442–1483
r. 1461–1470,
1471–1483

Elizabeth
Woodville
c. 1437–1492

Edmund
Earl of Rutland
1443–1460

Elizabeth
1444–1503

Margaret
(*Meg*)
1446–1503

Henry VII
1457–1509
r. 1485–1509

Elizabeth of York
(*Bess*)
1466–1503

Edward V
(*young Edward*)
1471–? 1483
r. April–June 1483

Richard
Duke of York
(*Dickon*)
1473–? 1483

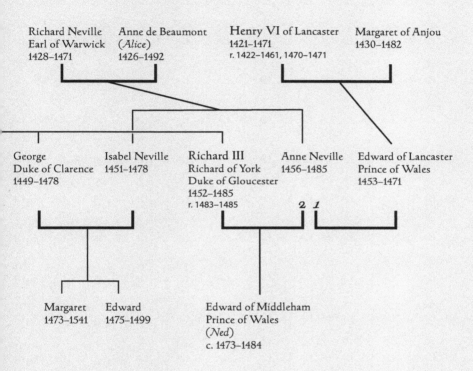

Richard Neville
Earl of Warwick
1428–1471

Anne de Beaumont
(*Alice*)
1426–1492

Henry VI of Lancaster
1421–1471
r. 1422–1461, 1470–1471

Margaret of Anjou
1430–1482

George
Duke of Clarence
1449–1478

Isabel Neville
1451–1478

Richard III
Richard of York
Duke of Gloucester
1452–1485
r. 1483–1485

Anne Neville
1456–1485

Edward of Lancaster
Prince of Wales
1453–1471

*2 1*

Margaret
1473–1541

Edward
1475–1499

Edward of Middleham
Prince of Wales
(*Ned*)
c. 1473–1484

# Benediction

Benediction

# Benediction

# Prologue

Journal of Thomas Hobbes, Court Physician
August 22, 1485.

*Richard is dead.* The defeat of the King's army reached Westminster this evening in somewhat reliable form after a day and a half of conflicting and nearly incoherent rumors. I must face the fact that I may well be dismissed from service. Even those of us with few ambitions had loyalties Tudor might find offensive. I loved Richard: might I not therefore use my knowledge of herbs and potions to poison his successor? Idiocy. But an irregular succession brings men circling for power like kites after carrion, and I suppose the new king may be forgiven if he fears any man who served Richard loyally and well.

But for the moment I may stay where I will, and I choose to sit in the king's chamber, writing at the king's table as dusk falls in our great city. Through the wide windows overlooking the palace gardens, I can see across the Thames all the way to the spires of St. Paul's. In early summer, roses filled the room with their heavy fragrance and an occasional wandering bee. This late in the season, only a few late-blooming herbs grace the garden, and their scent is too faint to reach the window.

On so fair an evening, one usually would see people of the court strolling about—ladies in gowns of red and gold scattered like flowers on the green lawns, and lords walking in pairs, talking about the price of wool or the tedious journey to their country estates. But tonight the palace grounds are empty. People are in the taverns mourning or celebrating, or quiet in their homes, sitting on their opinions and hatching plots.

Beyond the garden walls, the Thames flows wide and green in the fading light, its surface broken by ponderous barges and the needle-like masts of sailing ships. In the distance, the roofs of London stack up toward the sky—heavy timbers of great houses and guilds, thatch of cottages, and the graceful stone spires of cathedrals. Edward, God bless his merchant's soul, loved the sight of London spilled at his fingertips, all her glories displayed *like the bounty of a great estate. To Richard, northern in his heart, London was a whore with a jeweled throat and honeyed voice, skirts sodden with mire, breeding ambition like Scotland breeds thieves.*

*Now Richard is gone, like his brother Edward before him, and poor mad Henry before both. A new Henry will take the crown. An unknown Welshman, king of England! Like the virgin birth, the impossible is made manifest.*

*From Henry to Henry has a certain symmetry, a closing of the circle. A comfort, I suppose, for those who find meaning in such things. I do not. I see only sadness and waste, so many good men dead before their time.*

*I will make myself a riddle. Why do men die? No, that is only a question. I will make a true riddle. What is as invisible as the wind, as soothing as tincture of tansy, and brings more men to their graves than the Black Death?*

*My answer has nothing to do with humors, fluxes, miasms, or any of the ailments I am trained to treat. Men, particularly kings, die of forgetfulness. Henry died of his poor dim wits, Edward of too much wine, rich food, and fornicating, and Richard in battle. All three let themselves believe that obtaining power means keeping it. Conquer France, she stays conquered; subdue Scotland, she remains cowed; court a Stanley, he honors his word.*

*Why must men throw away their lives because they cannot pay attention? Even I, a physician, know that holding power is like battle, constant vigilance. Most kings are soldiers first. They should know that better than anyone, but put a crown on their heads instead of a helmet and they forget it all.*

*The ringing of the bells has ended now. Their awful din ceased moments ago, and the silence is unearthly. It is as if time itself has stopped, history hanging suspended like the summer sun in a noon-day sky. And like the sun, history would scorch and shrivel us if it didn't move. But events pass; their shapes shift and become familiar. Before that happens, before we become accustomed to the losses of the past few years and turn them into food for singers, I want to see some pattern in what happened, some ordinary image the whole of which will be comprehensible once the pieces are turned the right way, like bits of a mosaic.*

*I came to this chamber because of the traces of the men who ruled here, objects I hold up to my memory like shards of glass to the light. The jewel-toned carpet beneath my feet is worn in furrows where Richard moved his chair to follow the path of the sun. Edward's tall-backed chair stands against the wall as though waiting for its owner to enter the chamber. The long oak table on which I write holds stacks of paper, some signed in Richard's bold vertical script, candlesticks and candles ready for work far* into the night. He read all those petitions himself, every word and comma, intent upon solving the often conflicting claims of justice and legality. Edward's practice was simpler: he decided what he wanted done and asked his lawyers how to make it legal.

I recall a night perhaps ten years ago, when Edward was king. I had taken a late supper with him, Will Hastings, and Richard, down from the north. Richard's voice was resonant, a fine deep timbre, but unemphatic. He would not use his passions to sway others, as he wanted the justice of his words to stand without persuasion. Hastings was the other side of the coin. He needed the attention of other men, had to impose on them the force of his being, even when his words were hollow. And there was Edward, growing heavy in the girth and jowls, his famous beauty already rotting.

Edward's younger son, as hale and golden as his father once had been, came into the room. Little Dickon at first sat quietly by the hearth, then, growing bold, climbed onto his father's lap. As careless a father as he was a king, Edward brushed his son off with a broad, bejeweled hand. Dickon tried a few more times, as undeterred as a puppy, then finally stopped and looked about, as if trying to gauge the most promising wall to next besiege.

Richard beckoned the little boy over to him and pulled him up on his knee, his hand on the child's shoulder while he argued with Hastings. There was such affection in the gesture that I thought: there is no fairness in the distribution of children in this world. Edward treated the very young as most men do, as creatures of little rank and therefore little importance. Richard extended to them a grave courtesy, as though they were couriers from another realm.

Now I have come to that which haunted me throughout Richard's reign, doubts I buried a hundred times beneath my regard for him, which I now exhume with all their foul odors. Does such a man become a child-killer? Did he murder his nephews?

I shouldn't think a man could change so much. But the fact remains: Edward's sons have not been seen in over two years. If Richard was not the agent of their disappearance, who was?

I could never put that question before him. I told myself that if he were innocent, I could not inflict upon him the wound of my suspicion. The truth is otherwise: if he were guilty, I couldn't bear to know. Indeed, I believe he tried once to tell me what he knew of his nephews' fate, and I would not listen. I told him he must seek another time to talk, as I had patients to attend. May God forgive me. That time never came.

# Book One
# King's Cradle

1485; 1452–1467

# 1 *The Great Knight*

arket Bosworth was a peaceful village, deep in the midlands of
England. The land rolled easily from low hill to low hill, green
slopes scattered with yellow cinquefoil, tiny deep blue milkwort, and
the brilliantly colored Joseph-and-Mary. In daylight, flocks of sheep
roamed the hills, the hollow thunk of their bells the animals' audible shadow. But on this evening, August 21 of 1485, the sheep were
penned for the night, and the meadow flowers trampled under the feet
of a great host of men.

The men were divided, not altogether evenly, into three separate
armies: King Richard's forces nearest the town, the invader Henry
Tudor's troops along the moor, and a third force commanded by
Thomas Lord Stanley, roughly equidistant from the others.

None of these commanders was as easy in his mind as he would
have wished, even granting that peace of mind is never plentiful on a
battle's eve. Henry Tudor had lived his life in exile, had never led an
army or fought a battle. But it was in the nature of the peculiar, quar-
relsome English that he should have been courted, persuaded back to
this land that had cast him out.

That amused him. Henry, like half the nobles in England, claimed
royal lineage. His mother was descended from a bastard line of John of
Gaunt, middle son of King Edward III. And Henry's father, Edmund,
dead these thirty years, had been the son of Catherine of Valois and
Owen Tudor, groomsman of Catherine's dead husband, the ever-glori-
ous Henry V. That made Edmund Tudor half-French, half-Welsh, and
the bastard son of a groomsman. Now England was so desperate for a
successor as to seek out Edmund's son, penniless exile and twice-over
fruit of bastards, begging him to reunite the country.

Such were the vagaries of fortune.

There was little else amusing about his situation; if he were not crowned tomorrow, he would be killed. One way or another.

Henry knelt before his chaplain, his joints already stiff and aching. Sweat crept under the high collar of his tunic and ran in rivulets down his spine. The Host was in his mouth and the chaplain's calm voice in his ears. A facile calm, Henry thought irritably. The good man of God was not going into battle tomorrow.

*T*homas Lord Stanley stood under the folded-back flap of his tent. A small fastidious man who had made a career out of changing loyalties, he was Henry Tudor's stepfather and King Richard's pledged retainer.

In times of conflict, opportunities ripe and sweet as Spanish oranges awaited a clever man, and Stanley intended to fight for the victor. But therein lay the problem: this victory was not easy to predict.

Prediction should have been simple. The king had won battles while still a youth, whereas Henry Tudor was a pig-in-a-poke, bought blind. Yesterday Tudor had gotten himself lost. His army, mostly mercenaries, had all but deserted. The fool found the way back to his camp by evening, and order resumed.

But Richard was a tired man, worn with grief and his intense dislike of the intrigues and dissent that had plagued his short reign. Stanley smoothed his beard, pointed and neatly trimmed, and smiled. The man who had no stomach for the machinations of power had not the nature for ruling, and earned no pity from him for thinking matters should be otherwise.

Still, Richard's troubles were not the issue. Stanley's hand moved from his beard to his harnessed sword, and his smile dissolved as he tried not to think of what might happen to him, should he miscall the outcome and yet manage to survive.

*K*ing Richard sat at his narrow camp table in his tent, the map he had drawn spread before him. Cannon boomed in the distance, and he glanced in the direction of the noise as if he could see through canvas.

Poor Market Bosworth. The little town rarely saw more excitement than its Wednesday market. Tonight was Sunday. Monday would see the battle, and Richard doubted that any of the nearby villagers would have their minds on corn and eggs two days later. There would be men to bury, the wounded to tend, livestock to recover— and pillaging. Battlefields yielded coins, jewels, and the odd memento.

A brief walk could bring a careful searcher several times the cost of a stray sheep or two.

Richard turned his attention back to the map. Henry Tudor should never have been allowed to penetrate so deeply into the heart of the country.

An $X$ for Tudor the Welshman.

Thomas Lord Stanley had refused to commit to Richard. He had refused to commit to anyone. No doubt he hoped that both commanders would notice only that he had not committed to the other.

An $X$ for the uncertain Lord Stanley.

The equally uncertain Henry Percy, Earl of Northumberland, was just now riding in. With or without the men of York.

No mark for him—yet.

Richard tossed the lump of charcoal back into its pewter box. His head pounded. Through the open tent flap he could hear the pawing of horses' hooves and their impatient neighing. Hammers clanked on steel, and a sea of voices rose and fell. For an instant, the hammers and cannon hushed, and the plaintive voice of a flute wove its way through the voices. A lament, mournful and slow. On his walk through the camp earlier in the evening, he'd heard none of the rowdy laughter and bawdy stories that he remembered from the times before other battles.

He wouldn't sleep tonight. To sleep was to muster the dead: Will Hastings, Harry Buckingham, Anthony Rivers. Young Edward and Dickon—perhaps the saddest of all the sad, useless deaths. They were only boys, but they were the fulcrum of power, and it had to be broken.

Neither would he pray. He had not asked God's permission for his actions; he had no right to ask forgiveness for them. But he wanted to know: Was there anything he could have done to keep them all alive? Shouldn't a man know the extent of his sins before he was called to account for them?

He was sick to death of lies. All the tangled strands of half-truths—more half-truths than the shrines of England had saints' fingers. Most of all, he was sick of his own.

# 2   The Paper Crown

*Ludlow, England*
*October 1459.*

All that summer, a stream of messengers rode in and out of Ludlow. Good news meant musicians and mummers after supper and the children going late to bed. Ill news meant the seclusion of the duke and his companions behind closed doors and Richard's mother falling oddly silent. One autumn day, he came upon his father and mother standing in the niche of a window. His mother raised a hand to her cheek, and Richard thought she was wiping away tears. She said a few words to his father in a quiet, strained voice. Then his father tried to put his arm around her, but she stood stiffly, and after a moment his father turned and walked away, one hand clenching and unclenching at his side.

A few days later, Richard lay warm in his bed, listening to the sounds from the bailey—horses' hooves clopping on cobbles, grooms calling. A dog barked and a chorus of yelping voices answered. Probably a hunting party preparing to depart. Only the faintest streak of light shone through the chinks in the shutters, and no one had come to rouse him and George and see that they were dressed and groomed for breakfast.

Then he heard other sounds. Squeaking wheels of wagons, men shouting, gates opening to the clatter of more horses and impatient neighing. From inside the castle came a sudden burst of doors opened and closed, boots striding in the hallways and out again. Richard looked to see if George was awake and found his brother's startled eyes meeting his own. They ran to the window and opened the shutters to see the courtyard below filling with men and horses. At last Richard saw his father and brothers among the press of men, Warwick and Jack close behind. He shouted out to Edward, but his voice was drowned in the clamor below.

Then he remembered he had a new skill, one a stable boy, older and clever with animals, had taught him. He leaned his head out the window, put two fingers carefully spaced in his mouth, and blew.

Ahhh. Even better than he had hoped. Not one of the thin wheezing whistles he sometimes produced, but an ear-splitting blast the groom himself would envy. Edward stopped and turned, finally saw his brothers in the window and raised both hands in an exuberant salute before running to catch the others.

Richard was still trying to keep sight of his father and brothers in the clot of riders and wagons passing through the gate, when he heard someone enter the room.

His mother. Oh no. Good cheer, Mother. Whistling is not so rude a thing as that!

She didn't like him playing with stable boys; she certainly wouldn't be pleased that he practiced their uncouth habits. Then he realized that sound carried far better through an open window than through stone and oak. Whatever was wrong, it was nothing he had done.

"We are riding into the village," Cecily said. "Dress warmly." She smiled, the same false smile he remembered from when he was really little, and sick.

On the ride to the village, he could see smoke rising in the air. There was always smoke rising in the air but this was heavier and blacker. He rode close to his mother's side. "Mother?" All is well, she would say, and then he wouldn't have to be afraid.

But she didn't say all would be well. "Hush," she said. "We must hurry."

When they reached Ludlow's market cross they dismounted and tied their horses to posts. Richard had been in the village dozens of times the past summer. He knew where the baker's stall was, the butcher's, and the weaver's house. He knew where on market day people brought their baskets of wool, their eggs and chickens. The baker's wife had teased him and told him how fast he would grow if he ate her bread. The yeast would make him tall and fill him out, just as it swelled the bread. He had eaten half a loaf that day, and it gave him a stomachache that lasted through the night.

But this was not the village he knew. All through the streets men spurred their horses, riding almost on top of each other, breaking down doors, upending wagons, slashing open sacks of flour and grain. His teeth clattered like marbles in a bowl. His pony, a gentle little sorrel mare, skittered as if the fires of Hell were under her feet. "Ho there! Be still!" A servant yanked on her bridle. The mare braced herself, pulling back so hard Richard thought her reins must snap, her hide trembling from neck to flank. He wanted to go to her, pet her, and talk to her the way she should be spoken to. He wouldn't, though. He could see the chickens and dogs dead in the street, their blood mingling with wine from broken casks, flowing around the cobbles and soaking the edges of spilled heaps of grain. The smell of smoke was so strong it stung his nostrils.

A pig ran past, squealing. Two soldiers chased after it, threw their arms around its fat smooth body. Finding no purchase, they fell face down in the dirt, laughing. The animal fled down the street, where other men yelled and swore and waved it back. Again and again they waved the animal from one end of the marketplace to the other, until it stood, spent, sides heaving, and snorting for breath.

An archer loosed an arrow. Thunk. The arrow hitting flesh. Sickening sound. Richard had never heard that before. The pig fell, shrieking and bleeding, rose again and stumbled, the arrow quivering in its rump. A second man's arrow took the pig in the chest and killed it. A half-grown dog began to bark. One of the soldiers called, and it trotted over to him. The soldier's sword moved, and for a moment there was a red line on the dog's belly. Then the line opened, and there on the ground were purple-black coils, like snakes. The dog was full of snakes. It whimpered a moment, then let out an agonized whine, twitched, and lay still.

Richard tugged at his mother's skirt. It's time to go, now. Mother, it's time to go! He thought he said the words aloud, but if he did, she didn't hear him. She kept scanning the men in the marketplace as if looking for someone she knew. Finally he realized that she was afraid too. She was looking for someone to fix things, to make the evil go away.

Up the street, rioters ran between houses, hurling torches through windows and open doors, and the smoke in the air grew darker. Sometimes, above the roar and crackle of the fire, hoarse shouting voices and screams rang out. Richard's fingers weren't like ice any more, oh no, but his teeth had started to clatter again. A man on horseback was dragging a girl by the wrists away from one of the burning houses. He stopped when he reached the cross, dismounted, pushed the girl to the ground and dropped to his knees over her. Keeping her wrists in one hand, the man reached with the other for the knife in his belt. No.

No, please don't kill her. Richard huddled into his cloak, wanting to melt down into the ground.

A knight trotted up to his mother. As the man reined in, she grabbed his saddle. "Who is your captain? I must speak to him."

"Lady, for God's sake. . . ."

"I am the Duchess of York, and this town is undefended."

"Take your children and your servants out of here! There is nothing you can do." He had started to pull away when a man came up behind Cecily and grabbed the hood of her cloak. The hood came off in his hands, and the coil of her hair fell loose. The knight wheeled his horse, shouting over his shoulder, "Let her go, you fool! She's the Duchess of York! Leave her alone."

The man laughed and jerked Cecily's hair, dragging her backward. The young knight kicked his foot, stirrup and all, into the face of the man, and the man fell backward, howling, his hands covering his face as blood poured through his fingers.

The knight jumped down from his saddle and touched Cecily's arm. He was shaking so much his hand danced on her sleeve. "Lady. . . ."

"It is well. I am unhurt."

"Duchess, what do you here? This is madness."

"This town is undefended, sir," she said again. "No one you seek is here. My husband and all his men rode out at dawn. You must stop this."

"I, Lady? Look about you. It would be worth my life to try. I have no authority here."

"Who does? Who is in command?"

"The queen, madam."

"The queen? The queen has permitted this?"

"Nay, madam. Not permitted. She has commanded it."

"No. Oh, God have mercy." All the eagerness went out of her face, as if she just then fully understood the danger in which she had placed herself and her children in her vain attempt to save the town. Richard thought how strange it was that he had known from the start that they should not be in the wrecked and burning village, and his mother had only just now understood.

"Now," the young knight said, "let us take you out of here."

Cecily pushed back her hair. "Yes. As you say."

Servants gathered their horses. The knight lifted Cecily onto one, George onto another, and started to lift Richard up behind George, but changed his mind and mounted, settling Richard in the saddle in front of him. "You folk ride out, too," he told the servants. "Stay near until we're out of town, then go wherever you will."

Richard's pony was still standing white-eyed at the post. What if someone shot her? Even if she came to no harm, who would untie her and take care of her, give her grain and water? He wanted to cry, cry, and never stop. Instead, he closed his eyes and tried to imagine he was back at Fotheringhay and that the young knight, studded jerkin hard against his back, was only one of the grooms, taking him up and riding him around the stables before his legs could reach down a horse's ribs.

After the pillage of Ludlow, the Duke of York was declared an enemy of the crown. For nearly a year, Richard, George, and their mother were placed in the custody of others—the church, one of Cecily's sisters, and finally the Pastons, a London merchant family, where Edward often came to visit them. No one seemed to know where the Duke of York or his son Edmund had fled. Even Edward claimed not to know.

Richard dreaded sleep. In his dreams, he would see over and over again the poor frantic pig, the man ripping open the dog's belly, the tip of the sword flashing silver, then red. Sometimes it was not the dog the soldier killed, but his pony or even his mother. He saw the flames devouring the town like greedy tongues, licking the doors of houses, the boots of men in the street. Sometimes he woke believing he had seen something still more terrible, but the memory crept into the dark corners of his mind, where it huddled like a leper in shadows, ringing its bell if he came too close.

His mother and sometimes the host families and servants all seemed to believe he should have amusements to pry his mind away from thoughts of Ludlow. But he couldn't, and the effort to pretend only made him sadder. So he hid—behind the curtained window seat in one house, in the chilly attic of another. He discovered that if he took a toy or chapbook with him, adults usually could pretend he was up to something worthwhile and left him alone in his sanctuary.

Whatever else happened in those houses, the faces of his tutors, the people who sheltered his family, he didn't remember. Except the Pastons. He remembered them.

*London*
*December 1460.*

Richard and George slept together in a small room on the second floor
of the Pastons', which may have been a storeroom before a bed was
put in to accommodate the young sons of the Duke of York. It had a
window to look through, and the chimney from the hearth in the parlor bisected one wall, so that side of the room kept reasonably warm.

Snow had fallen for two days. It piled in windows and on roofs
and lay thick in the streets, broken only by narrow tramped-down
paths. Unrest crept through the house, but there was no point in
asking Dame Paston anything. She didn't believe in children asking
questions. She had a narrow, pinched face and talked to her husband
and servants alike as though they were always about to impose on her,
the best prevention being a sharp tongue.

Christmas arrived and left unheralded. Before the Twelve Days—
which should have been full of feasts and singing but were not—were
over, there came a day when the servants murmured constantly to
each other. Dame Paston sent the boys to bed early, before dusk, even
in this season when the days were shortest. It could not have been
much past three o'clock when she told them to go upstairs, and on no
account to get back up, nor disturb their mother with any foolishness.

Richard didn't think he would sleep. The evening was still early,
and he was afraid of his dreams. But the room was cold and his bed
warm, and all he could see were ice crystals on the thick glass of the
window, and, through the small space that he rubbed clear with his
sleeve, snow and more snow. He slept. After a time he woke, thinking
at first that he had dreamed of horses galloping in the silent street.
Then he heard strange voices. Perhaps he hadn't dreamed the horses.
He lay still in the dark and made himself hardly breathe so he could
listen harder.

He heard voices he didn't know and a chair scraping the floor.
Why would such common sounds seem strange? Then he knew. Usually, voices rose in laughter or argument, cupboard doors opened and
closed; no one tried to be quiet. So it must be very late. They were
only trying not to wake anyone. That was all.

Or perhaps not. Perhaps someone strange and dangerous was in
the house, someone the Pastons wanted to keep secret. Or the people
in the parlor were thieves, keeping themselves secret from the Pastons.
Maybe the visitors weren't people at all, but wizards and devils. No.

He tried to think more calmly. Wizards and devils wouldn't make any noise if they didn't want to.

Richard looked over at his brother. George might know what they should do. But he was afraid George would laugh at him, and somehow he knew that if anything needed to be done, he and not George would have to do it.

The voices stopped for a moment, and Richard heard another sound. Crying? Yes. Not quick and noisy like when he fell and hurt himself, but a terrible keening that made him sad just to hear it. He reached over and shook his brother.

George was angry, of course. "You woke me!"

"George, listen. Someone's crying downstairs."

Even half-asleep, George could mock. "Poor little brother. Does that frighten you? Go to sleep. And don't wake me again."

But Richard could not imagine sleeping. He got out of bed and walked to the door, the wood floor cold under his bare feet. The latch clicked when he opened it and again when he closed it behind him, even though he was as quiet as he could possibly be.

There was a landing about two-thirds of the way down, where the stairway turned; from there he could look across the hall and through the wide double doors into the parlor. The doors were only partly open, and he could see just half of the room: the scarlet tapestry that hung on the near side of the hearth, the hearth itself, one end of the narrow table at which the Pastons sometimes took a private supper, and two chairs.

In the chair at the end of the table sat a large man, his thick legs pressing against the wooden arms. And he, that huge man who looked as if he could snap into kindling every person in the room, was the one crying. His elbows were on the table and his head in his hands, forehead and eyes completely hidden. Dame Margery stood beside him, a hand on his shoulder, and for once she looked soft and kindly. John Paston stood by the hearth, and next to him a man sat in the other chair, looking as if he would melt out of the chair at any moment, as though his body had no bones. His face was dirty, and his eyes were red like coals in ashes. And it wasn't late at all—everyone was fully dressed.

A voice from the end of the room Richard couldn't see said Christmas peace. Then came other words: surprised them; took him at the bridge; unarmed; slaughter. He knew all the words, but couldn't put them together in a way that made sense.

37

"We heard rumors all day," Margery said.

Rumors were like gossip, things you were not supposed to hear. The red-eyed man said, "Lady, those were not rumors. We were there."

The big man lifted his head and said in a hoarse, pained voice, "I couldn't help either of them. I couldn't reach them in time."

"We heard Edward was killed, too," Dame Margery said.

"Woman, we did not!" Richard had never before heard John Paston, that cold distant man, speak in fiery anger. "Cannot you understand? Edward was not killed. He wasn't even there."

Paston stopped and looked down at the floor, as if he had startled himself, but his wife surprisingly didn't seem offended. She took her hand from the big man's shoulder and walked over to her husband, who put his arm around her just as though he hadn't only the moment before been shouting at her for a witless fool.

"Poor Cecily," Dame Margery said. "Poor children."

Richard didn't understand all of what had happened, but two things were clear: it was something terrible, and it had to do with him. Fear and guilt clenched like a fist around his stomach. He remembered how fiercely Dame Paston had instructed him to stay in bed and thought that the very course of the sun around the earth might depend upon his returning to his room without anyone noticing him. If he could climb the stairs and go back to bed without anyone seeing him, the voices would stop and the strange grieving men would go away. In the morning Dame Paston would be cross and tart, and Sir John coldly reserved, as they always were.

But as he started to turn, the exhausted courier raised his bloodshot eyes and saw him, rending with that one glance the curtain between truth and dreams. Richard scurried up the stairs, heart thumping, and pulled the blankets close around his ears so he couldn't hear anything from below. Clamped his eyes shut, too, for good measure.

*I*n the morning, Dame Paston explained to Richard and George the news the strangers had brought in the night. There was a Christmas truce, but the enemy didn't honor it. Their father, their brother Edmund, and many of their father's men were killed, a number of them unarmed, as they foraged for food. Edward had not been present at the disaster.

No Plantagenet could rest until dim-witted King Henry and his wife, the wicked Queen Margaret, were defeated, Dame Margery said.

Edward would avenge his father and claim the throne; then all would be well.

All day Richard thought about what Dame Paston had said and the tales of the Great Knight that his mother had told him. Everyone was in the stories—the feeble-minded king and cruel queen. Surely those were King Henry and Queen Margaret. And his father was the Great Knight, his mother the sorrowing lady who watched him ride away.

He was stupid not to have known that the Great Knight was his father. For that whole day, he hated himself for his ignorance. But he hated his mother more. Why couldn't she have told him the truth? All that time, he had listened to stories of the Great Knight when he could have been hearing about his father.

## Wakefield Green, Yorkshire
## December 30, 1460.

As the Duke of York fought outside the walls of Sandal Castle, he knew this was the last morning he would ever see. For himself, he had a sense of watching something that had already happened, but he called to Edmund to run and hoped profoundly that honor was not too deeply imbued in his son.

Edmund, who had lost his sword and had only the small knife sheathed at his belt, reached the bridge before he was overtaken. He fell to his knees, one hand gripping the bridge's escarpment, the other trying futilely to extract his knife even as he begged for mercy from the four men around him. He had time for two thoughts before the tip of the sword penetrated his leather jerkin and reached the flesh between his ribs. The first was that his mother had been wrong about the scratch on his cheek; it had left a narrow white line, and that would sadden her. In that instant his bowels loosened, and the second thought came: he was going to die not only in agony, but in shame.

There was no grave for the men of the House of York. The body of the duke lay where it fell, crumpled in the snow. In a cold gray sky, huge flakes drifted down as lazily as feathers, as one of the soldiers stopped where the duke lay, and, with accuracy many a headsman would envy, in one blow struck the head from its shoulders.

The body stayed to freeze in the snow at Wakefield, but the head traveled back to the city of York. They made a crown of paper and set the parody of the King of England over the gates of the city he had loved. "So York can look on York," they said, and, "York keeps a more level head now than ever he did on his shoulders."

$\mathcal{A}$t night Richard lay huddled in his bed trying to solve the puzzle. "So York can look on York," the voice in his head repeated. Could the dead see? Perhaps only what was buried was truly dead. Perhaps his father's head could see and think and talk.

$\mathcal{H}$e tried once to ask the Pastons' maid about it. She started to cry, then knelt and gripped him by the arms. "Don't ask your mother that. Never, never tell her you heard that. Do you understand?" She shook him. "Richard, do you hear me?"

He had asked her quietly, feigning indifference because he didn't want her to know how important her answer was to him. "Why, no, Richard," he had thought she would say, "Dead people can't see," as easily as saying, "Cows don't fly." Then he could have said, just as easily, "Oh, I knew that. What does it mean, then, what people are saying?" But her passion frightened him, and he nodded quickly, suddenly wanting nothing more than to be out of the room.

She shook him again. "Richard! Are you listening?"

"I hear you!" he shouted, breaking free from her grasp.

That night in their attic, Richard lay silent while George talked on and on, filling with his words the sparsely furnished room and the empty spaces in the world where their father and brother had been.

# 3 Prince of the Realm

*London*
*January 1461.*

People stirring in the house. Footsteps on the stairs. Richard sat up, but the door was already opening. A candle wavered into the room and lit his mother's face as she leaned over him. "Richard, you must get up."

"Master George. Wake, now." John Skelton's voice. Skelton was one of the handful of servants who had remained with Richard's family after their escape from Ludlow.

"Dress quickly, children," Cecily said as Skelton brought their neatly folded clothes from the cupboard and laid them on the bed.

"Where are we going?" George asked, his voice muffled as he pulled his singlet over his head.

"Abroad. We are leaving England," Cecily said.

"Hush, don't trouble your mother," Skelton answered at the same time, although Richard didn't think his mother seemed troubled. Her face, in the candlelight seemed . . . he tried to think, . . . certain, the way she looked when she was directing him to do something important. Certain, but not troubled.

"Where, abroad?" George's head emerged from the singlet and he struggled to push his arms through the sleeves.

"Burgundy. We have good friends there who will keep us safe," Cecily said.

"I don't want to go to Burgundy," George said. "I want to go home."

All motion stopped. George stood with his head and one arm poking out of his tunic. Cecily and Skelton exchanged a look. Then Skelton shook his head.

"We have no home," Cecily said. "Not at present. Now hurry, dears."

Richard dressed in silence. He hadn't talked for days, hadn't said a word since the day he had shouted at the Pastons' maid. He could, of course, but he didn't want to. Back when he had talked, people either didn't listen or they answered his questions with lies. Anyway, he had nothing to say.

So far, no one had noticed his silence. He answered questions with a nod or shake of his head, responded quickly to directives, and stayed close to George. Like the two faces of a coin, they were opposite but inseparable, each worthless without the other.

Neither of them had cried. Their mother had, though. Richard could hear her if he stood by her chamber—she never cried where anyone could see. He would sit on the floor by her door, listening to her sobs, rough grating sounds that seemed to tear at her throat. He would stay until the crying stopped and he could hear only silence, and then he could leave, because she wasn't sad any more.

The last few days, he thought, she had not seemed quite so sad. It must be because they were all going somewhere better. Maybe they were going to be with Edward, wherever he was. Richard remembered how Edward had hoisted him under his arm and swung him around gaily: Edward's smile and his laugh. Surely no harm had come to Edward.

"Aren't the Pastons our friends?" George asked. Skelton had put more clothes from the cupboard into a small chest that a servant carried out.

"Yes, dear," Cecily said.

"Then why can't they help us?"

"They can't. That's all."

"I'm hungry."

Skelton patted a burlap sack. "Your breakfast's here, Master George. Come along, now." They went silently down the stairs. Both Dame Margery and John Paston were standing at the foot of the stairs. Dame Margery embraced his mother, and John Paston took Dame Margery's hand. "It's best," Paston said. Richard's mother nodded.

They went out into the street, and there was a faint easing of the darkness along the eastern sky. A horse-cart and driver stood waiting for them, the small chest and another coffer waiting in the cart. Skelton helped Cecily onto the seat beside the driver, and Richard scrambled up beside George in the rear of the cart behind the trunks. The horse's hooves clopped down the empty street, Skelton striding briskly alongside. Richard put his hands around his neck, touching finger to finger and thumb to thumb.

George nudged him. "What are you doing, silly, choking yourself?"

Richard lowered his hands to his lap. His neck was so little, his enemies wouldn't even need a sword. They could cut off his head with a kitchen knife. One stroke and his head would be gone. He shuddered, broke the circle apart, and sat on his hands as he watched the Pastons' house disappear.

"We'll come back to England soon," George announced. "We'll be rich as lords, and we will go anywhere we want."

Richard frowned. They were lords, weren't they? Their father had been a duke.

"We are lords, already, of course," George said. He had developed the habit of answering his own comments, as if he could read Richard's thoughts. "But we can't claim our fortune until Edward defeats King Henry."

Soon they could see the walls guarding the old square castle that had come to be known simply as "the Tower," even though there were four towers, one at each corner. The cart entered a narrow street darkened by low stone buildings on either side, the buildings' entire lengths broken by a handful of windows. When they came out into the open again, the street had become the wooden planking of the wharf, with the whole wide Thames flowing beside them. Ships rode all up and down the river, pale sails furled, dark masts standing bare against the dawning sky like the trees of a ghostly forest.

The driver drew the horse to a halt. Cecily and the boys stepped down, and a tall man in a fur-lined burgundy cloak came walking toward them.

"Captain?" Skelton said, extending his hand.

"The same." The man clasped Skelton's hand and removed his hat, bowing to Cecily, who was standing as still and quiet as Lot's wife turned to salt.

"Fine ship you have there," Skelton said, turning his hat in his hands.

The captain laughed. "She's not the fastest ship I've sailed, but she'll do."

"You have been a seaman long?"

"When I was not much bigger than these lads, I served as cabin boy in the king's navy. Those ships sailed close to the wind. This one," he jerked his thumb over his shoulder, "carries wool to Calais, and she'll be hauling back bales of velvet and such."

"Trade is good, then?"

"Not as good as in old Henry's father's time—him whose navy I served in. The ports of Europe were bustling then, as perhaps they are beginning to, again." He cleared his throat. "Here now. There's a reason these lads are booking passage, and we've not time to stand and talk."

"Where will the boys lodge?" Skelton asked.

"Why, they'll travel like princes, which, God willing, they soon will be."

Skelton had started to lead them up the gangplank when Richard realized that his mother remained standing on the wharf. He and George glanced at each other and, in perfect accord, ran back to her. George reached her first and tugged at her hands. "Mother! You must come! We're leaving now."

"No, son. I am not going."

"But you must," George protested. "Our enemies will find you. You said so."

"I am quite safe. I will never make a king." She put her hands on George's shoulders and kissed him before turning to Richard. "Oh, my poor little lord," she said, crouching down and pulling him close so that his face was turned into her shoulder. Her voice wavered, as if it were caught somewhere down in her throat and couldn't quite come up to her mouth. "Don't be sad, dearest. We'll be together again soon."

Richard stood stiffly, his arms rigid against his side. Why would she tell him not to be sad, when she was the one crying? She had lied to him before, and this, sending them away without her, was worse than a lie. He didn't care; he wouldn't listen to her again. But he wondered: was trying to be king such an evil thing that men should hate and kill his father?

Once on board, the captain took them down to the sailors' quarters, where a sheet was hung between the officer's hammocks and the other end of the cabin. "Put your things here." He turned to Richard and George. "You boys have never been aboard ship? We'll be casting off soon. You'll want to be on deck for that."

Richard stood beneath the cold bright sky watching the land recede and the wharf grow smaller and smaller as the ship made its way downriver. Finally, the city became only a faint blur on the horizon. His mother was clever to send them across the sea. He understood that now. Without roads, no one could follow them. He turned his face into the wind and filled his head with the cold sharp smell of the sea as the wind stung his cheeks and blew his hair back from his forehead. Then he grimaced and let the air whistle cold through his teeth. The ship rolled a little from side to side, dipping down and rising again to ride the surface of the sea. All around him were the gray-green expanse of water white-tipped with waves and the raucous calls of seabirds. He almost believed he could jump into the air and rise like the gulls, sailing on the wind forever, and tightened his grip on the railing to keep himself from testing that notion. In a moment he noticed that the miraculous floating, rolling, sinking, rising motion of the ship on the sea could also describe what his stomach was doing inside him.

One of the sailors seized him by the arm. "You're turning green, boy." He hurried Richard down the steps to a small compartment with two bolted-down beds. He sat Richard down on one bed and placed a wooden bucket between his feet. "That's good. If you get too weak to sit, lie down and hang your head over. Just be sure your aim is good. We've enough to do without cleaning your foul mess. And believe me, you won't want to clean it yourself. You won't even want to raise your head." The man drew out the last few words and chuckled.

Richard was soon heaving himself inside out. He would have thought he was dying, except that then the sailor surely wouldn't have laughed, would he?

### Flanders, Duchy of Burgundy
### January 1461.

"What handsome lads we have here." A lady with white hair and bright red lips and cheeks smiled down at them. Richard could hardly understand the people in Bruges. Their speech had an odd moist rich sound, as though thoughts of food simmered in their brains, no matter what they spoke of. Only a few people spoke English as he was used to it, this lady among them.

George smiled and answered. "Thank you, my lady."

"And what a quiet little man you are," the lady said to Richard. "Are you always so?" She had empty eyes and a smile as sad as his mother's.

Skelton said, "Richard? Answer the kind lady."

He met her eyes and nodded.

"Such a perfect, mannerly child." She turned to Skelton in a low voice. "The poor lads have endured enough. That affair at Wakefield was a terrible, terrible thing." She glanced at the boys again. "I pray every day that your brother may triumph and your sojourn here be brief." The woman's eyes blurred as she spoke. She wore a gown of scarlet, trimmed in miniver, but when she turned to walk away, he saw the fur didn't quite meet at the back of her neck, and there were frayed patches on the velvet skirt.

Skelton put his hand on Richard's shoulder when the woman had gone, "Next time, you must speak to the lady, Richard. That poor, good, unhappy soul."

"Why is she unhappy?" George asked.

"Her husband fell at odds with Queen Margaret, though it galls me to call such a woman a queen. It would be worth their lives to go back to England; the French bit . . . sorry, lads . . . witch would have the man hanged the moment he set foot on the docks. If Henry weren't such a dim-witted, spineless eel, he'd have kept his wife in line, your father wouldn't have died, and all the exiles in Europe could go home."

"Exiles?" George said.

"People who must live abroad because they have displeased the king."

"Like us?"

"No, Master George, not like us."

Exactly like us, Richard thought.

### Flanders, Duchy of Burgundy
### March 1461.

Richard drummed his heels on the window seat. George had found new friends his own age. When you were nearly twelve, you didn't like to play with children, especially children who didn't talk. George was hunting today—the Burgundians had fine horses and hawks—or practicing archery at the butts, things Richard was not quite old enough to do. He missed George and his talk, even though Skelton often lost patience with his brother, telling him to cease his "senseless chatter."

Richard liked George's chatter, especially lying in the strange bed in a country they might never leave. They had endured many troubles, George said. Their father and Edmund dead, Edward hiding like a common thief. But George was never discouraged. They could make a strategy, he said, one for staying in Burgundy, another for if they returned to England. A strategy was good. It was redress—paying back—for the past and it gave you hope for the future. George's strategies were secret, though. He said Richard would have to make his own.

Richard slid down from the window and wandered across the hallway to a partly open door. He had walked in that hallway and sat in that window many times. He had looked through the door, but had never found the courage to walk in or even knock on the door. He would like to, though. A glimpse through the crack of the door told him the room was full of books, such a trove of riches that it would take him days to see it all.

He was peering through the gap a foot away from the door, just as he had done every day since discovering the room, when a man frightened him by flinging the door wide.

"Well, child, you're here again. Why don't you come inside and stare?" The man was tall and thin with sparse gray hair reaching to his shoulders. He wore a tunic and ill-fitting hose, both a dull brown. His fingers and tunic were stained in dark patches, black and a reddish brown. All the other Burgundians Richard had seen dressed finely, "wearing their fortunes on their backs," Skelton had said with a touch of scorn. Skelton dressed plainly, too, but he was a servant. Richard couldn't imagine what office this strange, rumpled man could hold.

"You're one of the Duke of York's sons, aren't you, boy?" the man asked.

Richard nodded.

"We've seen plenty of the likes of you." He waved one arm. "If you don't like the temper of the times, come to Burgundy! But even Duke Philip's generosity wears thin eventually. You'll find out if you stay long enough."

He leaned down toward Richard. "And you, child, want to see the library. Are your hands clean?"

Richard extended his hands, palms up.

"Come in, then." The strange man motioned Richard closer and made a deep bow before closing the door behind them.

"I don't let many children see this room. Not that many want to. It's the duke's library. The Duke of Burgundy, that is. Duke Philip.

Not his great library, mind you, but his private one. My name is Anselm. I'm the mender of the duke's books." The man's voice was proud, whether of his skills, or the library itself, Richard couldn't tell. But he did seem pleased to have an interested visitor, even a child.

Anselm looked pointedly at Richard. "Well? You have a name, too, I suppose." He paused for an answer.

"Have you nothing to say, child?"

Richard shook his head.

"Never mind. It's not important. A silent child is better than a rowdy one. Look around, but don't touch the books on my table. Some are badly in need of repair. If you're very careful, you may turn the pages of the books on the reading tables. Nothing else." He wiped his hands on a rag and put on strange gloves with the ends of the fingers missing before turning to his work.

There were more books in that room than Richard had seen in his entire life. Thick volumes bound in red and green and brown leather with gold-stamped covers lay on shelves, sat on narrow slanted reading tables with benches, and covered a good part of Anselm's table, along with unbound pages and pieces of leather. And this wasn't even the duke's great library.

He climbed up on one of the benches and carefully opened the book before him. Around every page were borders of fruit and every variety of flower imaginable—cornflowers and poppies and many more that he couldn't name. There were creatures no human eyes had ever seen: a woman with a serpent's tail, a bagpipe-playing sheep, a goat-legged man.

The goat-legged man was playing an instrument. Richard bent his head closer and drew in his breath. Sorrow overtook him so quickly that tears stung his eyes before he realized he was weeping. He wiped his eyes on his sleeve, having nothing else, and laid his face against the open page. In a moment he felt a hand on his back. Anselm turned him around and slid the book a little distance away. "The copyist would be flattered you find his work so moving, but the book won't tolerate it. A tear is a flood to these old inks, son."

Richard quickly slid off the bench and left the room. He knew what had made him cry, but he wasn't going to tell Anselm. He wasn't going to tell anyone.

*H*e thought about the book the rest of that day. The next day he had a strategy. He could never hope to own a book like the one he had cried over, with its beautiful illuminations, but there must be one book in that room that no one would miss.

*I*n the morning the library door was open. Wide. Richard entered and stood silently in the doorway until Anselm lifted his head. "It's you, again. So you have a fondness for books already? Well, come in. See that you don't wash the pages this time." He didn't sound annoyed, though.

Richard walked around the shelves and rows of tables, taking his time. The book he wanted would be small and plain, with a good leather binding. After a few moments he saw one that fit his needs, but when he approached the table where it lay, he saw gold clasps on the spine of the book and a chain running through a ring on the top clasp. He couldn't see the other end of the chain, and slid under the table to find where it was fastened. He could hear Anselm was muttering to himself, the sound of the knife cutting leather, and the rustle of parchment. He found the bolt that held the chain, and tried with no success to turn it.

He sat for several moments trying first to loosen the bolt, then attempting to spread open one of the links in the chain, with no success, before he noticed that the room was completely quiet. He could no longer hear Anselm's mutterings or the whisper of the knife. When he peered out from under the table, he saw the librarian's legs in their baggy brown hose. The man stooped down, hands on his thighs.

"What are you doing, boy?"

Richard shrugged.

"I said, boy, what are you doing?"

Richard shook his head.

"So nothing to say today, either? Come out from under there."

He crawled out, hastened by Anselm's hand tugging on the front of his shirt, the librarian glaring at him.

"You're a bright lad; you must be, if you like the books so much. But you know the chains are here for a reason, don't you?"

Richard nodded.

"The reason being to keep nasty little thieves like you from stealing them."

Stealing was a sin; he knew that. It hadn't seemed important when he made his strategy, but then his strategy had not included getting caught. His eyes swam in tears. He longed to explain to Anselm that he had meant no harm.

"What have you to say for yourself?" Anselm's hand gave Richard's shirt a shake. "Well, boy? I said, what have you to say to yourself?"

"Nothing!" The word rattled out.

"So the little mute has a tongue. Go. I've no time for thieves. Come back when you think you can let the books stay as they are."

Richard had reached the door, holding his head up, not crying, when he heard a weary voice behind him. "Come back, child."

He turned around but didn't come any further into the room. Anselm was standing at his worktable. "You wanted a book badly enough to try to steal one."

Richard nodded.

"Why didn't you ask me? And none of that silence. You can speak and should be ashamed of yourself, mocking those who can't."

"Yes, sir," Richard said. That seemed safe enough, although he had never thought to mock anyone.

"Then tell me, lad."

Anselm didn't sound angry, and Richard stepped further into the room. "I wanted a book to take with me. To have in my room."

"Why that book? It's extremely valuable; that's why it's chained to the table, but there are many more even prettier. Don't you want a beautiful one?"

He shook his head.

"Tell—never mind. You are a strange child, but I don't suppose you meant to be wicked. Would you like this?" Anselm took up a small parcel of pages. "The illuminations in this are very fine, but a good deal of it is missing. It will never make a book again. You may have one of the pages. Is that what you wanted?"

"Thank you, sir." He made no effort to take the page.

"Well? Is that not enough?"

"Yes, sir."

"Then take it, boy. What ails you? I said you may have it."

"Could I have that, sir?" He pointed to a scrap of worn leather on Anselm's table.

"What? That's just an empty binding. Or was, once. "

"Yes, sir."

"Very well." Anselm picked it up, turning the torn leather in his hands, finally handing it to Richard.

Richard slipped it inside his jerkin. The next part of his plan was to hide it under his pillow to have next to him at night. "Thank you, sir," he said, and smiled.

Richard began to "help" Anselm, mostly by pressing his hands down on a book while the librarian applied glue and a clamp. Anselm had been too modest; far from only "mending" books, he was a skilled artist and could copy pages so well that they were hardly distinguishable from the original. Occasionally he would allow Richard some paints and parchment—only the most common colors and the smallest scraps, for everything in the library was used and used again.

You have good hands. Very sure, for a child," Anselm told him.

Richard smiled. He only talked when he had to, but his silence had changed. It was the silence of contentment. The library was the first place he went after breaking fast, and the place he left before evening devotions.

He didn't tell anyone what had made him cry that first day in the library, what made him want a book to hide under his pillow and hold next to him at night: the smell of the bindings, the rich aroma of leather, brought back the memory of his father as his father had taken him off to bed.

Where are you going?" George asked. It was the first day in the weeks since Richard had discovered the library that George had not had pursuits of his own.

"I'll show you."

Anselm was already at work when Richard entered, dragging George along by the hand. George stared at the librarian's work table a long moment, then said, "What? That's what you've been about, watching this man fix books?" He didn't sound mocking, only bewildered.

"No," Richard said. "I help him."

Just then, a door slammed from somewhere outside the library. A moment later a sudden roar of voices surged amid an explosion of shouts and cheers.

"What—" Anselm stood and laid down his tools, and all three of them rushed to the door. All up and down the corridor, doors were opening, people coming to see what the commotion was. John Skelton was running up the stairs, two at a time. A crowd—men and women, courtiers and servants—was behind him, all of them laughing and cavorting. When Skelton saw the cautious trio standing at the library door, he grabbed George's hands and danced him in a circle. "It's your brother, boy. Edward's won the battle and taken the crown. He's King of England, God be praised!

"It's true. Your brother's king. You are princes of the realm!" He dropped George's hands. The cheering stopped and people on the stairway looked at Richard and George in wonder, as though, like Midas's daughter, they had turned to gold.

*R*ichard and George returned to London in fame and glory, a very different state from how they left, except for one thing. Whether exiled knave, whose life was not worth the shadow cast by the figure on a coin, or prince of the realm, seasickness felt the same.

# 4  *The Fairest Sight*

*Baynard's Castle, London*
*October 1461.*

It's time for him to go," Edward said. "His education is a disgrace. A merchant's son would have been better tutored."

Richard, Edward, and their mother were at supper at Cecily's home, Baynard's Castle on the Thames. Richard had thought wonderful things would happen after Edward had been crowned king. In his vision, he, Edward, George, and their mother would live together. He would have a tutor and sometimes read out loud to his mother while she sat at her needlework. He and Edward and George would all ride about the countryside on their fine horses, and soon he would learn to hunt and hawk. But reality had not aligned with his hopes. Edward lived "at court," which, Richard was starting to understand, wasn't a single place at all, but wherever the king chose to be—mostly the Palace at Westminster and the Tower—and the king's servants and followers went with him. Laughing, clamoring people and a continual hum of voices surrounded Edward wherever he went. People bowed to him, calling him Your Grace, smiled when he smiled, and ceased smiling when he frowned.

Richard preferred his mother's house to any of the "courts." Servants kept it fresh by changing the rushes and airing the carpets and tapestries, and by setting out bowls of fragrant spices and dried flower petals to sweeten the air. Daytimes, his mother sat with her ladies, while they talked quietly and stitched their fancywork. In the evenings, she often had a few friends in to sup with her and hear her musicians and singers. She had no clowns or players, which she considered lewd. She did, once, have a fool, who spoke not a word but could make you believe that he was climbing a rope or riding a stubborn mule just by the way he moved. Tonight, a lutenist was playing softly in the corner of the room, but no one was paying him much attention.

His mother had changed. She would work on her embroidery with a book of prayer or scripture at her side. Every now and again she would stop her work and lay her hand on the book's smooth leather cover, just as he had once seen her lay her hand on his father's cheek. And sometimes she would lift her eyes, and her gaze, wherever it fell, would glow. Her radiance had nothing to do with who or what she beheld. Richard knew this because once she had looked just so at him, and he had had to speak to her three times before she knew he was there.

Recently his mother and Edward had quarreled. And he knew what they quarreled over—him. His future, at any rate. Edward wanted him to be fostered at Middleham, his cousin Warwick's estate far in the north.

"He's too young," Cecily was saying. She was thin and pale. The square-necked gown showed her delicate collarbones sticking out like wings. She dipped her long fingers in the laver on the table and daintily wiped them on the linen. She seemed to be cleaning her fingers without taking even a bite of her food in between.

"He's nine now," Edward said, and mopped the grease from his mouth with a linen. Edward always ate lustily. He had grown taller and broader in the last year, as if he had decided a king ought to take up more space. His voice was stronger and his laugh louder. "The same age I was when I rode with my father."

"Has he a father to ride with?" Cecily asked. "He has only you; you cannot send him away. It is too soon. Send him to the church now. He can begin his studies here in London and be fostered out in a year or two."

"No, mother. Not the church." Edward's voice was tight. "We have talked of this before. You will never have him fostered. You intend to make the church his vocation."

"Your father promised him to the church. Would you betray your father's word?"

When his mother said "the church," Richard thought she didn't mean going to the cathedral to pray or make his confession. It meant growing up to be like the men people called father or brother, who had shaved heads and wore black cassocks, with crosses hanging about their necks and corded belts at their waists. It was strange to know that a course had been set for his entire life all this time, and he only just now learned of it when it appeared that course was not to be.

"That was before he thought to be king, mother. He had four sons' futures to think of, and not enough money to establish us all. " Edward made little stabs on the table with his finger. "Of course he wanted one less title, one less rich marriage, to secure. Anyway, Richard's knighted and titled now. How many priests do you know who are dukes?"

"Nobility have taken vows before."

Edward leaned back in his chair and folded his arms across his chest. "No. I have other plans for him."

Richard tucked his head down and poked at the meat on his trencher as Edward and his mother sat in chill silence. Everything was so complicated now that Edward was king. Where Richard spent his foster years was important not just for his own sake, Edward had explained. Having the king's brother as a member of a household was an honor and a mark of the king's favor. The Nevilles were the most important family in England, next to his own. Keeping close ties between the families was a way of ensuring they continued to work in harmony. Edward wanted his youngest brother allied with the Earl of Warwick, not secluded behind abbey walls.

Edward uncrossed his arms and took a deep breath. "Mother," he said, "he can ride with Jack Neville and his men when Jack concludes his business here. He'll leave in a fortnight."

"No," Cecily said. "Middleham is too far." She motioned impatiently for the lutenist to stop playing and leave the room.

"Christ, mother! It's not too far. He's already been to Burgundy and back. Jack's a sensible man. If Richard needs to rest, they'll stop." Edward had given up on calmness; furrows crossed his forehead and the cords in his neck stood out.

Cecily rinsed and dried her fingers again with no sign of impatience or hurry, and laid her linen on the table. "I am ashamed to have raised a son so disrespectful as to swear at me," she said, her voice as calm as her gestures.

When Edward didn't reply, she stood and left the room with her head high and her back straight. Richard heard the sound of a door closing.

"Oh, Chr—," Edward broke off, rising and following after her.

Richard glanced at the lace and velvet on his wrist, resting on the table. Now that he was knighted, he had fine clothes and castles of his own that he had never seen. He tried to remember what had made him happy, forever ago, when he and George had played their knights' games, before their father died, before Edward was king.

He listened but could hear nothing of what Edward and his mother were saying to each other behind the closed door. In a moment a servant appeared to ask him if he would like a frumenty to end the meal. "No, thank you," he said. It seemed to him that the meal had ended; the servant just hadn't noticed.

*R*ichard left the table and went to his own chamber, his favorite room in the castle. The walls were painted a pale blue, with stenciled gilt stars scattered on the walls. On bright days the sun came through the panes of the window and made diamonds of light on the floor. He took down from a shelf the little coffer in which he kept his most precious possessions—the page and binding Anselm had given him in Bruges; a small, beautiful entire book, also from Anselm; and a finely carved chess set missing a white pawn and the black knight, which he used for playing armies. He took out the chess pieces and lined them up on the floor. The kings stood at the head of the lines of pawns— their armies—and the queens and bishops and castles waited at the side for the battle to end and the outcome to be known.

A few moments later, his mother walked past his door, not pausing to speak to him. Another set of footsteps came and stopped at the doorway.

"Pack your things tonight," Edward said, coming into the room and taking a seat on Richard's bed. "I'll send someone to collect you tomorrow."

"Tomorrow? You said a fortnight."

"You will travel north in a fortnight. But you'll come to Westminster tomorrow. Your mother says she cannot bear to see you here, knowing she'll have to say goodbye so soon."

Richard knew then, although he could hardly put the idea into words, that his future was a kind of battle between his mother and Edward. Edward had won, but Cecily's refusal to have Richard spend his last few days in her household had been her own small victory, her way of showing that she need not bow completely to Edward's will, even if he was the king.

"You'll like Middleham, I promise you," Edward said. His voice was cheery and hearty, the bright false sound of a lie.

"Yes," Richard said, not looking up.

"Well," Edward said, as though he expected more of a response. When Richard said nothing more, Edward said, "Well," again and stood. "I'll be off now." He looked faintly relieved as he left the room.

Richard got up and went to the window to watch until Edward boarded the barge at the pier and disappeared. When he turned from the window, John Skelton was in the room. Skelton had been at the edges of Richard's life for so long it seemed strange to think of leaving him. "I'm going north to Middleham. George isn't going with me," he said.

Skelton's lips compressed. "Edward wants that boy near him, is my guess."

"Edward said I'd like the north." Richard knew the north was far from London, far from Fotheringhay or anywhere else he had been. Some people thought it wasn't as civilized as the rest of England and spoke slightingly of "northerners."

"You might. Some people do. Who knows?" Skelton winked. "Some day you'll be a man. Your brother will send for you, and you won't even want to leave, you'll like it that much."

Richard doubted it. He saw no point in arguing, though. "I don't want to stay here. I don't like London, anyway."

"That's as may be, Master Richard," Skelton said, looking doubtful. "The Nevilles are good men, at any rate. I'll have the trunks sent for, and you can pack tomorrow. It's too late now to think what you might need for the journey."

"Very well, John." Richard picked up the white king, feeling the carved stone cool and smooth in his hand. He waited until Skelton had left the room, then loosened his grip and threw it across the room. He had lied. He wanted with all his heart to stay. He just didn't know where.

Richard stood in the yard at Westminster before the night had begun to yield to day. Servants were loading the carts by lantern light while shivering, sleepy-eyed grooms, roused from their beds of straw, led the horses from the stables, their breath making little clouds in the cold air, impatient hooves striking sparks on the cobbles. The party was to get an early start on the journey before the roads clogged with carts. This was at Jack's behest, but Jack wasn't there yet.

*R*ichard had acquired his first squire, Jeremy, a sad-faced orphan his own age, whom Edward had made his ward when the boy's father died at Towton.

"Why are we here so early, if we're not to leave yet?" The squire piped. He was a tall, gawky boy with knobs for elbows and knees. His light brown hair was cut so straight and thick across his forehead that it made Richard think of a thatched roof.

Joseph, the old master groom, walked over to the boy and cuffed him. "Boy, that is your good lord you are speaking to. Mind your tongue." Joseph was gray-haired and so thin that his hose bagged at the knees. He smelled of grain and dust and horse-sweat.

He turned to Richard almost as fiercely as he had spoken to the squire. "And you, young sir. You must not allow such insolence."

Richard winced under Joseph's gaze. Why hadn't Edward told him how to manage a squire? He had for so long done what others told him that he hadn't given a thought to the notion that he could—must—order another person to do his bidding.

"My father said it was foolish to travel with carts," the squire said now, looking directly at Richard. "Packhorses can go anywhere a horse and rider can. Carts will cost you days. They break down. Wheels get stuck in mud. We'll be lucky to get there by spring."

The boy was deliberately baiting him, and Joseph was watching. Richard went over to the squire, looked him in the eye and said loudly, "Be silent! You may talk when I ask you a question." The squire blinked and closed his mouth. Joseph smiled. Jeremy caught the smile and made a show of wiping his face on his sleeve, as if Richard had spat on him. Stupid boy, Richard thought.

Just then Jack Neville came down the steps from the palace, followed by his men-at-arms, spurs and swords clinking. Jack was dressed as plainly as any yeoman, in hose and a high-collared tunic, with no gilt embroidery or cut sleeves, his fine boots his only concession to fashion. They were of soft brown leather, knee-high and cuffed to show the rich lining. Jack turned to Richard.

"Here you are, waiting for us. When I didn't see you in the hall, I thought sure I would have to send someone to turn you out of your bed."

"No, I'm ready."

"And impatient for the laggards, no doubt. Good. Then we are for Middleham." Jack caught sight of the squire standing sullen and silent. "Who is that boy? He's riding with us?"

"Yes, sir. He's Edward's ward. He's to be my squire."

"In that case, we've work to do. What's his name?"

"Jeremy."

Jack beckoned the boy. "Come, here, son. What's your family name?"

The boy moved slowly. "Owen."

"Very good, Jeremy Owen. Now pay attention. The first thing a squire must do is bring his master's horse. Hold it, and give him a knee up while he mounts. Well, lad?" Jack added when the boy showed no inclination to move. "Fetch your master's horse and be quick."

"The small black mare," Richard told him. Edward had given him a horse for the journey. She was bred, Edward said, out of a shaggy Scots pony and a fine palfrey. She had a pony's barrel-like body, but breeding in her small head, clean hooves, and delicate pasterns. A glistening solid black, no white star or stockings, she was called, inexplicably, Pearl, and Richard hadn't changed her name.

"When will we get there?" he asked Jack, as Jeremy moved to answer his charge.

Jack rubbed the back of his neck. "We might do it in three days, even two, if we were post riders. Which we're not, thank God. A week would be excellent time if we had no carts. But we do. Nine or ten days, then, depending on the roads. If the weather holds and none of the horses go lame." He frowned. "Look, lad, I'm no prophet. We'll get there when we get there. Why? Are you eager for your new home?"

"No. I just wondered."

"I wouldn't blame you if you were. It's wonderful country." Jack laid a hand on Richard's head, looked at him thoughtfully, but said nothing more.

Jeremy locked his hands for Richard's knee. As Richard was swinging his other leg over the saddle, Pearl laid her ears back and twitched her tail. He managed to find the stirrups and get a grip on the reins, and she quickly calmed, but Richard wondered what Jeremy had done to provoke her.

Jack swung up in the saddle and tilted his head back to appraise the weather. "Fine clear morning. We'll have good traveling today."

Richard stared up at the millions of stars. Here in London, Edward lay beneath those stars, and in Yorkshire, Warwick, too, at his far northern castle. And everyone in between, all the sleepers over the miles and miles of town, forest, meadow, and moor that he would cross. The stars shone on all of them, on all the dark earth. Wherever he would be tonight, the next night, and forever, the stars would go with him: the fairest sight he could imagine.

Jack spun a coin to Joseph, and they turned toward the narrow lane past St. Margaret's church, out the gate at High Tower and on to London proper, where they were to meet a companion for the journey.

By the time they reached Newgate, at London's west wall, the black of night had started to loosen and dissolve in the east, and a silver sheen of light lay on the Thames. A little man sat just outside the gate on a sleepy horse, the beast's head drooping and nodding, the man hunched over in the cold, hugging his arms against his chest.

"God save you, Brother Simon," Jack called. "Where are your wits, that you wait outside the walls before daylight?"

"First light," the man corrected, looking toward the horizon. "And any thief would know I was a poor prospect for filling his purse." He spoke true. In any light, he was shabby enough, with his coarse woolen gown and only one thin parcel tied behind his saddle. No fortune in the horse, either, Roman-nosed and with hooves as big as plates.

The sky was ringed with fire now, streamers and banners of red and orange. Richard spurred Pearl to get ahead of the carts, taking a position at Brother Simon's side. Few travelers were about yet, as they followed ancient Watling Street east from London toward Epping Forest, where pale leaves lay brittle on the ground. When a sudden gust of wind came through, warm as a summer breeze, the leaves rattled and rose up, flocking around the horses' legs like startled birds.

"I like not that," Brother Simon said. With the dawn, Richard could see him better. The man was all one color like an acorn, his gown russet, his face and hands burned by the sun to a deep reddish brown. Even the ungainly horse was chestnut-colored. "You watch," Simon continued, "a storm will follow hard by so warm a wind."

Richard was about to ask Brother Simon what he meant, but a sharp sting on his ankle stopped him. Jeremy, closer than Richard had realized, was now edging away, his eyes straight ahead. Richard pressed nearer. "Do that again," he said, "and I'll have you beaten."

"Coward," Jeremy said. "Can't beat me, yourself, can you?" He struck again; his boot hit Pearl's flank, and she pitched her head down and kicked her heels up with a nasty sideways twist. Richard pulled in on the reins and held on.

"Someone put pepper on your little mare's hay?" Brother Simon asked.

"No," Richard said. "Something stung her." Jeremy had dropped back to the far side of the carts. Richard waited a moment and then wove through the carts to Jeremy's side. He gave a dig at Jeremy's horse, and it lashed out to kick at Pearl, who bared her teeth.

"Here, here, you two. None of that." Brother Simon pushed his horse between the ponies. "Richard, ride up beside your good cousin. And you, boy, come over by me."

Richard and Jeremy rode without so much as a word between them the rest of the day. When they stopped for the night, the inn was nearly full. Jack's entire party shared one room. Brother Simon slept between Richard and Jeremy, who kept tugging the coverings back and forth between them, until Simon wrapped the entire blanket around himself until they promised to lie quietly.

Even then, Richard felt restless and uneasy. The bed was lumpy, and the room smelled of stale cooking smoke and something worse. He could hear the men on the floor grunting, snoring, moving restlessly, like old dogs dreaming. Laughter came from the main room below, loud voices, and then a thud like a chair overturned. A short silence, then footsteps came up the stairs along with cursing and the sound of a heavy object being dragged. Finally a steady scrape at the top of the stairs. More laughter, a door slammed. Richard heard someone singing loudly. "Quiet, you fool," another voice shouted, almost as loudly as the singing. The boots clapped briskly back down the stairs. Gradually the place settled into stillness and Richard eased into sleep.

# 5   *An Educated Man*

*Middleham Castle, England*
*October 1461.*

The travelers reached Middleham in midafternoon. Brother Simon had parted with them an hour earlier, riding alone up the lane to Jervaulx Abbey, whistling as he trotted away on his poor nag, as happy as if he owned the riches of the kingdom.

Richard's party rode up the steep winding road past Middleham village, a cluster of handsome stone houses sprawled just below the rise on which the castle stood. The wind had risen. Sharp gusts tore at them as they crossed the moat into the outer courtyard, and blew the porter's shouted greeting back down into the dales. The immense outer courtyard contained a number of houses and outbuildings, an orchard, tilled ground marked by stakes and the withered remains of a garden, and a small fishpond. The wide gate stood open onto a deserted inner ward. Maybe the castle would be deserted, too, Richard thought, cold and dark, populated only by owls and bats, like the remains of villages they had passed, ruined long ago by the Great Plague.

Jack dismounted and began to untie the panniers from his saddle.

"Well?" he said, looking up at Richard and Jeremy. "We're home, lads. Why are you sitting there like rooks on an elm?"

The boys slid down from their saddles. Standing on his own two feet, without the benefit of the horse's height beneath him, Richard felt no taller than a dwarf, his legs shrunken to nubbins, and he could still feel the horse's gait in his bones as he stood, looking at this place that Jack called home. *This* was what Jack loved so much?

Middleham Castle was a dull gray rock beneath a dull gray sky. Like all castles, it had been built for defense; unlike some, it had no delicate spires and traceries to disguise the fact. The keep was massive and fortress-like, with powerful square towers buttressing the curtain wall at all four corners. With the sun now dropping in the west, the narrow courtyard lay in shadow, black and opaque. Only the rampart above caught the lowering sun's weak light, touching the face of a guard on the wall. The only good thing was that they were out of the wind.

Richard's soul shriveled up inside him like a salted snail. He told himself he didn't have to stay here forever. He already had his own estates. He would claim them when he came of age, find the one he liked the best, and that would be his home—not this bleak, ugly place. In five or six years he would be a man. If he learned fast enough, he might even shorten the time.

Jack had begun to gather some of their smaller parcels when a door opened at the top of the steep stone stairs leading to the keep, and a boy emerged. He slammed the door shut behind him and ran down the steps, a sturdy boy, fleshy and solid, not at all ghost-like, with a high color in his cheeks as though his face were continually whipped by wind.

"I knew it was you, sir! I saw your horses from the tower." Richard saw that the youth was perhaps his own age, with bright red hair and freckles running together across his face.

"Hello, Percy," Jack answered. "I've been thinking these past three hours about a joint of meat before your fire." He looked around at the courtyard. "Where is everyone? Has the place gone to sleep with the pigeons, or could you rouse a groom or two?"

"I'll see to it, sir. Everyone's inside. Even the grooms. The countess said they might. But you're too late," he added sadly.

"Am I, now." Jack said. "Not a bite of food left in the place?"

"There's always food, sir, but you've missed the players! There was a man could jump through hoops on fire and a juggler kept six knives in the air. And musicians, too! Maybe you can ask them to begin again."

Jack laughed. "No, but many thanks, Percy." He turned to the Richard and Jeremy. "Courage, lads. I know you're weary, but better things await you."

They followed Jack up the steps the boy had come down. At the entrance to the castle's great hall, a hand clamped down on Richard's neck and another on Jeremy's. Jack's man, the older, gray one, hauled them back to the laver.

"Wash your hands and face first. Did they teach you no courtesy in London?"

Richard washed his hands and face, and took the linen the page handed him, before looking about him.

What he saw cheered him. Middleham's great hall was neither dark nor gloomy. An ornately carved oak screen stood beneath a four-paneled window in diamond panes of red, blue, and gold glass. Two huge chandeliers hung from massive chains at either end of the room, and horn lanterns flickered along the walls. Flames blazed high in a central hearth taller than most men stood, and hanging in the air was the aroma of roasted meat, garlic, and cinnamon, with a slight eye-stinging essence of woodsmoke, a mixture so heady and savory that Richard's mouth watered.

People stood talking in clusters as musicians gathered their in-struments. Servants carried away heaps of soiled linens, some white and others rayed in red, green, and gold. Still others were taking the boards from the tables and stacking them along the walls. A few hounds nosed among the rushes for bones, while a kitchen boy swept the floor under the tables.

The crowd of strangers before him were not so glittering and shining as the people at court, Richard noticed. These folk dressed in plain woolens and camlet, in shades of madder and green. Or in a dull saffron gold, the color of fallen leaves—that was the gown of a wom-an standing with her hands on her hips, talking to two little girls. The taller girl was fair-haired, with cheeks the pink of the inside of a large curled seashell that Richard had once seen. The younger girl stood partly hidden behind the woman. He could see half the child's face, the forehead and cheek draped by dark chestnut hair, and one dark eye beneath a fiercely scowling brow.

The woman saw them and came forward. Her skirts were dragging behind her, and she turned and gave them a strong yank, shaking the dark-eyed girl from the folds of her gown. "Child, stop hanging on me!"

She embraced Jack, then stood back and smiled at him, keeping one hand on his arm. She had a handsome face, russet hair pulled back in a simple coif, and a ring of keys belted at her waist.

Jack pushed Richard forward. "This is Richard, Alice, Cecily's youngest."

Alice. The woman was Warwick's countess, then, and the little girls must be his daughters, Anne and Isabel.

The countess smiled down at him. "Your cousin must think I am blind. Anyone could see who you are. You are very like your father. But then, I imagine you are weary of hearing that."

No. He could never hear it enough. The portrait he carried in his mind was already blurring. When it disappeared, his father would be gone forever.

She gave him a searching look, and turned to Jack. "But Jack, he's so small! What are Edward and Cecily doing, sending him up here? If Cecily had anything to say about it, that is. How old is he now, anyway? Eight? Seven?"

He was tired of hearing *that*. Tired of people commenting about his size as though it were time for him to do something about it.

"He's nine, Alice," Jack said mildly, "and he rides well."

She laughed. "Oh, excellent! He can sit a horse, therefore he's ripe for a soldier. Well, if men are fools, it's none of my affair. It's Giles's worry if the child can't heave a sword."

Then Richard saw the Earl of Warwick striding toward him. He remembered the young-looking face, burnished by the sun to a sheen like polished oak, the black silver-streaked hair and beard. He didn't remember the eyes, an unusual golden brown, almost amber, that seemed at a glance to be all fire and light, but that when he looked closely, showed nothing but his own image reflected back at him, like a highly polished shield.

Warwick looked down from his full height. "So Edward sent you to prepare for knighthood."

"Yes, sir."

"See to it that you acquit yourself well."

"Yes, sir, I will do my best."

Then Warwick startled him by breaking into laughter. "Why so serious?" he said. "God's bones, lad, you're here to learn, not to take office from the Pope!" The laugh was warm and genial, but something in Warwick's eyes seemed hard, almost angry.

"Enough, brother. We're for food, now," Jack said, guiding the boys to the kitchen, where his men were already eating, seated on stools around a table on which several fowl were laid out to be plucked. One man tugged at a wench's skirt as she passed, pulled her to him, and kissed her. "Another, sweetheart! I couldn't taste your lips for the grease." He wiped his mouth on his sleeve. She pushed at his forehead and spun away, laughing.

A cook banged a spoon on a kettle and pointed first to Jack's man, and then to the girl. "More of that, sir, and you'll go begging. And you, fool, I'll chain you to the spit."

Richard sat on a bench beside Jeremy. Someone handed him a plate of the savory-smelling meat. He took a few bites, but his hunger had passed. His empty stomach felt as though it had folded in upon itself.

After the others had cleaned their plates, a man came into the kitchen, calling, "Where are the green lads?" He was short, with curly brown hair and a gray-streaked beard. His muscular arms, long in comparison to his height, waved about as he talked. "Up, lads. I don't know why I should call you green, though, when you are as pale as any louts I've seen."

The man took Richard and Jeremy back across the courtyard to a door in the curtain wall, which he said housed the dormitory where they would sleep. "You'll also find the nursery, the bakery, the lord's offices, and counting room." He pointed to a wooden arcade joining the keep to the curtain wall. "That bridge leads to the lady chamber, which you will *not* find."

They climbed a flight of stairs to a large room where maybe a dozen beds lined the walls. Several boys lay abed, while others sat cross-legged on the floor, talking and laughing. Two lads were playing at dice by the light of a small brazier—the red-haired Percy and another youth that the man called by his full name, John Parr, as though it were one word.

"I had an older brother named John," the boy explained. "He was sickly, so when I was born, my parents named me John, too. My brother lived for a while, and they had to call us differently. After he died, the name stayed, anyway. Do you read yet?"

"Of course."

"Well, anyway," the boy said, as though Richard had not answered, "Bennett will make you an educated man." He pronounced the word in separate syllables, *ed-u-cat-ed*. Then he and Rob chanted in unison. "An ed-u-cat-ed man knows both, the Latin and the English, the sacred and the secular," and then laughed gleefully at their mimicry. Richard stood uncomfortably, uncertain what the jest was.

"Never mind," Rob said. "Bennett talks odd but he's a fair tutor." He pointed to a narrow cot next to the wall. "That's your place.

We've an extra bed just now. You can have it to yourself." He looked up at Jeremy. "You share with John Parr, here. He'll show you."

Richard saw that his goods had been brought to his bed and went over to undress. The odd bearded man had gone out, and the boy Percy talked without pause. Richard caught some notion of books, meals, and practices in a field, which were to become much more exciting, come spring, although he had no idea what fields and why they were exciting.

The short bearded man stuck his head through the doorway. "All right, boys. Into bed with you. No more dicing. If I see candles burning, you'll use their light to clean out the garderobe."

The boys groaned, but no one seemed afraid of the threat. Richard crawled into his bed. It was the first time since the days when his mother had told him stories that he could remember being alone in a bed, and he thought of how many times he had wished to be free of jabbing elbows or knees, of fighting for his share of the blankets. He hadn't always liked having George beside him, or Jeremy, on the journey, but the empty bed seemed huge, much too large for one sleeper, and cold. He would have liked a close body to warm his back against, someone to whisper to now that the candles were snuffed.

He shivered a little as he drew his knees up toward his chest, pulled the blankets tight around him, and closed his eyes.

*R*ichard was lonely. It wasn't that the other boys were unkind, or even that they ignored him. But what was simple pleasure to most people—idle talk and laughter—he found foreign. Laughter and gaiety were a second, easy, language that others knew and he did not. He scarcely noticed his loneliness at first. Unlike the time in London, when he and George were shunted from one place of hiding to another, the days at Middleham had a pattern both beautiful and comforting, an order as absolute as the seasons. Mass at six, followed by bread and meat and wine. Then, all morning, letters in the schoolroom.

Sessions began with recitations in English of the easy things, the "baby bookes," things everyone who wasn't raised in a barn should know.

*Do not blow on your food or quarrel at the table.*

*Do not scratch the dog, or your head, while you are eating.*

*Do not put your knife far into your mouth, nor wipe your nose on the tablecloth or spit across the table.*

*Do not sneeze or yawn at the table or belch unnecessarily.*

*Do not dip any bread you have been chewing into the common bowl.*

Then Latin, French, and logic. Philosophy and mathematics. The rituals of chivalry. History and policy-making.

The tutor, Bennett, was a small, dark man with a thin moustache that twitched when he talked, giving him a semblance to a nervous mouse. He spoke exactly as John Parr had in mimicking him. *"Do you wish to be an ed-u-cat-ed man, Master Richard?"*

Rob Percy was the poorest reader. His Latin agitated Bennett. The tutor would first tug at his moustache and then clutch at the hair at his temples as if he had a headache. After a few moments, he would sigh and tell Rob to stop.

"Richard, read," Bennett would say, and Richard did. He read eagerly, the way he had once listened to his mother's stories, but books were better. They held secrets that he hadn't the wisdom to completely grasp, but they did not laugh or lie, as people did. Somewhere in the histories and philosophies he read was everything he needed to know to gain his place in the world.

Dinner came at nine or ten. Then leave the books for riding, hawking, and training in knightly skills. Giles, the gruff, bearded man Richard had met his first night at Middleham, was master of the horse. Richard and his companions learned to handle lance and shield, lift and swing their swords, and cross swords with each other.

At the end of Richard's first practice with weapons, Warwick had presented him with a beautiful finely balanced sword, the hilt studded with small rubies—small, but a real weapon. "In honor of your brother and the respect between us," Warwick said. "May our houses long serve each other."

When Jack saw the sword, he held it up to the light, turning the blade so the sun flashed around it.

"Nice weapon." He lowered his arm and traced his fingers down two softly defined channels in the blade. "See these? They're for all the blood. For it to run in."

Richard felt his eyes grow large. Until the mention of blood, it had all been play. Now he thought he never wanted to see anything hurt as much as the men and animals had been hurt at Ludlow. Never wanted to inflict such hurt, but he supposed he would have to. That's what being a knight meant.

"No, lad. I have a willful humor," Jack laughed, handing him back the sword. "You must learn not to believe me too quickly. Now see," he said, guiding Richard's fingers down the channels, "these make the weapon a little lighter—easier for your arm—without weakening the steel."

Richard would have preferred a sword like those of the other boys, wooden blades hammered together. But it did not occur to him to put his splendid gift aside. He knew it was meant to be used, so he wrapped the blade in cloth when he practiced, trying not to injure while he was learning how to kill.

Soon they moved to practice the quintain—a post topped by a swiveling beam with weighted bags hanging from either end, the beam attached in such a way that the arm would pivot when a bag was struck. Rob gave the bag a shove. "You have to strike it hard enough to set it in motion. You try to make it go halfway around, then get out the way before the other arm comes and hits you. Try it."

Rob made it look easy. Richard took a run, but the bag didn't budge. On his second try, his shoulder hit the bag with such force that he lurched forward when the post spun, and then pitched headfirst onto the ground.

"Don't fret," Rob said. "Everyone does that at first. You'll get the feel of it. Wait until spring. We do the large quintain on the practice field. It's much more exciting. You'll like it."

Supper came at three or four, and evenings were for the gentle arts—music, dancing, conversing with ladies, and chamber games of chess, backgammon, and dice.

Richard liked the sessions in the schoolroom, and the work of physical skills went quickly, even if he was clumsy at first. It was in the evenings, when the everyone else welcomed the day's end, that he felt most alone. After supper and before bells rang for evening prayer, Richard went out onto the castle rampart. No one passed on the walkway except the watchman on his rounds, who paid a wandering boy no mind and expected no conversation. The darkness of sky and earth ran together, and the lantern lights shining in the windows from the village below seemed only one more constellation as Richard began his ritual. He let his mind be still and prepared to work the magic. A chill ran like a cold spoon down his spine, the night was so beautiful, as he squinted his eyes to fracture the stars' brilliance. Gold and white beams of light connected him to the firmament, splinters of light as close as his hand, and he pretended he soared among them, no longer bound to the crust of the earth.

## Middleham Castle
### January 1462.

Winter came, colder and bleaker than Richard remembered from Fotheringhay or even London. In the mornings frost sparkled in the sun. Bare black branches of trees waved starkly against the sky, and the castle seemed even more like a drab rock than on the day he had first seen it.

Servants cleared the coppices of dead wood, replenishing the supply for hearth fires, honing some to replace handles of axes and hoes, and carving smaller pieces into bowls, spoons, and an occasional toy for a child's pleasure.

In the evening, the men would sit before the hearth, their quick-skilled knives flashing in the firelight as they worked. Many of their chips and shavings fell on the floor, and the children made a game of finding the largest and smoothest of the pieces, gathering them before a kitchen wench could sweep them into the fire.

It was that winter that Richard began to notice how harshly Warwick would treat his younger daughter. Anne's eyes were often red from crying, her cheeks bore the mark of her father's hand, and Richard wondered how a child of five could make her father so angry.

Anne had saved the wood chips and splinters she had collected and gathered them into a small coffer. One day she showed Richard her "treasure."

"This is a pearl," she said, pointing, "and these are rubies."

"Rubies are red," he said, proud of his great nine-year-old knowledge.

"*This* one isn't," she replied.

Later he found her crying, the box of chips at her side. He bent to pick it up, but she kicked it aside. "But these are your jewels," he said. "Don't you want them?"

"No. They are just wood. They're worthless."

"Then why are you crying?"

"I showed them to my father. He punished me for lying."

In the spring, when the ground had partly hardened after the melting snow, the lads took up practicing on the large quintain. For a week now, they had worked with the ungainly device, charging it on horseback at a full gallop. The timing was far more treacherous than with the small quintain. Instead of two sandbags, a weighted shield hung from one arm. A rider had to hit the shield squarely and solidly for the arm to yield; if he scored a strong hit but moved too slowly, the sandbag could swing around with enough force to unhorse him.

Richard could never find the precise moment to strike—he was always too soon or too late. Pearl galloped faster than he could think, and in the instant he raised his lance, the quintain seemed to shift before his eyes, ready to smite him in the face. He could see himself fall and taste the sawdust before he ever raised his lance.

"Very good, Percy. Now do it again. Richard, watch." Giles lifted his arm. "Go," he called. Rob ran the course and left the quintain spinning almost as quickly as the time Giles took to lower his arm.

"Now, Richard."

Richard moved into place.

"Think clearly before you start, Richard," Giles said. "Move a little to your right. That's it. Fix your eyes on the shield. Good. Keep your speed until you have finished the course."

Normally responsive to his handling, Pearl had grown to hate the course almost as much as Richard did. She would try to pull left at the last minute and avoid the quintain altogether. Richard gathered in the reins, the right rein slightly more taut. He made certain his lance was level, his elbow close to his side, his heels down.

Giles raised his arm. "Go!"

Richard applied his spurs, and Pearl surged forward.

Again. Everything hurt. His back where the bag had struck him, and his hands, which had taken part of the weight of his fall. Most of all, his lungs, which felt hammered flat as parchment.

Richard pushed himself up first onto his hands and knees, and then sat back, gasping until his breath returned. Pearl stood placidly, reins trailing until Jeremy trotted off and retrieved her. Now a hand taller than Richard, and an effortless jouster himself, Jeremy refused to look at him until he stood and had dusted off the sawdust. Then he whispered, "Slow down. You strike too early."

Giles crouched down in his padded leather vest, callused hands resting on his knees. "Master Richard, what have I told you? You must strike quickly. Once you move, do not hesitate." He lifted one hand and chopped it across the other palm.

"I know."

"Then?"

"I will try." Poor Giles. Jeremy, too. They wanted so much to help, but all they could do was say the same words over and over. It didn't even seem strange that they had opposite advice. Richard was convinced that he was slow when he should be quick, and sudden when he should take his time. He didn't know how to make them understand that he wasn't so stupid that he didn't understand the words. What he didn't know was how to put everything together, and words didn't help.

One particularly bad day, as he was picking himself up, he saw Pearl yawn, a great horse yawn with quivering nostrils and thick lips pulled back from her teeth, showing all her pale pink gums. After he stood and gathered her reins, the first thing he did was to give her nose a sharp smack.

"Master Richard." Richard could tell from Giles's tone that the horsemaster was not pleased. "You do not chastise your horse for your failings. I don't suppose I need to explain that?"

"No, sir," Richard said, and gave the poor abused nose a stroke.

His next run was the worst he had made. As he lay on the ground, he felt the sawdust grinding under his cheek and thought he could not tolerate one more fall, one more failure. And why should he? Who ever heard of a real knight spinning around like a top after you struck him?

He spoke boldly, as soon as he found Giles alone. "I'm not going to practice on with the quintain again."

"No?" Giles raised one bushy eyebrow and waited.

"It's nothing like real battle, is it?"

"Not so much."

"Then it can't be important."

"I've seen plenty of quintain contests in tournaments."

"I won't ever joust in a tournament." There. That should settle the matter.

Giles put down the strap he was oiling. "Master Richard, you may be the king's brother, but I am the king's servant, and the king has bid me to train you. The time to decide what you don't want to do is when you know you can do everything, should you need to. Otherwise, you'll always act out of fear. That is what the quintain can teach you."

Richard went up on the ramparts that night, as he usually did, and looked up at the stars, but the magic didn't happen. There was no magic. He had only been pretending.

## Middleham Castle
### June 1462.

All summer the stern-faced men rode into Middleham, Some were dressed in coarse plain wool, axes hanging from their belts. Others were knights outfitted in sword and harness, squires at their sides, jeweled rings and ornamented buckles catching the sun. A handful one day, scores the next. They soon filled the great hall with their sun- and wind-hardened faces and their voices. Some of them Richard could hardly understand, their dialects heavy and ancient: a trace of the centuries-past Norse invaders, Bennett explained. At night, the men slept where they ate, indifferent to the servants around them and the hard stone floor on which they lay. The hall reeked of sweat and dogs, and the ladies complained that the stench ruined their appetites.

The men spoke of battles and killing in much the same way that Richard had overheard that night in Ludlow Castle. He heard again the names of King Henry and Margaret—the hated Queen Margaret, the French bitch. The same king and queen whose army had killed his father and Edmund. He had thought Margaret and Henry were dead, or gone to France. Eventually he pieced together, from rumor, from bits of overheard talk, what was happening.

Henry still had supporters determined to restore him to the throne. But Edward was king. How could anyone change that?

One day Jack rode in with a group of his knights; a few days later, all the men who had gathered at Middleham followed. *Where was Edward?* Richard finally had to ask: Alice nearly dropped the account book she was about to shelve.

"Poor gosling, do you fear for your brother?"

Gosling. That was her name for him. And sometimes she called him Shadow. The little ghost-boy who appeared from nowhere. He hated both names.

"No. I'm not afraid. I just want to know where he is."

"Child, he is in London, minding his kingdom. Where did you think he might be?" The countess was calm. Didn't she know what happened when men took their wagons of weapons and rode away?

Of course she knew. She was lying about Edward being safe, and he wondered why. Was she herself too afraid to see the truth? Afraid that Warwick might never come back?

At night Richard lay in the dormitory awake and alert, burdened by his terrible knowledge. He listened to the castle's night sounds, the boys stirring in their sleep, the occasional footsteps and muffled laughter out in the passageway, while he waited for the sounds that would wake him to grief and disaster. Except he wouldn't let them. This time, if he was to be taken again to watch some village burn, or be sent across the sea, he would not be caught unprepared. He schooled himself to sleep lightly, waking at every sound. At night the dreams returned, but he learned to pull himself awake from them, too. Sometimes, exhausted by the nights, he fell asleep in the schoolroom, until Bennett, at once disapproving and concerned, touched his shoulder. "Master Richard, find you Homer so tedious?"

Toward the end of summer, most of the Middleham men came riding back. Others were slung belly down over their horses, hands and boots dangling beneath the stained and blood-stiffened cloaks that covered them. The horses carrying the dead were at the end of the retinue, swarmed over by small clouds of flies, like meat gone rotten.

Oh. That's what men were, then, when they died. Dead meat. His father's head could not have seen or talked. Could not have looked on York, nor anywhere else. Dead was dead. How silly he had been to think otherwise.

Richard remembered how he had come to Middleham terrified by war. He had thought of battle as the wolf at the householder's door, something foreign and wild, bringing horror and destruction where there should be safety. Now he saw that, although unpleasant, it was a common enough beast. If you were strong enough, you might keep it shackled at a distance, but it was never truly tamed. And the crown was never truly won as long as there were other heads that would wear it and armies to help them.

That fall, Margaret's army seized the county of Northumberland. In January of '63, Jack and Warwick chased her men back to Scotland, and by the following spring it would have taken a ledger book to keep account of who held certain castles along the border. The one thing

Richard still could make no sense of was why Scotland, England's
ancient enemy, would protect a mad old English king.

## Middleham Castle
## March 1463.

By his second spring at Middleham, Richard could no longer remember when he had had his last nightmare. At bedtime he was so tired
that he couldn't think of whether or not he was afraid to close his
eyes, and no messengers came in the night to rouse him.

Even the quintain held no terrors for him.

At some point, he began to see how everything came together on
the field, how to manage a shield with one arm and a lance with the
other, how to feel his own weight and use it to his advantage. He
thought of all the times he had squinted at the stars, breaking their
pure and brilliant light into splinters. It was as if all his life he had
been squinting, then had opened his eyes. There was the light, and
what had been fragmented became clear.

On a clear spring day, Richard could watch from a hill as the dales
changed before his eyes. First there were the wide sloping shadows
that molded the contours of the land, layering the hills with alternating darkness and bands of sunlit green, like looking at night and day
at the same time. Then the clouds would shift and open the skies, and
the sun shone so brilliantly the turf seemed to glow with a golden
light all its own.

Even when the clouds grew heavy and black with rain, there were
still those occasional sliding sheets of light. If there were sheep on the
hills, you could watch the animals graze, heads down in the shadow,
moving close together for warmth. One of the moving pockets of sun
would catch a single sheep. The animal would lift its head and turn
its face into the warmth, chewing drowsily until clouds covered the
sun again, and then blink, baffled, in the bone-dense way of sheep,
before staring at the ground like a beggar who has lost a coin and
expects it to magically reappear. Finally, it would blink again and go
back to grazing, the dream of light forgotten.

On one of those bright spring days, Richard and John Parr
watched a lamb's birth.

They lay face down on the slope, the sun on their backs, half
hidden by the grass, their horses hobbled at a little distance. They had

followed narrow pathways all morning, paths that went in circles to spots like this one, worn bare, clearly an animal lair.

One animal, a laden, panting sheep, lay there when they came and settled quietly down, chins on folded hands. And now two: the lamb had come into the world before their eyes, and they watched the hind legs rise, fold and rise again, until finally they stayed upright, quivering sticks. Then the head and forelegs. Richard tried so hard to be quiet that it almost hurt to breathe, but he wanted to cheer at the same time, the little creature was so persistent in its efforts.

A voice came from behind him. "You, there! Boy!"

Richard raised up on one elbow. "I, sir?"

"*You*, sir! Is it your ears or your wits that are lacking?" Brother Simon labored up the hill, as nut-brown as ever, using his shepherd's crook as a walking stick. "Oh, it's you, Master Richard. And John Parr. You have found Clothilde for me, then?" He saw the lamb and let out his breath with pleasure. "Ahhhh. She has had her little one, I see."

The brother sat down on the grass beside them. "She's the last of my ewes to lamb. She picked a fine day for birthing, didn't she? There was some bitter weather for little ones earlier this winter."

Simon turned his face into the sun before speaking again. "A new-born lamb can take as much cold a grown ram, did you know? As long as it's dry, that is. If it stays wet, it will freeze. Think of that, lads! An hour old, it will have eaten and walked, and can sleep through weather a man wouldn't wake from if *he* slept. Wondrous creatures!"

John Parr said, "You called her Clothilde."

"Aye, that is her name."

"You name your sheep?" Richard asked. "How do you tell them apart?"

"You lords." Simon shook his head. "You name your fine horses, your hunting birds, your swords. Even your cups! But you cannot tell one sheep from another. For shame."

"But those things, they are all different."

"So are the sheep, lad, so are the sheep." Brother Simon stood, then stooped to pick up the lamb, and prodded Clothilde with his crook.

"Are you going to eat her?" John Parr asked.

"Oh, not for years. She's a good breeder. Just look at the size of the lamb."

"And the lamb?"

Brother Simon looked at the little creature in his arms. "Well, that's hard to say. We raise them mostly for the wool, you know. He may make a stew some day when he's too old and stringy to roast."

How good it felt to stand in the sun with Brother Simon. A cloud passed over, and as it did, Richard had a sudden fear that Edward could call him back at any time. This was not his to keep. His only to learn and know. Edward's will could send him anywhere.

### Middleham Castle
### July 1463.

One fine day in high summer, Warwick took Richard out to the bailey. The stable boys were gathered, talking among themselves with an air of expectation. Even the countess and her daughters had come out to mingle with the servants.

Richard was wondering what the occasion was, when Rob came from the stables, leading a horse. A full-sized man's horse, white like the gods must have ridden. The horse had a wide forehead, brilliant dark eyes, and a narrow muzzle. Its muscles rippled beneath a glossy hide, and it lifted its hooves briskly, as though eager to follow wherever it was led. When Rob brought him to a stop in front of Richard, the horse obeyed instantly, looking around with alert, curious eyes.

"He is beautiful, sir," Richard said to Warwick.

"Yes, is he not? The Brothers at Jervaulx bred him." Warwick then fell silent until Richard felt the pause. "You don't see it, do you?"

"Sir?"

"He is for you."

Richard was the king's brother and had untold riches, but he had never dreamed of owning such an animal. "Thank you, my lord." The response was inadequate. Any response would be.

He walked over and took the lead rope Rob extended to him and stroked the horse's neck and jowl. He knew the animal would be fast and, almost without thinking, knew the name it was born to have.

Mercury whinnied and pushed at Richard's face with his muzzle. Richard pushed back, a joy he had never experienced welling up inside him. He laid his cheek against the horse's neck, the sleek hide warm beneath his skin, smelling the good clean horse smell. *Mine. He is mine.*

When he lifted his head, he found Warwick watching him intently. He knew he was being measured, but against what standard, he couldn't have told.

*York*
*December 1463.*

In December, Edward came to York to sign a treaty with the Scots. Richard was to attend the meeting, his true initiation into the world of men, out of the schoolroom and tiltyard.

Many things were clear to him that had been mysteries. The first was that Henry and Edward were kin, descendants of some long-ago king; that was why they each claimed a right to the throne, and why Edward and Margaret of Anjou each named the other murderer, impostor, and devil's agent. The second was that as long as Edward had England, Margaret and Henry had the attention of the Scots, who, having envied the English for centuries, were now zealous to support the former king and queen for the pure pleasure of seeing England writhe. And last, that Margaret, former princess of Anjou, away from her homeland and married to an English imbecile, hated the English even more than did the Scots, and her blood rose up in joy at helping them shake loose the borders.

The once incomprehensible and complex now had the precise neutral elegance of a mathematical equation: hate balanced against hate, uncontaminated by either pity or piety.

There was one more side to the triangle, one that did not fit the equation so nicely. Louis, King of France, sat on his throne subtle as a spider in the corner of the ceiling and watched Margaret and Edward tear at each other like a dog and a bear in the pits.

Warwick believed Louis could be wooed, won from his alliance with Margaret and Anjou. Was not England the greater power? And was Louis not drawn to power like filings to a magnet, no matter how dearly he loved to scheme and postpone any satisfying resolution?

Edward disagreed. He thought Warwick played the fly to Louis's spider. You do not bargain with spiders; you sweep them into the fire. Besides, Edward had dreams of reclaiming the English holdings in France that Henry had let slip through his fingers, dreams of the day when Englishmen could hold their heads high, not only at home, but anywhere on the continent.

Pale gray skies sheltered the city's stone walls, covered in a mantle of snow. Edward's party stayed at a quiet inn on a street so narrow that the lanterns swinging across the lane danced circles of gold on the door of the inn as they approached, winter's fireflies. The king's officers had the best chambers in the place, of course. The innkeeper would have seen to that out of pride, regardless of payment. Unlike his predecessor, however, Edward rewarded hospitality with a full purse.

The Scots delegation returned home as soon as the truce was signed, having no wish to remain on English soil any longer than necessary, but Edward chose to stay a few days in York before making the long journey back to London. He was in his glory: the crown he had struggled so hard to gain was now truly his. Without the Scots to fight for Margaret, surely she could do nothing but turn back to France and give up all pretensions for her husband and son.

In the two years since Richard had seen him, Edward had acquired a calm detachment that replaced the deference he once would have shown to men older and more experienced.

Warwick must have noted the change too; there was a new constraint between him and Edward, as though both men had in hand a playmaker's folio, but their lines didn't match. Jack alone seemed unaffected, sitting relaxed, legs stretched out before the fire.

"Well, Ned," Jack was saying, "that was excellently done! About time the Scots had enough of dying for Margaret. If they had any sense, they would have made peace with you two years ago. Nothing to win by holding out, although I never knew good sense to rule them."

Warwick turned his goblet in his hand, leaned forward, elbows resting on his knees. "Yes, it was neatly done. But what did it really gain us? Nothing. I still have half the able-bodied men in the north watching the borders."

The air in the room was suddenly as stinging as smoke in the eyes. Richard didn't understand why, but clearly he wasn't the only one who felt it. There was Warwick, half his face bright in the firelight, the other half in shadow, fingers tense around the stem of his goblet, and Edward, standing at the hearth, pride in every inch of him, but with a stubborn shuttered look, as though he would say what was expected of him, but his thoughts were his own.

"Come here, Dickon," Jack said, for no apparent reason. Startled to hear the childish name, Richard went over and sat on the bench beside his cousin. Jack draped one arm over the back of the bench, his hand firmly on the boy's shoulder. "No one expects the borders to be calm." Jack looked off into the fire as he spoke, talking to no one in particular. "They haven't been since Arthur's time, why should they be now?"

"True enough," Warwick agreed. "But look, friends," he set down his cup and spread his hands. "Your confidence is riper than the peace you think you have. You," a quick look at Edward, "will not be secure in your throne until Henry is hunted down. Hunted down and killed. You can celebrate all you want tonight, and I'll grant you congratulations are deserved, but the work is not yet done."

"Cousin," Edward said, "I thought it was you who told me that if I had one contender for the throne, I may as well have a dozen. Why trouble with Henry when he still has a son for men to rally around?"

"Precisely my point, Ned. Kill him, too."

Edward made a sound of disgust. "He's a child."

Warwick smiled, a thin-lipped smile of no mirth. "He's Richard's age. Is your brother a child?" Richard felt Jack's hand on his shoulder tighten, as if Warwick and Edward were two dogs tugging at a bone, and Richard had been about to fling himself between them.

"You can't compare my brother with that changeling! Lancaster wouldn't know one end of a sword from the other."

"So you'd wait a few years first." Warwick leaned back. "Let the boy live for now, then kill the man? Like fatting a calf for slaughter, is that your plan?"

For the first time, Edward seemed uncertain. "Of course I'd rather meet him on the field. I have no appetite for murdering children."

"It's a mistake." Warwick spoke soberly, and so intensely that even Jack looked startled.

"What's your meaning, brother?"

"If the Scots won't help Margaret, she will take the boy back to France, and Louis will support him. Unless, of course, Louis decides it better pleases him to side with us than with Margaret. It is the French we should be courting, not the Scots."

Edward snapped, "Let Louis do what he will! If the French didn't learn their lesson at Agincourt, we'll teach it again."

Richard had heard tales of Agincourt, the battle on French soil half a century earlier, when English archers won the day—and a good part of French soil—against a host many times their number.

At Edward's small outburst, Richard began to understand that what they were talking about had nothing to do with the Scots, nor land in France, nor with killing anyone. It was a private contest between Edward and Warwick in which what the prize was did not matter nearly so much as the mere fact of winning. Now that Edward's composure was broken, Warwick seemed easier, almost happy.

"Sometimes I forget how young you are, Ned. Not every battle turns out as you wish it to. Surely Wakefield taught you that."

Richard tensed and felt Jack's hand tighten on his shoulder. Edward's face had gone white. How had Warwick the arrogance to speak of their father's death so lightly?

When Edward answered he had his voice in control, but there was an unmistakable warning in his words. "Cousin, let me make it easy for you to keep your friendship with me. There are two things you must never do. Do not talk to me as you would a child, and do not forget that I am king."

Warwick was thrown off balance, but he landed on his feet. "How could I forget? You are the king of my own making."

## Middleham Castle
### June 1464.

That summer, Warwick began to negotiate Edward's marriage. On a visit to Middleham, Edward discussed the matter with his cousin. Warwick told Edward bluntly that the time had come to choose a wife. It was well for a king to have brothers to guard the succession, but that he needed a queen and heirs of his body to secure the hearts of his countrymen. Louis of France had turned down Warwick's suggestion of Edward marrying Louis's daughter, but had offered the possibility of pledging his sister-in-law, Bona of Savoy, to Edward.

All the while Edward smiled agreeably. Yes, it was time he married. Yes, the king needed heirs. Indeed, the sooner, the better. Yes, a marriage between England and France was a matter of great import, a blessing to both kingdoms.

All yes. All smiles and agreement until one September afternoon when Richard was helping Giles sort through the weapons in the guard tower as Anne watched. The little girl had become his constant shadow. He didn't mind, as long as no one remarked on it.

"Here, Richard, take these. God knows what they are doing here." Giles handed Richard two short lengths of chain, such as might have held a man in leg-irons, thoroughly rusted. He gave Anne a quick glance. "Lady Anne, by careful. Your mother will have me flayed for allowing you up here."

Giles stepped into the tower and scuffed at a section of the floor that was dark with moisture, stepped back, and looked up at the roof.

"There's the trouble. We'll have to repair the leak before we store anything else in here. *Lady Anne!*"

Anne had disappeared. Actually, only her head had gone missing. Richard saw the rest of her, straining to look over the crenel, her head and shoulders hidden behind the merlin. She stood straight at Giles's outcry and pointed.

"Someone's coming!"

Richard turned and saw the dust raised by the galloping horse. It's nothing to do with you, he told himself. But he could not think of hard-riding messengers as bearers of anything but bad news.

Warwick called to him as he and Giles were crossing the arcade to the keep. "Richard, make haste. I must see you."

He followed Warwick into the earl's private antechamber. After closing the door, Warwick picked up a scroll from the table. "I have here a letter from your brother, Richard. What do you suppose it says?"

Richard was silent.

Warwick tapped it across his palm. "Well, don't you want to know?"

"Yes, sir."

"It seems Edward has chosen a wife for himself. He is married—has been married since May."

Edward four months married, and Warwick just now told? No. There must be an explanation. Edward would not do such a thing without good reason.

"Don't you want to know who the fair lady is?"

Richard could only nod, not trusting his voice, which was beginning to falter and crack when he least wanted it to. Edward's wife was not Bona of Savoy, that much was certain.

"Elizabeth Woodville of Grafton Regis."

So. It was a jest.

No. No jest. The look on Warwick's face was a warning that Richard would be wise not to smile.

"This is wrong, Richard. I hold the north in the palm of my hand. Where I lean, the northern counties lean with me. Your brother has much to learn, but I did not expect this! No one leans with him. Not the north, nor the midlands. Certainly not London. Do you understand? This woman brings nothing to the marriage. Nothing! Two half-grown sons who bring Edward nothing but grief. Oh, I know, the woman has sons, she must be fertile. Is that what you are thinking? The boys are seven and eight years old—they're proof of nothing at all."

"No, sir."

"Why, Richard? Why would your brother do such a thing?" Warwick's voice was soft, but his eyes were glistening and bright, almost as with tears. Surely not, Richard thought, but he had a sense of Warwick's composure maintained by great effort and could imagine the wound to both pride and trust that his cousin must have suffered.

"I don't know, sir." Surely Edward had cause for the marriage, had the good of the kingdom in mind.

"Well, Richard, have you *nothing* to say?"

"No, sir. I don't." Anything he said might be denying or agreeing to something he didn't mean. The tangle of grown men's actions was more than he wanted to try to undo.

*R*ichard found Jack in the empty chapel, gazing out the window. Jack turned slowly. "The weather's changing. Winter's in the air."

Richard didn't care about the weather. "Edward is married! Did you know?"

"Yes. Warwick told me." Jack was calm enough.

"Don't you know who he married? Elizabeth Woodville!" Mistress Woodville was *old*, having sons almost as old as he. But perhaps even more appalling, her husband had died fighting for Henry.

Jack was still calm. "What of it? Your brother will do as he will."

"Should he have married her? Was that wrong?" Richard stared as Jack struggled with his answer.

Jack shook his head slowly. "No, I can't say that. In a way, Edward did well. He is his own man, and Warwick was slow in seeing that. Edward couldn't allow my brother to lead him about like a pig with a ring in its nose. He would be seen as Warwick's puppet. That is a disaster for any man, let along a king."

Jack gave him a hard-edged searching glance. "Do you understand what I just said?"

Richard nodded. Of course he understood; it was exactly what he wanted to hear.

Jack went on. "Good. Now, let me tell you something else. Understand this, too. My brother is not wrong, either. He has a right to be angry. All these months of negotiation, and Edward said not a word. Warwick must be the butt of all the jests in France just now. No man likes to be taken for a fool."

"Why did Edward marry her, then?"

"For love, I suppose." Jack's mouth twisted in a bitter smile.

"Is love wrong?"

"No, but it is not always to be indulged"

"Who is right, then?"

"Right?" Jack laughed. "Oh, so that's it. You want to hold court, do you? You want your brother acquitted and mine convicted?"

"No." Yes. If it came to that.

"Look. What good would that do? Bring peace between them? Make it easy for you to stay here? That's what you want, isn't it? You want to stay here and serve them both, and you think knowing who is right will let you do that."

The sun was setting in the window behind them. In the fading light, Jack looked weary and depleted, the first time Richard could remember seeing him anything but hearty.

Jack sighed. "I can't tell you who is right. I'm not a clever enough man to know that. I will tell you what is true, though. Your brother and mine no longer love each other. Some day it will not be possible for you to love them both, either." The tone of Jack's voice, the same flat, heavy acceptance, was what Richard had heard in his father's voice years before. *England may well regret she has so many sons of kings.*

"But you do," he said. "*You* love them both."

Jack passed a hand over his eyes, as though he had just seen through the years and witnessed a disaster that all the knowledge in the world would not prevent, and finally shook his head, with a look of infinite sadness. "Time will come, lad, time will come."

# 6  *Transformations*

*Jervaulx Abbey*
*June 1465.*

"Good morning," Brother Simon greeted Richard and Warwick as they dismounted.

"To you, also, Brother," Warwick said, pulling off his gloves. The earl and Richard had come to look at the new crop of foals, and make arrangements to bring to Middleham the yearlings Warwick had selected the previous fall when they in turn had been foals. The horses would not be ridden for another year, but they would be handled and trained to accept halters, blankets, and finally saddles. By the time the animals were two-year-olds, they would accept without protest the weight of a grown man. At three, they would carry man and armor as though born for the task.

"Brother Simon," Richard nodded.

At thirteen or thereabouts, Simon noted, Richard had grown quite handsome. The lad had a quiet smile, and his eyes were level and direct. But he seemed watchful, not quite at ease, as if the rules of the arena in which he played were subject to sudden change.

"Come to the paddock," Simon said. "I think we have had an unusually fine season. I am anxious to see if you agree."

Richard ran his hand down Mercury's neck, ending the stroke with a pat before turning the horse over to a groom.

"The white horse still pleases?" Simon hardly needed to ask. Few horses had the particular blend of sweet disposition, quick intelligence, and willingness to perform that he had seen in this horse.

"The white horse," Warwick said, "is something of a *waste*."

"My lord!" Simon was stunned. "The horse does not meet your expectations?"

"Oh, not that," Warwick laughed. "The horse has talent to spare. It is the talent which is the *waste*."

"My lord?" He saw Richard's face go blank except for a spark in the eyes that could have been pain, anger, or even fury. But it was gone too soon to tell.

"My lord means," Richard said, his voice clear and steady, "that I don't use Mercury's abilities to the fullest. I don't joust."

"You don't like the tournament?" Simon asked.

"No. It seems a *waste*." Richard's eyes met Warwick's, and Simon could feel the charged air between them. "Of time, that is."

"I doubt that's all of it." Warwick's voice was calm. "I saw how you paled at the joust when Hadley met his fate. You'll see more blood flow soon enough. I suggest you accustom yourself to it."

"It's not that," Richard said. "It was the horse. Hadley rode poorly. If he wanted to waste his own life, that's his affair, but he should have spared the horse."

"And we shouldn't ride horses into battle? Must we think of their safety then?" Warwick pursued.

"No, sir."

"And that doesn't trouble you?"

"No, sir. It's of necessity, then. We must and they must, too."

"Well," Warwick said. "Now we know the truth of it." He clapped Richard lightly on the back. "You're right. We must mind the creatures that serve us, be they man or beast."

The grooms brought several pairs of mares and foals into the enclosure. The foals, round-rumped youngsters with liquid eyes, were still learning how to manage their stilt-like legs. The dams hovered close, nosing their little ones.

Simon watched the two of them, Warwick with his hand on Richard's shoulder as he discussed the merits of one foal against another, and Richard, the slight fiddling of one hand with the dagger at his side the only betrayal of his unease. So, Simon thought, that was where the boy's edgy caution lay. Richard could master his responses to the barbs; it was Warwick's blowing warm after cold that threw him off balance.

*R*ichard loved any excursion to Jervaulx. It was one of many Yorkshire abbeys founded by the white-robed Cistercians, for whom even the austerities of the Benedictines and Augustinians were too soft. The Cistercians had their own notion of a life of purity—one devoid of color and ornament, even of speech. But that was in the old

days, when the most a wanderer might expect was a terse sentence
of direction accompanied by a waving hand. Now silence was mostly
honored within cloister walls and at meals.

Bennett had explained about the plainness of the abbeys. "Not like
your great churches in London. No stained glass, only clear. And no
painted saints." But Richard admired their stark beauty. Their propor-
tions had been designed by men possessing an eye for grace. The gardens, too, were of a pleasing order, green rows carefully tended, laid
out as neatly as squares of tile. Even the abbey's names were beautiful:
Jervaulx, Rievaulx, Fountains.

"You are near thirteen now." Warwick's voice pulled Richard out of
his thoughts. "Before many years, you must marry. Have you thought
about that?"

"Marriage? No, sir." Richard had wondered all morning what lay
behind Warwick's invitation to accompany him to Jervaulx.

Of course he had thought of marriage. His wife would be whoever
best served Edward's policy. She might well be a foreign princess who
didn't speak his tongue, an infant, or an old woman. It would be no
matter if she were ugly, too. Nothing about the idea gave him pleasure.

Warwick turned in his saddle. "Perhaps you should do so. It is possible you will be a man grown before you take a wife. On the other hand,
depending on what alliances Edward needs to make, you could be married before you even see your bride. Has the king said anything to you?"

"No, sir. Has he to you?" He hadn't seen his brother in over a year,
but couldn't believe Edward would have begun marriage negotiations
before at least mentioning the fact.

"No, but you know how things are these days. An alliance between
us could pave the path for years of friendship." Warwick went on. "I
know your brother well. When the time comes to determine your
future, he will consider your wishes if it is possible to do so."

Then the earl said something Richard had never thought to hear
cross the man's lips. "Your brother married for love; he would surely
understand your having desires of your own."

Richard had thought often that Jack's warning about the enmity
between king and cousin might come to naught. For one thing, Elizabeth was proving not nearly so disastrous a queen as many had feared.
She had borne young Bess with admirable promptness. A son would
have been better, but since Elizabeth already had two strong young
sons, her ability to conceive males was not in question.

There were other signs, too. Warwick and Jack had tracked poor mad Henry to Lancastershire, where he had wandered with a handful of attendants. The old king was taken to the Tower, confined there, and allowed to receive the few guests who cared to visit him. There was no more talk of killing him. Edward rewarded Warwick with more land and grants and gave Jack the Earldom of Northumberland, the office formerly held by Henry Percy, the Nevilles' long-time rival, and Rob Percy's distant cousin.

Marry for love. That was what people said about Edward's marriage to Elizabeth, although they usually laughed when they said it. He understood the laughter now. The king's grey mare. Oh, how I'd love to mount the king's grey mare. Blood rushed to Richard's face—and to another part of his body that seemed to have a mind of its own. Just thinking of such things was enough to cause that inconvenient change in his body, a state the church said was sinful. It happened to all of his friends, though, and they didn't seem to feel unduly guilty.

He still couldn't make sense of everything, though. What his mother and father had done—and they had truly loved each other—and what Edward and Elizabeth did that caused the laughter were the same. The same, even, as what the soldier did to the girl that terrible day at Ludlow.

"I don't know about love," he said stiffly.

Warwick laughed. "Of course not. You are not expected to at your age, although that will change faster than you think. But tell me, how would you serve your brother after your time at Middleham is ended?"

"I don't know, sir." That was something Richard had not dared even to ask himself. In another two years or so, Edward would summon him back to London.

"Well, then," Warwick said. "Let us consider something. Let us suppose that keeping the north together were as critical to the peace of the kingdom as any foreign alliance could be. If I am correct, Edward would want either you or George to marry into a family that already holds much of the north. Such a marriage would provide the base of the king's strength here. Do you follow me?"

"Sir."

"I don't know what Edward would say, but I do know this: I hold the largest grants in the north, and I have two daughters your age." He glanced at Richard. "You look puzzled. What is it?"

"Are we not cousins, sir?" Richard silently cursed himself. Could he take nothing lightly? Warwick had just proposed an idea better than any gift he could imagine, and he had to look it over like fish from a disreputable market.

"You and I are cousins, Richard. My daughters are therefore one step further removed. You would need a dispensation, but they are granted all the time for kin closer than you and my daughters. And, need I remind you, the Archbishop of York is also my brother. Permission to marry would not be difficult to obtain. Now, which of my daughters would you choose?"

Isabel was meek and fair, with her gentian eyes and goldenrod hair. Anne was neither. The Teasel, Warwick called her—the thistle, the prickery one who went against the grain, who could raise her father's ire like a fuller's brush raised nap.

"Anne pleases me, sir," he said.

When they reached Middleham, both girls were sitting on the steps of the courtyard, their skirts prettily about them. "Daughters," Warwick said. Isabel gave a quivering smile. Anne looked up at her father with an odd expression, then turned away, as if she had been trying to recall whether she knew him or not, and had decided she didn't. She was barely nine years old and could infuriate her father with a glance.

Warwick frowned. "You have forgotten all courtesy? You should rise and greet your sire, not sit in insolence."

Both girls stood, and Richard saw at their feet, partly hidden by their skirts, traces of small animals—a tail here, tiny paws there.

"Move." Warwick grasped Isabel's elbow. "Stand aside."

There they were, three squirming little creatures, whelps of Warwick's favorite bitch, their eyes barely open.

"What's this?" Warwick asked. "I expressly told you not to handle them. Do you forget so easily?"

"No, sire." Isabel flushed and lowered her eyes. Anne was clearly thinking. Richard could see her face change as the possibilities passed in her mind, one after another, as precise and orderly as the rows of the abbey gardens. The trouble was, all that order sometimes brought her to strange conclusions, as if she planted carrots and harvested cabbage.

"They like it here," she said.

"What say you, daughter?"

"I said, they like it here. They like for me to pet them."

Anne's expression was utterly bland, as though she were completely indifferent to the effect of her words. For a moment, Richard thought the incident would pass, as Warwick moved a step forward. But then he suddenly turned and struck Anne a blow that jerked her head back and left the mark of his hand on her cheek. Anne had her father's gift of landing on her feet. She stooped and gathered all three pups into her arms. "Come, I'll take you back. My father says you shouldn't be here."

*Y*ou think that was cruel, don't you?" Warwick said, mounting the steps after the girls had gone.

"No, sir." He did, but he wasn't going to say so. He would learn all he could at Warwick's hand, and then decide for himself what was cruel and what was necessary.

"Come, I can see you do. It shows in your face. What I would have you learn from this, Richard, is that benevolence is no one's entitlement. It must be earned."

They reached the top of the stairs, and Warwick paused at the door. "You will have people beholden to you some day. Teach them early how to win your good lordship."

*A*nne was not in the hall at supper. Richard searched her favorite haunts inside the castle, then went outside. He didn't see her in the garden and finally wandered down toward the fishpond. He was about to turn back when he finally spotted her walking a little distance from the pond, kicking at the ground as she went. "Anne!"

She stood and waited for him, twining the tail of her braid around her finger. Her eyes were dry, but shadowed and red.

"You weren't at supper," Richard said.

"I didn't want any."

"No, Teasel. Your father beat you, didn't he? You can't sit down."

"I could if I wanted to."

They walked slowly back toward the pond. The reeds at the water's edge moved slightly in the breeze, and the sun turned the shallow water a golden brown. Richard picked up a stick from the ground and knocked it idly against the cat-tails. "Why do you make your father so angry, Teasel?" he asked. "He doesn't *want* to hurt you. If you'd said you were sorry, he wouldn't have touched you."

"If he didn't want to hurt me, then he shouldn't have done it. Leave me alone. I don't want to talk to you."

Anne turned to run. Richard let the stick fall from his hand and grabbed her braid.

"Ouch!" Anne looked at him curiously. "What are you doing?"

"Nothing. Your hair is pretty. That's all." He wrapped the braid around his hand, feeling it, sun-warmed and silky in his palm. When they married, would he love her? Would he enjoy touching her, long for her? He saw her tear-streaked face, how hard she tried to hide all hurt. Like me, he thought, and quickly let the braid drop, as though its warmth were enough to burn him.

## Middleham Castle.
## September 1466.

Francis Lovell came to Middleham in the fall of '66, a tall boy with a handsome, high-cheek-boned face. Actually, Richard thought, pretty. A little younger than Richard and Rob, Francis seemed a lifetime more knowing, certain of himself, and good at everything. An excellent swordsman, the better to protect that pretty face. The arrogant boy knew everything. He had read everything, too, always quoting someone important (unless he was lying, of course), and fluent in both French and Latin. Bennett, with his love of all knowledge, was smitten. To see his face as Francis read, you would have thought the tutor was listening to choirs of angels.

Francis was Warwick's ward and had married just prior to his arrival at Middleham. Jeremy tried to extend friendship to the new boy by mentioning that he also was an orphan and a royal ward.

Francis shrugged. "So the king's brother is your lord? What an honor. I congratulate you." There was a bitterness in the words that left Jeremy looking confused. "Even better, your lord is smaller than you. You can knock him down if you don't like his orders. Don't look so disapproving. I can see you wouldn't do that; you are bristling with honor."

Rob gave Francis the same introduction he had given Richard. "An ed-u-cat-ed man, the Latin and the English. . . ."

"Of course," Francis said. "The sacred and the secular."

"You've already met him?" Rob asked.

"Who?"

"Bennett. Our tutor."

"Don't be a fool. Everyone knows. Latin for the sacred, English for the rest."

All the lads in the dormitory would fight sleep as long as possible, playing dice until last light, or, in winter, by dying firelight. They talked about the Scots, about war, and women—about everything that fascinated them but about which they knew next to nothing, taking refuge in mocking what they did not understand.

In Scotland there were witches, murderers, and felons, but no churches. An unfortunate traveler was said to have noticed the absence and asked: Are there no Christians here?

Nae, the Scot said, we are all Eliots, Grahams, and Armstrongs.

Scotland was nothing like London, where smiles hid many an insult. When a Scot smiled, you knew it was because he was taking pure pleasure in the thought of slitting your throat.

They laughed about what the Scots did to the English and the English to the Scots. Steal cattle, burn villages, rape women. With regard to ravishing the enemy, the Scots clearly had the advantage over the English, your average Scotswoman being as ugly and hairy as a boar. Oh God, the thought of those prickly boar bristles touching their most tender and private parts. They fell into horrified laughter.

Francis groaned. "Have any of you ever been with a woman?"

Been with? Of course. Richard had sat beside them, talked to them. Long ago, he'd slept beside Agnes, and even before that, in his mother's bed. But that wasn't what Francis meant.

"What—" Rob began.

Francis cut him off. "Lain with, Percy, *lain* with. Tupped!"

Richard half expected someone—Giles or Bennett, or even the countess—to come in and drag Francis away by the ears and wash out his mouth, as though they were infants, when walls had ears and adults could see right through your skull into your thoughts. None of them was brave enough to ask Francis what they really wanted to know, but at full dark, Richard turned to Francis and asked, "Have you? Lain with a woman, that is? Your wife?"

"Don't be an idiot, Gloucester," Francis answered.

Did Francis mean that since they were married, of course they lay together? Or that he and his wife were obviously too young to bed? Richard waited, but Francis didn't elaborate. Nothing to do but keep quiet and not add to the demonstration of ignorance.

No one, except perhaps George, could mock as well as Francis, or give advice so calculated as to set a man's teeth on edge. Rob was most often the target.

"I don't mean to be cruel, Percy," Francis said, "but you cannot speak French with a northern tongue. It is like putting salt in sweetened sack."

Rob looked at Francis as if the younger boy were lack-wit. "Well, I can't speak at all, without it."

"Then better you should limit your conversations to those languages well-suited to a northern tongue."

"What might those be?"

"Surely not French. That's obvious. Nor Latin. Now I think on it, I doubt whether even the king's English sits easy on a northern tongue."

"Then you'd have me silent altogether!"

"Not so! You are most skilled at sounding all of men's most important pastimes. I have heard you belch and snore. You can surely strike terror in your enemy's heart by roaring—a northern tongue is most suited for roaring. And some day, Percy, even you will groan with love." Francis waited for Rob's response, which was never as heated as he seemed to hope. He turned to Richard. "What think you, Gloucester? Does a northerner need words at all?"

"I think if I were Rob, I'd beat you for the insult."

But Rob was never offended. Richard had never seen anything like the ease with which insults came to Francis's mouth, but to Rob, they were of no more significance than chaff blowing in the wind.

Francis clearly resented Warwick, and he barely tolerated Richard. But since they shared the bed, Richard decided to at least try to understand the new boy.

"How do you happen to come to Middleham?"

"Well, you see, my father fought for King Henry at Towton. He lived for a long time with his wounds, but he never healed."

An enemy, Richard thought. No wonder Francis hated being at Middleham.

"He was fighting for his *king*, you understand," Francis went on. "That's what Henry was, then. Your brother was the usurper. After that battle, my father continued to name himself a loyal subject of the king, who was then your brother. But it was too late. Warwick hated him. He probably hates me, too."

"Then why did he agree to be your guardian?"

"Your brother paid him, of course." Francis hesitated. "I know my father's estates and all their retainers. We could have managed—mother and I. I didn't want to marry, but the marriage makes me richer."

Richard was sorting through what Francis had told him when Rob asked, "Why would Edward pay Warwick to support you if you have property of your own?"

"It doesn't take a wizard to understand that." Francis flashed a disdainful look at Rob. "Look. If someone takes me off my estates, the crown can claim those lands. Or at least the revenue from them until I reach my majority. Let me tell you, I don't eat what Edward pays Warwick, and my keep is a pittance of the estate's income to the king.

"I am a bargain for them both, you see. The wars killed my father. Wars are only good for kings." There were tears in Francis's eyes. "And of course I may not live to reach my majority and claim my inheritance. But I won't make my father's mistake. I won't fight for any king. I won't *die* for any king."

It was the first chink in Francis's armor. The second came one night when Richard was awakened by a faint movement beside him. Francis was crying. He wasn't making a sound, but Richard knew about heaving shoulders and what they meant. He lay beside the new boy, thinking. Obviously Francis wanted no one to know of his distress. But he was suffering, and it was hard to lie there and do nothing.

Finally Richard turned over, his back to Francis, close enough to touch, shoulder to shoulder. Francis could make of it whatever he wanted, accident or comfort. If he didn't like it, he could move away. Richard felt the younger boy's body tense, as though he were holding his breath; after a moment the thin back relaxed and settled against Richard's own.

After that, when Francis's sorrow overwhelmed him, half asleep, Richard would move closer, or lay a hand on the other boy's shoulder. They never spoke of it or in any way acknowledged what passed between them when Francis was taken with grief, but a corner had been turned, and they both knew it.

In March, Jack asked Richard to ride with him to York to sit on a commission of oyer and terminer. The strange words sounded like the names of monsters in a myth—Scylla and Charybdis—but they meant only a hearing of complaints and grievances. It was to be Richard's first experience in the duties of a lord, outside of the schoolroom or tiltyard.

Some of these people think they are still living in the last century," Jack said. "If you want to know how your grandfather's father lived, you have only to sit at one of these meetings."

"What do you mean?"

"These are the quarrels of men who think their laws mean nothing, and might is everything. Destroy enough in your cause, and you can convince everyone that wrong is right. Watch. You will see what I mean."

Jack explained the cases on the way. The main one concerned grazing rights. The previous summer one of the wealthier citizens, Sir James Reade, appeared to have overshot the number of animals he was allowed to pasture on the commons. The constable, Peter Pennons, impounded the animals in his own enclosure, but then someone broke down the pens and dispersed the animals, including Pennon's own stock. In retaliation, Pennon's friends and supporters destroyed the hedges and gates around Reade's property.

From there, it was a matter of increasing violence and taking of sides. Both Pennons and Reade denied any knowledge of damage done to the other's property, but by summer's end, riots flared at the drop of a word. Mentioning a name in the wrong tone of voice could start a scuffle in a tavern or burn down a few out-buildings, and winter hadn't cooled the dissent. So far, the conflict hadn't cost any lives.

Richard was surprised at the hearing. He had always imagined such things to be mysterious and dignified—dry scholarly men like Bennett talking in serious phrases weighted with Latin. Now he thought, with a touch of contempt, that his first image of Scylla and Charybdis was more accurate. Both men were blustering and contentious. Reade said that his people were not responsible for the constable's losses: at least when his animals were penned, he knew where they were even if he couldn't get to them. Now they were scattered over the dales of Yorkshire. Pennon called Reade and his men arrogant tyrants who, if given the chance, would flatten any poor soul under their heels as surely as they razed his pens. Reade retorted that Pennon was an over-officious pomposity, and he could turn "Pennon's pens" into the ultimate ridicule.

The Middleham men were having supper in the inn after the day's hearing when a man burst in calling for Jack's help. Some fifty or sixty men were gathered in the commons. Several had clubs, and more had drawn knives. Only one man, a miller who had been unruly during the hearing, appeared to be wounded. His face and arm were bloody, and two of his friends restrained him, but the threats and jostling all were near eruption. Jack and his men rode uneasily among the quarreling throng, trying to quiet them.

Peace teetered on a fine edge. Richard could feel the wish for violence as sharp in the commons as the biting February air. No one taught you that, he thought. They taught you the law and soldiers' skills, but no one talked about this, how men long to use their power, however destructively.

Jack dismounted and spoke quietly to some of the men who appeared to be the leaders of the gathering. It was nearly dusk. The fading light and Jack's calm seemed to be dispelling some of the ill feeling when some poor fool was shoved and stumbled into Jack's horse. The horse shied, backing into the men calming the irate miller; the miller broke free and ran forward, knife raised.

Richard spurred Mercury forward, and man and horse collided shoulder to shoulder. The miller fell to the ground and lay there leaning on his elbows, gasping for breath.

"Go home," Richard said. "Put down your knife and go." He had no idea what he would do if the man defied him.

Dazed, the miller rubbed his eyes and looked at his knife, still in his hand.

"Put it down," Richard repeated. "Go home." The man rose unsteadily to his feet and let the knife fall from his fingers as he staggered away. And then, for no reason Richard could see, it was over. Jack had quieted his horse, and the crowd slowly scattered, grumbling as they went.

*R*iding back to Middleham, Jack said, "You did well, son. You kept your head there in the commons. Things might have ended differently without you."

They were riding at a sensible pace befitting the dignity of lords who had just spent days deciding the fates of men. Pride thundered in Richard's head as Mercury's hooves struck the ground. What he had sought all these years—to grow up, to act without fear—he had done. And in the future were Anne and a home in the north, hopes which he kept in his heart like jewels in a bag, to be taken out from time to time to gaze at in wonder, then carefully hide again, secure from covetous eyes.

A raucous joy filled him, and he pulled in on his reins. He had an old challenge to settle. Richard looked at his cousin's horse, taller than Mercury, a leggy beast that could cover ground, but he would swear that Mercury was at least as fast, and he knew himself to be considerably lighter than Jack.

Jack stopped, too. "What is it?"

"I'll race you to the next hill," Richard said, pointing to where a single tree stood on the horizon, black trunk and snow-sprinkled branches against a pale gray sky.

Jack remembered. "Ah, the gauntlet thrown back at me. You're better mounted today, I'll give you that. Just a moment."

Jack untied the panniers that were fastened behind his saddle and handed them to one of his men. He seemed to debate handing over his sword and harness, too, but kept them. "I'm ready."

"Wait." Richard looked at the countryside around them—rolling dales dusted with snow, a narrow bridge crossing the stream before the land started to rise again, two stone houses, and the snaking low stone walls. The road curved to the right around the houses, then swung back left to the top of the hill. Straight as the crow flies, a rider would have to leap the stream and several walls. The jumps would slow him down, but the distance was a little less. "We don't have to keep to the road," he said. "Choose your own way."

Jack frowned. "You want an old man to take those walls?"

"You're not old."

"No, but I haven't jumped in years."

"Your horse jumps. You have only to stay on."

"Son, if you talk like that, you had better hope you win."

Richard waited, wondering if he had gone too far and had offended his cousin, but Jack grinned. "Very well. You win—I forget that you were insolent. I win, and you groom my horse for a fortnight."

"Done."

"And polish my boots."

"That also."

Jack laughed, shaking his head. "You don't contest the terms?"

"No."

Jack touched spurs to his horse. Richard first followed the lane, where it lay straight and flat, neck and neck with Jack's bay, and wondered if he might do better to stay there. If he wanted to cross the field, he would have to give Jack the lead in order to clear the wall running parallel to the road.

He let Jack get a length ahead, then pulled Mercury in a sharp left. Mercury cleared the wall with a foot to spare, then crossed the ice-encrusted stream in a soaring arc.

Then over another wall, and from behind it a sheep ran out, startled and bleating. Richard glimpsed a blur of gray wool, and Mercury's hooves came down a yard away from the sheep, kicking up small clouds of snow. Richard was sure Jack had decided to stay with the road, but had no idea who was closer to the hill and wouldn't break his attention to look. He had only one more wall and then the rise. Mercury had reached a pace that seemed beyond effort, the horse's neck stretched forward, his ears were turned back by the wind of his own speed. As they started up the short rise toward the tree, Richard could feel the sound of other hoof beats drumming in his ears.

Richard reined in Mercury and for a moment had the hill to himself. He stretched his spine and jarred a branch of the tree, sending a spray of snow down the back of his neck.

As he watched Jack crest the hill, he could feel his blood beating everywhere, in his heart, but also in his fingers and behind his eyes. He had never felt so alive and would have traded places with no man on earth. He felt a shudder of fear. Surely he was loving this place too much. He had heard nothing from Edward about plans for his life.

## *Middleham Castle.*
## *May 1467.*

Finally the plan for Richard's life came. It came from Edward, as Richard had thought it would, but in a form he had not expected. Warwick had continued his long-standing obsession of peace with France and believed his efforts alone were responsible for keeping France within her boundaries. Then Edward arranged the marriage of his sister Margaret to the Duke of Burgundy. Richard scarcely remembered Margaret, who was much older, and had grown up in a different household, and he had certainly forgotten that his rarely thought-of sisters could also be used in games of policy. As with Edward's marriage to Elizabeth, the message of this betrothal was clear: France and the Earl of Warwick were nothing. Edward's will was the king's command, and Burgundy was the ally he wished to cultivate. Edward tried to salve Warwick's pride by giving him a place of honor in the train that was to escort the new Duchess of Burgundy to the coast to sail to her adopted home. Whatever Warwick thought about the insult, he didn't say.

*R*ichard! Where are your wits? Attend, please. Chess is not merely a game. It is a great teacher of strategy. Your strategy is deplorable." Warwick rapped a knuckle on the edge of the table.

"Your pardon, sir." Richard dragged his attention back to the game. He hated chess. It was one skill he had not mastered. He disliked its tedium, the infinity of moves one must consider and discard. Trying to keep in mind the ever-expanding possibilities gave him a headache. Perhaps he could have borne it if there were a time limit allowed for each move—as much, say, as the blink of an eye. Whatever you could think of in that instant was what you did.

"Peace, husband! Leave off the talk of strategy." Alice sat beside them, embroidering. The wools—sapphire, crimson, and green—lay in the basket at her side like jewels in the sun.

"Lady?" Warwick's voice was both surprised and angry.

"The musicians are beginning. How do you expect the lad to heed your instruction now?"

Richard had seen no other woman challenge her husband as Alice did Warwick. Warwick glared at her, but she held his gaze, unflinching under his displeasure.

"Oh, very well." Warwick lifted his hand and leaned back in his chair. "Go, Richard. I suppose this can wait. Anne, come. You can pick up Richard's place."

Warwick had taught the game to both his daughters. He expected them to be as expert as any lord's sons in everything but knightly skills. At first he had restrained his skill, letting the girls learn without the shame of constant defeat. He would praise Isabel for her beauty and demeanor, which were greater than her skill, and Anne for her deft mind. "I am checked! Anne, that was brilliant." The more Anne matched her wits with her father's, the more harshly Warwick treated her. But as Anne grew older and ever more capable, her successes seemed to strike a searing pain in her father, and all his praise took on a rasping edge.

In Richard's first days at Middleham, Warwick's harshness to his younger daughter made no sense. Intelligent and determined, Anne was a daughter to make any man proud. She even bore her father's stamp upon her face—the precisely molded features, the unusual amber eyes. But now Richard understood. Anne was everything Warwick wanted in a son and heir. Warwick could not forgive her. Perfect in all save being female, she must have seemed like Fortune's spite.

Richard saw her face light up when her father called her. She took her place at the little table, her eagerness and love dimming when Warwick hardly glanced at her. How she wanted his love and admiration! Richard made no effort to move closer to the musicians. Something was in the air of the hall that he did not trust, an unease that had persisted through the early spring.

"Your move, daughter," Warwick said.

Anne studied the board, making no haste. Finally, she made her move. The earl turned to Richard. "What a clever woman the Teasel will make. Ah, but what man would want to marry such a one?"

Who beside himself? Just about anyone, Richard thought. Anne could have been as ugly as a bear, which she certainly was not, and half the men in England would have been pleased to marry the daughter of the Earl of Warwick. Warwick had not mentioned marrying Anne since that ride back from Jervaulx, and Richard doubted Edward had heard anything of such a plan.

Now he studied her. Her white, rounded forehead, the dark brows like a raven's wings, the erect posture, even when she must be cringing inside. The quietness that somehow made her feel like kin, a soul sister. Yes, he wanted to marry her, not just over Isabel, over anyone. He wanted her, for herself. The straight posture, the quick little curtsy— not just because she came with Middleham. He wondered how she would look at his age, fifteen. He hadn't known how much he cared for her, and the fierceness of the knowledge made his stomach hurt. How dare Warwick hurt her, bait her? Was Warwick trying to tell him something? That Edward would not approve the marriage? That Warwick had someone else in mind?

He couldn't bear to watch. He walked over to the alcove where Rob and Francis stood listening. The musicians weren't particularly good, and he had nothing to say. He went upstairs to the dormitory.

"The game is over?" Jeremy asked.

"For me it is." He wondered if Edward perhaps had made plans Warwick hadn't told him of. He couldn't shake the feeling that something ill was in the wind, something brewing, a change. Warwick's edginess, Edward's silence. He wonder if Edward and Warwick had spoken of his future. Was Warwick trying to tell him something, tonight? He was fifteen now, and Edward had said nothing to him.

*W*arwick entered the schoolroom the following morning. "How do these lads?" he asked.

"Very well, sir." Bennett's courtesy did not falter, but Richard caught a flicker of puzzlement in his eyes. When had Warwick inquired after the progress of his wards in the schoolroom?

"You may go," Warwick said as Bennett waited. "I have come to speak to Richard."

Bennett nodded and departed. Francis stayed seated, an open book on the table before him, his head bent over his book..

"Did I ask you to remain, Lord Lovell?" Warwick asked.

"No, sir."

"No more did I. But no matter. Stay if you wish." Warwick walked over to the table. "What absorbs you so?"

Francis looked up. "Virgil, sir."

"I have been wondering about kings and subjects. What has Virgil to say on the matter?"

"Sir?"

Slowly, deliberately, Warwick reached across the table and closed Francis's book. "Well, it may be that poets have not the answer to my question." He shifted his gaze. "Richard, perhaps you could tell me. Where should I read to understand a king who refuses all counsel and risks the country's peace to satisfy his lust? Or allies himself with a weak and petty power to give his sister a rich marriage? I would like to understand if such a man is fit to rule."

No need to guess what king Warwick had in mind. "I don't know who writes of that, sir."

"Of course, we speak in riddles, Richard. But your wits are quick. You know what I am asking. What think you of your brother's policy?"

"I make no judgments on Edward's policy, sir. It is not my place."

"I see I must be even plainer. Edward must do as he sees fit. The consequences will accrue. I am asking you where *your* loyalty lies."

"You have been my good lord these past six years, and Edward is my liege and my brother. I would do you both good service."

"But you train to be a knight *here*. Have you eaten my bread and learned from my tutors only to raise your sword against me?"

"I hope not to, sir."

"You hope not to?"

"Well, cousin," Richard said, "I cannot answer you for certain until you tell me where *your* sword will fall."

Their positions had somersaulted. Now it was Warwick whose honor and integrity were questioned, and he knew it. The silence that followed was leaden, and Richard was suddenly afraid.

Francis answered. "You asked another question a moment ago, sir."

"Yes, Lovell?"

"I can't tell you much about kings, but I can tell you what people say about those who make them."

Francis was smiling and all courtesy—so much the worse. Richard willed his thoughts to enter Francis's head: *This is not your battle. Don't fight it.*

"Go on." Warwick's voice was deadly calm.

"Why, they say, sir, that the making of kings is a game for men who make no sons. And that, unlike mere men, who never outgrow their Maker, kings sometimes do, and then that game is done."

"That is vile, Lovell."

"Yes, sir."

Richard closed his eyes. *God in heaven. Francis, you fool.*

Warwick clasped his hands behind his back and looked off toward the corner of the room. "Well, I have it. Only an ass would conceive such a saying, and only a lout would repeat it." He moved close to where Francis sat and leaned toward him. "Get you out to Giles and tell him I said he knows how to deal with little louts before they grow into large ones."

Francis was as white as linen.

Warwick went on. "Tell him there is to be no shamming. He loves you lads well, Lovell, so tell him I will want to see what he has taught you. Now go."

Richard turned to follow after Francis, but Warwick stepped quickly in front of him, blocking his way. "No, Richard. You will stay here. Your presence at that lesson is not called for."

*R*ichard found Francis in the empty stall at the end of the stables, where the grooms kept the herbs and salves for treating horses' ailments, as well as ropes, blankets, and halters. And whips.

Francis sat on a stool, his arms folded on the edge of the grain bin in front of him. Giles was spreading ointment from a jar onto

Francis's back, and Francis's skin twitched violently whenever Giles touched him. Giles's usually placid face was heavy and gray.

Richard went over to them and leaned down, trying to see how badly Francis was hurt. He heard someone else enter the stable, and then Anne was beside him, taking in everything at a glance. "Francis! What happened?" She turned to Richard. "Who did that to him?"

Giles answered quietly. "I did, Lady."

"Giles! You?" She went at him in a fury. He put down the jar and seized her wrists and held them. "Softly, Lady Anne. I have not hurt him."

"Not *hurt* him!"

Richard spoke. "It was your father's order, Teasel."

"Master Richard, hush." Giles was stern.

"Giles whipped him, but your father ordered it." Let her know. Let someone tell the truth here.

"My father? Why?"

"He was angry at me. And Edward. So he took out his wrath on Francis."

Anne stopped struggling and stared at them as though they were all madmen. Francis had collapsed against the grain bin, his head hidden in his arms.

Giles released Anne and wiped his hands. He lay one heavy cal-lused palm very lightly on the back of Francis's neck. "I'm sorry, Lord Francis. I know you'll not credit it now, but you will be surprised how soon you will feel better."

"Go, Giles. I'll stay," Richard said. After Giles and Anne left, Richard looked more closely at Francis's back. It was raw and red, cross-hatched with welts, but perhaps the lashes weren't deep. How did a man become so skilled at such a thing? "I think Giles was right. It should heal quickly."

Francis's response was to bury his head still deeper in his arms and choke with sobs, as much with shame and misery, Richard guessed, as pain.

*M*ay I speak with you, sir?" The conversation with Warwick was overdue. In the few days since Francis's beating, Richard had looked at the incident from every vantage point, and there was only one thing to be done.

Now he would never marry Anne, never live at Middleham, never put what he had learned about the north and the border country to use. Perhaps he would serve on the Welsh marches. He must begin again to find a place for himself. How strange that this place he had come to in fear and pain and loneliness should have become, in fact, home.

"Yes, of course, Richard. What is it?"

"You were right, sir. It is time I stopped imposing on your generosity."

"Indeed. I don't recall saying that to you."

"No, sir. Not in those words."

"I see. Where do you propose to go, may I ask?"

"London. At least until I know what Edward wants of me."

Warwick turned back to the papers spread before him. "Well, Richard, do as you think best. There is no urgency in the matter as far as I'm concerned."

"No, sir," Richard said feeling hollow. His future was destroyed, turned to dust.

*R*ichard closed the lower half-door of the stable behind him. The dusty warm odor of grain and straw greeted him, a smell so thick he could almost see it. The light coming through the open upper door lit motes of dust; ladders of light fell between chinks in the roof and flashed around the rafters. All the sounds were hushed. Pigeons flew from beam to beam like neighbors come calling, and the sound of their cooing mixed with the flutter of wings and the whispery shuffle of hooves as the horses shifted their weight.

He walked down the aisle to Mercury's stall. One of the stable cats, an orange-striped tom with golden eyes, peered at him from behind a grain sack. Mercury lifted his head and snorted, spraying grain-flecked saliva. Richard led Mercury out of the stall and into the corridor and light. He brushed the horse's coat until it was gleaming and combed the mane to lie slick and smooth. He was lifting a hoof to check the shoe when he became aware of another presence in the stable.

"He looks fit for a procession," Warwick said, walking forward. "You've a good hand with horses, Richard. But don't the stable boys care for him well enough to suit you?"

"Yes, sir. They do very well. I enjoy grooming him myself."

"That's good. I like to see a man take pride in his animals." Warwick leaned his shoulder against a post and said softly. "You will miss him, won't you?"

Miss him? Richard's breath caught. It could be a jest. Warwick could laugh, clap him on the back as he used to, and say, *You had better take him. You don't mean to leave him here to eat my grain, do you?*

"Ah. So you won't miss him that much. So be it. He stays."

*Damn him.* Richard turned his face away to keep from giving away the rage and pain he felt. Warwick started to leave but stopped again at the door. "Oh, by the way, you could have had him, you know. You had only to ask. I admire a man who has the courage to demand what is his. One who lacks that deserves his loss."

All this Warwick said cheerfully, as though he were discussing some friendly but dissolute neighbors. "Godspeed, Richard," he said, and was gone, through the doorway and out of sight, his sure tuneful whistle falling on Richard's ears like salt on a wound.

For a moment, Richard almost called after him, as he stood there trying to fight his tears. As shameful as begging would have been, what he had done was worse: he had betrayed Mercury.

Moths don't return to the cocoon, but some transformations don't hold. He thought of the ride back from York, when he had raced with Jack and felt like he had owned the world. It had been a long climb from the child who did things all wrong to the youth who held the world in his hands, but only a short fall back again.

He heard someone move and spun around. Anne edged around the door.

"Oh, Teasel. It's you. What do you want?" Richard wiped the heel of his hand across his eyes. "What are you doing here? Get out. Go on, get out."

She didn't move. "My father shouldn't have done that. He was cruel not to let you have him."

"He wanted me to beg. Maybe I should have."

"I don't think so, Richard. It wouldn't have helped."

"Don't be a fool, Annie. You heard him. I could have taken Mercury, if I'd begged for him."

"It wouldn't have made any difference. *Listen,*" she said, as he drew breath to protest. "If you had begged, he would have said no and shamed you for that. He would have hurt you, no matter what."

The truth of Anne's words lanced his last illusions about Warwick and rid him of their poisonous hope. "It doesn't matter," he said, suddenly weary. "Teasel, do me a favor. See that he's taken care of, will you?"

She nodded, and looked so close to tears, herself, that he was curt again. "What's wrong? He's just a horse." He wondered if Anne had even known she might have been his wife some day.

*R*ichard and Jeremy were riding with a handful of servants to York, where they were to join a party of pilgrims traveling south to Canterbury. Their baggage was packed, ready to be loaded in the morning.

Pilgrims! Richard wished at least that, if he had to go, Jack and Brother Simon could be his companions again. He kicked a cobble and sent a pigeon flapping away. He wanted to stay, or would, he corrected, if Warwick were to vanish. An accident. A sudden illness. Alice would turn to him as to her own son. *Richard, there is no one who knows my husband's estates as well as you.* Rot, the voice in his head retorted.

Richard walked through the courtyard, over to the entry steps, and sat down in the sun.

He hated Warwick, hated himself, hated everything. He remembered how he had pleaded with Edward to let him stay in London and his disbelief at what John Skelton told him. *Some day you will be a man. Your brother will send for you and you won't even want to go.* Skelton had been wrong on two counts. He was not, quite, a man. And Edward hadn't sent for him.

A shadow fell on his back. He turned and started to rise, but Alice stooped and put her hand on his shoulder. "Don't get up, Richard." Alice gathered her skirts and sat down beside him, her hands clasped around her knees, like a girl. "You will have fine weather for traveling. And good companions. Safe." She smiled at him. "We will miss you. Bennett and Giles are losing their most diligent pupil."

"I won't need tutors any more."

"They are your friends. You always need friends," Alice said quietly. Then, in a different voice, "Don't let Edward make you into a soldier too soon."

"It is what I came here to learn, Lady."

"So it is." Alice sighed and leaned back, her elbows on the step behind her. "Ah, but you will be too busy to be fighting all the time. London is full of fair ladies."

She confused him. First she talked to him as though she were his mother; now she seemed to be teasing, except that there was a hint of displeasure, almost anger, in her voice.

"So I've been told, my lady."

"So you've been told! You've been told there are ladies in London." She spoke in a mocking, sing-song voice. "Richard, don't be a goose. What do you *want*, child?"

Right now, he wanted to get up and run to the stables, but that would let her know he was a coward as well as a goose. And a child. Feeling nine, when he was fifteen. "Edward has made me Lieutenant of the Marches. I will serve him well and be a great lord." He felt the blood rush into his cheeks at the ridiculous boasting he had fallen into.

"No doubt." Alice smiled. "But I wish it were here that you could practice your greatness. I had hoped to see you married to my Anne." She rose and shook the dust from her skirt. "Think of us kindly, Richard. I would things could have been different."

*F*rancis's back had nearly mended. He would groan softly as he turned from one side to the other in bed, not even waking with the slight discomfort. Lying beside his friend on his last night at Middleham, Richard could not still his mind. Warwick and Edward would still have to work in accord, he supposed, even if their friendship had cooled. He himself might have occasion to ride north on Edward's affairs. He might even see Anne—and her husband, whoever that should prove to be. He turned his mind from those thoughts and began to remember, one by one, all the things he had loved—the dales, the faces, Mercury, —to find a place for them in his memory, and that proved the most painful of all.

When Richard and Jeremy went down to the courtyard early the next morning, the pack horses were loaded and Jeremy's horse saddled. "What horse have I?" Richard asked.

"What horse do you wish, sir?" the groom asked. "My lord said you may choose from any in the stable."

"You mean any but Mercury."

The boy looked puzzled. "That is not what he said, sir. He said, *any*."

Richard should have been happy, but he felt only anger. Warwick's kindness, if such it was, came too late. "Saddle Pearl for me."

"What?"

"The small black horse I came here on."

The groom was shocked out of propriety. "But she's a pony, sir."

"She's small, but sturdy."

The groom walked off, and Richard looked up at the sky. Dawn was breaking, and only a few stars were still visible

"I wish I could go with you." Francis had come down to the court-yard to see them off.

Richard almost wished Francis had not come. He could pretend indifference to the countess, to Warwick, but his grief was too near the surface to withstand assaults of love and loyalty. "I wish so, too."

"When I am sixteen, I can go where I will. If I came to you, would you have me as your man?"

"Gladly. But I don't know where Edward will send me or what I will be about."

"It's no matter."

"Then I will look for you," Richard said. They entered the stable together, and Richard unbuckled the ruby-studded sword Warwick had given him and hung it on the wall by Mercury's stall. He was ap-palled at how the gesture saddened him, when he had never even liked the gift. He changed his mind and handed the sword to Francis.

"Take it. It's yours."

"Not forever," Francis said. "Until we meet again."

"Until then."

Scotland

❋Middleham

*Yorkshire*
Towton ✧❋York  Pontefract
Castle

✧Doncaster

England

Nottingham ❋
Castle

Ludlow✧  Coventry✧  ❋Fotheringhay Castle

Wales  Tewkesbury
✧
Gloucester✧  Minster  Barnet✧
Lovell✧  Epping Forest
Sodbury  London❖✧
Hill

Beaulieu Abbey✝
✧
Weymouth

Burgundy

France

# Book Two
# King's Brother

*1467–1471*

# 7   The Kingmaker

*London*
*November 1468.*

"Your brother," Elizabeth said, "is watching your wife."
 The queen spoke loudly enough for Richard to hear every word. Of course. Baiting him was her favorite pastime, especially at supper, when he must sit at Edward's table, or rumors would arise that the king and his brother had fallen out.

Edward laughed. "I have the most-watched wife in all England. Should I take offense that my brother also notices her beauty?"

Who could *not* look, Richard wondered. Everything the queen did was meant to draw men's eyes to her. Tonight she wore a gown of blue satin with cloth-of-gold sleeves that set off her silver-gilt hair so it shone like moonlight. She brushed Edward's cheek with her lips, leaning forward so that her breasts swelled against the low neckline of her gown. Richard supposed he was meant to notice that, too, and envy Edward for his beautiful wife. He didn't envy his brother; he pitied him.

He had come to London prepared to love Elizabeth for Edward's sake, and at first her perfect face had awed him. But now he knew her beauty to be shallow and her soul corrupt. This woman had snared Edward, and cheated Richard of his future. Without her, there would have been no split with Warwick and Jack, and Richard might still be in the north with his friends, not breathing in London's rank air.

The story was that Edward had tried to persuade Elizabeth into his bed. When she refused, saying she was too good to be any man's mistress, he married her. Handsome, shrewd Edward, who could have bedded any woman in the country *except* Elizabeth—had been clay in her hands. And then he had sold his kingdom to satisfy her huge family.

Richard ticked off the marriages and honors in his mind. Seven marriages and one betrothal that benefited only the Woodvilles, giving them titles and land they could not have hoped for on their own. One match was particularly despicable: young John Woodville had been married to the Dowager Duchess of Norfolk, old enough to be his grandmother. If Richard hadn't known of the marriage first-hand, he would not have believed Edward capable of making such an arrangement.

One of Elizabeth's brothers was appointed governor of the Isle of Wight, two were made Knights of the Garter, and one made Bishop of Salisbury. Richard could almost understand Warwick's rage at Edward's marriage. Richard understood now why people laughed when they said the king married for love. Some said plainly that Edward was led by his lust. Some said he was led by something still ruder.

"No offense, my lord," Elizabeth said, turning her famous green eyes on Edward. "But surely such behavior indicates a lack in his life. Your brother has been with us a year now and has neither lover nor occupation. He must find it difficult to fill his days."

Richard bent his head over his plate. Breathing in Elizabeth's presence was difficult; sitting at table with her night after night was difficult; keeping silent when he wanted to shout at her to take her kin and go back to Grafton Regis was difficult. *Those* were the difficult things. He'd left the best part of himself at Middleham, the part that had the courage to stand up and ride away. Now he stayed at court with Edward, hiding every thought and swallowing bile. Life stretched before him in infinite boredom. *Now* he was the shadow, the ghost boy, not at Middleham.

"He has occupation enough," Edward said.

"But don't you think the lad needs a sweetheart?" the queen asked.

"Perhaps he already has one," Edward answered, looking bored.

"No," Richard said, looking up squarely at first Edward, then Elizabeth. "He hasn't. Nor does he need one."

Elizabeth smiled. If you didn't know her, you could almost think it was a kind smile. "It's rude, don't you think, Richard, to speak when you are not addressed?"

"I think, lady, that it's rude to speak about a person in front of him, as though he were not there." Richard grasped the hilt of his dagger, where it rested in his belt, both his hand and the dagger hidden by the table linen, and began reciting verse silently in his head. Sometimes he counted, anything that kept him steady until the anger passed.

Elizabeth probably thought he was holding in check his desire, if she noticed anything. Her vanity was that great.

Pages began clearing the tables, removing platters of bare white bones. The brilliant peacock feathers that had adorned the roasted birds so that they almost looked alive were sodden with grease. Now came trays of comfits, the small dainty sweets, thankfully not the ghastly towering impostures of subtleties that Richard detested— spun sugar in the shape of swans, castles, stags, and hounds. Why would anyone try so hard to make something appear to be what it wasn't?

"Your brother does you little honor in how he speaks to me," Elizabeth said, taking a comfit from a tray and biting it in half. She fed the rest to Edward, keeping her hand at Edward's mouth a little too long, as if waiting for him to lick her fingers.

"Richard's not to blame. You drive a man mad, Bess," Edward kissed his wife's neck, but he hardly looked mad with lust. He looked like a man trying not to show annoyance. Then Elizabeth leaned toward him and whispered something, kissed Edward just below his ear, and blew soft puffs of breath along his jaw, and Richard could see his brother soften. Edward put one arm around his wife's neck, and his hand crept down her shoulder and caressed her breast.

Elizabeth leaned closer, laid one hand on Edward's leg. A softness and shine had come into her face, and the anger faded from Edward's eyes, replaced by a doting, foolish gaze. Edward pinched her breast, so the nipple stood up under her bodice. They were nuzzling each other, their hands sliding everywhere.

Embarrassed, Richard pushed his plate away. How did lust take hold of a man, move him from indifference to foolishness? How did it make him forget that he had a kingdom to rule?

After a moment three musicians in mulberry and gold parti-colored tabards paraded through the hall and mounted the steps to the upper dais, laughing and jostling each other as they went. Once on the dais, the musicians huddled together. The horn player blew a muted note and the other two men plucked their instruments and adjusted strings. Abruptly Richard laid down his napkin and stood. "I beg your leave, Lady. Brother."

"Already, Richard?" Elizabeth asked, looking at him. "The entertainment has not begun."

"On the contrary. I have had a surfeit of entertainment already." He spoke with malice and perfect courtesy, a skill he was learning from her. He noted with satisfaction both her frown and the fact that she had no response to throw back at him, at least not before he left the table.

*G*et our cloaks," he said to Jeremy as he strode out of the hall.

"Where are we going?" Jeremy asked when he returned, cloaks in hand.

"The stews. We'll find a ferry."

"Why?"

Richard stopped. "There's only one reason men go to the stews, isn't there?"

"I meant why now, tonight?"

"No reason. Any reason you like." He was past sixteen now, a man. He would find out about lust, experience it for himself, end his ignorance. "Have you been there, before?" he asked.

"A few times."

"Good. You will know where to take me."

*Y*ou have to knock. The door is kept locked." Jeremy had found the house with no trouble. It stood across the Thames on Cock Lane in a row of many such houses. The courtyard in which they waited was attractive enough, with its arched façade overhanging the entrance, but suffered from neglect. Several of the tiles underfoot were broken, and the boxes in the windows at either side of the entrance held brown and desiccated remains of what had once been greenery.

After being admitted to the house, they found themselves in a large parlor lit by smoky tallow candles. Almost immediately a woman came from an inner door, through which Richard glimpsed steam rising from oaken tubs. In and about the tubs were men and women nude except for their heads, which were wrapped turban-like in white linens. Some people had pinned the wrappings with jeweled brooches. How strange that, birth-naked, people should still find means to display their wealth.

"Did you come for the baths?" the woman asked.

"No. Just two rooms, please," Jeremy answered. She cited a sum, which Richard paid, then admitted them through another door without explanation.

Several young women in various stages of undress looked up when they entered. Some wore only night robes or shifts. Others wore shoddy finery, and would have been fully clothed except that the necklines of the gowns were halfway to the waist, exposing the women's breasts. A girl Richard judged to be not much older than himself, with hair the color of flax and fair skin dusted with pale freckles, smiled at him. He tried to keep his eyes on her face, and not the robe slipping from her shoulders. *Fool.* Here, he was supposed to look. When he hesitantly returned the smile, the girl walked over to him, took his hand, and led him upstairs.

He followed her to a narrow, sparely furnished room. A lantern stood on a shelf; a small commode held a basin and ewer. There was a screen behind which he supposed she tended to her personal needs, and a bed, the coverings pulled up neat and smooth to the pillows. He stood awkwardly just inside the door. What had possessed him to come here? He felt no lust, no desire, only a fierce urge to leave. He should say he had made a mistake, that he had come only to keep company with his friend, who tended to get into trouble. He could wait for Jeremy in the courtyard.

The girl pulled him further into the room. "There, sir," she said, pointing him toward the commode, as the door closed behind him. It was too late to leave. May God have mercy on him.

He dropped his cloak over a chair-back, removed his gloves, and folded back his sleeves to wash his hands, the girl gazing at him the whole time. He plunged his hands into the water, then picked up the towel on the commode. The girl seemed to be waiting for him to do something more.

"It's your first time, isn't it, sir?" she said quietly.

"Yes. You know that by the way a man washes his hands?"

"Well, the water, sir. It's not for your hands." If he'd heard the least mockery in her words, he would have given her his purse and fled, but her voice was kind, almost soothing.

"What—?" It took him a moment to understand what she meant. No. *That*, he wouldn't do—touch himself in front of her, but he couldn't bring himself to say so. As he stood, furious at both what she had asked of him and his own embarrassment, she came to him and took up the task herself, talking as easily as if they were old friends.

"Sometimes I say it's my first time. Men often like to think so, especially the old ones, even if they don't truly believe it. I'm twenty-two, although I don't look it. I've been here five years, sir, but it's been longer than that since this place has seen a virgin. Except for the young men, that is."

Standing face to face, he saw she was much smaller than he had realized downstairs. The top of her head reached just to his nose. Between that and her ease in undressing him, he felt less foolish, and began to notice the pleasant effects of her touch. When she had finished, he wore only his singlet, which he shed as they made their way to the bed. "And you?" he asked, lying down and touching her gown as he pulled her down beside him.

"There's no need, sir. I'm ready." She opened her robe.

"No. Take it off. I want to see all of you. Please." To touch all of her, too.

"That costs more."

"I don't care."

Then she was naked, and she no longer had to instruct him. He knew the places he wanted to touch, and did so, which she seemed to like; when she touched him, he didn't have to think about what he should do next. He was only surprised that, once started, the act was over so quickly. He laughed at his own surprise and at the sheer joy of what they had done, and that surprised him, too.

For the first time since he had come to London, he felt no anger, just a crumbling of walls he hadn't known defended him. In that moment, he didn't hate Elizabeth, didn't resent Edward or despise his own ignorance. He marveled that a girl could touch him and take the bitterness out of him. And the girl seemed happy, too, cuddling closer and stroking his chest.

He lay a while drifting in and out of sleep. When he came fully awake, the peace had vanished. The girl's body had a tart-sweet smell, like roses mixed with salt brine, which had pleased him at first, but which now seemed too pungent, and the small room seemed close and shabby.

He got up and retrieved his clothes and purse, then realized he had no idea how much men paid for such things. He settled the question by holding out his hand with a selection of coins, not caring so much that she would cheat him as that she would think him a fool. The girl looked up into his face, took two of the coins with great deliberation, then closed his palm around the rest and pushed his hand aside.

"Listen, sir, it's very late. You'd best stay the night here."

"They will open the gates for me."

"They'll open the gates of Heaven itself if you've enough gold, but you have to get there first. There're cutthroats between here and there." She pulled her robe around her, and started to rise. "I'll find your friend and tell him you're staying."

"No. I'm going."

The girl shrugged. "Please yourself."

Then, because he had been curt with what was only an attempt at kindness, he asked, "What is your name?"

"Kate, sir."

"Then, Kate, I am . . ."

"I know who you are. Come back any time you've a fancy." She gave him a sad smile.

The night they had just spent, the only such night he had yet known, was only one of hundreds for her, one instance out of an unvarying, numbing repetition, the same act, night after night, year after year. How could she bear it? This was not the life for someone like her, young and kind and pretty.

"Why do you do this?" The words lurched out.

"Do you think I have a choice?" The girl's shoulders slumped under the flimsy gown.

"Couldn't you marry?" He had pulled on his doublet and was fastening his belt.

"Who would I marry? Someone young and kind like you, sir? Do you think there is such a man on this earth for me?"

He stared at her. "No, not me, but. . . ."

"What do you know about it, a king's brother who will never want? Keep your words to yourself. We took our pleasure and you paid your money. Let that be enough." In that moment she looked every one of her twenty-odd years.

He picked up his cloak and left.

$\mathcal{T}$hey met no cutthroats, and the porters opened the gates and closed them without a blink. But not without a word, apparently.

At breakfast, Edward asked, "Who's your sweetheart?"

"I don't have one."

"Come now, you weren't coming back from hunting in the king's forest that hour of the night."

"No. I was coming from the stews."

"Oh." Edward seemed proud, amused, and puzzled all at once. Maybe even a little sad. "You don't have to pay for women, you know."

Will Hastings said nothing, just watched intently. Hastings was Edward's Lord Chamberlain and mentor now that Warwick had abandoned the post. Richard didn't quite like Hastings, who seemed to him pompous and self-important, as though he had taken on the mission of reflecting Edward's greatness back at him.

"What do you mean?"

"God's bones, you're the king's brother! Half the women in London would bed with you on that account alone, even if you weren't young and passably handsome."

"Why?"

Hastings shot a puzzled glance at Edward, as if to ask: *Did this lad appear to have all his wits yesterday?* When Edward seemed to have been stricken dumb, Hastings answered for him. "Well, Richard, because of favors."

"Such as?"

"Access to court, sometimes," Hastings said. "If the girl is exceptionally fair and witty." He shrugged. "Gifts, almost certainly."

"Gifts?" Richard looked at Edward.

"Gifts! Jewels, gowns, all the foolery women love. You know these things. Why are you asking me?"

"That's not paying?"

Edward shrugged. "Different coin."

"Better a coin than a kingdom."

*Please let him have imagined speaking. Let the words he could hear in his head as clearly as if God had uttered them be only his thoughts.*

But he had spoken, with all the distaste, judgment, and disapproval his words implied.

Edward rose from his chair. "Stand up."

Richard stood and laid down his linen. Edward had come around to the other side of the table. His fists were clenched at his side and a vein on his forehead was engorged with blood. "Step away from the table," Edward said. "Are you a coward as well as malapert?"

"No," Richard said. "I'm not a coward." He moved apart from both the table and chair. He didn't know the severity of the punishment for what he had just done. What *had* he just done—spoken a moment's glib insult, or committed treason? With both of them unarmed, given the difference in height and weight, Edward could kill him.

Edward slapped him with an open palm, although the force was hardly less than if he had used his fist. The blow snapped Richard's head back. He reeled, lost his footing, reached blindly for the chair, and grasped air. Dizzy, blind, and nauseous, he pushed the nausea down, dropped to one knee, and tasted blood. The blow had left the side of his face full of burning needle-points and blotted out his sight except for visions of stars and cannonfire. He expected to be hauled back up to his feet by his shirt and hit again. No one touched him and after a moment, he blinked and saw the floor and toe of his boot, instead of stars. He cautiously straightened and stood.

Richard's breathing steadied as he glanced around the room. The servants had gone deaf and blind from the look of them, turned to stone in mid-breath. Hastings's glance was directed toward the corner of the chamber, the blank joining of walls and ceiling. Edward was leaning over the table, palms pressed flat. He picked up a linen from the table and tossed it at him. "Here. Don't bleed all over yourself." Edward appeared to be trying to smile, but his hand was shaking, and he looked pale and ill, like a man with a deadly secret exposed, as he fumbled for his chair. "Never impugn my wife again," he said.

"No." Pride kept Richard standing. I didn't impugn your wife, he thought. I impugned you. He kept the words to himself this time.

## Westminster
## February 1469.

Richard and George dismounted, and George handed his horse off to the groom. "Take him. I want to watch him with a rider."

The groom mounted and took the horse off at a smart trot. On the second lap, the man tucked his heels closer and eased his grip on the reins, and the horse moved effortlessly into a canter.

"You'd hardly know he was only a three-year-old," Richard commented.

"Wait until the spring tournaments," George said. "He will be unsurpassed." It was late February and the sky was the color of dull steel. The month had been bitterly cold; this was the first temperate day in a fortnight. As the groom came full circle a third time, George motioned him to a stop. "That's good for today. Take him away."

"Shall I stable your horse, too, sir?" the groom asked Richard.

"No. I'll do it. The walk back will do me good."

Richard held open the gate for George and the groom, then led his horse though and shot the bolt after.

"You should compete," George said.

Crowds and noise. People drinking too much, getting sick and pretending to enjoy it. Unnecessary pain and good animals damaged. "I'll consider it."

George laughed. "That means you won't."

"I suppose so."

"You should take more pleasure in life," George persisted.

"George, how can I take more pleasure in life by pursuing what doesn't please me?"

"What? Never mind; don't explain. I'll tell you something that *will* please you." George spun around so that for the moment they were walking face to face. He had recently given up the gaudy slashed sleeves, parti-colored hose, and spiked shoes that were all the fashion. These days, even at court, he chose plain surcoats and the dark boots he wore for riding, but his hair was longer, curled, and perfumed. The effect was one of youth and, oddly, innocence, a man who by accident had picked up some of the style and richness of court, but put them together with the untaught eye of a child stringing beads.

But George did nothing by accident.

"What?" Richard felt a wave of weariness. George's passions were short-lived and unpredictable, and often left a trail of destruction in their wake. He felt the older of the two, by far, now, although he couldn't have said how or when the change occurred.

"I have been in correspondence with Warwick," George replied. "I have decided to marry his daughter."

*I think I'll marry Warwick's daughter. Tell the Pope to step down, why don't you? That was equally likely to happen.* "You can't do that."

"Brother, you're not listening. I have just said I *will* do it."

"Very well. Which daughter are you marrying?" His heart was clamoring. He hoped George couldn't hear it.

"Ah, I knew you would be interested." George smiled his brilliant, pleasant smile. "Don't worry. Warwick has two daughters—one for me and one for you."

"Yes, George, I can count, too. Which one are you marrying?"

"The choice is Warwick's, of course. Do you mean to tell me our good cousin never approached you with the idea?"

"Some time ago. When I was at Middleham. Who does Warwick choose for you?"

"Don't worry, brother. I don't have my eye on your little pet. I'd marry Isabel, of course. She's the elder."

"Have you said anything to Edward about this?"

"Not yet. And you must not, either. But believe me, some day he will be glad to have made peace with Warwick again."

Richard pulled a dried apple from his jacket pocket and fed it to his horse. Hope was cutting through him like a knife. "Is that what Warwick said?" he asked, not looking at George. "He'll reconcile with Edward if you marry Isabel?"

"Not in so many words. But he'd have to, wouldn't he?" George said.

"No, George, he wouldn't have to," Richard sighed. "He could turn against Edward completely, and then what would you do? Who would you give up, your wife or your brother?"

"Good God, Richard. You make everything so serious. Think of this. The fair Elizabeth has borne Edward three children. All girls. What say you to that?"

"That you would be wise to wait a few more years before you make overly much of it." He rubbed the horse's velvet nose and glanced up at the sky. The sun was making a wavering attempt to penetrate the gloom.

"No. The point is this. Until Edward has a son, *we* are the heirs of the kingdom. We could be king one day. It behooves us to mend the breach with Warwick."

"*We* could be king? George, one king must die before another reigns. Has no one explained that to you?"

George held up a hand. "Do not mock me, brother."

"In fact, as things stand now, marrying Isabel is treasonous." Richard heard himself starting to shout and fell silent. He might as well reason with the stars.

## Westminster Palace
### June 1469.

Richard turned his neck first to one side, then the other, easing the tightness accumulated during the past four hours at the table. Edward's clerk was ill, and Richard had been filling the office. He didn't mind. He liked the feel of the pen in his hand, liked seeing it lay down the broad neat strokes. Dusk was falling; the heady scents of lavender and roses were borne on the summer air from the garden below.

Someone was playing a lute; the song ended with a ripple of strings and laughter.

Neither Richard nor Edward had spoken of the morning after Richard had gone to the stews. The incident lay between them like an unmarked grave, around which they cautiously moved, not wanting to step on it, knowing its presence but uncertain of its dimensions. In an odd way, Edward's blow had given Richard power, as though Edward's was the greater of their offenses, for which he must make silent amends.

Spring had begun in violence. Suddenly, as though Edward had not ruled a stable country for eight years, rebellions erupted, protesting his reign. The disaffection spread wide, but the heart of the trouble seemed to be in the north. Jack Neville quickly subdued the risings and observed Edward's own policy of executing leaders and sparing commoners, who were usually of little menace on their own. But with summer, the revolts flared up again like tinder fires never completely extinguished. A sheaf of letters from Edward's retainers bore witness to the disorder.

"Is this justice?" Edward asked. "A new hawk, a fine day, and I must spend it inside, deciphering the words of men who can't be plain." A servant poured more wine from a gilt flask which, like the new hawk, was a gift from their sister Margaret. He sighed. "So was it my reeve who was burned, or an effigy?"

"I can't tell," Richard said.

"Read it to me again."

Richard had read no more than the first sentence when Edward interrupted. "Enough!" Richard put down the letter and waited.

"God," Edward said, blowing out his breath. "There *is* a difference between flesh and blood and a sack of straw. Write the man and tell him to be clear."

Richard dipped the quill. "Jack did you good service in the north," he said.

"Yes." There was caution in Edward's voice.

"Far better than Henry Percy would have done."

"Yes, I know. Why are you telling me?"

"Because you might have lost sight of the fact."

"Are you my conscience?"

"No."

"Why are you looking at me, then?"

"No reason."

Edward sighed. "Look. You will have noticed that land and a title given to one man must have come from another. I take Northumberland from Henry Percy and give it to Jack, and months later trouble breaks out all over the north. Is that coincidence? I don't believe so."

"No."

"Good. Now, Henry Percy may not have initiated any of the trouble. Perhaps his followers did it on his behalf. It doesn't matter; the trouble's *there*."

"You can't be thinking of restoring Northumberland to Percy?"

"I'd be a fool not to think of it. Thinking of it doesn't mean I'll do it. Where were we?"

There were a dozen quills on the table, a knife, fine sand to dry the ink. Richard sprinkled sand over the letter and blew it off the paper.

*A* week later, Richard began tidying the table after another round of letters, when there was a knock at the door. The servant opened the door and admitted a page with a dazed look.

Richard put the quill back into its jar.

"Well?" Edward said.

The page gave him a quick nervous glance. "There are two men without the door, sir, who say they have heard the king has need of men." The boy blushed and stumbled over his words. "They will ride anywhere, but their price is a bag of gold, women for the journey, and the ransom of any prisoners they capture."

"*What!* Who would demand such terms? Why are we listening to this?" Edward turned to the servant. "Throw them out."

"Forgive me, sire, but there is more—"

Edward cut him short. "Send them to John Howard if they insist on talking to someone. He will deal with them. I'm tired. Well, what now?" The page remained by the door.

"They say, sire, that they are the terror of the north. That when they are finished, there will be none of the king's enemies with their heads still on their shoulders."

"Did you not hear me?" Edward had half risen from his chair. "Go! I have no time for such folly."

"Wait." Richard thought he knew now who the fools might be. "I'll see them now, if they are brave enough to discuss their terms with me and the king at once."

Edward groaned. "Very well. Bring them in."

The page rushed out. In a moment John Parr and Rob Percy entered on their own. It had been over a year since Richard had seen them. Rob was almost as tall and broad as Edward, but John Parr was still small, as dark as one of the old hill people. Country boys come to court, large-eyed and awed, holding their hats before them like an offering.

Rob whistled. "Look at you!"

Richard hadn't thought of his dress as anything close to sumptuous, but now he was aware of the richness of his velvet, even if the deep wine color was discreet, as was the heavy gold chain he wore. He put out his hand to Rob, who pulled him closer and whacked his shoulder, and the moment's awkwardness was gone. The three of them embraced and laughed and thumped each other's backs and arms until finally Edward's voice recalled them.

"I take it you know these men."

Richard introduced them then turned back to his friends. "Francis is still at Middleham, then? I don't imagine you came up with such demands yourselves."

John Parr smiled. "He did give us some counsel."

"Francis said to tell you he fares well," Rob said. "He has managed to get himself beaten only three or four times since you left."

"Ah, yes," Edward interrupted, "Middleham." He sat forward, every trace of languor gone. "Have a seat, men. Tell me about my good cousin. What is Warwick about, these days?"

"Little, my lord," Rob said, seating himself, "if you can trust what he says. But many people think his hand is behind most of the trouble in the north."

"Why?"

"Well, it's true that Henry Percy is discontent. And it is easy enough to tell when Percy's people are involved. Many people think he wants to pressure you into restoring Northumberland to him. But some of the uprisings seem to start from nowhere, begun by men who have no connection to him. There are plenty of folk who say that Warwick is behind those."

"Suppose that's so. What is he after?"

"He may be only spiteful, sire, and wish to cause you annoyance, but the rumor is that he is trying to make enough disturbance to incite people against you and restore a Lancaster to the throne." Rob paused a moment. "Who he thinks to crown I can't say, with Henry in the Tower and Margaret and Lancaster back in France."

Yes, Richard thought. But they were both alive. He remembered Warwick's warning after the Scot treaty was signed in York. *Kill them both*, Warwick had said. The only way Edward's throne would be safe, even after all this time.

Edward pounded one fist into the other palm. "That is much as I thought. We'll know soon enough if we are right." He motioned the servant to pour wine all around. "We can surely use your services, men. Ride with us, if you can bear to retrace the journey you just made."

*Olney*
*August 1469.*
They were in the midlands when word came that George and Isabel were married. Warwick had bribed the papal council to obtain the dispensation. Edward was enraged but grimly amused, too. "My legate bribed by my own brother. The next time I see the ass, I'll tell him that since he prefers George's gold to mine, he can change paymasters permanently."

Richard wondered anew what Warwick might have in mind for Anne. She would be twelve, now. George and Isabel's marriage might well be only a thumb-your-nose at Edward, but surely Warwick wouldn't spend both his daughters' marriages on spite.

*E*dward's small army rode on to Nottingham, where they stopped to await Edward's friend Lord Herbert, who was raising his own muster. Two days later, Herbert hadn't shown, and Edward decided to go on without him. They were all uneasy; it wasn't like Herbert to fail in his obligations. At Olney, one of Herbert's men reached them. Warwick's army had laid into Herbert's men. Warwick had tried and arrested Herbert and his captains for treason. They were found guilty and executed. Edward sat and listened to the names of the dead: Elizabeth's father, Anthony Woodville, and her young brother John; several men of Herbert's family. "It can't be treason," Edward said, disbelieving. "*I'm* their king."

There was more bad news. Warwick's brother George Neville, Archbishop of York, had exchanged his vestments for armor and was approaching Olney with a large host. August was cold and wet that year, as melancholy as most Novembers. The soldier who brought the news was little more than a boy. The lad's fair hair was pasted to his forehead by the drizzling rain. Edward stood with his head bowed, his hand on the reins of the lad's horse. When the boy had finished his message, Edward shook his head as though he were trying to rid himself of a persistent and annoying fly. Finally he looked up. "Thank you. Can we feed you before you ride on?" His voice was flat.

The boy declined. "I'm near home, sire."

"Go, then. God be with you." Edward released the reins and slapped the horse.

Edward, Richard, and their household knights went inside to sit before a cold hearth and listen to the sound of horsemen galloping through the village, first the remnants of Lord Herbert's army, then, in increasing numbers, Edward's own men.

John Howard came up the stairs dripping and walked, unthinking, to the empty hearth. Edward growled at one of the knights, "Get the innkeeper in here to kindle a fire. What in blazes does he think we are paying him for? Well, John?"

"They are leaving in droves, Ned. What would you have me do?"

"What *can* you do?"

"Beastly little." Howard stepped back to let the servant approach the hearth. "Make some threats. Hang a knave or two as an example."

"Let them go." Edward sighed, and looked around at his companions. "Gentlemen, I have led you into a pretty pass." He turned to Richard. "Here is a puzzle for you, brother. Why would Warwick want our dear brother, the most changeable man in the kingdom, for a son-in-law?"

Richard understood everything now, what all the pieces meant, as if he had been looking through a colored window, panel by panel, intrigued by the brilliant hues and odd shapes, and then had stepped back far enough to see the pattern. It was the design of Edward's destruction. For Warwick to rule the ruler, George must be king. Therefore Edward had to die.

A cold silence filled the room. Richard imagined what Edward had to feel just then, betrayed by his own cousin. How could Warwick have turned against him so completely?

"What's the matter, can't you say it?" Edward asked. "It's perfectly plain. If I die, the earl will be the father-in-law of the king. *When* I die, that is." Edward slammed his fist down on the table. "God, I have been a fool. A child should have seen what he was about. Start a few revolts in the north, lure me away from London, then make war on the men who ride to join us, a few at a time."

"How many men have we here?" Hastings stopped pacing and addressed John Howard, but Edward cut short the tally.

"Save your effort, Will. Warwick's three times our strength." He lifted a hand. "Ten times, a hundredfold. What does it matter? I won't send any more men into slaughter."

No one had mentioned Jack. Richard wondered whether he had joined Warwick or was keeping to himself, hoping for the miracle that would free him from choosing.

"Well, it's a long ride to Fotheringhay, Ned," Hastings was saying, "but we might reach it before they catch us."

"No," Edward said. "I won't be cut down on the road or hide at Fotheringhay. Or anywhere else for that matter. We won't be trapped like beetles in a bottle."

"What then? Forgive me, Ned, I just don't see. . . ." Hastings let his words trail off.

"One beetle, Will, trapped in the bottle. Just one."

"You'll be in danger, Ned, wherever they take you."

"Thank you, Will, for your concern. However, I don't retain you to tell me what I already know."

"For God's sake, Ned, think about it! What's to stop Warwick from poisoning you and saying you died of a fever."

"He won't poison me, and he won't stab me in my sleep."

"You can't know what he'll do."

Edward smiled bitterly. "Why, friend, that's true. The only thing we can be sure of is death, and even that comes when it will."

"Richard?" Hastings's voice was irritated. "Can you not reason with your brother?"

Richard took a breath before answering slowly. "No, sir. I think he's right."

"You *think* he's right? You are willing for Edward to risk his life on a *thought*?"

"No, sir. What I think has nothing to do with what he should do. But he's right that Warwick won't kill him. Our cousin would be dead within the hour."

"I am dealing with madmen," Hastings said.

"Let him go," John Howard said, as if Edward weren't there. "The lad always had more brass than sense."

*T*he sounds of retreating hoofbeats yielded to silence, and the silence to a rumble like the thunder of an approaching storm. One of the guards burst into the room. "My lord! Archbishop Neville is at the gates."

"He's expected," Edward said, with a heavy sigh. "Ask him to wait below. Tell him I'll be with him presently." Edward turned to his men. "Put up your swords, gentlemen. No blood will stain them today."

Richard watched his brother transform himself, shedding regret and fear like a shabby cloak too disgraceful for further wear. By the time George Neville had ignored the message and clattered with a half-dozen knights up the stairs in full armor, red-faced and wheezing, Edward had such command of himself he might have been a host receiving troublesome guests, pained but too well-bred not to greet them graciously.

He was standing at the window, one foot propped on the ledge, gazing out at the distance through the mist and rain. When his visitors entered, he took his foot down, turned and smiled.

"Archbishop. How good it is to see you again. It appears you hurried rather more than you need have, however. Won't you sit and catch your breath? No? In that case, I'll not detain you." Edward turned and started to walk toward the door.

George Neville drew his sword with a flourish and a clang. He extended it until its point touched Edward's stomach. "You are not leaving here."

"Oh? Perhaps I misunderstood." Edward took the sword between his thumb and forefinger and delicately lifted it aside. "I thought you wanted me to come away with you."

Neville's mouth gaped like a beached flounder. "Yes, damn you."

"Then you had better let me get my horse. I would ask you to enjoy my hospitality before I partake of yours, but, alas, I am ill-equipped to serve so large a host. It is better that I not offend you with an inadequate attempt. Shall we go?"

## Pontefract Castle
### October 1469.

Edward was conveyed first to Warwick Castle, then to Middleham, and finally to Pontefract.

The king's men ringed the castle's outer walls, and when Richard and Hastings approached the gate with a score of knights, the porter merely saluted before admitting them.

A page took them to the prisoners' chambers, where a guard sat by an open door. Inside, Edward and Warwick were playing chess.

Chess? Richard wondered. He and Will Hastings had gathered six hundred men to disrupt a game of chess? But Edward looked up and beneath the bland agreeable mask, his face was strained and tense. He was thinner, and there was a wariness in his eyes as though he were not certain he could trust what he saw.

"Lord Hastings. Richard." Warwick greeted them civilly enough. "So you've come to fetch your king and brother. How many men have you brought?"

Hasting answered. "Six hundred, give or take a score or so."

"That should suffice to escort any man safe to London, no matter what the condition of the kingdom." Warwick was almost as good as Edward at playing at indifference. "As long as you are here, may I offer you supper and a bed for the night?"

Edward grasped a rook tightly in his hand. "Yes, cousin. You can feed all my men and their horses, too, but I'll be damned to Hell if I'll sleep another night behind these walls."

After arranging food for his men, Richard came out of the kitchen to see a man in a plain dark doublet and high Spanish boots disappear up a back stairway. He bolted up the stairs and caught up just as the man was about to enter one of the private chambers.

"Jack?"

The man stopped and turned.

Richard would have stepped forward and embraced his cousin, but something in Jack's manner, cautious and stiff, stopped him. Jack recovered, smiled and offered his hand, but by then Richard had had time to wonder why a man he loved and who he believed had loved him would have made no effort to find and greet him. Worse, to intentionally avoid the meeting.

Jack withdrew his hand. "Don't apologize. There's no need to explain. I told you myself to be careful whom you trust when families start to fall apart."

"Yes. But. . . ."

"Well, let us say that I thought someone should keep an eye on our brothers. I'm glad to report that they were most civil the whole time. Not even a suggestion of killing each other."

"Not that." Jack was either still a friend or he was not. "What I meant to say was, did you know I was here?"

"I did."

"And you wouldn't have spoken to me?"

Jack slowly rubbed his chin as though it were the first time he had considered that his behavior might seem odd. "I suppose there might be a quiet corner here where old friends could talk for a time."

"You know this castle better than I. But I would rather be outside, if you please."

"By all means."

They sat on the steps of a small outbuilding by the stables. The golden afternoon was yielding to twilight, but the sun still held enough warmth to bleed through the bright crisp air. Jack picked up a piece of straw and twirled it between his fingers. "If I were a magician I could turn this into gold. That would be a talent to have, wouldn't it?" He fell silent and seemed far away.

Finally he said, "You are looking well. London must agree with you."

"You jest."

"Oh? My eyes deceive me, then. You are not healthy and a hand taller than when I last saw you? You have not two eyes, all your teeth, your head still on your shoulders, and the command of a band of soldiers as well-fed and armed as I have seen?"

"You are laughing at me."

"Ah. So then you thrive, but are not content."

"Content! Are you?"

Jack shrugged. "Who of us is, these days?" He looked down at the straw in his fingers. "It's not the same world as when we were at Middleham. I'd be the last to say it was, or that I like the changes. And the older I get, the less heart I have for quarrels and bloodshed. Thank God this affair looks to end peaceably."

Richard agreed. "I can hardly believe we have come to this. I'm not sure what any of it means. Sometimes I feel as though I'm dreaming, coming here where my brother is prisoner and saying to yours," he cleared his throat and lowered his voice, "I've come to release the king. Do you give him over to me or do I make war on you?"

He continued in his normal voice. "All the time I was thinking, what if I *did* start a war?"

He had surprised himself by saying so much, but there in the stable yard, surrounded only by pigeons and straw, it seemed possible to talk of all things. "I used to think it would be different if my father were alive. That he would have taught me."

"Taught you what?"

Richard shook his head. "I don't even know. What he would do in my place, maybe."

"Do you ask Edward?"

"Sometimes. You know how he is. Decide what you want, then do it. He says I am too much conscience and too little certainty. Except, of course, when I disagree with him, then it's all reversed." Richard laughed, a little embarrassed that he might have seemed to be playing for pity, when it was the last thing he wanted.

But Jack seemed to understand. "For some men, everything seems simple. I have never been one of them, either." He hesitated. "Do you know what Edward intends to do with Northumberland?" There was a rough edge in the steady voice.

"No." Richard looked down at his hands, glad now that Edward had not told him.

"Never mind. I should not have asked you that. You are not accountable to either of us for the other." Jack leaned back, resting his elbows on the step behind him, one hand still dangling the straw. "Now, about you. I am told you are the steward and chamberlain of all Wales? And Constable of England, too? Ah, so it is true, then. That is much responsibility for a young man's shoulders. Edward must have a high regard for your abilities."

"Maybe. Do you remember when I was knighted?" Richard asked. "I promised to serve God and king. I thought that meant rescuing widows and children from infidels. It isn't like that."

Jack laughed. "Let me tell you something. *Nothing* is ever what you imagine it will be. Congratulate yourself; you have learned life's most important lesson." He put his hand on Richard's shoulder. "Listen, son."

Son. Heart-stopping word. It was only a manner of speaking, Richard knew, but he was almost afraid to breathe, lest the universe shift.

"I don't know where any of this will lead us, but I doubt our troubles are over." Jack's voice was very low. "Our paths may take us separate ways. In fact, our brothers may call upon us to do things neither of us would wish. Both of us," he stressed. "You, too. You do know that, don't you?"

"Yes." *Stop, please. Don't say any more.*

Jack tightened his grip for an instant, then took his hand away, and what he said was entirely different from anything Richard could have imagined. "I just want you to know that I think well of you. That if you were truly my son, I would be proud to call you so. Whatever befalls."

Well. They sat in easy silence. If there were times when no words sufficed, there were also times when a very few were enough to right the wrongs of the world.

## Westminster
### December 1469.

Richard heard voices as he approached the door to the king's chambers. When he stepped inside the room was silent, but the air felt splintered, as unnaturally still as cracked crystal, waiting for the breath that would reduce it to a pile of rubble.

He knocked on the door to the inner chamber, and Edward's voice called out for him to enter. As he closed the door, a small object hurtled across the chamber in front of him. Edward and Elizabeth stood in the middle of the room, Edward's hand clasping one of his wife's wrists. Edward was smiling, Elizabeth glaring. She turned to Richard, her cheeks as red as pomegranates.

"What are you doing here?"

"Edward sent for me. Have I interrupted you? I would be glad to wait outside until you have finished whatever matter is at hand."

"Do not trifle with me, Richard."

He walked over to the side of the room to see what she had flung and picked it up. It was a silver hairbrush, the handle still warm from the heat of her hand.

She moved to retrieve her property and stretched out her hand. "That is mine."

"So it is." He laid the brush in her palm and she strode out, hair and gown flowing.

"Ah, Bess." Edward's eyes followed his wife's retreating figure. "She does not understand the needs of statecraft, but her protestations are amusing. Be seated." Edward sat down on the edge of the bed; Richard continued to stand. "I thought you would want to know that Warwick and George have accepted my terms. They will celebrate the peace here at Christmas."

"Do they mean it?"

"Oh yes. Now they mean it. Now they are most sincerely, abjectly contrite. Will they mean it tomorrow? Who can tell? I hope so. I don't like the idea of declaring them traitors. I do not like that at all, Richard. As much as they deserve it, I would hate to name my own kin my enemy."

## London
### December 1469.
Christmas. Time for lords to lay down enmity. And time for gaiety and color to warm the cold year's end. Deck the doorways with holly, the walls with banners of scarlet, gold, and green. Hang horn lanterns by the hundreds and bring out the best wax candles. Time to heap the fires high, butcher the boar and dress his head with apples and mint for the king's platters. Lay the tables with seedcake and spice wine, and lace the dancers' boots with bells.

In the midst of the celebration, it was easy to miss the fact that Elizabeth's family sat on one side of the hall, and Warwick's on the other. Richard barely noticed the coolness between his brother and his cousin. He was watching Anne. Surely the years between eleven and thirteen encompassed more change than any other such span in a maid's life. The little Teasel was lovely. There was the beginning of a woman's form in her body and a woman's gravity in her manner. She still wore her hair in a single long braid uncovered with coif or veil, dignified by a small circlet around her forehead and plaited with ribbons of green and gold. All through dinner his eyes were drawn to her, and he thought he caught her glancing once or twice at him, but when he turned to be sure, her eyes were engaged entirely with the feasters at her table.

Finally the remains of the feast were carried off, and the musicians came out to end the evening, all the singers and the players of flutes and pipes and viols. When the music ended, Anne left the hall, disappearing before Richard could reach her.

The next day he saw Anne with her mother in the midst of a flock of the court's ladies, admiring the new gown of one of the women. Anne did not look up when he approached. Her impervious concentration ironically made him sure that she had felt his presence. Her reserve, so different from what he had expected, gave him confidence because he thought he understood. She wanted to be seen as a serious young woman, one who had more important things to do than look at him. Which must mean he was important.

He walked over to her. "Anne. You have not even said hello to me."

"Hello, Richard." The face she turned toward him was very grave, not stern or unhappy, just utterly solemn.

"Will you walk with me in the gardens? I would hear the news from Middleham."

Anne glanced at her mother, who nodded. "Take your cloaks, children." Richard caught the amusement in Alice's smile. The gardens in December: well, it was the best he could think of at the moment.

*T*hey walked down the lane that passed the little cemetery of St. Katherine's and stopped for a moment by the abbey fishpond, where a monk was breaking the ice with his staff.

"I saw you at supper last night," Richard said, "but you left before I could talk to you."

"I wasn't sure you would know me."

"Not *know* you!"

"I was little, then. Back at Middleham, I mean."

Said it with pride, implying that now she was not.

The monk turned to look at them and in silent agreement they left the abbey grounds. When they came to the waterwheel, they crossed the bridge over Southditch and walked vigorously, feeling daring, like truants or vagabonds. There were few travelers on the road. The fog was rolling in and river mists were said to be unhealthy, but they paid that caution no mind. They felt wrapped in a secret world

Even in winter, the Thames was alive with ships: Venetian galleys bearing velvets and spices, Flemish caravels and Spanish merchantmen, barges toting the goods of local travelers. Richard told her what ports the ships came from and what they were carrying. Soon he was telling her things he had told no one, how he had thought he would die of seasickness sailing to Burgundy, and about the library he had visited in Bruges.

"I couldn't keep my promise to you," Anne said.

"What promise was that?"

"You remember," she said, frowning at him. "To care for Mercury."

"What happened?"

"My father sold him. For a while he let me ride him, even though he didn't think I could handle a great horse. But then he said he was too valuable an animal for a woman's palfrey."

"Oh." Richard had not thought of Mercury in a long while. How could he have ceased to miss something he had once loved so much?

"Don't be sad, Richard."

It was the second time she had comforted him, and both times were over the horse. He gave a small bitter laugh. "It doesn't matter, Annie."

Finally Anne told him that Francis talked of the time soon when he would come to London. "He sent you something. Wait." She reached inside her cloak and pulled a folded parchment from the pocket at her waist. "He said to give you this."

Richard slipped the letter inside his doublet. The wench. Ignoring him all evening when she knew she would eventually have to seek him out. "When were you thinking of giving this to me, if I had not come to you?"

"I would have given it to you."

"When?"

"When I was ready." She ducked her head so that her hood fell forward and he could no longer see her face. Their easy friendship vanished as if it had never been. Anne was almost entirely silent, answering his attempts to regain their companionship with a terse word or a nod. When she lifted her head and pushed back her hood, he remembered how clearly her face showed when she was thinking. He just wished he could know *what*.

"Richard?"

"What is it?"

She took his hand, stepped in front of him to stop his stride, and kissed him. He hadn't guessed what she was about, so he didn't make her task easier by bending his head, but he was only a little taller and she didn't have far to reach. A woman's sureness, but a child's kiss, as soft as a moth's wing brushing his cheek. A very cold moth's wing. She looked at him, assessing the effect. She must have been satisfied, for at last she smiled. "I want you to do something."

"Of course. I'm at your command."

"Not that kind of thing." Anne frowned, then looked away.

A mistake: his too-generous compliance had reduced her request to child's play. The matter was clearly serious. "I'm listening. Tell me."

She drew a deep breath and let it out. "Tell your brother you want to marry me. Tell him while he and my father are still friends." The words tumbled out in a rush. By the time she met his eyes, it was too late for her to see his first, naked response. Perhaps she had intended that.

"Wait," he said. "Wait a while. Let us see what happens."

"George and Isabel didn't wait. Edward forgave them."

He waited a moment before answering. "You can't imagine how much I would like to."

"You're wrong," she said in a small voice. "I *imagined* that you might want to marry me badly enough to do it." She waited, silent, until they both knew he had made her wait too long, and she stood before him exposed and shamed by his failure to respond.

She turned and walked away from him. He caught up in two strides and took her hand again. She wrenched it free and started to run.

"Wait, Anne." He reached her again and grasped her arms. "Listen. When Edward can rest and know who is foe and who is friend, then I may know what path I can take." He loosened his grip on her. "If I married you, and your father fell out with Edward again, I couldn't turn against my brother. I couldn't let you go, either. I would tear you from your family. You wouldn't want that."

"No. No, you are right. I see that now." Her face was stricken, and her voice so low he could hardly hear her.

He'd made her face the truth. He wished he could feel any way but miserable over having done so. In silence, they resumed their walk. In silence, he reached for her hand, expecting her to pull away again. But she tightened her hand on his, and they remained clasped, both of them clinging hard to hope.

*London*
*February 1470.*

Rain hammered on the roof and spat at the shutters. Richard parted the bed curtain and looked out. The room was still black, but it must be close to dawn. The hope that had raised its head at Christmas was dead. Stone-cold, irrevocably dead. Warwick, shamed and defeated after his humiliating scheme to kidnap Edward, was like a hawk with its wings clipped. When the feathers of pride grew back he began to soar again. Some day, though, like Icarus, he would fly too near the sun. Richard wondered only who else would be scorched and take the long hard fall to earth with him. Anne, of course.

Richard put his head through the curtains. "Jeremy? Are you awake?" Foolish question.

"Yes, my lord."

"Light a candle, will you? I'm getting up."

"Yes, sir."

They dressed and went downstairs, where they found the hearth ablaze and servants about in the kitchen and asked for wine and a plate of meat. While they were eating, Edward came downstairs, rumpled and bleary-eyed.

"Good morning, sire," Jeremy said.

Edward sat down and rubbed his eyes. "Morning! It's the middle of night."

"Why are you up?" Richard asked.

"Thinking what to do. Why are you?"

"The rain woke me." It was as good a lie as any.

"Who would have believed Warwick would go to Margaret after all this time?" Edward glanced toward the rain-lashed window. "May the storm reach the coast. Let his ship sink in the crossing. He can drown and George with him, for all I care. The Devil take the lot of them." He looked over at Richard. "Oh, sorry. You liked your little cousin, didn't you?"

# 8   The Pawn

Anne curtsied before her father. When she straightened, his eyes met hers, not sliding over her as they usually did. His face was thoughtful, attentive. Anne caught her breath. What had she done, that he would look at her so?

"Anne. Come here, my dear." Warwick sat at the long oak writing table in the chambers their family shared. They had been in France two weeks. Heavy with child, Isabel had gone into labor on the voyage, alternately retching and screaming with pain. The child was born dead, and Isabel was so wrung out that they feared they would lose her, too. Once on French soil, however, she began slowly to recover. Alice paced. She tried to occupy her hands and mind with needlework, threw it down, and paced again. Anne brought Isabel her meals and waited.

Warwick spent time every day talking with Queen Margaret, and there were jests that the former queen of England kept the duke on his knees the whole time. What they talked about, precisely, was unclear. Anne thought perhaps her father was offering to help Margaret free Henry from the Tower, but could not see what Warwick would gain from that.

Warwick reached forward and took her hand, holding it between his own. What a handsome man he was! There were streaks of silver in the black hair at his temples, and his bronzed face was still almost without lines. Today he wore a velvet doublet of a rich dark blue the color of the night sky, paler blue hose, and gray boots. Her mother must have been overcome when she saw the man who was to become her husband.

"You look handsome, daughter."

"Thank you, sire." Everyone said she looked like him, with her amber eyes and angled face.

"You have been well?"

"Yes, sire." The conversation was growing stranger. When had he concerned himself with her health? And when had she not been well, except for the times he chastened her? He released her hand and leaned back in his chair. "Come here, child. I do not talk to my men with a table between us. How should I do so with my daughter?"

Anne's chest tightened around her heart as she moved beside him. Was it possible that he did feel a tenderness for her?

"How is it you have grown so, and I have hardly noticed. You are how old now? Fifteen?"

"Fourteen, my lord."

"You are of marrying age. Did you think I would neglect to arrange a husband for you?"

"No, my lord."

"Well, you are very fortunate. An extraordinary marriage awaits you. You are to be queen of England. What say you to that?"

Queen of England? Edward had a queen. Elizabeth was very much alive. Had her father gone mad, then? His eyes had an odd brightness and he seemed both exultant and agitated.

He was waiting for her to answer.

"To be queen is indeed an honor. But who is to be the king my husband?"

Warwick put back his head and laughed. "A queen needs wit, daughter. You will do very well."

Now that he had taken her bafflement for wit, she could only wait quietly and hope he would reveal himself. She lowered her eyes. Modesty covered many a confusion.

"Anne, my dear, you will make Lancaster a fine wife."

She looked up. The room blurred and wobbled in her vision and her stomach felt as though it were dropping down a well. Lancaster? The son of old King Henry? Anne wanted to laugh, to let him know she was quick enough to catch the jest, but her throat felt stuffed with wool.

Warwick suddenly appeared more relaxed, as though relieved at her silence. "You may be somewhat surprised," he said, "that Queen Margaret and I have come to terms again. However, it is clear that no matter how distraught poor King Henry has become, he was the lawful king of England. It is only just that now, in his disability, his son should reign in his place."

Anne looked at her father's handsome face and felt a disbelief so violent she feared she would be ill. How could Lancaster be king when Edward was alive?

"Lancaster is not king yet," was all she said. "Am I to marry him before or after he is crowned?"

"You will be wed immediately, as soon as the queen and I agree on some final terms."

"Forgive me, Father, but how can this be? You were the lady Margaret's bitterest enemy." She was desperate to find a flaw in his reasoning.

"Yes, yes." Irritation roughened Warwick's voice. "Of course, but that is past. Are you going to stand there and quibble about quarrels that are of no consequence now, when I have just said you are to become queen of England?"

"I am to be Margaret's hostage." Anne spoke quietly, but she was beginning to understand. Her father's notion of putting George on the throne had been discarded as the idiocy it was; there would be war again; Edward must die. And her importance to her father lay only in her worth as a pawn. Who would not rejoice to find a farthing changed into a fortune?

"What are you talking about, girl?" Warwick was flushed, his hands clenched into fists, thumping a soft beat on the chair arms.

"I mean, until you have killed Edward and brought Lancaster to the throne, I am the promise you will not betray your word." Anne was beginning to feel an enormous calm, as if she would never be afraid again, now that she had nothing to lose. "And what if Edward kills you? That could happen, could it not? Then what will I be, sire?"

Warwick stood suddenly and she felt the sting of his hand on her face. Her eyes were watering, but that was only from the blow; she wasn't crying.

"Father." She spoke in as calm a voice as she could manage. "I will obey you, of course. But I wonder if Margaret knows the sort of man she makes this pledge with—a lord who would strike a lady for speaking the truth."

Now her father was losing his flush; he was in fact quite pale. What an interesting effect she had on his complexion. "Would you like more truths, father? Since you force me to the marriage, I don't care who kills whom. It's all one to me."

Mother of God. Had she said that, told her father she didn't care if he lived or died? She made herself keep her head up. She expected a second slap, but it didn't come. Instead, Warwick made a mocking little bow and addressed her in a voice that far surpassed hers for calm and contained fury. "I am honored to have such a child, one that recognizes the value of truth above all other virtues. Good day, daughter."

After her father had left the room, Anne found herself trembling and then sobbing. She went over to sit in the window, drew up her knees, and huddled next to the sun-warmed glass. For a moment she had felt free and wild when she had defied her father, but now she was sick with remorse. She didn't want him to die; she could hardly bear to think about how she would feel if he did. But she didn't want Edward to die, either, that handsome god that Richard loved. And what of Richard? What was his part in all of this?

The sun had eased into a velvety twilight when her mother came to her. Alice sat down and drew her daughter into her arms, stroking the damp hair and hot wet cheeks.

"Did he tell you, Mother? He's going to make me marry Lancaster." She heard her mother's sharp intake of breath, the slight hesitation before she spoke.

"Yes, dear."

So her mother had agreed to it: there was no more hope. Anne said tonelessly, "Father hates me, Mother. I made him hate me." She didn't say what troubled her the most—that either Edward or her father would die. Either way, she might never see Richard again.

"Nonsense, Anne. A father does not hate his daughter." She lifted Anne's face. "And the marriage is not as ill as all that. Lancaster is a fine-looking young man."

"Mother! He goes about boasting of lopping off people's heads and running them through."

"He's very young. Men take longer to grow wise than women."

Anne rested her face against her knees. If her mother said so, perhaps it was true. Lancaster wasn't old, and he wasn't ugly. Perhaps they would come to like each other. She was too exhausted from crying to think well. Maybe even the anger that had passed between herself and her father was a whim, forgotten tomorrow. Then a bitter thought entered her mind, a thought as clear and cold as a diamond. "You knew already, didn't you? You knew what he was going to do before we came to France."

Alice didn't reply, and that was answer enough.

$\mathcal{M}$argaret of Anjou sat on a cushioned bench, her spine so stiff as to imply that chairs with backs were made for invalids and sloths. Anne straightened her own back, then caught herself. She wouldn't give Margaret the satisfaction. She walked forward a little slower than was proper.

A proper curtsy, of course. Very low. The queen couldn't bend so low; Anne had heard she was plagued with aching joints. Why did people say Margaret was beautiful? The queen's skin was as white as fish-flesh, and she wore a gown of solid black, which accentuated her pallor. An elegant gown, Anne had to admit. It had a low square neck, and tight sleeves that ended in points at the wrists, and it fitted her body closely from shoulders to hips. Margaret had dark eyes with beautifully arched—plucked, no doubt—eyebrows, lashes of extraordinary length, and a nose also exceptionally long, with a little point at the end. A nose like a parsnip. Anne stood demurely after rising from the curtsy, her arms at her sides.

"Lady Anne," Margaret began. "Your marriage to my son is the promise of great joy for us and for England."

"Yes, Lady." *Liar, it's the price you had to pay.*

"The throne will be restored to its proper steward. You will be queen of England, and your father will enjoy the respect and position he deserves."

Steward? Anne hoped her face showed less amazement than she felt. Didn't stewards care for and tend what had been entrusted to them? And herself, queen. Why should that make her happy? All she wanted was to go home to Middleham. If Richard had married her, she might be safely there now, but Richard had too much honor for that. She had no use for men's honor: they took it on and off like a hat.

"As my son's consort, you will enjoy a position of great stature. On course you will conduct yourself in a way that warrants such regard." Margaret's eyes traveled Anne's person, up, down, back up. The faintest smile touched her lips. She means that, Anne thought. She doesn't like my father or anything about this match any better than I do, but she believes I won't disgrace her family.

"I'm sure you are aware that this marriage brings you many benefits," Margaret continued. "Presumably you are anxious to assume the position in private as well as public life. However, although you will exchange vows immediately, you will forego the pleasures of your union until after the coronation."

What was she saying? That she thinks I can't wait to share her son's bed? That she expects an heir in the making as soon as Lancaster is king? Anne shuddered inwardly, and felt the blood drain from her face to her throat.

*A*nne was treated exactly like a piece of furniture: as long as she was presentable and in the appropriate place, she elicited no notice whatsoever. If she made a misstep, she received the same impersonal anger directed at a footstool one tripped over. Anger and pride had sustained her through her interview with her father and kept her from withering under Margaret's scorn, but she could not survive on those forever. If she was not to die of loneliness and despair, she must have someone to whom she was not invisible. It required no great wit to determine the person most likely to receive her attempts at friendship.

*E*dward of Lancaster was a tall thin boy who looked much younger than his sixteen years. He had his mother's dark hair and eyes, as well as her pride. He showed Anne his favorite horse, his coats of arms, and his sword, explaining them to her as though she had never seen such things before. For all his pompous strutting, he clearly wanted Anne to like him.

She began to smile when she was seated near him at meals. When their eyes touched and lingered for the first time, he looked at her in a way no man had before, and she felt a an odd prickly sensation on the back of her neck. What have I set in motion, she wondered, and felt a shiver that was half nausea, half excitement.

# 9 *The Beggar-King*

*Doncaster*
*September 1470.*

Clatter and clank of weapons gathered and armed men running through his sleep. Richard opened his eyes and raised them to see a silver sickle of new moon in a sky full of stars. But he hadn't dreamed the sounds of war. The camp was stirring to life, men kicking out the banked remains of their fires, and going for their horses.

He stumbled to his feet and rubbed his eyes, which burned and itched as though his eyelids had been lined with sand. Idiot, he told himself. You don't spend the night in a hay stack and then grind in the chaff. It hadn't been much of a night, though. More like two hours for himself and Edward, only a little more for their men. He shook the dust from his cloak and put it on.

Edward was hurrying toward him, sword in hand. "See to your men! Jack has betrayed us."

*No, Jack, not yet.* Richard felt a shock as powerful as if he had been hit in the stomach. He took a step backward, nearly lost his footing in the hay, and his effort to keep erect steadied him. Ever since Warwick had married Anne to the son of Henry VI, war had been inevitable. Richard and Edward had spent all summer recruiting men. Jack was in the north, also gathering men for Edward's cause. But at summer's end, when Warwick sailed back to England with a fleet manned and supplied by Louis of France, Jack's loyalty seemed less certain. Jack was traveling south—every inn and village told of the great army some friend or brother had seen—but no messages came, no word of a meeting with Edward. Now, a hard ride in the middle of night, soldiers fully armed, could mean only one thing: Jack was riding not to join Edward, but to attack him.

"Betrayed," Richard said, not disbelieving, just tasting the idea before he swallowed it.

"Almighty God, what would you call it?" Edward was turning away. "Move! We've no time to argue about this."

"I'm not arguing with you." But what was he supposed to do? Arm his men? Dismiss them? "What are we about?" What could they do but fight where they were, even as outnumbered as they must be?

"Burgundy, if we can find passage."

"*Again?*" Richard said stupidly, as if it had been only yesterday. His weariness changed into a cold hollowness that reached all the way through him. Exile. He had come home from exile once before. Edward had been victorious before; he would be again. Think of that, Richard told himself. Leave room for no other thought. But he had never heard of a king in exile. How could Edward ever regain his kingdom from across the sea?

"Well?" Edward stopped where he stood. "Have you any better ideas?"

"No." Not one.

*E*dward's army rode for the sea. With forty miles to cover and no chance of changing horses, they pushed hard at first, then slowed their pace; horses ridden into the ground did not take you anywhere, and Jack's own steeds would tire first. They took only the briefest respites for water and reached the Wash at dusk. At least half the men Edward had brought together had scattered along the way. A storm was gathering and the fishing boats were docked. Edward found the owner of one of the boats, and Richard could see his brother's angry gesturing, while the other man simply stood, his arms crossed, shaking his head to everything Edward said. Finally, Edward stopped gesturing, reached into his cloak, pulled out a pouch, and put it into the man's hands before stalking back to the diminished circle of his men.

"Blasted idiot," Edward said. "He wanted me to *buy* the boats."

"And did you?" Richard asked, thinking of the size of the bag.

"Half," Edward said. "The rest in our horses, which we couldn't get across anyway."

By the time they embarked, night had fallen and the stars were winking out one by one. A bitter wind chopped at the waves and knifed through their cloaks. Richard hoped time might have seasoned his stomach, but they were only minutes on the rough sea when he felt the first rise of nausea. Shoulder to shoulder between Rob and John Parr, he put his head down between his knees, not wanting to spew on them. Within moments, so slight a thing as seasickness made little difference, to him or anyone else. The wind tore open the sky and battered the sea until it buckled, the deluge from above hardly distinguishable from the heaving water beneath them.

When they reached Portsmouth, drenched and chilled to the bone, half the men in convulsive shudders, they hired merchant ships to take them to the continent. Richard was on his feet—the crowd of men pressed close around the ship's small cooking hearths allowed for no other position if he wished to warm himself—but still too sick to care much whether he reached France living or dead. Gradually, the voices around him penetrated his misery, and he realized that several men in their midst had been with Jack.

"It was passing strange," one man was explaining to Rob. "When my lord called us up, we understood we were to fight for the king. Then on the road to Doncaster he tells us his brother Warwick has landed and now they are going to put old lack-wit Henry back on the throne!"

A second man laughed. "Just like that, can you fancy it? All of us gathered to do the king's work, and he says the king is that sad lump of flesh that hasn't seen an unbarred sky for a decade."

"How did you come to be with us, then?" Rob asked.

"Why man, he gave us leave. He said any who would fight for King Edward should go. That's how he put it, too, like he'd forgot who he'd just said was truly king. None would get an arrow in the back, but they'd best be quick because he would draw his sword on any man he found along the way, and no talk first.

"He's been a good lord," the man went on, "and his gold's as good as any man's. A lot stayed with him." He shrugged. "Not me. Edward's reigned for nigh on ten years now. If you ask me, it's a poor time to decide he hasn't the right."

Richard wondered just how much of Edward's gold remained—that huge purse to the fisherman, the pay to men who by now must have reached their homes. He had a small purse himself, and many of the others might well have, but Duke Charles would have to be a very generous man to enjoy his brother-in-law's arrival in Burgundy.

## Flanders, Duchy of Burgundy
### January 1471.

Hour after hour, day after day, Richard sat with Edward in Duke Charles's antechamber. When Edward spoke of soldiers, Charles answered with talk of trades and ports. Pages filled wine cups and hid

yawns behind their sleeves, watching for the exact moment to turn
the hourglass resting on a corner cabinet. The cabinet stood next to a
mechanical clock with all its wheels and pulleys. Charles's great pride
was to demonstrate the accuracy of the new device by keeping the
two side by side, and a page in constant attendance.

Now Edward was reminding Charles that the two of them had
agreed to stand together against France.

"I was not aware, brother," Charles said, "that we were at war with
France."

"You are correct, brother, as always. But Louis has put France at
Warwick's disposal."

Charles lifted a hand. "The merest dregs and crumbs of France."

"Some of those dregs have washed across the channel." Edward
leaned closer to Charles. "Warwick will have Lancaster crowned. You
know what that means to Burgundy. The boy is the son of Margaret
of Anjou. When a half-French king sits on the throne of England,
how long do you think it will take for Louis to wage war against
Burgundy?"

"Alas, brother, I must consider more than your cousin's outrageous
posturing. Our too-cool and wet summer brought a meager harvest.
Poor Burgundy will suffer a lean winter; all her resources must be
closely husbanded." Charles's face was dark and heavy-jowled, hung
with self-righteous melancholy.

"If our situation were reversed," Edward said, ignoring poor starving Burgundy, "I would have troops here without hesitation. I myself
would lead them. Surely you can see that." The whole purpose of
Meg's marriage to Charles was for Edward and Charles to stand together against mutual enemies, principally France. But Edward was a
king without a country—a beggar with possibilities. As far as Richard
could tell, their sister's marriage had given Edward nothing more than
the right to come to Charles's court and pretend he wasn't begging.

"Perhaps you would." For the first time that afternoon, Charles
smiled. "The English are ever rash. *Here*, we must bide our time more
judiciously."

Edward closed his eyes and emitted a barely audible sigh. When
his eyes opened again, they were glazed with the effort of hiding his
impatience, and the muscles along his jaw were bunched into tight
knobs. Richard would have liked nothing better than to see Edward
grab Charles by the collar, shake him out of his self-important gravity,

and urge him to the benefits of English directness. Perhaps dangle him from the parapets to hasten his decision. The clock struck two, and the upper globe of the hourglass was empty. The page received an angry look from Charles as the boy hastened to his task two strokes too late. As a child, Richard had been entranced by hourglasses. Each grain was eternity, the seed of everything that would eventually happen, all the days and years of the world waiting to be born. Now, fatigued with boredom, he watched the mountain of sand on its endless circular journey and thought it could just as well be dirt on the grave of all that would not happen, their dreams stillborn in Charles's council chamber.

Margaret came one evening to her brothers' chambers, attended by one of her ladies-in-waiting, a very young maid with a heart-shaped face and a narrow crescent of auburn hair showing beneath the demurely concealing wimple.

Edward drew up a chair for his sister and sent a servant for wine as if he were the host and she the honored guest. The maid stood, eyes lowered, at her mistress's side.

"Have patience." Margaret smiled at Edward and sipped her wine. "My husband will give you what you want." Anyone would have known Edward and the Duchess of Burgundy as brother and sister. They had the same ripe wheat hair, the same high fair coloring and strong jaws. In Margaret's face, however, the bones were lean, which gave her a look of spare strength, like the stone ribs of cathedral pillars, while Edward's face was showing the effects of too much wine and too little activity.

"Ah." Edward could put a whole discourse into a sigh, this one full of disbelief, even disgust. After a quick dismissive glance at his sister, he stood and stared into the fire with his arms crossed over his chest.

"Give me quill and ink, sister," Richard said, after a long moment in which Edward made no attempt to respond. "If your husband is so great a magician, I'll make my petition quickly, while Edward thinks on it."

Margaret laughed. Richard looked up to see the young maid watching him openly with interested gray eyes and a smile both radiant and poignant. For a moment the fatigue lifted and his heart swelled with longing.

"Then what would you, Richard?" Margaret asked.

"Nothing," he said. "It was only a jest." He felt the warmth of the maid's gray eyes and hoped he wasn't blushing. Edward noticed every slight detail that passed between his brother and a woman and wouldn't fail to comment.

"Tell me, Meg, how you come by this knowledge." Edward turned from the fireplace and hovered over Margaret's chair. "Is it the way your husband smiles warmly at me? Perhaps it's the great sympathy he extends to our plight."

Margaret said nothing, just sat calmly, waiting for Edward to go on.

He sighed and rubbed the back of his neck. "Your pardon, sister. You bring us cheer and good will, and I mock you. But I am at the end of my wits. I understand Charles must think about all of this, but I can't tell him how it will go. He is either with us or he is not; more time will only make matters worse for all of us. I would have the thing decided and done with."

"That is what I am telling you, brother. The matter is decided. Charles will give you what you ask." Margaret's face was serene and a little amused.

"Be plain, Meg. I have had a surfeit of subtlety."

Margaret reached out an elegantly slippered foot and tapped Edward's boot. "Think about this: What will you do if Charles refuses?"

"God's mercy, Meg, that is what I try day and night *not* to think about! Richard and I are dead men, should we ever set foot on English soil without an army behind us. Without Charles's help we will be in bloody exile forever. Don't you see that?"

"Edward, dear, I see it clearly. It is you who do not see what is before you."

"Forgive my dull mind, Meg. I have been meeting with Charles every day, but I seem to have missed any hint of his helping us."

"Charles is very fond of you, dear, but he doesn't wish to have you guests of his court forever. Of course he will help you. How many men do you need?"

"Ah." This time, a sigh of a different nature. "As I told your husband, five hundred men would be excellent, three might suffice. We need only enough strength that men will have confidence casting their lots with us. If we can land in the north with a strong show of arms, by the time we reach London we will be a mighty host."

After Margaret and her maid left, Edward turned to Richard. "That girl likes you, did you notice?"

"How do you know?"

Edward laughed and poured himself another glass of wine. "I thought you learned something during those years in London."

"I didn't say I couldn't tell. I asked how *you* knew."

Still laughing, Edward shook his head. "I sense these things. The question is, what are you going to do about it?"

"Nothing." Edward had taken one of the courtiers' wives as his mistress. Everyone seemed to know, and no one seemed to mind. In fact, if court gossip was to be believed, nearly everyone was sleeping with someone else's husband or wife. Except Charles and Margaret. Richard heard no gossip or slurs on the reputations of either of them. But Edward thought any interest in a woman was an itch to be scratched. He was wrong: there were itches and there were longings, and some longings were too deep to scratch.

Edward said suddenly, "You are like Edmund." It sounded like an accusation. Edward drank from his wine and stared at the violet dusk through the window.

"No," Richard said. "I'm not. I saw him at Ludlow, don't you remember?"

"Not in appearance. In your mind. Edmund thought about everything. He always wanted to know whether God would approve."

"*I* do that?"

Edward answered as though he were talking to himself. "Me, I have no time for that. The king may be the arm of God, but I'm not His mind, am I? He needs to make His will clear when he deals with me."

He put down his goblet. "Another way Edmund was like you. There was a girl he liked. He wanted to marry her, even though he probably could have had her any time he wanted."

A servant came in to close the shutters and tend the fire, then left again.

"Poor young fool," Edward went on. "I hope he had a taste of women first. He had no bastards that I know of, though. How many bastards have you?"

"I have two. You know about them."

Once Richard began learning about women, he had learned quickly. What Edward told him was right: many women thought it a great honor to sleep with the king's brother and sought his loins as a passport to wealth and position. He learned about the emptiness of flattery and how it could take the joy out of the simplest human act. And one day, he had learned he was to be a father.

The mother was the daughter of the owner of a tavern he and Jeremy frequented, a shy dark-haired girl named Elinor, who reminded him vaguely of Anne. Richard passed time with her because she was pretty and because he felt sorry for her. Her sweet nature and eagerness to please brought only greater demands from the tavern's patrons. But he had no wish for a mistress at court, and when he made that clear, saying that he would nevertheless provide everything the child and mother needed for all time, the girl's father was pleased, but Elinor was wounded. The hurt in her face was so naked that he knew it was more than the loss of a life at court that she mourned, and felt the pain, himself, of having inflicted that particular wound.

When she asked him what he wished to call his daughter, he said the first name to came to his mind. "Kate."

It took him a moment to realize why he remembered that particular name, and when he did, he almost clapped his hand over his mouth. He would have taken it back—how could he even consider naming his daughter for a whore?

But Elinor said, "I like it. Katherine."

Richard swallowed. "Very well, Katherine."

Thereafter, he spent little time with any one woman and was careful not to like any of them too much. When, a little later, he learned he would have a second child, by another woman, he named the boy Jack, for his cousin.

Edward had been distressed by the second child. "I suppose you'll care for this one, too."

"Of course. He's mine."

"Brother, sire as many bastards as you wish. It's nothing to me. It's fine that they should not grow up in need, but you should not be so hasty to provide for them. You invite claims on you that should not be made. You see that, don't you?"

"Yes, of course. Don't concern yourself." He had already made up his mind on that account. He didn't intend to sire more bastards, and there was only one way he knew of to be sure he didn't. It didn't seem much of a sacrifice. He had never recaptured the short-lived joy he had experienced with the whore. He flirted, touched, and kissed, aware that he had become a prize in a not very pretty game.

"Still only two?" Edward asked. "Well, I'm blessed. Do you still provide for them?"

"Yes, of course." And, as long as they were on the subject, "How many have you?"

"God knows. At least I hope He does. I keep no count." There was a heaviness in Edward's voice, and he drew a hand across his forehead, as though he could wipe away whatever thought was there. He was silent for a long moment. "It was a black time when Edmund died. I mourned our sire, but Edmund was like a part of me. I can't say it better than that. I trusted him.

"I trust you, too. You don't know how few people I truly trust. Do not betray me, brother. If ever you decide to go against me, stab me in my sleep, instead."

What a strange thing for Edward to say. Richard would give his life for his brother, whatever their differences. Surely Edward knew that. "Did you trust Warwick?" he asked.

"Oh, in the beginning, when we fought together. I never thought about it. It was always fight like Hell, see if we were alive after the battle, then take what came next. He was good to fight with. In battle I trusted him."

Now, Richard thought, to the point, perhaps. "What about Jack?"

"I never understood him. A good man, but slow to make up his mind, and moved by things I never saw." Edward thumped a hand on the table. "Did you know what Jack was going to do? Just before we left England. *Did you?*"

The bitterness and intensity in Edward's voice startled him. "How could I know? I haven't seen him since he came to court a year ago Christmas." Richard still regretted that he had only talked to Jack in passing. He had not taken the time to seek him out. "'*Not yet,*'" Edward said.

"What?"

" 'Not yet.' That's what you said at Doncaster, as if you'd known all along what Jack was going to do. If you knew anything, you should have told me."

Richard said, "I knew nothing."

"Don't lie to me."

"I'm not."

What did a man in Jack's position do, tied life and honor to two horses, one galloping east and another west? If he had any sense at all, he would cut the rope that bound him to one and try to ride the other. Of course he had known what Jack would do; he had just not known

how or when. They had forgiven each other the future that afternoon
by the stables at Pontefract.

*N*ews from England reached the Burgundian court almost daily.
Warwick released Henry from the Tower and paraded him through
the city streets, then summoned a Parliament in the old king's name
and proceeded to be ruler in effect while he awaited the arrival of
Margaret of Anjou and her son. Now it took three men to make one
king, Richard thought—Henry for the right, Warwick for the wit,
and Lancaster for the future—a badly made machine, overly complex,
with too many vital parts to long succeed. But nothing they heard
suggested that people in England were troubled by the arrangement.

Finally, there came news of a different kind. A page summoned
Edward and Richard to Charles's chambers, where the duke greeted
them with an air of expectancy. The servants stood attentive and
watchful. Margaret and a man dressed in Edward's livery had tears
in their eyes. The messenger started to drop to one knee in front of
Edward, but Edward grasped the man's arm. "What is it? Tell me."

Tears were now streaming unrestrained down the courier's face.
"You've a son, sire. A thriving, healthy boy."

"God." Edward took a seat at the table. "A son, you say." He had left
England not even knowing Elizabeth was with child.

"It is a sign from God, sire. You are meant to take back your crown
and kingdom."

Richard sat down on a bench along the wall. Everyone was crying
now, except for Charles, and even he seemed pleased, sending the page
out with orders for the best wine.

"All England rejoices and waits for your return," the messenger said.

"Well, not all. I would hardly be here if that were so." Edward had
little taste for flattery these days.

"Most, sire. Enough. Begging your pardon. . . ."

"Speak out, man!"

"Sire, it is this. Your subjects have always loved you. But men are
weary of the quarrels. In London, they saw your cousin's actions as
something you might have better controlled. I speak boldly, sire."

"Go on."

"One of the difficulties has been that if anything happened to you
in the strife, it was the Duke of Clarence who would succeed you. I
think you will find that having an heir of your body will make a great

difference. There are men who will stand beside you now, who might have hesitated before.

He paused. "Come home, sire. Come home and reclaim what is yours."

# 10 *Time Will Come*

In Yorkshire, every city and village greeted Edward with men who wanted to join his cause. A few joined on the spot; more promised to meet him in London. Still, in spite of Charles's gifts of gold and archers, Edward's success was far from certain. Two of the ships had wrecked, costing them both men and and horses. And they didn't know where Warwick was. Rumor had him first in London, then in the west. Edward's gold was running low: he had no credit.

When they approached Coventry, they saw a throng of riders just outside the city walls. The sun was just dropping low and the sky glowed with streaks of gold and red. The horsemen didn't move, and after a moment a single rider detached from the group and rode toward them at a good brisk trot, and then a canter. He rode up to Edward alone, the sun at his back and clouds of dust rising behind him.

Jack? Richard wondered. Had he had a change of heart?

Edward reined in and held up a hand, then his posture changed. He laid one hand across the other, resting both lightly on the pommel of the saddle. Richard saw Edward's face, the look of resignation, the slightly lowered head, and understood. George. Of course.

George pulled his mount up short, the horse's hind legs skidding to a stop, George's cloak furled behind him. He dismounted, his feathered hat doffed and broadly swept, gold curls catching the glint of the sun.

"Brothers!" George said, beaming.

"George," Edward said. "What brings you to Coventry?"

"Why you, brother." Richard saw George's boyish face, the quick smile. Edward's face was unreadable.

"I'm touched, George. Who are those men behind you?"

"Two hundred of the finest who decided, with me, that Warwick's cause was false."

He turned to Richard. "And you, Richard? Have you no words for me?"

"Greetings, George." How easily George changed sides. Takes what he wants, smiles, and Edward forgives him. How many times would Edward forgive? Seven times seven, the scripture said, but all that really meant was more times than men could count.

"Kiss and make amends, brothers," Edward was saying.

Richard saw the joy in Edward's face, though he was trying to be solemn. He saw himself, serious, constant—and unimportant. Edward hardly noticed his presence. Like a shadow. If a man loses his shadow, he would note the oddity, and then go about his affairs, never missing it.

"And if I don't accept your—ah, pardon me, George—somewhat dubious assistance?"

"I have two hundred men who beg you, as do I." He waved an arm behind him. "Tell them to leave. They are at your command to keep or dismiss. I also am yours, your man or your prisoner. Whatever comforts you most."

"George, I have not a single man to spare for guarding you. How can I make you my prisoner?"

"Then you must have me, brother." George spread his arms, palms lifted toward the sky.

"I would say that *you* have me." Edward was smiling. "Idiot. I would never turn you away. You know that."

George smiled. "As you wish."

Richard hardly looked at George

"What's wrong with you, little brother?" George asked. "Are you not happy to see the prodigal return? Oh, I forgot. The loyal brother doesn't welcome the prodigal. That's not how the story goes. Understandably enough, I must say."

"I'm glad to see you."

"Well then, come down from your steeds, brothers, and welcome me. I hunger for your embrace!"

George struck a fist on his chest.

Richard dismounted. "That's your *heart*, George."

"Why, so it is! It's my heart that suffers, little brother. My stomach is easily sated."

Richard held himself stiff and awkward for a moment, then relaxed. He could not keep his anger alive. It was like staying angry at a child. George meant no harm. He just went happily about his life, taking what he wanted, never exactly taking *from* someone else, but never seeing the damage that could arise.

## Barnet Heath
### April 11, 1471.

Now Edward's army was camped at the edge of a broad plateau, waiting for dawn. The plateau sloped down onto a common bounded on one side by a marsh; beyond the marsh were hedgerows and the woods. The night was shrouded in a thick mist that from time to time would part and reveal from across the common the pale blurs of light that were Warwick's campfires. The earl's archers sent volleys of arrows, overshot and falling harmlessly to earth beyond Edward's men. Cannon boomed to the left and across the meadow, wildly inaccurate even for those unreliable weapons.

"Let them fly, cousin." Edward stood under the open flap of his tent, shaking his fist in the direction of the enemy, and laughed.

An archer, a thin boy who had never even seen an army, asked, "Do we return fire, sire?"

"No, tonight we'll let them rest easy." Edward was in great high spirits. "This is my cousin's last night before he burns in Hell. It's the least we can do for him."

Some of the soldiers grumbled. It galled them to lie there and take Warwick's insults, even without injury. Allowing the enemy a night free from noise and terror went against their grain. But Edward was the general. His army did not return artillery and did not light fires. They had eaten cold and would sleep cold. But Edward knew the precise location of both armies, and Warwick knew only his own.

The one light in all Edward's camp was the lantern in his tent. In the soft glow of its light, Edward's height, his fair hair and unscarred face, which had lost the fullness he had had in Burgundy, made him seem as ageless and inviolable as an angel as he hovered over the table.

He took a lump of charcoal from a white bowl and drew rough geographical features on the parchment—the hill where they were camped, the road to Barnet, and the positions of the armies, making three Xs on the line of his own forces. "The center is my own battle, of course. The left flank," Edward pointed to one mark and spoke to Hastings, "is yours, Will."

Richard prayed he wouldn't have to fight Jack. But even if they didn't meet on the field, that was not the end of it. As Constable of England, he would be the one to pass sentence on any surviving enemy captains. Jack would understand, he knew, and forgive him. Whether he could issue the order—or forgive himself, if it came to that—was another matter.

"Richard, you will take the van," Edward said, breaking Richard's thoughts.

Richard's head jerked up. That had to be a mistake. Lead an army, not just fight a battle. But Edward met his eyes as if to say, yes, you can do this. It had never occurred to him. Why did Edward believe he could do it? He glanced at John Howard, saw Howard gulp, cover the surprise that ran across his face. Surprise ran around all the faces. But that was like Edward, not to let people in on his plans until he was ready to implement them.

"You have the worst ground, so take care. If you get to Dead Man's Bottom, you have gone too far. All of you take care. If the fog doesn't lift by morning, it will be easier than you know to end up where you don't want to be." He paused. "I presume Warwick commands his center, but I don't know who is leading the flanks." He paused long enough for John Howard to admit to the tent an old man with fine white hair, who looked too frail to do much but sit by a fire, until you saw his eyes, which were bright unclouded blue and fiercely alive.

The old man took off his cap and nodded to Edward before walking over to the map.

"The center is here, sire." He pointed. "Just as you thought."

"Warwick's command, I assume?"

The spy stroked his chin. "No, sir. It doesn't appear to be. It looks as though Warwick's brother, Lord Montagu, will lead the center."

"And the flanks?

"The Earl of Oxford commands the van and Exeter the rear."

Edward frowned. "Where is Warwick, then?"

"Well, sir, it appears that Warwick will lead the reserves."

"*Lead* the reserves?"

"In a manner of speaking, sir. And that's not all. It seems that Warwick's men were uneasy, thinking perhaps he and Montagu might not pull together. The spy cleared his throat. "Both of them having been friends of yours once, you know."

"Yes. Go on."

"The tale going about is that they could desert their own cause and come over to you if the battle turns badly for them. Or that one might turn against the other."

"Let them try it," Edward said. "They will see what I think of their last-ditch love."

"Yes, sir. Anyway, the humor in their camp is not that cheerful. Men are looking over their shoulders at a breath and jump at a twig breaking."

"So now Warwick reaps the harvest of his treachery," Edward said. "I can't say I pity him."

"No, sir."

Richard stepped outside Edward's tent and started toward his own, a few paces away.

"Walk with me for a time, son?" John Howard asked.

"Of course, sir." The battered old soldier had been one of Edward's commanders at Towton, Richard remembered. What would Howard say to him? That Edward had made a grave mistake, that Richard had no business leading a battalion? Howard could be offended at being passed over for the command tomorrow.

"We won't use the horses in this weather, that's certain," Howard remarked, coming up to Richard. "Just as well. There's only one thing I hate more than killing injured beasts, and that's not killing them and watching them suffer."

"Yes, sir." The fog was growing thicker. A cloud of dragon's breath. They picked their way slowly, speaking of small things and stopping when visibility became too poor to keep the tents in sight. Richard wondered what they would do if the fog didn't lift by morning.

Richard wondered too many things: Why do soldiers follow a commander instead of running? What would he do if they didn't follow? How afraid would he be; would he want to run, himself? Worst, what if he was so afraid he would run without even knowing it?

They had walked only a little distance from the tents when Howard stopped. "Your first command," he said, as if he'd known what Richard had been thinking. "I remember mine. I thought I would burst with pride if I didn't die of fright first."

"Yes, sir."

"I'm an old soldier," Howard went on. "Do you know what old soldiers want?"

"Sir?"

"They want to stay alive. Honor and glory, all those things that stir you youngsters' blood don't mean so much any more. My pride doesn't bleed. Do you follow me?"

"Yes, sir."

Howard fell silent for a moment, then went on. "Tell me something. This isn't only your first command; it's your first battle. Do you fear it?"

How could anyone know before the fact how they would feel? He had yet to put a blade through a living being.

"I don't know, sir."

"God save us, your learning has done you wonders! All that Latin and Greek, and you can't tell if you're afraid." Howard swung around in front of Richard, his battered ugly face not eight inches away, and put his hand on Richard's chest. "How does that feel, there?"

"What do you mean?"

"Can you feel your own heart beating?"

"Not just now, sir."

Howard took his hand away. "You put too fine an edge on things, lad. You feel your heart banging around like a bull trying to break down a pen, that's fear. You don't feel anything at all, that's fear, too. It's all the same. There's no shame in fear, remember that. There's no shame in asking for help."

"In battle, sir?" He wouldn't have thought there was time enough to ask for anything.

"Sometimes time stops on the field. You will be surprised."

"Could I ask you something?"

"Ask away."

"How do you know who you are fighting, sir?"

"Well, the livery and pennants, lad." Howard's voice was puzzled.

"I know, sir. But can you always see those?"

"No, son."

"Then what keeps men from killing their own without knowing?"

"Sometimes nothing. Sometimes we do kill our own."

Richard took that in. A mistake of that magnitude, and men couldn't always avoid it.

"We'd best be getting back now," John Howard said, his voice gentle. "Rest easy. Morning comes soon enough.

*F*rancis came out of the tent as Richard and Howard parted paths. "What did Lord Howard have to say?" When Edward's army had reached London, Richard discovered that Francis had left messages for him across the city.

"He said it was all right to be afraid."

"Are you?"

"He says I am." Richard waited, then, "I lead the van, Francis. It looks like Jack commands Warwick's center."

Francis understood. "That's one thing to be thankful for, anyway."

*J*ack reined in by the tent he shared with Warwick and handed his horse to his squire. "You know where to take him."

"Yes, sir." The boy took the reins and hurried off.

*Bright lad*, Jack thought. *You don't want to stay to witness this.*

Warwick strode toward Jack, calm and smiling in the lantern light. "You have seen to the horses?"

"Yes. I had them taken to the wood," Jack said.

"The wood?" Warwick's face was blank as stone. He would understand soon enough.

"Wrotham Wood."

"Your horse is in Wrotham Wood?"

"My horse. Your horse. All the horses. The horse park is there."

"That was not my order."

"I know. It was mine."

"You countered my command?" Still more disbelieving than wrathful.

Jack pushed by his brother into the tent and Warwick followed. "Your soldiers believed me," Jack said. "That's how."

"What? You deliberately changed my orders? In God's name, why?"

"You bloody well know why," Jack spun around to face Warwick. "The word in this army is that you are wondering where I will be if the battle goes hard tomorrow. Now you know. I'll be beside you or dead. I hope your mind is at rest."

Warwick stepped in front of the tent opening, his body blocking the dim light from the fires outside. "I could hang you for this." His voice was quiet but there was no mistaking the menace in it. Ah yes, he was beginning to understand.

"Well, brother, the men seemed to like the idea, their commanders taking the same risks as the lowest foot soldier. No riding for Scotland while they are cut down. Maybe it's your commitment they are worried about, not mine. Had you thought of that?" Warwick remained speechless and Jack went on. "In any case, we can all rest easy about betrayal tomorrow, every knight, archer, and yeoman of us. The most cowardly soldier malingering in camp would have to have wings on his heels to reach his horse in time to flee."

"You treacherous fool. Do you know what you have done?"

"Why, I would have thought you would like the idea. Burn your bridges—or slay your horses—behind you. Isn't that your device? This way you don't have to draw your sword." Jack started to step past Warwick to reach for the wineskin on the table, but Warwick stopped him, an arm across his chest.

"I cannot believe this. My own brother. I could execute you on the spot. I *should* execute you. I would have any other man's head."

Jack's anger was waning. "You could. Do it. That will clear your mind of all doubt."

Warwick stared. "I see it now. You hate me for making you choose."

"I don't hate you," Jack said, "but how can I have stayed beside you thus far, and have you still wonder if I will betray you? Still let your men know that you doubt me?"

"You loved Edward. For some men, it is very difficult to make war on past friends."

It astonished Jack that Warwick could say that with no embarrassment. With no thought of the cost of his brother's loyalty. "Yes. It is difficult. This is not the most pleasant thing I have ever done."

"Damn it, man. I would send you from me this instant rather than wonder about you. Everything rides on tomorrow."

"I know." Jack sat down on his cot and dropped his head into his hands. "I know, I know, I know." He looked up. "I'm here. What else do you need from me? Can you possibly think there is anywhere else I could be? Shall I go to Edward now? You know how he would welcome me, find a log and have my head." He stood up and was aware of how tired he was, more in spirit than in body. "I'll send someone to bring the horses back. I'll say I misunderstood."

"You can't do that. The thing is done. Leave it." The rage had gone from Warwick. "Just pray for us, brother. You have narrowed our lives to a hair's breadth."

Jack laid his hand on his brother's arm, and Warwick surprised him by placing his own on top.

"Come," Jack said, "enough of this. We must rest if we are to be strong tomorrow."

After Warwick had wrapped his cloak around himself and lain down for a few hours' rest, Jack stayed awake, ate, and drank a little wine. A little more than he should have. He sat with his head in his hands. A fine thing he need never have worked as a mercenary. There wasn't enough gold in the world for him to enjoy fighting for what he didn't love.

That was just the trouble. He had loved both Edward and Warwick, but now the love was mixed with pity and shame, nothing that could give a man the spirit to fight and count the risks worth taking.

He had always thought of himself as a worldly man, in the simplest sense of the word. If a thing did not rob him of the food on his table or the roof over his head, he saw no purpose in taking offense. Pride was of no earthly use that he could see.

Therefore it shocked him to discover just how much pride he had. He was rich enough to never want, but he couldn't bear having been given Northumberland just to have it taken away again. Edward could not even see that he had sold a sure friendship for the illusion of surety.

Jack asked himself what he loved enough to fight for. Nothing that stood him in good stead tomorrow, and that was the bitter truth. The children. Anne and Isabel. They were so beautiful when they were little girls, their flower-bright faces full of joy and hope. Both of them married to fools now, fools he hoped with little confidence would not mistreat them.

And Richard he loved like a son. In truth, he knew the boy better than his own children. What kind of country was this that would take a man's children from him just as they reached the age when he might take great pleasure in knowing them?

He had tried to persuade his wife that they should not be fostered out, but Bella had declared it was proper, and he had not had courage

enough to insist. He simply stopped looking on his wife with pleasure and gave his love to other men's children.

The thought of coming face to face with Richard on the field tomorrow was grotesque. A man does not kill children he loves. Surely
out of thousands of men, he could find someone else to cross swords
with. If the gods of battle were with him, he would be spared that
particular trial.

Jack stood up. There was one thing yet to be done before the
battle, something between himself and his soul. He listened to Warwick's breathing to be sure his brother slept, then quietly changed
into a fresh tunic. He yawned and lay down but did not intend to
sleep. Tomorrow was a day he would face alone, no matter how many
men fought beside him.

*T*wo hours before dawn and Richard had not slept. He rose from
his cot, parted the tent flap and stepped into the night. Still misty
and cold. He thought of what John Howard had said about fear. And
Giles, back at Middleham.

*Fear purifies you. It can help you concentrate. You must find a balance,
though. If you are too afraid, you will draw yourself into danger. But you
don't want to be too calm, either. You can't be thinking of your lady's kiss
after the battle.*

He had been too young to have a lady, of course, but he had understood what Giles meant.

Jeremy and John Parr had carefully laid out his armor, but Jeremy
continued to pick up each piece and apply the polishing cloth.

"Leave it," Richard said. "It's ready."

"The damp will rust it."

"It won't have time to rust. I'll be giving it back to you before the
morning's over. Help me arm now."

Jeremy picked up the greaves and the padding worn under them. "I
don't think I can do this in the dark."

"Light a candle. They will know where we are soon enough now."
Richard stood still, feet spread apart, arms lifted, as his squires began
to array him. Older knights, who had fought in enough battles to
know, thought the armor of the day the finest yet, as perfect a compro-
mise between protection and mobility as could be made. Plate of the
arms and upper torso overlapped downward to deflect blows, while
that of the ankles and feet lapped upward for ease of movement. His

was a fine Italian suit, strong but light, its weight so well distributed that he could walk comfortably, even run a distance. The real danger was from sweat and sun, which could turn the best armor into a knight's personal stew-kettle.

Richard could not persuade himself to endure the armet—the one-piece helmet and neck-guard that attached to the body armor by sliding rivets, rendering the head virtually immovable. Frontal vision was limited to the slit of the visor; side vision was nonexistent. He and Edward had argued about it.

"Do you want to be blinded?" Edward had asked. "Your face is an invitation for the ax in that thing," *that thing* being the simple sallet Richard preferred.

"At least I have a chance of seeing a blow coming," he said. He couldn't tell Edward how, when the armet's visor was closed, he felt the world closing in and couldn't breathe. Couldn't think, either, about anything but getting the helmet off.

"Take a good look, then, because it's the last thing you will see."

They had compromised. Richard's helmet had a well-constructed, closely fitting visor, independent of the body while still protecting the throat and neck. He could bear the visor, just.

Jeremy fitted Richard's gauntlets and secured the sword in its harness. Richard picked up his halberd. He might not use the sword at all; the halberd could penetrate armor far more efficiently. No shield. His armor was his shield, and he needed both hands for weapons.

Outside, the dawn was gray and dim. Rags of fog drifted thick and opaque, distorting the soldiers so that they appeared as ghosts of the battle they had not yet fought, disembodied limbs rising from the field. An armless hand reached through the mist; a head floated by, laughing.

A herald trotted up on a dark horse tossing its head and snorting with impatience. "His Grace requests you to form your battle, sir." He hesitated, then said, "Your brother also said to tell you, God be with you."

"Thank you. Tell him the same. Tell him I'll drink with him, after."

"Yes, sir." The herald wheeled his horse and was gone.

The men took their positions, columns of knights and archers flanked by wings of more archers, standard bearers and trumpeters to the fore. Flags hung limp from the poles, and cannonfire pummeled the air around them. Horses pawed and shrilly neighed from the horse park. From all directions, cannon and handguns boomed.

Richard was definitely queasy. Some men stepped aside to retch, then calmly stepped into line again and he heard someone near him curse, *"I've shat myself!"* Then laughter.

The trumpeters blew the call to advance out over the lines, their call hardly distinguishable from from the great racket all around. At the trumpet's call, the division fell in, and Richard started his men down the slope. He could see only three or four men on either side, but he felt the earth shudder under his feet, as though it had a pulse of its own. His mind divided into two parts, like the floors of a building. The lower level, around his eyes and ears, took note of the trumpets and the call to advance and the ground he walked on. The upper part was pushing against the roof of his skull as if it were trying to get out, and he could hear it clamoring: *All these men here with you? There are just as many coming toward you. All those swords clanging now? They will slit you from top to bottom as if you were made of silk.*

But his feet kept moving down the hill as Giles's words came to his mind. *Hold your ground, don't let your men march into their shields.* Whole armies had drifted off course because soldiers had veered left, walking into their own shield cover. He didn't have a shield. He could keep his men on course.

*Remember the simple things; everything else will come to you.*

*Giles, I sincerely hope you were right.*

Arrows swarmed into the air, in range now. A man on Richard's right took one in the neck and pitched face down onto the ground; sounds of fighting rolled like thunder around them. More arrows found marks; cries and screams rose up as soldiers dropped to the earth. The lines parted around fallen men, not even faltering as they came together again.

Richard kept moving toward the sound of fighting. He began to feel uneasy that he had not yet made contact. The ground became steeper, which didn't fit the land as he remembered it. He recalled Giles's caution about veering left and was nearly certain he had not done that, but somehow they had lost their course. He looked about him, trying to find something familiar that could serve as a compass point. *You've been here before, on this very spot. Try to remember.* But there was nothing, only his own men and the fog around him.

Abruptly, the land leveled out. The ground was soft under foot. Then wet. Water seeped between the steel plates and through the seams of Richard's boot. *Dead Man's Bottom.* The very thing Edward had warned him about. His sense of disorientation was so strong that for a moment he was giddy with dismay. He heard someone near him shouting something about the fog, *The fog, it was the fog*. He thought it was John Howard. Then his mind calmed and he was able to think what might have happened. In the fog, the armies were misaligned from the beginning. He must have marched right past Warwick's flanks, could probably have shaken hands in passing. *Someone miscalculated; it doesn't matter who. Just get it right, now.*

He swung his men left. They leaned into the face of the hill, taking the air in gulps. Richard's sweat rose like steam in his helmet. If Exeter understood what happened before they reached the top, he would knock them down like pins on a bowling green. He talked to his men, in his head. *That's good, hurry. Crest the hill.*

Nearly there now. The crest of the hill made fresh men of them all. They ran up over the top, and he gave a savage shout as they surged forward. Exeter's men paused in shock and confusion. They had had one of Edward's regiments for two of theirs, and now they had one at their front and another at their side.

*Make the most of it.* Exeter would realize soon enough that he was not outnumbered. Richard swung his axe into the first man he reached. It cut into the man's belly; he doubled over and fell. Not so hard to kill, after all, it happened so fast. He felt strangely light-headed, almost elated.

Exeter's flank recovered from their shock and rallied. The field was swarming and disordered; fighting met with increasing difficulty as men were felled and bodies clogged the line of impact. Men tried to step over or around the fallen soldiers. At times they had to scramble over the dead and wounded and wait for still others to fall to have a place in the fighting. It was next to impossible to know who was the enemy. Muddied and bloody, pennants had grown indistinguishable in the dim light.

A few arrows pelted down from a long way off. They seemed harmless, like rain. Richard brought his axe down on a man's arm. It missed the joint in the plate; the man shoved him back, and he nearly stumbled over two soldiers grappling face to face on the ground. He sidestepped them and a body fell between his feet. He lurched and was jolted forward. When he had his feet under him again, he was fighting someone else.

*T*he sun was fully up now, and a murky yellow light shone through the remaining shreds of fog. Richard fought with a kind of mechanical endurance. His arms burned and ached but they kept moving as though they were things apart from him. He felt as if he were standing still, that the ground beneath his feet was moving, flowing like a river. He had lost all sense of time and seemed to have been fighting one man forever. This was not good, fighting the same person for so long. The steady rhythm could lull you, especially when you were already tired.

The man Richard fought was tall and powerful, with a long reach. Great efficiency of movement. Too much efficiency, his moves cost him little effort. He could fight a long time without tiring. There was a game the boys had played at Middleham: think of the worst things that could happen, every gruesome and horrible thing that could befall you, and imagine it in great detail, because what you thought of seldom came to pass in exactly the way you dreamed it. It was a kind of magic with them; think of the thing precisely enough, and it would never be. They were wrong. He had not seen how simple it could be, no decisions to make at all. *This man is going to kill me.*

Each time the other man's sword came a little nearer its mark. Each time Richard felt himself to be a little slower and clumsier. The sword came at him, he lunged forward and thrust his axe upward. The axe glanced off the sword and ground into the other man's shoulder, cutting deep between the plates. The knight dropped slowly to his knees. The ax went with him. Richard grabbed at it and pulled, and the man came forward. Stuck? *Please, no.* Yes. Richard put his knee against the other man's chest and pulled back. Metal grated against metal, and the knight screamed, but stayed on his knees and lifted his head. He wore an old-style helmet with a nose plate and no visor, and his eyes were agonized. Blood ran down his armor into a pool around his knees. He was absolutely still, not even swaying.

Richard released the axe, and the man tilted forward. Richard still had his own sword, and he glanced from it to the other man's weapon on the ground, as if he were deliberating over wares at market. He watched himself do it, as though he had until noon to choose. He stood there at the calm center of the storm raging around him, thinking, shall I take this one or the other, and the fighting didn't touch him.

Then time moved again. A mace came from nowhere full at Richard's face, and he knew he couldn't move quickly enough to escape it, but somehow the blow fell clumsily on the side of his helmet. His head echoed inside the steel and he felt a hot line of pain running down his temple. A short heavy knight lay before him, a knife in his back. The knife belonged to John Parr, who had appeared from nowhere and now stood over the fat knight. The squire was standing there one moment, and the next, was clutching his side and tumbling over Richard's sword to the ground. Richard grabbed for him, then let out a startled cry as the wound at his temple raked against rough metal and blinded him. He had a moment of absolute helplessness and terror. Then people were around him on all sides, and he realized they were his own men, acting as a living shield while someone carefully removed the helmet. Richard made himself breathe. The mace had apparently struck just at the joint of helm and visor, sprung the rivet, and battered the edge of the helm. He was cut along the temple, but all that had blinded him were sweat and tears.

God. He knew fear now. He saw the eyes of the knight kneeling in his own blood and John Parr falling over his sword and was weak with it.

John Howard was right. Thinking was the trouble. If you could keep moving and not think, you were all right. He started to push back into the fighting and heard someone shouting.

"Gloucester! Wait!"

It took him a moment to realize the name was his own. A herald with Edward's livery ran toward him, half stumbling. *Please, not bad news,* he thought. Then, *Don't think.* He waited for the boy to reach him and get back enough wind to talk. "His grace says to tell you he will send his reserves."

"No, we'll hold." Richard looked at the lines. But there were no lines. There was only a field black with blood, broken by the dead and the writhing wounded and by clots of men that could have been either fighting or embracing. Two men near him leaned on their swords, watching each other, each letting the other be the first to move.

The herald was waiting. "No, sir, you don't understand. His grace is sending you reinforcements."

"We'll hold," Richard repeated. He started to turn away, but the herald stopped him. The boy spoke with great precision, as though from rote or as if he were talking to a madman. "His grace King Edward sent me to tell you he is sending part of the reserves. They should arrive any moment."

"Tell the king," Richard began, then stepped closer, "tell Edward to use all the men he has and finish this. We don't need more men, we need to stop fighting."

The boy first looked startled, then as though he might cry, straightened his face and opened his mouth to try again.

"No more," Richard said. "Go back and tell the king, before those men start over here. If he doesn't like it, tell him you gave me his message three times and I threatened to kill you. If we get his reserves I will personally look you up and run you through."

He watched the herald disappear, then turned and pushed back into the fighting.

It seemed to Richard that he could hear more clearly. Sounds were separate, not layers of a great clamor. No cannon now. Hoofbeats came from a distance. He felt a faltering in the men he fought. *Push now. Don't think who's in retreat. You'll know soon enough.*

Soldiers began to break from the center of the fighting, first a few, then a deluge, like a rupture in a dam. His own men were shouting and running, pressing on the other army. At first, he couldn't tell who was retreating and who pursuing. Then, more quickly than he would have said it could happen, the chaos assumed a shape. The men fleeing wore Warwick's livery. They dropped sword and shield as they ran, sometimes gauntlets and helmets, any piece of armor they could fling loose. It was over.

Richard looked around for friends and didn't see them. John Parr was almost certainly dead. He hadn't seen Jeremy since the beginning of the battle, and could not remember seeing Francis or Rob at all. He had no idea what had happened on the rest of the field. He pulled off his gauntlets and hooked them under his belt, then crouched down to pull a handful of grass to clean his sword. He stood and slid the sword back into its scabbard. His whole head was beginning to throb. He felt carefully along the edges of the wound; it ran along the hairline from his eye down to his cheekbone, and seemed to have stopped bleeding.

There was no excuse for what had happened. There was something he should have done. He would think later what that was. An archer was picking up arrows from the ground and tying them into a bundle. The man's face was so dirty he was unrecognizable.

"Christ bless us," the archer said, looking around him, "that's a sight to make a man thankful to be whole, isn't it?"

Some of the fallen men were gathering themselves and moving with purpose, sitting up and crawling. Some stood, slung between friends, and were half-carried away. There was a continual din, like the buzzing of thousands of flies. It took Richard a moment to identify the sound as moans and cries for help. Kites hovered and settled on the field. The smell was that of a charnel house, excrement, blood, and a smothering sweetness, as if the air there would never again be pure, never carry the smell of grass and spring air.

Sunlight fell through the remnants of the mist in white shafts, like in paintings of Easter morning. It occurred to Richard that it was, in fact, Easter morning.

"God's radiant candle rose over earth."

Richard turned toward the sound of the voice, and behind him were Francis and Rob. Not wounded, thank God. "Poetry, Francis?"

"Yes," Francis said. "Not mine, however. It's an old battle chant. Very appropriate. God's glory above man's carnage. Things haven't changed, have they?"

Francis's eyes were bright and large. "Go to my tent and get something to drink," Richard said.

"In a while." Rob had started to pull Francis in the other direction, but Francis shrugged off his hand. "I came to tell you we've won. All of Warwick's divisions were broken."

"We saw Jeremy," Rob added. "He wanted to come with us to look for you but I sent him to the surgeons."

"He was wounded?"

"Nothing serious. I think his arm is broken."

"Oh," Richard said. "Well." He was so glad to see these two alive he was losing the power to speak intelligently. "Do something for me. I'm not going back to camp just yet. I want to see if I can find John Parr." He unbuckled his sword and handed it and his gauntlets to Francis. "Take these. Tell Edward I'm whole and I will be there soon. Then find the heralds and help take a count of the dead. If you don't know the man, and the herald doesn't recognize his device, find someone who does." He turned to include Rob. "Disarm first. There is no rush. We'll be here all day."

Richard walked down the road that led to Barnet and into the center of the field. The road was no less littered than anywhere else; the fact that it was free of hedges was the only way to know it as a road. Must be after nine, now. He was sticky and filthy. It was going to be a mild day, after all.

*H*e found John Parr lying on his side, one arm flung out, the other draped across his stomach. Except for all the blood, looking at ease, a nap in the sun. Richard could see his squire's chest moving in and out, and breathed a prayer of hope.

He knelt down. "John?"

The boy was indeed breathing, but his expression didn't change.

"John Parr?" Richard said.

John Parr's eyes moved as though he were trying to find the source of the sound, then widened, probably only to let in the last light of a dimming world, but they looked as if they were exploded by the brightness they beheld. *Tell me what you see.* Then John Parr's eyelids quivered, and he let out his breath and did not take another.

Richard touched his squire's face. *You saved my life.* A squire's duty, but he need not have died. *I was dreaming on my feet. Forgive me. God speed your soul.*

Odd to look on the dead face. The spirit was gone, but the face still held so much that was John Parr. What did that mean about the soul? Too big a question. Richard stood up and went on.

He came to Edward's tent and went in. His brother was stooped over a basin on a table made from boards on trestles, splashing water on his face. Two squires worked on his armor. Edward wouldn't stand still for them, and they followed his body as he moved. Will Hastings sat on a cross-legged stool by the king's cot. "Your Grace," Hastings said, and inclined his head to Richard.

"Will," Richard acknowledged. It made him uncomfortable when Hastings treated him so formally. He suspected Hastings knew, and that it amused him to do it.

A squire put a linen in Edward's hand. Edward wiped his face, threw down the cloth and turned to Richard with a grin. "Brother! I'm glad you're still alive."

"Not as glad as I am. Have you fresh water?"

Edward tossed him a wineskin. "I couldn't have said that your life mattered to you. I thought perhaps you were trying for sainthood." There was an edge in his voice.

"What do you mean?"

"Hah!" Edward pulled off his breastplate and tossed in on the table. "My herald said you threatened to kill him if I sent you help."

"I didn't mean it. He wouldn't stop talking."

Edward shrugged. "He thought you were mad. You did very well, though, you and your men. Another time it might not work. Remember that."

Richard put the stopper in the wineskin. It was fair wine, but warm, and he would have rather had water. "What are you talking about?"

Edward blinked. "You had nearly all of Warwick's reserves at your throat. You frightened him into committing most of his reinforcements to your division. He must have thought you were the main army. Didn't you realize the kind of numbers you were fighting?"

"I didn't count, no." Richard said. Already, he couldn't remember the battle clearly.

Edward was out of his armor. He shook himself like a horse rid of its saddle and pulled his shirt in and out from his chest, venting it. He turned to Hastings. "Did you hear that, Will? Not bad for a green commander, is it?"

Hastings crossed his arms over his chest and rocked back on the stool. "Not bad at all, young man. Half my men were routed."

"What happened?"

"The battles weren't aligned properly from the start. Surely you discovered that?"

Richard nodded.

"Oxford wrapped around us from our left and pushed us into Jack Neville's center. A good portion of my men panicked and ran for Barnet."

"Oh." Richard set the wineskin on the table. He thought about washing and decided the water was too dirty to be of any use.

"We've more water," Hastings said.

A squire poured the basin out on the ground and refilled it. Richard gasped when the water touched the side of his face.

"You know better than to fight in an open visor," Edward said.

"I wasn't." Richard didn't even try to explain what had happened. He went over and sat on Edward's cot and started to lean back before he remembered the wall behind him was made of canvas.

Edward ignored Richard's denial. "You're fortunate you didn't get your brains scattered. How many men did you lose?"

"I don't know. A lot." He hesitated. "Is George all right?"

"Yes. He remembered which side to fight for. That helped."

"Sir? Pardon me." A voice from outside the tent.

"Yes, what?" Edward called.

Rob Percy stepped inside and inclined his head to Edward. "Sir," he said again, then stopped.

"Well, what is it, Percy?"

"Could you come, sir? I think we've found Warwick."

"Can't your men—" Edward began, then frowned. "You know Warwick, Percy. What do you mean?"

"He's dead."

"Not in battle?"

Rob shook his head. "He was run down trying to get to his horse."

"I gave orders to spare him. Who killed him?"

"Our men, sir. From the van. They didn't know who he was. Now they want to know what you want done with him."

Edward glared. "God damn it, Richard, your men are zealous today. I wanted him taken alive if he survived the battle. What do I care what is done with him now?"

Richard got up. The trembling seemed to have stopped. "I'll go talk to them." Probably what they really wanted to know was what Edward was going to do with *them*.

Hastings lowered his stool back onto four legs. "Be careful what you say to them. You can't let your men start thinking it is acceptable to ignore the king's orders, even unintentionally." He glanced at Rob. "You're certain it was accidental?"

"Yes, sir. They weren't looters. They probably had never seen him before. They hadn't started taking off his armor when I got there."

Hastings nodded. He pulled up a blade of grass and bit at the end of it.

"Don't worry, Will," Richard said. "I will make clear to them the gravity of their offense." The sharpness of his own voice startled him. Hastings rocked back on the stool again and chewed his blade of grass.

Edward said quietly, "I think you meant to say something else."

"Just that it seems useless chastening the soldiers. Warwick dies a few hours sooner, and by the sword instead of a headsman's axe. What's the difference?" What did Edward think to do with Warwick, set him free?

Edward laughed. "He's right, Will. It doesn't matter. Who would I ransom him to? Henry? Margaret? Maybe I could have let him keep company with Henry in the Tower for the rest of their natural lives. Now I will not be responsible. For once, the king is not responsible. Your men did me a favor." He pointed at Richard. "You don't tell them that, though. We'll take his body to St. Paul's. Maybe Margaret would like to burn a few candles for his soul."

*S*oldiers were crowded around the body, unbuckling the armor. They stood and stepped back when Richard came up. Warwick lay spread-eagled on the ground, half under a hawthorn hedge. His horse, or someone's horse, grazed a few yards away, the reins trailing. Richard looked down at his cousin. *No great gestures today in the name of glory and the king?* He thought of the story told of Warwick. That the earl had stabbed his horse at Towton, claiming he would rather die with Edward than flee. It had seemed as heroic as the old epics. But no matter how Warwick's loyalty had been corrupted, he hadn't supported Margaret as he once had Edward. Warwick would have given the kingdom for his horse, today.

Richard stooped and ran his hand over Warwick's eyes, closing them. What would become of Anne now? He started to rise and found that his legs had gone weak. "Give me a hand, Rob," he said. He pulled himself up and turned to the soldiers. "Finish stripping him. Make room for him in one of the baggage carts; we're taking him to London."

Richard walked on in the direction of his tent. Clerks and heralds were examining livery and trying to make lists of the dead. Men were stacking the armor in huge heaps, one for pieces undamaged enough to use or sell, and one of battered and broken plate that would be melted down.

Already scavengers were rifling the dead for valuables, quick as cutpurses. Some local people, mostly women, were slowly walking the field. A pretty young woman knelt by a corpse, her hands cradling the hand of the dead man. She pressed it to her cheek and then to her lips, her head bowed, tears streaming from closed eyes. The gesture was so tender and private that Richard turned his eyes away. He wondered what it would be like to have someone who loved him like that waiting for him, and imagined what such a woman might do when she found him still alive. He felt a moment's envy for the dead soldier, then despised himself for it.

"Richard. Wait!" Francis was hurrying to catch up with him. Francis's face was still grimy, and he looked exhausted and grieved, but at the same time more like himself.

He reached Richard and stopped and caught his breath. "They found Jack," he said finally.

"Oh?" Dead, Richard supposed. He was sad for a moment, but, as with Warwick, it could only make a few hours difference. Then he remembered who would have to oversee the trial and execution of the enemy captains, and all he felt was relief.

"He's dead," Francis confirmed, "but there's something odd you should see." He seemed to want to say more.

What could be odd?

"Did he try to change sides after all?" Richard hoped not. Jack had made his choice. Let it be one he was able to live with to the end.

"I can't tell you." Francis brushed tears from his cheek. "You must see."

*A* squire sat on the ground beside his late lord, face in his hands, sobbing. Edward was striding up as Richard stepped forward. Jack lay stretched out on his back, armor removed, the once-ruddy face unmasked. Arms at his side, legs straightened. A huge bloody wound just beneath his heart, the blood nearly obscuring the rising sun. *The rising sun of the House of York.* It was sewn on Jack's tunic, next to his skin, out of sight until his armor was removed.

*Time will come, lad, when you cannot love them both.*

*But you do.*

*Time will come, time will come.*

*If you cared that much, why didn't you stay with us?* But he knew. Jack's heart was one place, his loyalty another. The sun wasn't an emblem of regret; it was a message of love to men he could not serve. He touched the squire's shoulder. "Did you see him killed?"

The boy nodded, starting to sob again.

Edward said, "Get hold of yourself. What happened?"

The squire gulped. "Oxford's men dispersed, chasing some of your troops. When he gathered them back, they were coming from the wrong direction. His banner looks a lot like yours, sire. My lord's archers fired on them before any of us understood who they were. Both sides were shouting treason. Oxford and my lord both saw what was happening, but they couldn't get their men to stop fighting. It was one of Oxford's men killed him, sir."

Richard looked up at his brother. Edward was wiping tears from his face.

"Damn," Edward said, "damn Warwick for all of it. Bloody waste." He shook his head. "Send his body home. No, take it to London with Warwick."

"Edward—" Richard began. He couldn't bear to think of Jack lying exposed and collecting flies.

Edward sighed. "He'll get a decent burial, brother. Warwick, too. But not before London sees what happens to traitors to the King's cause."

Richard stood, stumbled, caught himself. Edward's hand was out to him. He ignored it. He saw the two faces, both loved. One living, one dead. The dead face bled white, dark hair matted with blood and sweat. A still face, showing nothing. Perhaps at peace. The living face, begrimed and weary, but beneath the exhaustion, a look of triumph. A smile, damn him. Under it all, a smile. *Your fault. This is your fault. He loved us to the end. He would have stood by you, had you given him any cause at all.*

He had to get away before he said something unforgivable. He took Rob's hand and stood. Away? Everywhere he looked were dead and wounded. Thirty thousand men, maybe half of them dead. Away was anywhere Edward wasn't. Anywhere he could think. Jack had warned him. Warwick and Edward were the clash of two great prides. May he never have such a pride. But humbler men like Jack were crushed between them.

He walked quickly from the little knot of men around Jack. He remembered the mist-wrapped morning when he had seen his men rise and follow him, and had felt that odd elation. Now he saw dead men all around him, stripped of their armor, pulled out of their crumpled positions and lined up like sides of meat at market. Men walked among the fallen horses, dispatching those that still breathed. His mind felt hollowed out, his skull occupied only by a searing white light. How did a man live with what he'd seen that morning?

To his right, in the shadow of a dead horse, he thought he saw a glint of color, a flicker of gold, and walked over to see what it was. There was a single primrose, whole and untrampled, untouched by even a drop of blood. He sat down on his heels and stared at it.

Except for this flower, the new spring meadows were as broken and torn as the men who lay upon them. But the earth didn't care. It would open and accept the bodies of men carried to their graves and of horses dissolving where they lay, blood and long white bones sinking deep into the ground. He sank onto his knees, crossed his arms over his ribs, and wept.

# 11 *Kill Him, Too*

"None of the outriders have come back yet," Richard said. He dropped down to sit beside Rob on the blanket spread on the ground. The earth was still wet from the rain that afternoon. Finding wood dry enough to burn had taken several hours, but now the fires of Edward's army flared all along the base of Sodbury Hill.

Margaret of Anjou had touched land in Weymouth two weeks ago, the day of the battle outside Barnet. With her was her son, Edward of Lancaster, and, Richard supposed, Anne Neville. The news of that defeat would have sent most women back to France in the time it took to board the ship, but the Duke of Somerset, who had commanded her troops at Barnet, had persuaded Margaret to fight again.

For several days Edward remained immobilized, waiting to learn whether Margaret would march on London or strike out for Wales, where she might receive support from Jasper Tudor. But when she finally moved, her direction was hardly clear. She took an irregular course, partly to receive supplies from towns sympathetic to the Lancastrian cause and partly, no doubt, to confuse the enemy. For the past seven days the queen's army had led Edward in a chase of feint and dodge across England, as he had tried to guess when and where she would engage.

Margaret's army—or part of it, as was now apparent—had occupied the hill earlier in the day. The army had vanished by the time Edward had reached Sodbury, and the brief Lancastrian occupancy of the hill could now safely be judged a diversion by a handful of troops while the main army had disappeared. Edward sent out riders in all directions while he wasted an afternoon's march waiting for information.

Richard kicked back into the fire a log that had fallen aside. "We're here for the night. Where are Francis and the others?"

"Tending the horses." Rob gestured toward the horsepark. "Or rather, Jeremy is tending the horses. Francis is tending Martin. Whatever induced you to bring him?"

"Edward," Richard said. "A favor to Martin's father." The son of one of Edward's clerks, red-haired and freckle-faced Martin was training as Richard's squire, but the boy had no skill with animals and sat a horse with all the grace of a sack of flour.

"Why didn't Edward keep him?" Rob asked.

Richard shrugged. "It was easier to hand him to me." Edward almost always did what was easiest, and most of the time that meant handing the problem to someone else. Richard hadn't realized until he heard himself speak how often that someone was him.

In a moment, he could hear Francis's laugh rising above the hum of voices around them, and Jeremy, explaining something to Martin as they approached. Jeremy's arm was bandaged and splinted, but he had wanted to come, and even one-handed he was more help than Martin.

"The horses are watered and hobbled," Francis said "Anything more?"

"No. Get some sleep. We're hoping for word before morning."

Richard lay back and settled himself. He remembered the years at Middleham, when the five of them—four, now John Parr was dead—were boys. Now they were men, and likely to take separate paths when this conflict was over. Francis had a fine estate in some of the most beautiful country in the realm and a wife said to be a beauty, too; Rob had ancient family holdings and a wife he had married when he was a child and she hardly more than an infant. Francis never mentioned his wife and didn't seem to care if he ever saw Minster Lovell again, while Rob knew his lands by hill and stream, knew by sight which stock belonged to which tenant. He spoke with shy pleasure of his Joyce and their life as man and wife now that she had come of age.

What made the difference? Maybe twelve was a bad age to marry, neither child nor man. Maybe you ought to be very young, so that you didn't mind accepting someone else's choice, or else fully mature, so you understood the need of it.

What if Warwick and Jack had lived? He could be comfortably married to Anne. Or, if Edmund had lived, Richard might have found himself in the church. A saver of men's souls rather than a snuffer of their lives. He could not imagine it. And now, he hardly dared to think what his path might be. All the men he has killed. Uncounted. He might, if Fortune was kind, kill no more. Peace might reign and he might find a way to serve justice. The long-ago dream at Middleham might still come to pass. Middleham was ownerless and Anne was a traitor's daughter. All Warwick's and Jack's lands and titles were forfeit, the property of the king. The countess was still alive, but that didn't matter. Isabel was married to George and *that* mattered. What would George think was his fair share of the attainted property?

Richard moved to fit himself more comfortably to the earth. There was a rock under his spine, but at least the fire had taken the damp from the blankets. He shifted onto smoother ground, and after a while he slept.

*R*ichard woke well before dawn. The fires sputtered low and the night seemed colder than when he had bedded down. He lay still a moment, trying to identify what had awakened him, then heard it: the puffing breath of a winded horse. As he sat up and pulled on his boots, he saw in the moonlight a horse and rider carefully threading their way through the camp. Edward was on his feet, too; the entire camp was coming to life as the rider slid down from his horse.

"The Frenchwoman is headed for Gloucester. Your other man passed me on his way back. I came straight to you, as my horse was fresher."

"Hurry, men," Edward said. "If we catch Margaret before she crosses the Severn, we can make her fight on our terms. If not, we'll have to battle Wales, too."

Martin and Jeremy took off for the horsepark while Richard, Rob, and Francis rolled up blankets and loaded the wagons. Richard had buckled on his sword and spurs when Jeremy returned leading four horses, not including Richard's big black Rex.

Jeremy started to hand the reins of all four to Rob. "I'm sorry, sir," he said to Richard. "Martin's having a bit of trouble. I'll go back and help him."

"No, I'll go," Richard said. "Francis, come with me." A *bit* of trouble hardly seemed apt, if one-armed Jeremy could gather four horses while Martin had failed to retrieve one.

They walked through a stand of ash toward the edge of the meadow. The catkins, leaves still tightly furled, showered dew down on them as they passed. The two squires' horses, saddled and bridled, walked loose, dragging their reins.

Richard nodded to Francis. "Get them." Rex stood in the meadow, followed by Martin carrying the bridle and moving quietly, like a cat stalking a mouse. The horse lifted his head to watch the squire, let him come within a yard or so, then moved away to graze.

"Martin," Richard called.

The squire turned. "My lord?"

"What happened?"

"Sir?"

"The horse. How did he get away from you?"

"I took away his fetters, and he moved before I could bridle him."

"God save us, didn't they teach you any better than that?"

Martin rubbed his nose on his sleeve. "I can't remember."

Richard stared at him. How was it possible to be so ignorant? "Well, what's done can't be helped, but you're going about it wrong. Stay here until I call you." He walked up to his horse and spoke quietly. Rex's ears pricked forward as Richard touched the horse's back, slid his hand along its neck, and had a firm hold of the mane. "Bring me the bridle. Move quietly. Don't hurry."

Martin handed the bridle to Richard and had at least sense enough to wait until Richard had the bit securely in the horse's mouth and the strap buckled before speaking. "Won't he kick you, coming from behind like that?"

"Don't come from behind. Come to his side and talk to him. Let him know you're there." Richard lifted Martin's hand and slapped the reins into the palm. "Do you know how to saddle him?"

"Yes."

"Then take him to the wagon and do so. Next time bridle him before you let him walk out of his hobbles. You're lucky. Some horses would have been in the next county by now."

*E*dward pressed his men to as fast a pace as the infantry could keep. By midmorning dust furred their mouths and many of the soldiers were faint with thirst. Rain and the crossings of the other army had stirred the streams into a vile mix of mud and manure. They took small sips from the water and wine they had carried with them and cupped their hands to share the meager supplies with their horses. Only one stream was clear enough to be potable, and even that was soon corrupted by the sheer number of men and animals needing to drink.

Sometime in late afternoon, Tewkesbury Abbey came into view, and Edward's scout confirmed that Margaret's army lay just out of sight, having found both Gloucester and Tewkesbury barred against her. Sick, weary, and out of provisions, she had been forced to give up the race for Wales. Her only course was to stop to rest and prepare to fight on the morrow.

*T*he night sky was brilliant with stars. Richard lay with his hands under his head and looked up.

Men said the first battle was the hardest. He hoped so. He couldn't imagine anything harder than what he had experienced at Barnet. But he did know one or two things that he hadn't known then, which in theory should make tomorrow easier. He knew, for example, that while the waiting was not the worst part, strictly speaking, it was the hardest to do. Fear requires movement. If you moved and didn't think too much, you could do what was needed.

But he also knew this: afterward, everything came back. By this time tomorrow, he would have more unwelcome memories, more ghosts in the already crowded graveyard of his mind.

He no longer dreamed of Ludlow. He had pushed down those memories, held them under the weight of time. He had memories of Barnet. In time, those, too, he would press down. But what he wanted to know was this: didn't happiness ever weigh enough to crowd out grief?

He didn't want to sleep and perhaps dream. He didn't want to think of tomorrow and the battle. He wanted to keep his mind clear and floating in the cool night air. When that proved impossible, he began to count the stars.

*R*ichard stirred out of a half-sleep to a touch on his shoulder, and sat up to find John Howard sitting on the ground beside him, Francis and Rob rousing, too. "Would you men like to share my breakfast?" John asked.

*R*ichard shook his head, then changed his mind. "Yes. What have you there?"

Howard held out a leather bottle and hunk of bread. "Are you all right, lad?"

"Yes." Richard reached for the bottle, wondering why Howard would ask, and drank. The wine was good, tart and cool.

"I don't know what we're fighting for," Howard said. "The game was over when Warwick died. Somerset ought to know that. Does he think that little monkey Lancaster can hold the throne without Warwick nearby to wipe his nose?" Howard broke off part of the crust of bread and passed the loaf around. "Warwick made a fair hell of this, if you want to know my opinion. What's the poor young lady to do, now?"

"Anne?"

"Her." Howard tore off another bit of bread. "Margaret won't have her, now Warwick's dead, I shouldn't think. But we needn't worry. If Margaret puts her son on the throne, I won't live to see it, because I'll die to stop it happening."

Edward of Lancaster on the throne. Anne was of no value as his wife, now her powerful father and uncle were dead. And then the thought came, brutally clear: *if Lancaster's on the throne, boy, you'll be dead.*

*D*awn shone pearl gray above the eastern hills. A beautiful morning and some of the worst ground imaginable for fighting. Hedges and dykes crossed the fields. An open meadow gave way to a small hillock and a thicket of hawthorn and briar where Somerset had positioned one of his divisions, the brush and scrub trees hiding the size and exact position of Somerset's battle. A wooded knoll to Richard's left sheltered a flank of Edward's spearmen. Beyond the knoll, the river Avon flowed into the wider Severn, a glistening golden brown in the sun.

No use deploying archers; Richard thought. They couldn't see for the trees. And impossible to get to Somerset's division if he chose to stay hidden. But he wouldn't. Too slow. Siege warfare. So how to get him into the open was not the question.

Richard gave Rex his head and started the big horse down the hill, his men following. He saw the flash of the sun off the enemy's armor in the midst of the thicket—something solid to fix his mind on.

He kept his men steady until they reached the meadow, and the enemy swarmed from the thicket. Then the spearmen came down on top of them, and Somerset's men, startled and confused, lost their impetus. The battle was a frenzy of killing, driven by something Richard had never known, not even at Barnet. The screams of the wounded and the crack of broken bones became part of the drum that moved him, that moved them all. Slay a soldier, slay him again from the other side. Nothing held him back when a man was mortally wounded.

The enemy ran for the river, flinging themselves into it fully armed, turning the river red with their blood before they drowned. Richard's mind told him to stop, but he couldn't make his body obey. When finally it was over, and the wave of killing left him, he drove his sword into the ground and leaned over it, grasping its hilt with his two hands to stop them from shaking.

$\mathcal{M}$artin was killed, poor ignorant youth who couldn't even catch a horse and probably didn't know a petard from a pikestaff. Edward of Lancaster died, too. His body lay face down in the grass.

"Henry's pup," George said. He nudged the boy's leg with his toe, then smiled at Richard. "Well? Are you not glad?"

"How did he die?"

"Richard, I asked you, are you not glad?"

"Yes, George. I'm glad."

"I hope so. Since I took such pains to make you so."

Richard's head was swimming. Now that the battle fury had left him, he felt all his strength ebbing away. He should sit down. Thinking clearly seemed beyond him. "You killed him? In battle?"

"No, just now. He was fleeing and I took him down. The fool should have never left his mother's side."

Revulsion crawled like a poisonous insect along Richard's skin. But how was he different from George, considering what he had done in the last few hours?

George was asking him something, his voice pleasant, conversational. "How does it feel to be the one man who could have prevented all this?"

"What do you mean?"

"Why, brother, I mean you. Think, Richard. When I tried to persuade you to marry Anne—if you had, she wouldn't have been free to wed this child. Warwick would have had nothing to gain from helping Margaret. That alliance would never have been. See what your fine conscience allowed to happen?"

Richard turned away, but George laid a hand on his arm. "I'm sorry, brother. This is a poor time to jest. I didn't mean to trouble you. I thought you might be glad to know, is all. You should learn not to let such fools as I agitate you."

Was he agitated? He didn't think so. He just wanted a place to lie down and get George's voice out of his ears.

*That* evening, Francis could not stop crying. No one had seen Jeremy, whom Richard had ordered not to fight. He was not waiting for them at the camp, but neither had they found him among the dead. Rob went back to the field one more time to look. Richard and Francis were sitting on the ground, taking a meager supper of hard bread and wine when Rob returned with Jeremy slung over his shoulder.

"He was in the center," Rob said. "Not your flank." He eased Jeremy to the ground, cradling the squire's head between his hands to let it rest gently on the earth. From the infinite tenderness with which Rob handled him, Richard thought for a moment that Jeremy must be alive. Then he saw the cavern that had been Jeremy's belly.

Richard looked from Rob to Francis. "What should we do?" He was trying to decide whether they should bury Jeremy there on the field. Middleham was a long way away, and God knew how long it would take them to reach London. Ah, Jeremy was an orphan; what did it matter where his bones lay?

"I need another squire now," Richard said, and was horrified to hear grief and laughter bound together in uneasy alliance in his voice.

"Oh, brother," Francis shook his head. "That is a hazardous office. You might find it harder to fill than. . . . " he stopped suddenly.

"What is it," Rob asked.

Francis's face was blank, as though he had been about to say something important and had totally forgotten. Then he wrapped his arms around himself, hunched forward, and sobbed.

Rob bent over him. "Francis?"

Francis wept.

"What shall we do?" Rob asked.

"I don't know." Richard crouched down in front of Francis. "What is it? Are you hurt?"

But all Francis did, beside weep, was shake his head, whether in answer to the questions or in response to sorrows in his own mind, they couldn't know. In a while, Richard and Rob carried Jeremy a little distance away, wrapped him in a cloak they took from the field, and buried him in a shallow grave dug with axe blades.

When they came back, Francis was lying down, still sobbing. Richard lay beside him as he had done long ago, not out of any belief that his presence changed anything, but because it was the only comfort he had to offer. He finally fell asleep with Francis's ragged breathing in his ears, and dreamed of standing in a crimson stream he took for light through a stained-glass window until he realized it was blood in which he stood, and that he was drowning in it. When he woke, he found Francis still beside him, silent and sleeping like a stone.

### Tewkesbury
### May 6, 1471.

Two days after the battle, the surviving enemy leaders were dragged from sanctuary. Edward was enraged because he had pardoned the men who sought refuge in Tewkesbury Abbey, thinking they were common soldiers, then was told that Somerset and several more enemy leaders had hoped to escape notice among them. The clergy of the abbey were horrified at the violation of sanctuary: as Edward saw things, sanctuary had already been violated by the deception.

"They deserve hanging," Edward told Richard. "Worse, actually. But it's up to you. You're the constable."

Beheading would suffice. No hanging and quartering. Not because he was necessarily more merciful than Edward, but because he hadn't the stomach to watch that degree of degradation to living flesh. And because he *would* watch. The deaths of traitors were an example, were they not? The constable could not mock the king's justice by refusing the lesson for his own eyes.

But most of all, he would watch because if you ordered a man's death, that was the least you could do. He could watch anything for an hour.

Francis and Rob stood with him, watched the blade come down, the incredible gush of blood, the pathetic twitching of the body, and smelled the sudden stench of loosened bowels. Richard wondered why, when only two days before, he had pushed wounded men off his sword to gasp and turn the Severn red with their blood, he found these deaths so difficult to witness.

That night it was his turn to be undone. He was shaking, silent, and morose as he sat before the fire, turning himself like a roast on a spit. Whichever side of his body was near the fire felt half-cooked, but the warmth didn't go through. Francis stayed awake a long time, talking to him. "You and Rob were so worried. I wanted to tell you not to mind me. I thought I *did* say it. Over and over. It was clear in my mind, but the words didn't come out. I wanted to tell you I was all right, that I was just so tired and there was too much I wanted to say. Sometimes there is no reason for what you do, but you can't help it, you know?"

Richard didn't know why the executions should have unmanned him so. He just knew he would have paid a prince's ransom to get out of his own skin that evening.

*London*
*May 1471.*

When they returned to London, Edward met with his council on the matter of the former King Henry, confined again to the Tower. But it was clear that with the son dead, the father must die, too. The end of all contenders for the throne and another task for the constable.

"How do you want it done?" Richard asked. He kept his face calm.

Edward looked up. "Brother, that is the privilege of the constable. You decide how you want it done. You can even decide you don't want to decide and leave it to your executors. You can do it however you will so long as you understand the cause of his death is pure displeasure, grief after Lancaster's death in battle."

Richard understood. Nothing must show. The body would be taken to St. Paul's with all the dignity due a late monarch, and old mad kings who died of displeasure did not have misshapen skulls or a second, gaping mouth beneath their chins.

"Pure displeasure! Who will believe that?"

Edward sighed and laid down his quill. "You are so guileless. People don't need to believe. The world is not as you would have it."

"Jack told me that, once."

"Jack. Well, I'm not sure his understanding of the world is to be envied, but if he said that, he spoke true."

*W*hen Richard entered Henry's tower chambers with James Tyrrel and another of Edward's men, Henry was sitting quietly in the chair by the window, his hands lying palms up on his lap, as if waiting to receive a blessing. He smiled at them as they came in.

*I*t's done," Richard said.

"How does he look?"

"Dead. By the way, the instrument appears to have been something weightier than 'pure displeasure.' It left a groove an inch deep in his skull."

"What!"

"The back of his skull. Nothing shows in his face."

"Do not give me such a fright. Come here," Edward said, motioning Richard closer, like he might a child. "Sit down."

"No."

"*Sit down!*"

Richard sat. He didn't bother to cross the room to pull up the other chair, but dropped to the floor where he stood, wrists resting on his knees, hands hanging loose. Limp, like a dead man's. He curled his hands into fists, leaned his head back against the wall, and closed his eyes.

Edward said quietly, "You despise me as a common murderer."

"No."

"Yes, you do. Do not deny that. You may love me. You may even forgive me. Nevertheless, that is what you think. Look at me, please."

Richard opened his eyes.

Edward held out his hands, palms lifted and spread apart, as if he were supporting something both fragile and of great weight. "How can I make you understand that this was not a wanton act? For your own sake, think about it. Have these past few years taught you nothing? Would you leave Henry alive to inspire more uprisings? You have lost friends. Should you lose more before your conscience is at ease? Before you can say, *now Henry dies, now it is time.*"

Edward flung an arm wide. "Maybe you would have me publish it, post it on the church doors, that I ordered his death. Three-quarters, no, nine-tenths of England has been praying I would do exactly what I have done, but if I owned the deed, there would be an inquiry. Our people are sick to death of war and strife. Do you think they would like to see their king tried and clapped into prison? Or perhaps taken to the block. Is that how you would have it end?"

"That would never happen."

"No." Edward sighed. "But all the bishops and lawyers would have to meet and debate it and find some words to make it legal, and the holy men would make me walk barefoot to Canterbury.

"Anyway, it is not your hands the blood stains, it is mine. The sin is not upon your head, nor the man who wielded the club, nor even the man who knows and pretends otherwise. Not the bishops and lawyers who are spared the necessity of passing judgment. It is mine. No one else's soul has to suffer for it. Now do you understand the joys of being king?"

"Yes." Richard got to his feet, angry that there was truth in what Edward said. Angry that things were as they were.

Angry that he had no answers.

*R*ichard had not seen Anne since her return to London. He wondered how the past two years would have changed her. He tried to see her face as it had been that day along the river. He wondered if they could recapture those sweet, early feelings, which now seemed hopelessly childish.

Alice had remained in sanctuary at Beaulieu Abbey, and Isabel was reunited with George at Le Herber, Warwick's London manor. Anne had apparently accompanied her sister there. Richard didn't know what to say to her. Some message before he appeared on the steps of Le Herber seemed a minimal courtesy, but none of the words he could think of seemed right.

*I'm sorry your father and uncle are dead. My heart is heavy, too, although I helped to kill them.*

*Good riddance to your husband. Will you marry me?*

*Oh, yes. That would do nicely.*

In the end, he rode over unannounced and asked the porter to summon her. The man told him that Anne and Isabel were both unwell, recovering from a strenuous voyage and the deaths of their father and uncle. Richard didn't know whether to believe him, but was not surprised when on the second visit he was given the same message.

On his third call, he only asked the porter to tell Anne that Edward was sending him to Scotland again to deal with the endless border wars, and he would call on her when he returned. He did not insist on seeing her because he was afraid of the look he might see on her face, a look more wounding than words, that would tell him she wanted nothing to do with him or anyone else that had joined in the fight that had ruined her family.

*London*
*October 1471.*

When Richard returned from Scotland three months later, George calmly told him that Anne was no longer at Le Herber.

"I see. Where is she?" He expected George to tell him that Anne had gone to her mother at Beaulieu.

"I don't know."

"George, don't jest. It's not amusing."

"Believe me, I do not jest. I don't know why you doubt me. The girl was ungrateful. My hospitality meant nothing to her. I have no idea where she has gone."

Richard was tempted to provoke George into a quarrel for the satisfaction of breaking his brother's calm indifference, but reason told him that someone had to know Anne's whereabouts, and a more profitable use of his time would be to go to Le Herber himself.

$\mathcal{M}$y lord, I know not where the lady has gone." The porter stood so stiffly and spoke so righteously that Richard wanted to wreak violence on him, too, just to see if he was truly human.

"Someone here must know. She didn't set out on a pilgrimage and tell no one. What would it take to freshen your memory?"

He meant a bribe, of course, but the porter took it otherwise. "My lord, this is your brother's house. You cannot harm me."

"My brother is at court, as he is most days, so perhaps I should see the duchess. Please tell Isabel I am here."

"Sir, I don't believe the lady knows anything that could help you."

"Then she can tell me that herself." Richard stepped past the porter as the noise of their encounter drew Isabel to the head of the stairs. She looked thin and drawn, almost haggard, but she smiled when she saw him, and descended.

When Richard put out his hand to take hers, she greeted him with warmth, stepping into his arms and embracing him. "Richard, how good to see you! I was wondering if you would ever call on us."

"I did. Didn't you know? I was told you were ill."

"Oh? Well, it's true. We were very weary for a while. The child died at sea, you know."

Richard grasped her shoulders. "What child?"

"Our little son, George's and mine. It was born too soon, on the way to France."

"Isabel, I'm sorry. I didn't know." He called her gently back to his purpose. "Where is Anne? George says she left without telling anyone she was leaving."

Isabel recoiled as though he had slapped her. "I thought she would have told you."

"No, Isabel. I've heard nothing from her." He asked to see where Anne had been, as if that could turn back time, and Isabel took him to a second-floor bedchamber, unremarkable. Some few things gave witness to a young woman's presence—a basket of ribbons, an embroidered surcoat more ornate than anything he had seen Anne wear, nothing that told him anything he wanted to know.

When he started to leave, Isabel seized his hand. "Find her, Richard." She started to cry again, and he held her for a moment while his thoughts ran riot.

"I will. Don't fret. I'll find her."

*H*e worked his horse to a lather on the return to Westminster and stormed into Edward's chamber, where Edward, Hastings, and George were standing around a bright fire, drinking sack. Life returned to normal, time for hunting, jests, all the ordinary pleasures. Nothing had changed for any of them. He couldn't bear their bland unconcern to what ordeals other lives had suffered.

He stood in front of George. "I have just been to Le Herber. You will tell me where Anne is."

"I have told you. I know nothing of her whereabouts."

"I don't believe you."

Edward put his hand on Richard's arm. "He has said he knows nothing. Can you not leave it?"

Richard stepped back. Edward's protection of George baffled him, but he might have left the matter as Edward asked, except that George said, in that quiet, mannerly way he could affect when he chose, "I have spoken truly. I don't know where she is." Then, "Richard I must ask you something. For all the times I pressed you to ask for Anne's hand and you refused, this is very curious. Why all the hue and cry now? There are hundreds of girls in London. One wench is as good as another."

Richard put his fist into George's jaw, and George crashed to the floor.

"God's teeth," Edward said, staring at Richard, "What's got into you?" Hastings, urbane and ironic as always, only lifted an eyebrow. Richard stood rubbing his aching hand, surprised by two things. That he had done what he had done. And that George, leaning back on one hand and wiping blood from his mouth with the other, looked not at all distressed. Richard had expected rage, even hate, but what he saw in his brother's face was satisfaction.

*Maybe George is truly mad.* The thought stared him down: he turned his eyes from the full implications of what such a truth could mean. Holding his injured hand against his chest, he extended the other to his brother. George reached for it and rose unsteadily to his feet.

# 12  One Wench

*London*
*June 1471.*

The window in the second-story room where Anne was lodged was her only amusement. Le Herber was one of the great houses of London, and it stood near enough the heart of the city for her to witness the commerce on the streets and the tradespeople going to and from their shops.

She pushed open the window and knelt in the seat. Below her walked two men in black, lawyers, austere as crows, but rich, with heavy gold chains around their necks. They bowed slightly to a tall woman dressed in a coppery brown gown. The Widow Crofts. She walked with a long smooth stride, like a man. Anne leaned further forward. That woman intrigued her. Like herself, a widow. No lord to defend and protect her, but she had such freedom! She ran her late husband's business and walked the street as boldly as any man.

The woman greeted the lawyers as forthrightly as any man, too. Anne watched how she took the hand of one, held it between her own two and laughed. She was a handsome woman; she could marry again if she wanted. But Anne thought she would not, for then her business would become her new husband's.

Anne sat back in the window. No one really cared what Dame Crofts did, she guessed. She envied that woman.

She swung the glass pane so she could see herself. Her reflection looked back at her, and the curve of the glass made her face look all cheeks. Her coif was too tight and hurt her forehead. She pulled it off, and her head still hurt. Maybe one of the pins that held her hair was the problem. She pulled them all out, running her hands through her hair, and pressed her fingers to her temples.

She felt ill with boredom. She had tried to accompany the maid on her trips to market. *Don't trouble yourself, Anne.* She asked George if she could arrange a visit to her mother. *No, I don't think that would be wise.*

Mother said that men started wars when they were bored. Of course they did; she felt like starting one, herself. She had never experienced such tedium before. It dulled her mind: her brain must have become as white and heavy as a slab of lard. At the same time, she could feel a rage within her, like a hibernating bear, dreaming tormented dreams, snarling and clawing in its sleep. The duller her mind became, the more angry the sleeping bear grew, until she felt she must be shredded from the inside out.

She laid her cheek wearily on her folded arms. The afternoon sun shone hot in the window, and her despair was so heavy it seemed to drag against her very skin. Her door wasn't locked, but it might as well have been. Every time she stepped out of her room into the hall, some servant's too-solicitous face appeared. *Is there anything you need, my lady?* They never let her out of their sight. They followed her to the kitchen, to the parlor, politely conversing, always seeming interested, and there was always someone beside her when she talked to Isabel.

She hadn't had this sense of confinement in the beginning. Of course, then she had been too numbed to care what anyone did. She wanted to sleep, to cry, to be left alone. Now, the better she felt, the less she was allowed to do. She had thought a hundred times of sending word to her mother, but she could not be sure she could trust any messenger. Besides, her mother had no power now.

*S*everal evenings later, George brought her dinner tray, instead of the servant who usually fetched it. "My poor Anne," he said as he set it down. "You must have found life hard to bear of late. Never knowing who you can trust." George reached over and covered her hand with his. "I wish I could tell you that was over. Unfortunately, we have come to a new difficulty. But don't be troubled. I have found the solution."

She wouldn't ask, wouldn't show him her curiosity. Or her fear.

So he went on. "You don't entirely trust me. I don't blame you, but I have done only what was necessary. I hope you will not hate me. I hope it will not be too uncomfortable for you. It's hard to imagine anything could be more so than your confinement here. At any rate, it's not permanent. That much I can promise you."

He took her chin in his hands, turned her face to look at him, and smiled. "Promise me, sister, that you will try not to hate me. And that you will listen."

Anne let out her breath and nodded. She had not promised to trust him, so she had not lied.

"You probably know that your father's and uncle's lands will be apportioned between my brother Gloucester and myself, the exact settlement not yet agreed upon." George stood up and walked to the window, leaned against the sill, and talked to the air outside, as though he could not face the news he bore her. "The most unpleasant part is this. Gloucester needs to secure his portion of your father's estates. If you would marry, your husband could claim them on your behalf."

That was simple, she thought. Let *him* marry me.

"He could ask for your hand, of course." George might have read her mind. He shrugged, as though Richard's thinking were too obtuse for him to follow. "But it seems he feels your father's treason precludes you as a choice of marriage partner. I'm sorry, Anne. I know Warwick has left you a bitter inheritance. There is nothing in Richard's decision that is personal to you, I can assure you of that."

There was a sincerity and simplicity in George's words that she rarely heard. "Since you cannot marry without your husband posing a threat, Gloucester suggests a religious vocation for you. However, I am not satisfied that it is safe to rely on that. Oh, please, I don't mean to say that Richard could think of harming you, but there are accidents. Others might take such an action upon themselves, believing it was in his best interests."

He crossed over and sat by her again. "Here is the heart of it. Richard has become increasingly forceful in demanding your surrender. I can no longer shelter you here. I have arranged for you to stay with the family of a gentleman I trust. You will act the part of a servant, to eliminate curiosity on the part of the household. After the matter of your father's estates is settled, you will have nothing to fear from Richard and you may resume your life as you see fit."

His words were empty. She would have no dowry, no property, no husband. No home. What was it that she was supposed to resume?

George's hand covered hers. It was smooth and perfectly groomed. A huge emerald ring circled the middle finger. She stared at the ring as though the answer were hidden in its brilliance.

"When do I leave?"

"Now. As soon as you finish your supper."

*A*n hour later a cart stopped at Le Herber, accompanied by two richly dressed men. They waited while Anne's belongings were loaded, then assisted her into the cart and rode beside her, one on either side. They volunteered no information on the way, and she was afraid to ask questions whose answers she might not want to hear.

They arrived at a house on the other side of London from Le Herber, and not as grand. One man helped Anne from the cart and took her elbow to lead her around to the side door of the house. She looked over her shoulder to see if her trunk was being unloaded. The man caught her glance, and answered impatiently. "Yes, yes. Don't worry. The servant will bring it."

The man sent the boy who answered his knock for the mistress of the house, and presently there appeared a large woman with a florid face and a ring of keys at her belt.

"Here is your charge, madam. Anne Neville, late of Middleham."

"Yes. Anne, here you will be known as Madge of Ripon. I am afraid there is no disguising that you are from the North. It is in your speech."

Too fast. She didn't even know where she was, or what she was to do, and already she had lost her name.

"Madam. If I might retain my name, 'Anne,' that is. I fear there is so much new here to put my mind on, if someone called for Madge, I should not hear it."

The woman rubbed the brass key ring. "Well, well. Anne's a common enough name. I don't suppose there's harm in it. I will show you where you sleep. Servants rise at matins and take their breakfast in the kitchen."

"Madam?" Anne asked.

The woman stared. She had heavy brows that gave her a fierce look. Anne felt like an odd insect spotted in the corner, worthy of a moment's attention before it was squashed.

"Madam, I am truly grateful for your shelter. I do not wish to seem rude, but I have little knowledge of the office."

"You will learn." The woman picked up the key ring and slapped it across her palm, "you will learn."

"Yes, I am a willing pupil. But won't my lack of skill cause comments?"

"I have thought of that. I have prepared an explanation. You were a lady's maid, but you were caught stealing one of your mistress's jeweled rings. The lord of the house would have cut off your hand, but your mistress prevailed." Anne felt the blood leave her face. Could that really happen? She had seen thieving servants beaten and dismissed from Middleham, but no worse.

"You were to be sent to another house, and not trusted near valuables. Here, you will be a scullery maid, and all will know you have no experience with that work. Your thievery has the added advantage that the other servants will keep themselves removed from you. You will receive little in the way of curiosity."

"I see." Anne was too bewildered and stunned to fully comprehend the consequences of her new position. She was recovering, a little, from imagining losing a hand, but grasped the fact that she was to be deprived of human warmth and friendly contact. The one thing she would have wished for was her mother's shoulder to rest her face against, and her mother's arms around her, but a soft word, a word of compassion from anyone, would have instantly reduced her to tears, so it was just as well none were forthcoming.

The tall man handed a small pouch of coins to Mistress Brown, which she slipped into the pocket hanging next to her ring of keys.

"If her goods are unloaded, that will be all."

The man bowed and touched his fingers to the brim of his hat.

*A*nne followed the woman to an attic with small high windows at either end.

Dame Brown pointed over toward the window. "There. There is a spot for you."

Anne looked in the direction of the pointing hand. There were no real beds, only several pallets on the floor, all occupied.

"Use your cloak tonight," the woman said. "Perhaps tomorrow we can find an extra pallet and more blankets." She lowered her voice. "It is well if you can make friends with them. Nights are turning chill, and it is warmer sleeping close. I will acquaint you in the morning with your duties."

She turned and left, fondling the pouch with its load of coins. Anne had to wait a moment before her eyes adjusted enough to see her way to cross the room. A few heads lifted to observe her.

"Are you Madge?" A voice asked.

"Yes." So much for Anne.

"Did you really take those things?"

What an introduction, and before they could even see her face. Well, so much the better, perhaps.

"No."

"Oh."

Hearing, if not a welcome, at least a lack of hostility, Anne walked toward the voice. She was already shivering, and a night on the bare floor was too grim to face.

"If you will share your pallet, my cloak will cover us both." She felt the need to add more persuasion. "It's wool."

The girl moved and Anne crept down beside her, spreading the warm cloth over them both.

Anne would have sworn she had only been asleep a few minutes when she was awakened by stirring all around her. It was not dawn yet, just a lighter gray at the windows. She was cold and sore; her shoulders ached; her back was stiff. She could not imagine being more uncomfortable than she was at that moment.

By evening, experience had accomplished what imagination could not. She had not known such degrees of fatigue were possible. From the time she had a thought to the time she found the words to express it, the conversation—or the plate of food she was about to ask for—had dwindled to nothing. If an assassin came to kill her now, she would think, oh glorious, a moment of rest while he drew his dagger.

She ate half her supper and stumbled upstairs. From her trunk she took another gown and slipped it over the one she already wore, putting the back in front so she could lace it easily herself. She lay down on the edge of the pallet and spread the heavy cloak and did not wake when Sarah crept in beside her and claimed her half of their bed.

*D*ay followed day, and Anne lost track of them. She lost count of how many days she had worn the same gown, and she hadn't bathed since she arrived. She saw plenty of water, though. She drew it from the well, carried it, spilled it, splashed it on her face, her hands stinging where it touched open blisters. She kept back rags she was given to clean the pots and wrapped them around her hands when they grew too sore to hold even a spoon without making her flinch with pain, and discovered that if she also wrapped them around her feet at night she slept warmer. Having no idea what details Dame Brown might have added to her story, she confided in no one. When accused of any ineptness, she made no excuses, merely acknowledged the complaint and tried to correct it.

Anne was too weary at day's end to need stories to soothe her to sleep, but she didn't suffer either the terrible loneliness she had felt in France, or the raging boredom of Le Herber. She was frightened only when she thought that her life could go on like this forever, so she did not think of it. In a way, she dreaded an end to the negotiations over her father's lands, rumors of which reached them almost daily, because it would mean that something *could* happen, and if it didn't then, it never would, and there would be no more hope. As long as Edward and his brothers debated, an end was possible.

After a month she began to reach the dinner hour with enough vigor left to secure her share of the simple servant's fare, and even to laugh with the other girls. Middleham moved far back in her mind, a place she visited in her sleep, nothing more.

One day as she was coming from the larder, she saw a stranger, a tall man whom she thought might be the man who had brought her there, but his back was toward her and she could not be sure. He was handing a pouch of money, not to Dame Brown, but to the smith, a powerful man who always looked dirty, the dust of steel embedded in the pores of his skin. Some inner warning made her stop. Maybe the tall man brought news from court. Maybe the dispute was settled. But she didn't like that man paying the smith. Whatever for?

"Half now. Half later. And how will we know the deed is done?"

The smith laughed. "I'll send a sign. Do you think I'll forego half my wages?"

"How will you do it?"

"Sir, it is too simple. The poor girl runs away, gets coshed on the head. Thieves throw her into the Thames. Or maybe she throws herself. Think of the shame, a highborn girl like that gone slattern."

Anne didn't need to be told who the highborn girl was. Such a fear seized her that she leaned against the wall to steady her trembling. Then the thought that not only could she be disposed of like an annoying insect, but that no one would even know of the injustice, took some of the edge off her terror and she began to feel instead a rage so immense she doubted she could contain it. How dare anyone think it would be that easy? Anne set down the cheese where she stood and walked away. She walked quietly, sure her very breath would call the men's attention, and then started to run. She didn't know where she was running. She had no cloak, no money, nothing, but she would think of something.

*Beaulieu Abbey*
*October 1471.*

Alice Neville, formerly Countess of Warwick, had chosen the most austere and also the most serene chamber to which she had access for her meeting with Richard. The room was small and narrow with a high ceiling and walls all of white. At the end of the room a double window stood open, its fine glass as clear as water, giving a view out over the courtyard below.

She poured herself water from the pitcher on the sideboard, and sat down to wait. The abbey was a peaceful place. The nuns were kindly and did not further assault her unhappy mind and bruised spirit with demands of any kind. The food was simple, even monotonous, but carefully prepared. Monotony, like the nuns' blandness, pleased her. She thought, in sorrow, how like children we become, clinging to the familiar. As little girls, Anne and Isabel had been passionate about routine and the continued appearance of loved possessions. Anne had worn the same gown nearly every day for a whole summer and cried when it was too tight to lace around her. And Isabel insisted on having her milk poured out of a particular small pitcher and howled with rage if the servants forgot to set *her* pitcher on the table.

She had solitude. Her bed was at the end of the guest dormer, so she had a companion on only one side, and often not even that. She couldn't complain. But now she was beginning to grow restless. She missed her own things, her own tasks, and she hadn't known she could be so homesick. Would she ever see Middleham again? Perhaps, but not likely as her home.

What were her possibilities? An abbey, this one or another. That would be bearable. There would be some pleasures in that life. Books. But no romances, no stories—just history and holy works. How could people live without love and laughter? Life was dreary enough without turning one's back on pleasure when it appeared. Gardening, perhaps. If she had a white room, some privacy, and a garden, she could survive.

Some abbesses had great power. But surely one would have to start earlier, and Alice knew she had no true vocation. But she had skills;

she might earn a respectable position. One does not manage an estate like Middleham without learning something.

What else? Live with Isabel and George? That was possible, too, but they were Londoners now. She didn't want to live in the city. What would she do—meddle in her daughter's kitchen, give the servants two mistresses? It was different the other way around, when the daughter shared the family estate, but Le Herber was George's house now.

There was one other possibility. There, she had said it. Now take it out and look at it. You are a traitor's wife, Alice. A dead traitor's wife. A dead traitor's wife who has an estate of value and no one but herself between a king's greed and that estate. And no convenient legal means of parting her from what was hers.

Sometimes traitors' families met unfortunate accidents. Or just disappeared. There was no justification for her death or imprisonment, but she would have to be a fool to deny that such things had happened. She hoped Edward wouldn't think such measures were necessary. George, after all, was still married to Isabel. And there was nothing to which she had a claim that couldn't easily be taken from her, legally or not.

Well, nothing like thinking of dying to make you realize how grateful you'd be to live *anywhere*.

She heard horses in the courtyard and got up to stand beside the window. Not in it, where she herself could be seen. Some impulse made her want to get whatever knowledge of Richard she could before they faced each other. She could not imagine what he had come for, other than to tell her of her future, and she would have preferred to hear that news from anyone else, an impartial messenger, rather than this boy she had known and once had liked.

There were two young men in the courtyard, the man with Richard familiar, too. Oh yes, Francis, Warwick's ward. Francis gave Richard's arm a quick cuff, an obvious wish-you-well gesture, then led the horses over to the green around the well, where he sat down and loosened the grip he had on the reins to let them graze.

Richard glanced up briefly, then started up the steps, a young man's springy gait. He lowered his head in concentration, or perhaps self-consciousness, but his determination was obvious in the way he took the steps, leaning slightly forward, his hands gripped into fists. She turned from the window, and sat again.

Footsteps sounded in the hall, a quick brisk step like boots, and a softer step muted by the rustle of gowns, one of the nuns. Sister Agatha opened the door. "The Duke of Gloucester is here, madam."

Richard stepped inside the room and walked over to her. "My lady." He started to extend a gloved hand, then stopped, chagrined that he had not thought about his gloves and now had to choose between taking her bare hand in his gloved one or making her wait while he removed them. He shrugged, then smiled.

She had forgotten what a disarming smile the boy could have. Well, a man could smile like an angel and still be a knave at heart. There were things she knew now that she had not known when she was sixteen, that being chief among them.

In his youth, Warwick could smile. Oh, could he smile. The most devastating was a particular combination of affection and rue, as though the smiler could not help loving—loving her, loving the tired old world, even though it was as clear as the midday sun that both were flawed, imperfect. A man who smiled like that always seduced her into believing he must be of a kind and tolerant nature. Worse, she had believed such benevolence would be extended toward her. It was just such a smile, half kindness and half regret, that she saw on Richard's face now, and she determined not to succumb to its false promise.

"Richard." She remained seated from long habit, although now she should have risen, but he didn't seem to notice.

"Countess." Now he had his gloves off, and he took her hand and kissed it. "You are looking well."

"Yes," she said, "I am well. Very well, considering all that has happened."

"I am glad for it." He seemed to say it simply, without irony or false brightness. She looked at him, trying to take his measure.

It had been two years since she had seen him. He appeared to be a little taller than she was, had grown broad in the chest and shoulders. His face had matured into a kind of grave handsomeness which softened when he smiled. Today he was dressed richly but quietly in a linen doublet of deep green, with black hose and boots. Clearly he made no attempt to rival his brother's brilliance. Maybe—she took a second thought—maybe he made an effort not to be compared to Edward. In anything. Perhaps that could be useful to know.

He stood before her, calm but a little awkward, one hand holding his gloves, the other at his side, giving in to a slight agitation. "Countess? May I sit?" He gestured with the gloves.

"I'm sorry. Of course. May I offer you some wine?"

Richard crossed the room not to the bench, but to the deep window, where he half leaned, half sat. He cleared his throat. "Just water, please."

She allowed herself a leisurely time for getting cups from the sideboard and pouring water for him and wine for herself. He set his gloves down beside him and sat turning the cup in his hand. Some nervousness or unhappiness there. He was not finding it easy to begin what he had to say.

"I hear you have become quite a soldier." Alice meant to say it kindly, even as tribute, but she heard the edge in her voice, and the challenge. What an awful thing to say, she realized, what could he possibly respond to that?

He was flushing a bright red. "My God, Alice," he said, "don't praise me. I did what I had to do. You don't mean to tell me it was a task well done."

It was a barb, whether or not she had intended it, but since it sank, she could not resist tugging on it. "Warwick would have been very proud of you."

A small muscle clenched along his jaw. "Well, yes, countess. People say I did well enough. At Barnet, my flank suffered more casualties than Oxford's and there were fewer of us to begin with. At Tewkesbury we had the worst terrain and the worst position, but we held. John Parr died at Barnet, and Jeremy at Tewkesbury. They had been with me since Middleham. You may remember them."

Richard's voice was tight, and his eyes cold as slate. He must be very angry, she thought, to offer such a long defense.

"I know what it is like to lose loved ones. I lost my husband at Barnet. *You* may remember *him*." She could never hold her tongue entirely. If she checked the hammer force of her temper, it came out in little silver daggers, all the more deadly for being carefully honed and polished.

"Not by my hand, countess."

"Your war." That was not fair. Neither fair nor true.

Richard took a long breath and blew it out. "I didn't come here to fight you, Alice. You were always kind to me, and Middleham was more my home than any place else I know." He ran a finger around his neckband, as though he were hot, but made no move to leave his spot in the sun.

At that moment he looked both very young and very miserable. He is so much the boy he was, after all, Alice thought: mannerly, distressed in the face of another's discomfort. It made her sad, and to her surprise, frightened. What kind of world was this, that a young man could go to war, kill old friends, and remain unchanged? In these troubled times, that he could and would find it necessary to do all those things was, unfortunately, as certain as breathing. But to do them and not be altered was, to her, chilling.

She sighed. "Forgive me. Grief has made me testy. My husband chose his own path; you are not to blame for where it led him. Anyway, it is not his loss I mourn now, so much as my home. But I will survive without it, I'm sure."

Richard's eyebrows lifted. "Whatever gave you the idea you would have to? Edward will probably grant Middleham to me, and he wants me to marry Anne. That is why I have come, lady. To ask if you could tell me anything that would help me find her."

Well. Fortune certainly took its twists and turns. Those were not the words she had expected him to say. "I don't know where she is, Richard." Alice turned her face away. "Men fight their wars. Your brother is alive, and my husband dead. I bear no grudge. It could just as easily have been the other way around. And I care not a fig who rules England." She hugged her arms to her body. "Let any ape be king who can hold the crown on his head. I am sick to death of all the bickering. But why can't my children be left in peace?"

"Alice," Richard said. "Once you asked me what I wanted. I didn't know how to answer you. I know now."

She gave him her attention.

"What I want is a place to keep for my own. Not to be beholden to any man. I will have that. If I can find Anne, I will take her back to Middleham, and you and she will have the peace you seek."

God spare her the magnanimity of young heroes. The poor boy believed it was that simple. Was that how it usually began, men's quest for power? Just give me enough to keep me and mine safe, I won't ask for more.

# 13 *Sanctuary*

Brother Lawrence listened to the girl's tearful story as she begged for sanctuary. His first thought was: *What little liar have we here?* The daughter of the Earl of Warwick, indeed. Her speech had the ring of the north, however, and it was rumored that the dukes both Clarence and Gloucester were searching for the girl.

Lawrence ran his hand over his skull, a gesture from the long-ago time when he was young and hair had flourished on his now gleaming pate. He did it these days when he felt young again, which was to say lacking in wisdom and inadequate to the task at hand. How was he to judge? Even if the girl was who she claimed to be, her story was preposterous. Plots of murder and kidnapping! In the end, it was the hint of disbelief in the child's voice, as if she could scarcely believe such wickedness herself, that convinced him.

He sighed. Poor little maid, she still thought her wants mattered in the midst of the affairs of kings and greedy lords. Well, perhaps this once they did. Cats, dogs, orphans, runaways, every stray in London seemed to know that there was not a soul less able to turn them away.

Lawrence left the room to bring milk from the larder for old Saul, the chantry cat, and a mug for the girl, as well. When he returned, he didn't see her at first, and thought she must have deceived him after all, and fled. But she had only tucked her feet up under her and fallen asleep, slumped over the arm of the bench. When he put down the milk and lifted her, she was so limp and light that he had to watch her breathe to reassure himself that she was in fact only sleeping. He carried her to his cell-like room and laid her down on his cot, old Saul brushing against his legs the whole time. After he had settled the girl to his satisfaction, he returned to the parlor and sat before the dying fire trying to think what to tell Philippa.

The girl slept until well past noon. When she awoke, to Lawrence's relief she ate heartily and seemed in good spirits. He explained his plan while she ate, and shortly thereafter, Lawrence and what appeared to be a young monk, hooded head turned humbly toward the ground, set out from St. Martin to one of the wealthy houses of Candlewick Street.

Philippa Carter surveyed her brother's latest stray. She took one of Anne's hands and turned it over, palm up. The girl had done hard service; that much was certain. "So you were a scullery maid."

"Yes."

"Were you competent?"

"I grew to be."

"You would do such work again?"

"It matters not what I do."

A strange girl, as silent and self-contained as an oyster. Philippa glanced at her brother, who shrugged. She knew his shrug: the problem was out of his hands and into hers. He may have collected the unfortunates, but it was she who truly rescued them. She sighed and released Anne's hand. "We can find work here less strenuous than what you performed before. Can you serve our family and guests their meals?"

"Of course. But will I not be seen by more than your household?"

"My dear, no one will give you a thought as long as you attend to your work and speak little. What shall you be called?"

"Sarah. Why am I here?"

Philippa stared.

"I mean," the girl said, "how will you explain my presence?"

"Oh." At least the child wasn't lack-wit. Nor entirely without humor. Perhaps they would get on. "Why were you in service the last time?"

"I was a lady's maid caught thieving, thrown out of the household, and grateful to have kept both hands."

"Then you shall be an honest lady's maid this time. One who refused her lord's advances."

"Very well." The girl gave the slightest hint of a smile. "Thank you."

George fought Richard's every petition for the northern lands with arguments so strictly reasoned and impenetrable they might have been written by lawyers. Edward listened to both brothers, made bequests, and changed his mind. One grant was certain: Richard would have Middleham, and he would marry Anne. If he could find her.

"Write out for me everyone your parents knew in London," Richard asked Isabel.

"You believe she is here, then?"

"I don't know. But we have to start. I'll have your mother do the same."

"I'll help," George said.

Richard looked at George, the pleasant face and smooth voice, remembered the man kicking Lancaster's corpse.

"Thank you." At first he had been sure that George had had a hand in her disappearance. Then he sensed a frustration and bewilderment in his brother that seemed genuine. Indeed, George offered every assistance in finding her even as he struggled to grasp every inch of Warwick's lands that he could, a contradiction that no longer surprised Richard. He was growing used to a brother whose nature was as many-hued as Joseph's coat.

Shall we each take a part?"

"No, I don't think so."

"It's a waste of time. We should go separately."

"Humor me, George. I'd like your company, and I'm sure you'll think of things to ask that I wouldn't." He rolled up the list that Isabel had written.

George rode steadfastly with him every day, helped with plotting their route, but their efforts were fruitless. After they had exhausted everyone in London whom Warwick's family had known, they made inquiries into all the abbeys, hostels, and guesthouses. Richard even sent letters with post riders to Middleham, in case she had somehow managed to return home.

"I think we must face it, brother," George said, "she is either gone from this earth, or doesn't want to be found."

After Anne had been in the Carter household several months, Philippa summoned her to the parlor. "Close the door, Anne." If the girl had tensed at the summons, she all but froze at the use of her rightful name.

"What have you done to poor Tom?" she asked.

"Madam?"

"My gardener, once a most industrious and affable young man, now dreams over his work. If you are anywhere near, he blushes and stammers as though his tongue were tied. My dear, I believe he loves you."

"I know, madam." The girl didn't even blush.

"Have you given him reason to hope, child?"

"Hope, madam?"

"Anne, you know what I am asking you. I will have no laxity among my servants, and you cannot intend to marry a gardener."

"No, madam."

*Yes, madam, no madam,* and you still had not a clue what she thought. "Anne, I am trying to say that you cannot stay here forever."

"Have I displeased you with my work?"

"Oh, no!" Philippa sat down in exasperation. She could find no fault with Anne. The girl's labor was easily worth her board. "I would all my servants were as diligent as you. But you were born to another life. My conscience hurts me every time I look at you. Are there not people—your mother, at least—who should know where you are?"

"No, madam, there are not. If your conscience troubles you for my sake, I would that were not so. I am content here, and wish no other occupation."

Soon after her arrival in the Carter household, Anne had cautiously asked Mistress Carter for paper and pen and a room where she might write unnoticed. She emerged from the room an hour later, the pen undipped, the paper unmarked, and returned them to Philippa without a word.

Then she had gone out to the small garden behind the house and stood by the apple tree dry-eyed and rigid. She could never be certain that a messenger would not betray her, nor know whose hands might receive the letter. Nor that her would-be assassin was in George's hire and not Edward's, or even the agent of someone whose identity she could not bear to suspect. She finally understood that her father had been only the first of many who might benefit from pawning her. The jest was that now her father's wealth was the prize for which her life would be bartered yet again.

She thought of Richard and what George had said about him. She doubted she could believe a word George said. One man proving a sinner, however, did not prove another a saint. However fond she might had been of Richard once, she didn't know what manner of man he had become. The more she thought, the stronger grew her conviction that her only true freedom lay in keeping her silence and forgetting that she had once been the daughter of an earl.

The longer she stayed at Mistress Carter's household, the more comfortable Anne grew, and the more likely it seemed that she would indeed be there forever. She might, with time, fancy herself the wife of a gardener, bearing his children and telling them tales of the great folk who lived in castles. Sometimes she let herself forget that she must be invisible as well as silent, and boldly walked outside, even, on rare occasions, tending to a quick household errand. And if there had not been one day as rare in an English autumn as a jewel washed up on the shore, a day so brilliantly clear, gold and blue, that she could not keep herself inside, Richard might never have found her.

The hunting party was leaving the long blue shadows of the forest, and Richard could see the walls of London at a little distance. The hunt had been a wretched misuse of a glorious day—two hounds and a horse dead as well as the boar, and the horse's rider badly wounded. The man had been fool enough to urge his horse into the melee of hounds and mortally wounded boar. The boar had summoned enough strength to break free of the hounds and rip the horse's side, as well as the leg of the rider, before dying. The man had sat on the ground moaning and wailing as his squire cut the horse's throat.

Richard was in an ill temper. Until Anne was found, or at least her fate discovered, his claim on Middleham was not secure. For the first time, he began to look forward to the border wars and fighting the Scots again. That would happen soon enough. Give the borderers a few months sitting by their fires and they would welcome spring with new and even bloodier ideas for tormenting each other. He didn't see a hair's difference between the Scots raiders and the English.

Now he could cap the day fending off his sister-in-law Elizabeth's barbs. Richard turned in his saddle. "Francis, let's ride into the city for supper." Court was at Westminster just now, a good five miles from London proper. He would put off returning to Westminster for a few more hours, and perhaps there would be an amusing minstrel later. He called to his squires to take his hounds in, and Francis drew up alongside him.

"My father used to especially like hunting boar," Francis said. "Ugly things. He said they were the bravest animal. They keep going and going with the blood pouring out of them. Men sit down and hold their wounds."

"If you have a leg knocked out from under you, it's easier to stand on three legs than on one," Richard said reasonably.

"I suppose. But I just don't like watching anything die." Francis's face looked bleak, like a man revealing a shameful secret. "My father made me watch a hanging and quartering once, some felon. I must have been about eight. He threatened to whip me if I turned my head."

"God, Francis."

Francis went on, but he was looking at the sky. "He didn't seem to enjoy the idea, himself, but he said it was no kind of man who couldn't watch the final battle. That's what he called it. I think he was deathly afraid I would grow up to be a coward. He said my mother indulged me too much, that she had ruined me.

"He was proud of me that day, though. When we came home, he told my mother what we had seen, and how brave I had been. I never blinked, he said."

He turned to Richard. "My mother cried to think of it. Then I cried to see her crying. I can still see my father standing there, watching his wife and son cry over what he thought was a triumph. He looked so . . . so defeated I felt sorry for him. I had hated him all that afternoon, but then I felt sorry for him."

"What did you do?"

"Do? Nothing. If I'd shown him pity, he'd have beaten me for sure."

How strange men were, Richard thought. Francis's father worrying about his son, themselves thinking of death on a beautiful day, the likes of which they might not see again for months.

"Ho, brother longface!" Francis said suddenly. "It was my tale, and you are sadder than I. It was years ago. Where do we go tonight?"

"The Boar and Thistle?"

"That's fitting," Francis said. "The Boar it is. Race you to the gates."

Richard called to his squires to take his hounds with them, and he and Francis galloped the half-mile to the city wall, sending up dust to choke the foot travelers they passed, reining in hard just as they reached Moorgate, where they received a sour glance from the porter. Riding recklessly so near the wall would get back to Edward, not that Edward would care.

*F*rancis noticed the girl first. She was filling a bucket at the well of a house across from them. She had a narrow waist above a beautiful curve of hips, like the swell of a viol below its neck. She wore a simple gown of dull brown wool that followed the smooth line of her hips and thighs. Her straight back and the careful way she set the bucket down without spilling a drop, although it was clearly heavy for her, moved him. A girl who took such care with her work would be tender with her pleasure.

After filling the second bucket, she turned her face toward the sun, put her hands on her hips and flexed her back. Her hair was bound in a long braid, and as she arched backward, the braid swayed between her shoulder blades. In Francis's mind, a little girl's skirt swished through a door, and a long braid, one he was chasing to pull, swung above it.

Francis caught his breath and reined in his mare so abruptly that Richard's horse walked into her rump and snorted in annoyance.

Richard hardly gave her a glance. He could predict the whole sequence of events. They would cross the street, Francis would find some implausible reason to speak with the girl, which she would nonetheless believe. If she were bold enough, or her mistress lax enough, Francis would convince her to leave her house and meet him at the inn. A few cups of wine, then Francis would take a room upstairs. Unless, of course, the girl was married, but Francis never believed in presuming the worst.

"It's a girl, Francis. You've seen one or two before."

With a sweep of her skirt, the girl settled herself on the stone bench surrounding the well, as calm as a lady waiting for a carriage. "Go on, go talk to her," Richard said. He would ride to Crosby Place and have supper with his mother, instead of returning to Westminster.

"What?" Francis shot Richard a puzzled look, then laughed. "Come here. Look!"

The reason for the girl's composure in delivering the water became apparent. A tall young man in a leather jerkin came up to her, then leaned down to speak. She turned her face up to him and smiled. Richard's shock at what he finally understood lasted only a moment. He was on the ground and halfway across the street, weaving between carts, before he thought to hope that Francis had sense enough to take his horse.

"Take my horse," Richard called back as he ran.

By the time he reached her, the smile that had lit her face was gone, and for an instant he even thought he was mistaken. This girl was taller than Anne, and there was a quality about her difficult to define, something in the way she looked at him, a lack of patience or modesty.

The young man stepped forward. If he recognized Richard's livery, he was not awed by it. "Do you know this man, Sarah?"

She said nothing, and the boy turned to Richard. "By your trappings, you are a gentleman of some estate." He put a mocking turn on "gentleman." The boy was younger than Richard had thought at first glance, his long limbs gangly and awkward. "Why don't you leave now and not cause Sarah any grief?"

Sarah, then. Not Anne.

But of course it was Anne, and of course she knew him, although there was no sign the sight of him was welcome. Her eyes were wary and remote, as opaque as tarnished silver.

By then Francis had crossed the street, horses in hand. "Annie?" he asked, peering at her. "By God, it *is* you."

Anne rose from the bench, and the youth put a protective hand on her shoulder. "Come, Sarah, these men can't hurt you."

Richard bowed to Anne, then to the young man. The next moment, he had knelt down on the pavement before Anne. He had no plan, certainly no intention of kneeling before her, but he was there, and had to do *something*. He lifted the hem of Anne's skirt, dusty and mended and kissed it. Why did I do that, he wondered. I have made a bloody fool of myself. From the crowd that had begun to gather around he heard murmurings of encouragement, even a few cheers, and then he knew he could have thought of nothing better to convey both possession and respect.

Anne flushed from her cheeks to her neck. The tall lad, who was apparently not dim, understood completely. He kicked one pail as Richard rose to his feet. Water splashed onto Anne's skirt and flooded the cobbles where Richard's knee had pressed.

Francis stepped forward. "Watch yourself, man. You offend the king's brother."

The boy ignored him and spoke quietly to Anne. "I will leave you to speak with these gentlemen."

"Tom, " Anne said, "Wait!" but he was striding toward the house. She turned to Richard. "What have you done? You have made it impossible for me to stay here." Her voice was fierce and despairing. She looked as if she were about to cry, then she spun away to run after the youth.

Richard looked after her, stunned. She was a servant. Her hands were worn, as was the gown he had touched, and her face was smudged. But she appeared strong and in good health. *She didn't care enough to send for you. Or just didn't want to.* If she hated him for her father's fate, there was little he could do about it, but he had to find out. He set out for the house, not hurrying.

"Go, Richard," Francis said. "Make haste! Whatever girls say, they are not won by hesitation. Convince her you are so enamored of her that only a fool would forego such a love, and only a heartless stone would reject the bearer of it." He continued talking right up to the door.

"Most girls cannot bear being found foolish, and those that can, cannot bear your thinking that they are heartless. Whichever, they will start to protest that they are not *something*, and that is where you press your hardest accusation. It is a fair weapon to use because they have put it into your hands themselves, do you see?"

"Francis!" Richard stopped. "Leave off."

*T*he house was a three-story timber frame with handsome decorations at the cornices and narrow jetty. From the absence of foot traffic around the front of the house, Richard judged the lower level to be not a shop but perhaps the offices of a lawyer or councilman.

"I would speak to one of your serving maids," Richard said to the woman who answered his knock.

"There's none but honest servants here," she said.

"Surely. Nevertheless I want to see the tall dark-haired girl. She would have been in your service no more than a year."

"Wait here," she said. She returned with a handsome gray-haired woman who seemed at a glance to disapprove of the young men, sweat-stained and splattered with blood, at her door.

"*Two* men," she said, "to speak with one poor maid?"

"Lady, you must know who your new maid is," Richard said. "She does not belong here. I would only restore her to her birthright."

"Would you? I suppose *men* might call it thus." Her eyes ran him up and down and Richard flushed.

Unexpectedly, then, the woman smiled. "Come in. I imagine she is expecting you to have followed here. Perhaps you'd care to wash, first?"

*A*fter Richard had done what he could with water and a towel, Dame Carter opened a door into what appeared to be a counting room. Thick books lay clasped on shelves along one wall. A writing table and a chair took up the middle of the room. Writing accoutrements and a stack of paper covered most of one end of the table. Anne stood in corner of the room where the shadows were the thickest.

Richard laid his hat and gloves on the table. "Come, Anne. Sit with me. I can't see your face."

She didn't move. "What do you want of me?"

"Want of you? Anne, Edward has given me Middleham. He wants us to marry—assuming I could find you, of course. Surely you have heard that." In every household there was gossip, and none better than that from court. "Don't you want to go home?" He hardly recognized this girl, so cool and indifferent, but to spurn a passport to Middleham and safety, away from all the intrigue in which she had been bounced like a tennis ball, would make her unlike any human he had known.

"To marry," she repeated, in an odd detached voice, as though what he said had nothing to do with her. As though he were talking about oranges from Spain. "Why do you ask me what I want? You have come to take me away, so that is what will happen." She walked to the table, but remained standing, across from him.

For two years, Richard had held in his memory the child who had kissed him on a winter's walk. That girl, he remembered, had been hurt by his refusal of her innocent attempt to woo him. Perhaps her feelings for him had died at that moment.

Maybe she had cared for Lancaster, or even the youth at the well. Maybe she hated him for his part in what had happened to her family. If she did, she could tell him so. If she counted him an enemy, he wanted to know from the start.

"No," he said. "I didn't come for you. I came to take supper across the street. I came to find an evening's respite from court. I saw you only by accident." He spread his hands. "Look at me, Anne. Do you think I would seek you out like this, covered with blood and filth?" He took a breath. "How long have you been here?"

"Six months."

"And before that?"

"I can't say."

"Won't, you mean. But never mind. What are you doing here now?"

"I'm a serving maid, can't you tell?"

He leaned over the table. "Not what are you doing, now you're here. An idiot could tell that. *Why* are you here, instead of a dozen other places I could name? *Why* did you send no word to someone, if not me, then your mother?"

"You come in here and announce that I'm to marry you. You command me to explain myself and ask nothing about how I've fared. Do you think I've enjoyed being here? You know nothing of my life, so don't pass judgment."

"Of course I know nothing! I know nothing because you have said nothing. Whatever drove you here, I know nothing of. But *you* knew. You knew I was searching for you and sent no word. Why didn't you at least let someone know you were still alive. If not me, then your mother. Just tell me that much." His face was only inches from hers.

"Stop shouting! You're frightening me."

"Frightened, Anne?" His voice was soft. "Let me tell you about frightened. I searched everywhere I could think of, talked to anyone who might know about you—your mother's friends, who were understandably unpleasant to me, although none actually slammed the door in my face. I wasn't sure they would tell me, even if they knew.

"For months, while you were safe and warm and well here, I walked the streets of London, searching for you. I saw the despair and fear in your mother's face every time I told her I had discovered nothing new."

"I haven't always been safe and warm and well." Anne's voice was sullen.

"I haven't finished. There is one other thing. I went to see a girl pulled dead from the Thames. The constable summoned me because there was enough of her gown remaining to make him believe she was of gentle birth."

"No."

"Do you know how many dead people I've seen, Anne? I've seen hundreds, thousands, after the battles. I've seen them killed in ways so horrible I still have nightmares, but I couldn't look at this girl. Do you know why, Anne? I couldn't look at her because she might have been you.

"The constable told me that I wouldn't be able to recognize her, anyway. He didn't know what color her hair was because it was dank with mud and filth. He couldn't tell the color of her eyes because the fish had eaten them away. They eat the softest parts first, you know."

"Stop! I won't listen to this."

"She had been in the water a relatively short time, however, because the rest of her flesh was intact."

"I can't hear you!" Anne put her hands over her ears.

"Don't you want to hear how I knew it wasn't you? I picked up her dead hand and held it in mine, just like I did yours along the Thames that day." He walked around to her side of the table, grabbed her wrists and pulled her hands down from her face.

"Is this how you treat me? Touch me with force?"

He dropped her wrists and lifted his hands, palms forward. "No." He probably looked as angry as he felt. "I do not force you to do anything. Touch you with force, make you tell me where you have been, marry you, return to Middleham. None of those things will I force you to do. You decide. But decide before I leave this house because if you tell me to go I will not return."

"You remember that day along the river?" All the fight, all the anger seemed to have gone from her. She looked as young and defenseless as she had that winter day.

"Your fingers are longer than hers," he said, remembering how he had finally gathered enough courage to pick up the dead girl's hand. "Yours were are almost as long as mine, even then." His anger was spent; he was exhausted.

She turned her back to him, burying her face in the crook of her arm as though ashamed, and sobbed. He went to her and pulled her into his arms.

"Anne, hush. It will be well. We will go home." Everything he said to comfort her seemed only to make her cry harder, so he stopped talking and stroked her hair. Some day she would tell him. It didn't matter when. They would be together and forgive each other's families. They would make something good out of all the sorrow and destruction.

# Book Three
# King's Man

1471–1482

# 14 *Treason's Children*

*London*
*November 1471.*

Ships were Edward's passion now. He was having three built in Portsmouth, which was said to have the best shipbuilders in the land. Three-masted merchantmen armed fore and aft, no broadside cannon. They could fight if need be, but their primary virtue was speed. He walked along the wharf with Richard beside him. Richard had been trying to tell him something. Edward was no more than half listening; he had thought only for his ships. Nothing on the river now would match his beauties. He had a moment's doubt about his decision to arm them so lightly but shrugged it off. Speed against defense. You always sacrificed something. The new ships rode low in the water and sailed close to the wind. It made his heart race to think of the riches they would carry back from the world's ports. Oranges and lemons from Spain. Spices from Egypt. A shrewd tradesman could grow rich in surprising new ways these days. The appetite for books was growing—not just the new, printed ones, but those of the ancients, too. If a man could lay hands on certain of the rarer old texts, he could turn a nice profit putting them into print and still keep the original valuable text for himself. And some men were sending messages by birds, of all things, exceeding even the speed of post riders.

How that system could be applied to commerce challenged the imagination. England would prosper more than ever, he knew it. He could feel it in his bones, in every fiber of his body.

"Edward."

"Later. Talk to me at supper."

"Better now," Richard said, "while we are alone." They were nearly even with the easternmost gate. Court had moved to White Tower while Westminster was given its last airing and freshening before the onset of winter.

"Christ-on-the-cross," Edward waved his arm toward the river. "Do you call this alone?" Dock workers, seamen, a merchant on horseback pacing, scanning the wharf with anxious eyes. On one of the docked roundships, two dark-skinned men, naked but for loincloths in spite of the chill in the air, were lowering a sail. Once, black skin almost always identified a man as a slave. Now, it marked nothing with certainty. A black man could be a freedman or even a scholar. Their languages were still gibberish, though, as far as Edward could tell. Richard smiled as though the question were too obvious to answer. "Of course. You know what I mean."

"No." But he did. For the moment, no one else was begging the king's attention. He had been enjoying one of the few moments of un-qualified pleasure he could remember of late. All the more reason not to listen. He did not want his sanguine humor disturbed; if Richard wanted his attention undivided, it could only mean he had something unpleasant to say. Edward swallowed a sigh.

"Very well. If you want my ear, get on with it."

"I am not going north just now," Richard said.

"What?" Edward barely slowed his pace.

"I'm not going north."

Edward turned and stared. "Of course you're going."

"No. I have decided to stay the winter in London. That is, unless you hand down a fair allotment of the Neville property before then."

They passed through the narrow gate in the outer wall that took them from the wharf onto Water Lane. It was late afternoon, and everything seemed touched by Midas's hand—cold, bright, and gold. Leaves from the great beech tree by Lanthorn Tower lay thick on the cobbles, crisp as parchment under their boots.

"Now." Edward put his hands on his hips, belligerent. "What is this foolishness about?" He was afraid he knew. Seven months since he had put an end to the hopes of Lancaster and his idiot father, and his brothers were still quarreling over the spoils like a pair of angry bees in a garden.

"I'll stay in London until we've agreed on the settlement."

"I want you up there now," Edward said, "not in the spring." He wanted Richard well established in the north by January, to be his eyes and ears during winter's idle months, find out just how much loyalty to Warwick and Lancaster still lingered there while the cold kept ambition and old grievances from flowering into their evil fruit.

Richard said nothing. Edward knew better than to mistake the silence for acquiescence. One brother married to a Neville heiress, the other about to be, why had he thought the settlement would be easy?

"What has your bride to say to your plan?" Edward could not believe that Anne, that little bird that had not budged from sanctuary, would delay going north.

"Nothing."

"Nothing?"

"I'm not marrying her."

"Good God, Richard! You yearned after the girl for months. Now you're the only one in the country who *can* marry her without the north rising up in arms. Of course you're marrying her.

"You want me in the north. Wait. . . ." Richard raised his hand to curb Edward's protest. "I want that, too. But consider. What you require of me there is that I win back for you the loyalty of Warwick's former retainers and persuade Henry Percy to submit to my authority. What right do you think I would have in the eyes of those men if you partition my holdings to appease George, who won't step foot north of Epping Forest?"

Christ, Christ, Christ. King of the most powerful nation on earth, and he could not command his own brothers. For a moment, the only sound was the rustle of leaves scudding about their feet and a thin wind carrying the scent of the river into the lane. "You want Anne Neville; you have her," Edward said finally. "You want Middleham; you have it. What more do you want?"

"A fair distribution of all the forfeited lands and offices."

"And you think that, as it is, the distribution favors George."

"Of course I think so. It does."

"Why should it matter so to you?" Edward asked. "You're rich enough." A pity that George had ever left Warwick's cause: he might have died with the rest of the traitors. Wishing his own brother dead: a man shouldn't think like that, he'd burn in Hell. But God knew it would solve a large problem.

Edward told himself he didn't believe George knew enough to be dangerous. A name, a face from twelve years ago. George had been only a lad; he would have no cause to remember.

Perhaps. That was the bind, Edward thought. To a troubled conscience, everything masked meaning—a glance, a frown, a tone of voice. Nine parts certainty, one part doubt, and the doubt would rule you. You tortured yourself wondering and imagining, and of course you could never ask outright, because then you would give them the weapon if they hadn't it already. There was one absolute certainty in this coil: if George knew, he would use that knowledge. Some day he would use it. Edward could count on that. He would not be left wondering forever.

"Why don't you ask George that?" Richard's voice was not quite mocking. "He's even richer."

Edward shrugged. "You know how George is. All things must be as he wants them, or he is malcontent."

"And that is reason to strengthen his belief that his discontent is a disaster to be avoided at any cost?"

"Then say I am weary of his discontent. That in this case, his content is worth the cost."

"But you're forgetting something, aren't you? In this case, the cost is mine."

"I suppose that's so," Edward agreed reluctantly. He looked at his brother's lean young face and thought how changed it was. There was none of the uncertainty about which he used to chide Richard; it was a face of stillness and determination. And amusement, Edward thought. Damn him, Richard was enjoying this.

"But why wait here?" Edward heard with disgust a tone in his own voice almost of pleading.

A shadow passed suddenly over them—a raven sailing down from the Tower to sit in funeral dignity on the outer wall, as if playing judge to their affairs.

"Because I weaken my position if I accept any part of the settlement before I am satisfied with the whole." Richard spoke slowly, finding his words cautiously, as a blind man feels his way. "You know that as well as I. You would do the same."

Edward felt the heat rise to his face. Richard was beating him at his own game, using the prize as weapon, flinging it back in his face to press him toward resolution. Richard was watching him intently, a look that Edward couldn't define, but that gave him a distinct shudder of distaste. "You would play me like a fish on a line?" Edward asked. "I might have expected it from George, but not you." He spoke in a cold flat voice. "Don't try it, brother, you haven't the nature for it."

"I'm not playing," Richard said, "and my demands are just."

"Just? Ha! It is not justice you are thinking of. I know. You are thinking how far you can safely push me. You play with high stakes, brother. I hope you are prepared to cover your wager."

"I'm prepared to give you however long you need to think about it."

Edward's shame at being bested was intensified by the fact that Richard had attempted to hide neither his victory, nor what Edward had at last identified as the look on his brother's face—compassion. Gloating would have been less offensive. "So my little brother has grown up at last, opened his eyes and seen what can be gained by a man who is willing to lend—I won't say *sell*—his soul. Well, I suppose I shouldn't be surprised." Edward smiled. His fine mood was soured and his smile bitter. His brothers drove him mad. Even thinking of his ships didn't abate his displeasure now.

## St. Martin Church, London
### December 1471.

Heavy rain fell as Richard rode to St. Martin, silver sheets of water blown by a gusty wind, November as seasonably cold and wet as October was falsely fair. He handed his drenched cloak and hat to the elderly servant who met him at the door. The old man smiled, revealing motley teeth, as many broken and black as strong and white, and a sepulchral breath that caused Richard to step sharply back. The servant gave the hat a brisk shake before the fire, sending droplets of water to hiss and crackle like beetles in the flames, and set about spreading the cloak to dry.

Richard stood and warmed his hands at the fire. He had taken Anne from Mistress Carter's back into sanctuary at St. Martin, although he hadn't known he was taking her *back*. She couldn't remain a servant, and she wouldn't consider any of the royal residences. Neither would she consider living with Isabel and George. When he mentioned that possibility, a look of such bleakness and fear came into her face that he had pulled her close and promised: never. Never again would she live anywhere she did not choose.

When they had reached St. Martin, Brother Lawrence cupped Anne's face with his fingertips. "Why child, you told me true. You *are* Warwick's daughter."

"Yes, Brother, I do not lie." Anne might not lie, but she was capable of monumental subtlety. Standing behind her, his hand on her elbow, Richard could not see her face, only the incline of her head to the priest. Brother Lawrence's smile change into a slight puzzled frown, followed by the light of comprehension. So Anne knew this man, but her connection to him was something she didn't want disclosed—at least not to him. A child could have seen it, and Richard had not been a child once for nothing.

But he put it from his mind. Happy men do not go searching for secrets.

George, of course, had secrets aplenty.

"Did you say your lady is found?" George asked. "How splendid for you! And where did you say she has been all these months?"

He kept asking until Richard lost his patience.

"George, you know I did *not* say. And don't trouble to ask again. I can't tell you since I don't know, myself."

The response seemed to move George to some mysterious satisfaction. "Ah. You don't know. Saints, that is curious, don't you think? That she would not tell you, of all people?" Now, if there was a language for giving bad news, Richard doubted he was fluent in it. He turned at the sound of the door when Anne entered the room, feeling his own smile as uncertain as hers looked.

No longer the kitchen maid, she was elegantly dressed in a gown he had not seen before, a deep rich red that made her hair and eyes look darker than he remembered them. She stood quietly, hands clasped in front of her, back erect as a pillar.

Standing in the glow of the hearth, surrounded by ghosts of the fire caught in the dark polished wood on the paneling behind her, she seemed wrapped in flame. Even her throat and the curve of her neck down to her shoulder had a warm glow. He played with the notion of abandoning what he had come to tell her; he wanted to talk of other things, not to talk at all. He wanted to touch her, to wrap his hands in her shining hair and feel it cool between his fingers, to slide his open palm down her neck and feel her pulse at the base of her throat.

"You look very fair," he said. "That gown becomes you. Is it new?"

Anne spread her hands and looked down at her gown. She seemed startled, as if she had just recognized an old friend she had not expected to meet. "Oh, no. It was made for me when I went to France. I grew so much that I had to have everything new. I sent to my mother for it. How would I have anything new here?"

"You can have anything you want, you know. You have only to ask for it."

"I wonder. What should be the fashion for ladies in sanctuary?" He could almost take the words for flirtation, except that her gaze was so solemn and intense. Probably she could see his thoughts. He thought that most women were part witch in their ability to know what men would hide.

He sent the old servant a sharp glance, and the man finally left the room after taking a few unnecessary tugs at Richard's cloak. He told Anne about the delay in their marriage and his possession of Middleham. Waiting for her response, he watched the candle flames in the brackets along the wall dance and waver in the draught. When he didn't look at them quite directly, shafts of light crossed like tiny swords above the slender wax columns. "This is your brother's decision?"

A dozen phrases came to his mind. But how do you comfort someone for what you do to them freely, of your own choosing, no dagger at your throat? And how could he tell her the truth that he was only beginning to understand, himself? *I am afraid, too. Of what is in my brothers' actions that I do not comprehend. Of whether my skills are enough for the task Edward has put before me. Smile at me, tell me you understand.*

It was a simpler truth he found words for. "No. It is my decision."

She considered that, and when she spoke again, her voice had lost some of its flatness. "Forgive me, my lord, I know it is not my place to ask . . ." *My lord* again. When had he become *my lord*? " . . . but what would you retain, if you yielded to the king's demands?"

There was no objection to her knowing. He shrugged and strung out the list for her: Middleham, Sheriff Hutton, Barnard Castle, some other minor estates. Office of Warden of the Marches, Constable of England.

"That is much!"

"Yes."

"But not enough."

"No."

A tremor of thought ran across her face, and when she spoke again, it was not what he expected her to say. "Sanctuary is just another word for prison, isn't it? For me, for my mother. I wonder why I never understood that before."

"Come, Anne. It's not forever."

"You say that George will not yield, that neither will you, and that the king will not intervene. In what other form may an end come?"

"That is too foolish to answer." Meaning, only a fool would give an answer when he had none.

"Then perhaps you will tell me, what price, exactly, would be sufficient to induce you to marry me?" Her voice was so calm and soft, it took a moment for the bitterness of what she had said to penetrate.

"Don't, Anne. It's no affront to you that I do this."

"Don't what? Every prisoner is entitled to know the sum of his ransom."

*F*inally, after Edward had taken and maintained for months a steadfast neutrality in his brothers' quarrels, Richard agreed to relinquish Richmond and the office of Constable of England, and dropped for the moment the issue of the Countess of Warwick, who remained at Beaulieu Abbey, although technically in the custody of George, Duke of Clarence.

Richard and Anne were married at last on the steps of St. Martin one cold March morning. Under other circumstances, given who they were, there would have been days of tournaments, jousting and feasting. At the very least, processions and a wedding banquet. There would have been crowds pressing together for a glimpse of the couple, the hope of a favor from a royal marriage, of largesse shared. So they married, hardly secretly, since the banns must be posted, but early in the morning. Anne had wanted that, and it was easy for Richard to honor her preference, never liking crowds himself.

She wore a gown of crimson velvet with ermine-lined sleeves, a sideless tunic of green, girded in gold. Her hair was braided the day before, then unbound to fall in waves to her waist, and crowned with a circlet of ribbons and leaves, and a few early spring snowdrops.

*T*he inn was noisy and crowded, voices and kitchen sounds bounding from wall to wall. It was the first night of their journey home, two months after their marriage on the steps of St. Martin. A man picked up a rebec and tried to get the others to sing along, but the notes were lost in the talk and laughter.

Anne stood up from the table. Richard started to rise, too, but she laid her hand on his shoulder. *Wait.* He thought that was the word her lips formed. In a little while he pushed his way out of the parlor, and climbed the narrow stairs to their second-floor room. He let himself in without knocking. Anne was alone in the room, sitting on the bed, her headdress removed, her hair over one shoulder as she gathered it into a plait. The smells of cooking grease and woodsmoke penetrated even their upper room.

"Where's Joan?" Richard asked. Two young women from Edward's court had been happy to leave London for the north.

"Gone." Anne was looking at the braid.

"Your other lady?"

"Sleeping."

She stood up and her garments started falling to the floor. Her braided girdle. Her linen collar with its lace fluting. Her embroidered pocket. Richard reached for the knot she was struggling with in her petticoat, but she shrugged his hand away. "Anne? What are you doing?"

"Undressing."

"Let me help you."

"I don't need help."

He reached for her hand and gently tugged her toward the bed.

"I've done this myself for a long time." She looked at him. "I can do a lot of things I never thought a lady would." Her voice was brittle as she released the knot and let her gown and shift fall to her feet. He could feel her stiffness, released her hand and stood up.

"Don't." He was angry and didn't know why.

"What? Don't you want me?" There was something sad and lonely in her face, and the anger left him, but now he knew its source. So far, everything had been on his terms. She had been made to wait in sanctuary while he and George wore each other down. And when the dispute was settled, everyone knew what her price had been. He had won his property. She was reminding him that he could not invite or ask anything of her because it was all already given. She was offering her body as a blood sacrifice and he wanted her heart, fragrant and luxurious as rose petals strewn on a hero's path.

"Yes," he said. "But not here." Whatever affection there might be between them felt infinitely fragile, as though he was walking through an invisible maze, where, if you misstepped, not only did you lose yourself, but you damaged the pathway so much that you might never go back. He picked up his cloak and laid it around her shoulders.

Sleep eluded him. He was like a child the night before the first day of Christmas, on edge with the anticipation of a too-keen delight,

needled by the fear that morning would bring nothing but evidence
of hollow hopes. He rose and opened the shutter to look out at
the courtyard pooled in moonlight. In this small inn, the smells of
cooking, of stale grease and woodsmoke, lingered even in the upstairs
chambers. Tomorrow he would ride into Middleham. His own. Still
not to be believed. For four years he had denied himself the memory
of the north country. He no longer had a claim on it, and he rejected its claim on him. Now he gave in to it completely, torn between
hope and fear, knowing how much he wanted the Middleham he
had known and how unlikely it would be for him to find it. He was
nineteen. He could command men, and he could kill them. He loved
doing one and hated the other, but they came together; he had no
illusions about that. Neither had he any false modesty about his skills.
For the past five years he had been gathering armies, fighting battles,
and languishing in exile. What did he know of running an estate? He
meant to find out. He meant to find out before anyone else found out
how little he knew. He was in water over his head, but a man could
learn to swim in deep water as well as shallow.

He left the shutter open and walked back to bed, the moon lighting
his way. In the dim light, Anne's naked shoulder was startlingly white.
He kissed it and lay down beside her. Toward morning, he slept.

# 15  *All but the Stars*

It was nearly sunset by the time Middleham's great stone keep loomed into view. The porter was not pleased to see them. He was a large man, clean-shaven but so dark-bearded his face looked as if it had been dusted with steel.

"Who be you folk and what be your business?"

The man's archaic tongue grated on Richard as much as his insolence.

"Where have you been, man, these last few months? I am Richard Gloucester and Middleham is mine now. Open the gates."

"If you'd come here a year past, we'd have hanged ye."

"A year past, I'd not have given you the chance."

"Where is Oliver?" Old Oliver, the porter Richard remembered, would have waved them in with a sweep of his hat and a broad hello.

"In the graveyard." The man hawked and spat. "For a year now."

They rode into the bailey, where pages appeared with torches and the grooms unloaded the horses and led them away to the stables. Richard was overcome with memory. Was it really five years ago that he had left this place? Eleven since he stood in this spot for the first time, a frightened and lonely boy? It could have been either yesterday or a lifetime ago. He was returning both as Anne's husband and as her family's destroyer. In this country where loyalties were as ancient as the hills and lakes, and men were strangers whose great-grandfather had not been born here, his boyhood years in this place hardly guaranteed his acceptance now.

Anne was watching him, her face troubled. "I don't know that man. What has happened here?"

"Don't be afraid." Richard brushed his gloved hand over his face, wiping away moisture that could have been either mist or tears. "Come, we're home. Let's go in."

In the great hall, fire roared in the hearth and torches filled the air with their resinous odor. Fresh herbs and grasses covered the floor. It seemed to Richard that the entire population of the castle must be in the hall. Someone must have watched long and carefully from the walls for this homecoming to occur with their arrival.

"Richard?" Anne gripped his arm. Her face was pale, and she looked as though she might cry. He wondered whether it was sorrow over returning to a home from which her family was gone, or fatigue. He was so tired himself that one good blow could probably knock his bones from their sockets, but he knew what had to be done in this moment.

"Yes," he said, leading her forward. "It is for us."

They walked to the lord's table in a blaze of light and a rowdy consort of cheers, shouts, and hats in the air. Richard found himself standing on the seat of the big armed chair that had been Warwick's, shouting something above the roar, and someone lifted Anne to the lady's chair. When they stepped down, people passed by, some leaning across the table to clasp Richard on the arm or touch Anne's hand. So many familiar faces he had thought never to see again. Hugh, the steward, came forward and bowed first to Richard, then Anne. He unfastened a large ring of keys from his belt and gave them to her. "It is a pity your mother is not here, Lady Anne. These are yours, forged especially for you."

Bennett was there, too, and Giles. Richard turned to receive Bennett's embrace, and Giles clasped his hand. Giles had not changed, but Bennett had grown silver-haired in those few years. But he was young, Richard thought, only a little past thirty. Bennett mistook his surprise. "You did not expect to find me here? For shame, sire. Did you think you were the only child in the world worth teaching?"

Richard laughed. "May God strike me dead as I stand here if I was that arrogant."

For three hours Richard and Anne managed to find the grace and strength to hold themselves upright in their chairs.

The purveyor brought the salt and presented it to the lord's table. The pantler cut the upper crust, round and delicately spiced. All the pastries were beautifully colored—red with rose petals, green with parsley, and gold with saffron. The butler poured the wine, to be tasted first by the cupbearer. There was little danger of poison: the gesture was one of respect, making no imposition on a new lord's trust.

The cook stood with his long-handled spoon hanging from his neck. The carver performed his art as gracefully as a dancer with his assortment of knives. Food appeared before them. Golden apples— meatballs wrapped in saffron. Subtleties of almond paste in fancy shapes. St. John's urchins, meat wrapped in carob pastry, shaped into edible quills. Anne shook her head as a page offered her an urchin from the platter. Richard stopped the page and put an urchin on Anne's trencher. "Eat it. You will feel better."

When the meal was cleared away, the revelry began: musicians, dancers, and mummers with their riddles.

*Green is gold.*

*Fire is wet.*

*Fortune's told.*

*Dragon's met.*

Richard remembered that the answer was the summer solstice, but was too tired to think why.

At length the meal ended, the musicians fell silent, and a servant led them through the stairs to the lord's chamber, which was as carefully prepared as the hall. Warwick's little chess table, brought from the solar and flanked by two chairs, stood to the right of the hearth. To the left, the lord's heavy oak bath, filled with steaming water and smelling of crushed lavender and rose petals. They stood in the doorway dazed with the prospect of yet another ritual. Servants to bathe them. Hands of others to disrobe them, eyes to watch—while trying not to seem to—how they watched each other. Watch, note, and speculate on the success of the marriage of the new lord and lady.

The air was heavy with ghosts. Richard would have liked nothing more than to be alone to face them for a moment and then sleep, and suspected Anne would have liked the same. But each initiation must have its ceremony, one for the making of a knight, another for the making of the lord and lady. He glanced at Anne. "It will be over soon. Be grateful you don't have to stay on your knees all night."

"What!"

"When I was knighted. We knelt and prayed from dusk to sunrise."

He gave himself over to the servants, sitting back and letting the bath ease the stiffness from his limbs and the dust from his skin until he was as red and wrinkled as a squalling babe. When his foot touched Anne's, he pulled back slowly, as though he had been about to change positions anyway, as if he was a man of resolution, no awkwardness or uncertainty about him.

At last, they lay in bed alone, the linen coarse and clean against their skin, the fire tamped down and the bed curtains pulled around them. Richard said softly, in the dark, "Your people gave us a fine welcome, Annie."

"*My* people. Now they are your people."

The tone of her voice was impossible to read. He couldn't tell whether her words were said in pleasure, sadness, or bitter resentment, and couldn't fight sleep long enough to find out. He said what he had never in his life said to a woman. "Sleep well, lady. I will see you in the morning."

## Middleham Castle
### June 1472. Lauds.

*The night belongs to the great birds. In the garden there is a scurrying among the leeks, then a thin animal scream that dies in the heavy whacking of wings.*

*Sleeping, all horses are nags, heads hanging, hipshot.*

*A water beetle lands on the mossy surface of the fishpond. It is courted by a deadly kiss, the whipping tongue of a frog, and disappears.*

*The scullion half-wakes, chilled, and pulls his blanket up around his shoulders. He opens his eyes enough to note the still undiluted blackness, and falls back asleep.*

Richard rested his elbows on the crenellations and looked out at the night. The village below him was quiet and dark, windows shuttered, candles doused. The night sky was ink black, Cassiopeia's Chair just above him. Oh God, the stillness. He could hear the wind, and some small creature noise, a frog or a cricket. He could hear himself breathe. It was his second night as lord of Middleham.

At last, he and Anne had completed their own ritual. Anne had stood quietly, straight as a soldier, as Richard began to undress her.

"Do you know how this is done?" she asked.

"I know something about it, yes," he said. He put his hands on the points of her bodice and began to loosen the knots. "Are you frightened?"

"Of you?"

"Not of me. Of what we are doing." Surely it was her first time. Margaret of Anjou would not have wanted a Neville brat until she was sure Lancaster would wear the crown.

"No," Anne said, "I'm not frightened. I know you will treat me well. As you treat everything you own."

Richard's fingers froze on the points as her words repeated themselves in his mind. "I don't own you, Anne." The quiet room with its carefully tended fire and fresh-scented linens suddenly seemed fraught with danger.

"Don't you? Middleham's yours. So are Bolton and Sheriff Hutton. You will need an heir for your estates. I think you must own me, too."

"It doesn't have to be that way." Richard made his fingers keep marching. The ribbon through the first eye. Then the second. Whatever abyss lay before them now seemed less disastrous than what they might say to each other if he stopped.

Her bodice undone, the dress slipped from her shoulders to lie around her feet. He began to untie her sleeves. "Does it matter so much," he asked, "that we had to take each other? I am *glad* it is you."

There were no tears, no fierce hungry kisses, no bodies trying to inhabit each other's skin. Their skin touched from belly to toes, but he rested his upper body on his elbows, careful of his weight pressing on her. A candle burned by the bed; in its wavering light he could see her eyes studying him, eerily, as though they were the eyes of a stranger, someone else watching them from a distance.

## Middleham Castle
### July 1472. Prime.

*A rabbit pauses by the raspberry canes, haunches pulled up neatly. A tuft of fur lies at its feet. It waits as though listening, then hops away.*

*The scullion yawns and scratches his chest, then fans the fire beneath the great cauldron. In the cauldron are three separate jars of food, capped with linen. In one, an oatmeal pudding, which will be the lord and lady's breakfast. The other two, veal to be later dressed with cucumber and mint and a venison and parsnip stew, will simmer throughout the day.*

*The lord's squire of the body carries away the basin of water and linens. He looks to see that he has left nothing behind before swinging the door closed after him with his toe, hardly breaking his stride.*

*In the chapel, white altar linens dazzle in the early morning sun
streaming through the windows. The lord and lady kneel there, absorbed in
their separate thoughts.*

$\mathcal{T}$here were changes at Middleham. A manor without a lord or lady
for a year and more will grow at least a few evils like mushrooms in
the dark: what retainers had leaner account books but fatter pockets;
who had keys they ought not to, keys to pantries, wine cupboards,
and accounting rooms; who bought fresh meat and served rancid.

The north had grown harsh. The untimely eviction of tenants
from their lands was becoming common practice throughout the
county, turning hard-laboring freeholders indigent at a landlord's
whim. Richard rode to his other northern estates, Sheriff Hutton and
Bolton, overseeing the repair of buildings, listening to tenants' complaints and good wishes, talking to their stewards and retainers.

York itself Richard found unchanged. He loved the small tidy city,
its white stone walls, parts of which had stood since the Romans.
York Minster moved him every time he entered it, as though it were
his first time. He could not see the minster's spires rising above the
city walls without a gladdening of his heart, nor enter its doors without a calm descending upon him.

He did not know why. It was no more possible to say why the
windows and columns of a particular structure moved him than to
say why the bones and eyes of a particular face gladden the eyes and
lighten the heart.

He loved the figures—gargoyles, cherubs, men and women—
carved on those particular corbels. Imaginary or human, they were faces that a worker a century past loved enough to render immortal. But
he loved best the sunlight streaming down from high rose windows,
shafts of light bright and intense at their point of entry, growing both
broader and fainter as they extended down toward earth. He could say
it was only a pattern of sun and stone, but could not help seeing it as
a parable of God's presence on earth.

He wanted his own presence felt everywhere. Peace along the
borders. His name the name of a man who would not be bought, and,
years in the future, the name of a man whose peace lived after him.

His children in the nursery, running through the halls, in the
schoolroom with Bennett. Eight or ten of them, as many as his own
brothers and sisters, under his own roof until they were old enough

to find their place in the world, not fostered out. He would not have them searching the faces of strangers for the image of a father.

The hands of his workers reshaping his castle. The time was long past when Middleham was needed as a defense against invasion. He would replace floor rushes with carpets, hang tapestries to warm stone walls. He would have more light. Above all, more light. Windows cut in walls. Perhaps another story added to the keep, tall enough to stand above the curtain wall, allowing daylight to enter the windows from dawn to sunset.

The guild hall was one of the last places Richard had been with Jack Neville. This time, Richard and the lord mayor sat at the head table, and the councilmen, all guild members, filled the benches that squared the room. The mayor crowded over the list of grievances and the record book, directing Richard's attention first to one item, then another.

Richard would have preferred to read alone, without the commentary, but couldn't say that without risking offense. The drone of voices, the rustle of parchment, and the scribe's scratching pen buzzed like a cloud of horseflies. The lord mayor's clerk rapped on the table. The noise lessened, then all but stopped. Guildsmen turned their faces to the table.

"Our good Duke of Gloucester," the mayor began.

Richard stood, thanked them, and sat down again. The mayor opened the session. The scribe dipped the pen in ink, scratched again, sanded the page. Laid his pen down to be shaved, picked up a new one, scratched some more. The air grew close. One of the guildsmen stood and opened a window.

The mayor appeared to grow anxious. Richard resisted the urge to pull both the record book and the agenda away from him. The scribe announced the next case and the porter admitted an elderly bald man in a rose-colored gown, the man and his gown looking as though one more scrubbing would rub them out altogether.

"Master Calthorpe?" Richard asked.

"Yes, my lord." The old man nervously twisted his hat in his hands. He complained that his neighbor had prevented him from working his own land for the past two summers.

"Who speaks for you?"

"I do, Your Grace." The speaker was a weaver, a red-haired man whose pointed face made Richard think of a fox.

"Is the defendant present?" Richard asked.

"No, my lord."

"Who speaks for him, then?"

"No one. His case speaks for itself," a candler answered.

"I see." Richard said. He wondered if he did. "The defendant's name?"

"John Glover, sir," the candler answered.

Richard turned to address the old man. "You have not had the use of your own land for two years. Is that correct?"

"Yes, sir."

Richard looked toward the weaver. "That is a way of saying that the ownership of the land is in question, I take it."

"Yes, sir."

"Is there proof of ownership?" Richard asked, puzzled. The case appeared so simple that a child could solve it, but he could feel the tension in the chamber.

"Yes, sir," the weaver answered. "Ownership appears to be clearly documented on the part of the plaintiff." And the defendant thought the case was so clearly in his favor that he needn't bother appearing.

The weaver sat back. A dozen pairs of curious eyes turned toward Richard.

So, he thought. Something he was not being told. Something they were afraid he would find out? Or were afraid to say, but hoped he would find out?

"We have here a man," he glanced toward Calthorpe, "whose land has been worked and harvested by another for the past two years."

"That is correct," the mayor answered.

"Then the land must be henceforth worked and harvested by its owner, Master Calthorpe," Richard said.

Some discreet clearing of throats, darting glances. The rose-gowned man ceased playing with his hat, and began to look as attentive as the fox he resembled.

"Is that not apparent?" Richard asked. "If the man owns the land, and his ownership can be verified, then the working of it and all its crops are his."

"Yes, my lord." This time it was the cooper who spoke. "There is also the matter of reparation sought for the past two harvests."

"Can you estimate the lost income?"

"Yes, my lord. That is not particularly difficult."

"Well, then?" Richard asked. No one answered. "Come, sirs. You present a simple case. In fact, you appear to have conceived a just resolution before you presented it."

One man coughed. They all looked at each other.

Richard leaned over the grievance list and looked back up. "Masters Widdrington and Salford, please come forward."

The cooper and weaver came forward. "Councilmen, Lord Mayor. What are you not telling me?" Richard asked in a quiet voice. The chamber was deadly still.

"Sir—"

"Yes?"

"The defendant is one of your retainers," The weaver said in practically a whisper, as if that explained everything.

"In what capacity?"

"He is the undersheriff of our city, sir."

"What of it? Does he owe the money or not?"

"He does." The mayor spoke. The other two men looked on.

"Lord mayor. The fine and cost of past crops must be assessed and collected from the defendant, the plaintiff paid, and the repossession of his land assured. Please enlighten me as to the difficulty."

The mayor smiled. His smile just missed mockery. "Yes, my lord duke, we will. If you are quite certain that is the course you wish to take."

"Councilmen." Richard laid both palms on the table. A more polite group of dissemblers he had never encountered. "Councilmen, we have here, what, six more cases to hear before we break for dinner? I have given you a decision which you concede is just. Please inform me what you expected me to do."

"None other, sir." The cooper, still cautious. "Only that it would not have been thus with my lord Warwick. If the defendant were his man, that is."

"I see," Richard said. This time he did. He turned to the scribe. "Please announce the terms of settlement."

He saw a score of doubtful faces, one beaming old face, the doubtful faces perhaps also amused, confronting what must have seemed to them an elementary, even naive, sense of justice.

*Oh, you're the new lord here? Wait. You are young. You will discover our ways are not so easy to know.*

*Nor our ills simple to correct.*

*August 1472. Terce.*

*The hay is cut and lies drying in the fields.*

*In the village, a pig foraging for food knocks over a basket of freshly picked vegetables, and the housewife drives him off with curses and the flapping of her apron.*

*Two boys thread a string through a moth wing. It follows where they pull it until they tire of the game and run off. The moth, wounded, tilts to the side as it flies raggedly, then falters.*

*Rain-cooled a few hours earlier, the raspberries on the hedge are now warm to the gardener's touch.*

*Middleham Castle*
*September 1472. Vespers.*

Richard and Anne had grown easier with each other. At night they would lie apart while they spoke quietly about the day's events. Having lived at Middleham more recently, Anne could sometimes give Richard a name to match with a face, or a history he could not know. They were like old friends sharing a bed.

When they touched, they panted, sweated, and sobbed for breath in each other's arms, and the old friends turned their backs and didn't watch. Once in a while, friends and lovers almost met. After loving, after they resumed the space between them, two hands would creep closer together, find each other, and hold while they said their good nights.

*Nottingham Castle*
*October 1472. Sext.*

*The horses are gone with the hunters; grooms clean the stalls, backs hunched from the weight of forks heavy with spoiled straw. They lay down the new straw, bright as gold, then flush buckets of water down the gutters and fill the mangers with hay.*

*A bubbling and hissing in the kitchen, fat being clarified for candles. The lad tending the cauldron leans too close and yelps when a drop of hot fat lands on his arm.*

*Wearied by the chase, the old boar can finally only turn and face the hounds. The pike, well-aimed and true, cuts the air in a neat arc before it slices the tough hide. The boar roars in pain and rage, the horn is sounded, and the pack leaps on the dying beast.*

*In the heart of the forest, undisturbed, young boars grunt and sniff among the leaf-mold, feasting on acorns and beechnuts.*

". . . . and then my hounds had him, his back to the rock, nowhere to turn. Aha! Now, Sir Boar, who is master of the forest? I draw my knife to finish him, but my hounds are in the way. I call them off. The boar feints and draws toward me. He thinks he may have fight enough left in him for a last charge, but I have him. Straight through the heart."

Henry Percy leaned forward and cut the air, barely avoiding knocking his cup on its side. "What think you, Gloucester? Have you ever seen a truer stroke?"

Certainly not heard the telling of it more times. Richard had to concentrate to keep his face sober. "As straight and true as I have seen, sir."

Like most of the Percy men, Henry Percy, Earl of Northumberland was large and ruddy-faced. Edward had arranged this meeting at Nottingham; he wanted Richard and Northumberland, the two largest holders of northern lands and men, to be in harmony with other.

"Here is your brother." Percy motioned to his servant and held up his cup for more wine. "Now, sire," he said, as Edward sat down, "as I was just telling my lord Gloucester here, of course I am his loyal subject, as well as yours, and will do him good service." Percy's tone of voice seemed to imply there was something else he *wouldn't* do.

"Of course," Edward pulled his chair closer to the table.

"But there are one or two small things I must ask in return, my liege."

"Yes?"

"Sire, have patience, I beg you. It is not easy to gather courage to ask favors of the king."

"Enough, Percy. Go on."

"I would have the assurance that my lord Gloucester will agree not to claim any of the offices I now hold."

"Percy, my brother's eye is not on any of your offices."

"Or any of my servants or retainers."

Richard spoke for himself. "I have no wish to claim any of your men."

"Nor any that ever have been."

Richard frowned. "I can't promise that. How can I know everyone who might have been in your service in the past?"

Percy went on as though Richard had not spoken. "Nor do you ever interrupt me or my servants on any of their business."

"God forbid I would deter any good north country man from his business. You have my word on it."

Northumberland nodded, satisfied.

"Any *legal* business," Richard added. He caught the twitch in Edward's cheek that betrayed the wish to smile, caught also the quick flair of annoyance in Northumberland's eye.

*H*e has not forgiven you," Richard said to Edward as they were undressing later that night, "for the insult of losing Northumberland, even temporarily." He pulled off his tunic and laid it on the chair. Edward sat on the bed, one stockinged foot planted on his squire's rump, the squire straddling Edward's booted ankle.

"He may not forgive you, either," Edward said, "for making sport of him."

"Sport?" Richard moved the candle farther from the bed drapings, surprised.

"Any *legal* business." Edward leaned back, applied more heft to the squire's backside.

"No sport. Only the truth."

"More truth than he wanted you to see. You're lucky if only half of his business is illegal." Edward's boot came off and the squire hurtled forward, scrambling to keep his feet under him. Edward grunted. "I'll say this: however Jack Neville betrayed me at the end, he was worth ten of Percy. Well, Percy's your worry now."

*Middleham Castle*
*November 1472. None.*
*Snow dusts the dales.*

*Pages walk the length of the passageways, lighting candles and torches. The days grow still shorter.*

*The north wind rattles the last leaves from the trees. The birds have all but disappeared; badgers and boars seek out their dens.*

*The threshers have flailed the grain, and stored the chaff in the bins for the harvest.*

*The husbandman straddles the sow, one knee on her neck. He plunges the knife into the artery, and the housewife holds the pan to collect the blood for pudding.*

*A*nne was sitting in her favorite window alcove. Her feet were drawn up on the seat, arms wrapped around her knees. "When do you leave for London?" she asked.

"Next week. Or at the latest, the next after that. Perhaps you would like to come with me."

She didn't answer, just smiled at him.

"Anne?"

"I was thinking of my mother. She must be losing hope she will ever leave sanctuary. Please try to persuade your brother to release her to you. I would have her here with me."

"It was in my mind to do that," Richard said, and saw the smile fade and her eyes suddenly wet.

"Thank you, my lord."

"What is it?"

She shook her head and wiped her eyes.

"If you came with me," he suggested again, "you could see your mother, whether or not she returns with me."

"No, Richard, I can't."

"Why not?"

"London is too long a journey just now. I am with child."

## London

"Sir." Richard greeted the queen's brother, Anthony Woodville, now Earl Rivers.

"And you recall my physician, William Hobbes," Edward said.

Richard extended his hand to the doctor. A fierce-looking man, well past mid-life, but tall and unstooped, with heavy white brows above deepset eyes and a hawklike nose. Hobbes could probably frighten his patients into health.

"A pleasure, doctor. I see your duties as king's physician have increased since I was last here." He waved a hand toward the chess table.

He would have expected Rivers to be Edward's partner, now that Hastings was in Calais, but Rivers was seated in a chair with a comfortable padded seat a distance from the chess table. The earl reached for a lute propped against the wall, and began to softly sound and tune the strings.

Hobbes laughed. "You flatter me. Your brother prefers my skills to those of my lord Rivers. Anthony does everything perfectly, while I can be relied upon to let my concentration flag under the influence of wine or a song. Both of which His Grace provides in plenty. There is purpose in his generosity, wouldn't you say? But perhaps I take your place," he added courteously.

"Oh no, doctor, not I. I never liked the game." Richard sat down on the settle by the hearth. Parliament would break for Christmas, and he must decide whether to go home and return in late January, or to wait out the interlude in London. He cracked a chestnut, hot and fat, and threw the shells into the fire.

True to his word, Hobbes seemed in no hurry to begin the game. "So you send your son to Wales," he said to Edward, "and you hope your regent will effect the peace there."

"Not Wales; Ludlow."

"The seat of the Welsh Marches; it is Wales he is to confine. Your brother, my lord Gloucester, in the north," a glance at Richard, "and your son in the west. The king's arm reaches far. Actually, who *is* to be your arm in the west?"

"My son. Didn't you just say that yourself?" Edward frowned at Hobbes, then spoke to Richard. "I assure you, he practices better medicine than logic."

Hobbes held out a cup for a servant to pour hot cider. "How old are you now, sir?" he asked Richard.

"I was twenty last month."

The doctor turned to Edward again. "Your brother and your son hold parallel posts. Your son is two years old. I would have said the prince was your emblem, not your arm."

Richard studied the physician: better medicine than logic? If that were true, the man would have the dead on their feet in no time. He answered Hobbes's question. "Parliament approved a king's council to accompany the prince and remain in residence with him."

"And my good brother Anthony has agreed to serve as tutor and governor of the prince's household," Edward elaborated.

Hobbes looked over at Rivers. "Congratulations, sir." Anthony smiled, dipped his head in a small nod, and continued his strumming, eyes half-closed.

"It is difficult to imagine anyone better suited for that office," Hobbes was saying. "May we now hope for the possibility of having a scholar king again some day?"

Edward roared with laughter. "Scholar king! I would like to see what a scholar would have done on the field at Barnet. Any field."

"Charles the Great did well enough on the field."

"Charlemagne? You call him a scholar?"

"Indeed. And in the most difficult of circumstances. He was his own tutor."

"William, I never claimed to be a scholar. Why should I, when they come as cheap as tallow candles? No offense, brother."

"None taken, brother." Rivers struck a chord, and laid down the lute. He had lost the post of Calais, a position of considerable wealth and power, to accept the relatively humble office of tutor. To hold in trust the future king's person and mind. A man of longer purpose and vision than many credited him with, Richard realized.

Indeed, a man who did everything perfectly.

*London*
*December 1472. Vespers.*
*The fishpond is crusted with ice.*
    *The meal is cleared from the hall, and bones tossed down for the dogs.*
    *From the gallery, the voices of lute and flute, rebec and bells, and a young man's high pure tenor.*
    *The ladies gather to hear the traveler tell tales of Alhambra, of streets paved with gold.*

*I*t was a warm wet winter. Repeated thawings had left the roads in deep mire, and Richard had stayed in London.

"Bess! Where is your nurse?" Edward asked his eldest child as she stood by Richard's chair. She was six now, tall like her father, and pretty. "You should you be in bed."

"She said I was to find the Duke of Gloucester. That is you," Bess said confidently to Richard.

Richard leaned down. "She? Your nurse said to find me?"

"No, sir. A lady," Bess explained with complete self-possession. "She said you were to come with me."

Edward looked at Richard. "Well, no wonder you have been declining the good doctor's place at the chess table, brother, since you have a better game afoot."

Richard knew he was blushing. "I'll see what this is about."

He felt Doctor Hobbes's shrewd eyes measuring him as he got up and let Bess lead him from the solar.

Children seemed to like him, which surprised him, since he never knew what to say to them. They disturbed and delighted him, going unarmed into a hazardous future. This little girl, taking his hand and chattering brightly away, had an ease already that he had never had and probably never would. "I remember you," she said. "You used to live in the palace. Until you were married. Then you left. My mother doesn't like you, but my father does." She took him to a curtained alcove of the gallery and waited dutifully for him to part the curtain and step inside.

For a moment he did not recognize her. Then he did, and wondered why this woman he had failed, and who had given him his first child, ever reminded him of Anne.

"You are looking well." That was only partly true. Elinor was dressed richly, but her face had lost its softness.

"Thank you."

For a moment he was afraid. "Kate? Is she well?"

"Very well. I had heard you were married." She played with the tassel at the end of her belt.

"Yes. To Anne Neville." Which she surely knew. "What can I do for you?" Richard asked.

"Nothing. I am well provided for, as you know. And now, I, too, am married."

Certainly her dress, fur-trimmed crimson brocade, as well as her very presence at court, implied a change in station. "I thought you must be. I am pleased for you."

"Thank you."

Now they had exchanged a dozen words, and it seemed that they must have said everything there was to say. "Forgive me, lady, but why did you send for me?" Richard found himself avoiding using her name.

"Have you children?" Elinor asked.

"No."

"A pity." Her voice said the opposite.

"We were married in March. There will be a child in May."

"Ah, a trueborn child. Much better than a bastard."

"I care for Kate."

"Oh, yes. I am certain you will even find a husband for her when the time comes. A suitable match for a bastard. Wealthy enough, and of good family. And old."

Richard began to understand. "As is your husband?"

"Of course, as is my husband. Who but a man old enough to have to pay for beauty would take a poor tavern-keeper's daughter with another man's child?"

Richard grew cold. "Bitterness does not become you."

The small gallery they were in was just off one of the lesser-traveled passageways. Footsteps approached, and they waited until they passed. "You wanted something I could never give, and didn't promise," he said, less harshly.

"No. I know you could never have married me, and we have both grown beyond childish fancies. But surely you are lonely sometimes." She risked a smile at him.

"Whether or not I am lonely, I am married."

"You are here, and your wife is in the north."

"I have no skill for such intrigue, lady. Nor any wish to learn it." His words sounded pompous and stiff in his own ears.

"I see. Very well." She didn't seem surprised at his refusal, seemed almost to have expected it. "Will you still support your daughter, now I am married?"

"Of course. Your marriage doesn't change her parentage, so far as I ever heard. How does your husband treat her?"

"He tolerates her. She is a pretty child, as you know, and it is easier than if she were a boy."

"Tolerates her. What does that mean?"

"He is not a harsh man. I have never seen him strike her. I doubt he loves her—she is not his child." A look of sadness softened her face and made him remember how lovely she had seemed when he was, truly, lonely. "But what would you, my lord? We did not think of that when we lay together."

Richard wanted to touch her, just her hand, acknowledge the bond that once joined them, and still did, through Kate, but was reluctant to risk being misunderstood. "I want Kate with me."

"Now?"

Would he like that? Yes, but that would surely be an ill-timed gesture, now while Anne was carrying. "No. When she is a little older. I will send for her later, if you agree."

*H*e was back at Middleham for the birth of his son, whom they named Edward. Richard marveled at the perfect hands, the curled toes like rows of tiny shrimp. How was it possible the seed of a man was contained in such a creature?

Everything was done for Ned as it should be for health and long life. The nurse of irreproachable virtue to feed and bathe him. His skin soothed with oil of myrtle, to ease his passage into this world, and his little limbs swaddled to help them grow straight and true. Sleeping, even by daylight, in darkened rooms, lest the light dazzle his eyes, but near the hearth. Let him sleep there as much as he would, to concentrate the warmth in his inner parts—heart, lungs, and brain so they would grow strong. For a man's extremities could grow no stronger than his center, from whence his spirit arises. Who has not noticed how hands and feet grow chill when they doze, all the heat moving inward? The body must protect its core.

When he creeps, have him followed closely, lest he creep into fire or water, bright glistening elements any child would want to touch. Or eat. And while man has humors made up of all of these and more, they must be acquired and balanced with care, not gathered in his hands and stuffed down his gullet, like a peasant's coarse meal.

Alice came to Middleham soon after Ned's birth, escorted north by Sir James Tyrrel, a lifelong soldier formerly in Edward's service. Tyrrel had eyes of a pure dark blue underhung with pouches of hard-living and drinking, a quick mind, and an inexhaustible supply of stories. He and Alice were fast friends by the time they arrived.

Alice embraced her daughter and bowed her head just perceptibly to Richard. "I understand I owe you my release. I am grateful." There was a coldness in her voice that Richard had never heard before, even when he had called on her at the abbey.

He replied in like manner. "This was your estate before it was mine. I am honored to have you here."

Alice turned away, blinking back tears.

There were no tears when she came to him the next day. "Richard. I could not reproach you yesterday, in front of the others, when I am so truly grateful for your efforts in allowing me to return here. *But what have you done?*"

"Lady?"

"Sir James tells me that *all* my estates are now in your name."

"Yes."

"*My* estates. Not my husband's. I did not believe him. I couldn't believe that you would ask for such a thing, nor that Edward would grant it."

"Edward was not easy to persuade."

"Not easy! Do you mean to say you take pride in what you have done? I almost thought I could expect fairness from you, but you are as poisoned by greed as every other fool who has raised his sword in the past twenty years.

"Or is it fear? Are you afraid that with my own lands I would raise armies against you? I assure you, Richard, I want no new strife in my husband's name."

"Alice. Please sit down. Consider this. How many daughters have you?"

"Do not be malapert, Richard! That you are married to my daughter and in possession of most of my wealth does not give you license for discourtesy."

"I mean no discourtesy. As I see it, you have two daughters. I am married to one; the other is married to my brother George."

"Oh." Alice took the chair he had offered, and they looked at each other in complete understanding. Richard need not have continued, but he did. "I think George could take from you more than he can take from me. Welcome, countess."

*A*nne had taken to bringing her needlework into the chamber where Richard worked, and they engaged in their separate tasks in amicable silence.

She walked to the open west windows, where the sun streamed in. "It is a fine day," she said.

"It is," Richard agreed, bent over his writing table.

"A fine day for riding."

He looked up. "Why do you not? There is no urgency in your fancy work, is there? Take some companions; perhaps your mother would like to go with you."

"I may."

But she sat down in the window, her embroidery idle in her lap. Richard wondered if she had something she wanted to discuss with him, but she was silent, and he returned his attention to the stack of letters and petitions before him. Of course, as soon as he had done that, she spoke.

"What do you read?" she asked.

"The usual complaints and petitions."

"What, in particular?"

"In this particular—" he said, looking up from the letter in his hands, "—the City of York is fining a certain Timothy Brandon for his fishgarths."

"Fishgarths? They were outlawed."

"Yes." The huge skeins clogged the river traffic and made the smaller nets of poor fishermen useless. The church alone retained legal use of them. "But this man is using them, nevertheless. His letter," Richard lifted it, "says he was my tenant once, and that I will surely recall him and speak of his fine nature and honorable intent before the council."

Anne laughed. "You could."

"You remember him, then?"

"Yes."

"Should I know him?"

"Perhaps, my lord."

He was beginning to understand her language. *Richard* was simple and direct, herald to a message that needed no translation. *My lord* was either formality or mockery. In either case, he wanted to shake her. "Well, what will help you decide? It seems that the fact that I am your lord is of little account just now."

"If you want my help, my lord, you must buy it."

"At what price, lady?" He could play the same game.

"You must tell me this; what will end the matter soonest?"

He tried to read her face. He could see mischief in her eyes, but mixed with an odd wistfulness. "What do you mean?"

"This. If I do not advise you, will you forget about the matter long enough to ride with me, or will you stay here thinking until your memory returns? On the other hand, if I answer your questions, will you reward me with your company, or will my service only allow you to be all afternoon solving the quarrel?"

Oh. A great many words to tell him something simple; she wanted him to put up his work and come with her. Why did she not just say so? He leaned back in his chair and considered his wife.

Unsure of their love, she had to poke and prod it as though it was a sleeping badger, to see how it moved before she decided if it was a creature she wanted to stalk. As he watched, the mischief receded from her face, and he saw only a cautious hope, at once guarded and naked, that her tenuously requested favor would not be rejected. Where had he seen that face before? Lord. In the mirror of his imagination, that was where, when he considered how he must appear to her.

He laughed and stood up. "You are as guileful as a lawyer, Teasel. Come. Let's ride."

*L*ove, like all Gaul, was divided into three parts—lust, liking, and courtesy, in approximately equal measures. Add a little jealousy, fruit of a wary heart. That is what he once thought, but no one ever loved by rote and reason. He remembered the moment he learned the price that love demanded, and it was nothing. Hardly a word was spoken, not a touch exchanged. He had come back from Sheriff Hutton a day earlier than he had expected by riding late into the evening. He could hear Anne calling to her lady before he reached the top of the stairs.

"Oh, Joan. . . ." There was such anguish in her voice that he ran up the last steps into the room. Anne was bent over the coffer in which she stored the goods from which her gowns were made. "Moths have gotten into the wool!"

When she looked up and saw who had come in, her dismay disappeared. She smiled, and there was a light in her eyes and a look on her face as if she had just swallowed something delicious and the taste of it still lingered on her tongue. Richard stood there considering the import of what he saw, then smiled back. He wanted to call the world in as witness: *Do you see that woman, the radiance in her face? I am the one who put it there.*

So love induced his vanity that easily. Just let one smile warm at the sight of him, one pair of eyes linger on his face, so long as they were the right smile and eyes, and soon a man would believe how wise he was, how handsome. And only wonder that the world did not see it sooner.

## Middleham Castle
## September 1473.

Richard stayed awake late planning the winter's border campaign. The previous year's tally: four hundred beasts stolen, run off, or otherwise lost. Fifty prisoners taken. Ten men wounded, five men and one woman killed. Six houses burned. Only God knew how much other property was lost or destroyed.

The coming season promised no better. Two signal towers were burned—in the summer, before the raiding season even properly started—and in daylight, when one of them had a watchman in it. One farmer missing half his cattle, and an eye, too, when he had the poor judgment to try alone to apprehend the raiders.

Why did they not tire of these feuds? The men rode and killed with a craving for vengeance as demanding as hunger. The women grieved for lost sons and husbands with wild lamentations that spoke of astonishment as well as outrage. As if death were not the constant companion of such habits, the only real question being what form it would take.

He knew what he would see. Burned huts. Bitter women and hollow-eyed children. Hanged men turning from their ropes, heads curled down from broken necks like question marks: Why? The inevitable, implausible question. Evidence in plenty that earthly joy was a fragile thing.

That struck him, that thin edge where those two faces of the blade of loving met, and he did not know which was sharper—the overwhelming delight in what was his, or the certain knowledge that what was loved could be lost. His wife and his son. The whole beautiful, bloody north. His own life, which he suspected he was beginning to value inordinately, for a knight pledged to service.

He put down the quill, picked up the candle and went into the inner chamber, where Anne lay sleeping. Parting the curtain, he leaned down and touched her shoulder. "Come," he said. "I want to show you something."

She woke quickly. "What is it? Is something wrong?"

"No. But come. You can only see this in the dark."

Richard took her, sleepy but obliging, out on the rampart, and stood with his arm around her. The night sky was as black, and the stars as brilliant, as he had ever seen them. There was a murmur of wind, and the short, breathy *ooo, ooo* of the owls from the coppice. Then came a single long quavering note, eerily beautiful, as haunting as a lover's sigh, and after, a silence that was absolute until he finally spoke. "Did you ever come out here?"

"Isabel and I played here all the time. We were told not to, but we did. In the daytime. Who would come here at night?"

"I did. When I was first fostered here. I used to come up here and dream that this was all mine—the castle, the stars, everything, as far as I could see."

Anne was not awed. She huddled deeper into her fur robe and leaned against him, yawning. "And now it is. All but the stars."

"No," he said, kissing her temple, and her skin was as cool and fragrant as the night. "Them, too."

# 16  *The Eyes of Cats*

*Jervaulx Abbey*
*1473.*

Richard had ridden to Jervaulx soon after he arrived at Middleham. The fine mist in which he had set out turned to a steady drizzle before he reached the abbey. Brother Simon was the same sun-reddened little man Richard remembered from his boyhood, if more wrinkled, his Adam's apple a more pronounced knob.

"Well, Master Richard! Although I suppose that is not a title I should use now, is it?"

"It will do, Brother, it will do. How do you fare?"

"Oh, well enough. These old bones should last a few more winters. But here, we are getting wet. Come into the hut." Simon stopped suddenly. "Perhaps you would rather go in to the abbey."

"There would be a fire on the hearth?"

"On a day like today, of course."

"And some of your excellent wine, hot and spiced, which you offered me very little of when I was a lad?"

"Indeed."

"And one or two chairs with cushions on them, that I would not mistake for the hardness of my saddle?"

"Yes," the Brother said, sighing.

"Then the choice is clear. Who but a woman or an invalid would choose such ease when he could test his endurance with rain and cold and misery? Brother, you have not changed at all! I feared age would have softened you."

Simon laughed, delighted. "A man cut from my own cloth. I knew the city could not have taken the country from your soul." Walking into the shed, he said, "I don't go indoors if I can help it, myself, while the sun is up. Except for my devotions, of course. I would not have you think I neglect those."

"Of course not."

The hut, low-roofed and leaking, was divided into two sides by a wooden gate. On one side was a stall with straw, a grain bin, and water bucket. The other held a bench and a battered table on which stood containers of powered herbs, jars of ointments, and purgatives for the Brother's beloved sheep. Simon kicked a stool out from under the table for Richard and sat down on the bench. "Well, once in a while I forget, if you hold me to the absolute truth. "

"If that is your worst sin, Brother, you will have a place among the saints."

"Well, that's as may be." He leaned forward and rested his elbows on his knees. "Let me look at you now—the small apprentice come back as lord. How do you find Middleham after all these years?"

"Very well, for the most part. Warwick left it in honest hands. I had to turn out a couple of retainers who had grown corrupt, and tend to some of the outbuildings, but the castle was in excellent repair and the larders not robbed bare."

"Your tenants were glad to have a lord again, I'm sure."

"The first month I was here, they all came with a sample of their plantings or livestock, to show me how fine their crops would be. Now, just the reverse. They bring every complaint and ailment for my consideration." Richard shook his head and shifted his position out of the way of a drip. "Now that I have been here a while, they seem to think I have supplanted God in the matters of sun and rain. Henceforth, any decline in their production will not be due to their labors, but to God."

"Isn't that the way of it? It makes me glad of my sheep. They are docile tenants. And what about you? Are you all soldier now, or is there still some shepherd in you?"

"Shepherd?"

"Do you not remember the day you and the Percy lad found my sheep for me?"

"I remember it very well. We thought we had found your supper."

"And were distressed for it, as I recall. I never saw lads go so long-faced as the two of you did."

"So you want to know if I remember the sheep. Bennett wants to know if I remember Virgil. Only Giles is satisfied. He thinks I remember everything he taught me, since I am still alive. He takes all the credit for that. If all the north were so easily pleased, this office would be simple, wouldn't it?"

"I suppose you must know it won't be. A year ago the Scots raided and burned as far south as Durham. They must have thought it was a fine time to try their luck, your brother not having had much time to get his kingdom under him again. The fleas go to the dog while he's down, they say. Or maybe I'm getting old, and the fighting only seemed worse than other years."

"It was bad enough," Richard said. "I was on the borders then."

"Were you? That close and you never rode here?"

"No offense, Brother. My own affairs were still not settled, and I needed to return to London as soon as I could. Anyway, I wasn't entirely clear where I would be welcomed."

"Nor are you yet, I imagine. If it is any consolation, the people here are probably wondering as much about you as you are about them."

"I come with no grudges. My brother wants peace and their present loyalty, no matter who they fought for."

"So you intend to do justice. Now that is a truly fine and noble ambition." Simon leaned back against the wall and clasped his hands across his slightly increased girth. "Tell me, what do you imagine justice to be, here?"

"What are you asking me?"

"Well, now. Look at us. We sit in this hut and look out at the rain. It's pleasant enough when we know we could have four walls around us and a fire to warm ourselves if we chose to walk across the cloister. But you have seen the huts of some of the border people. Turf and stone, hardly more time to build than to knock down. What do they know of justice and the king's peace?"

"I have no quarrel with them. They are not making the raids."

"No. But how do you tame the reivers when the country doesn't care? It's all the same to them, who rides over their pitiful hovel. And all the same to the Percys and Grahams whether it's you or King Jamie who hangs them."

Richard shrugged. "That is an old lament and one I doubt I will cure. But you were asking me about justice. I would say it was the same here as anywhere."

"Ah, not at all, my poor lad. I would have a heavy conscience if I let you leave me today with that delusion."

"Oh? A riddle, then? I thought you were a plain-spoken man, Brother, but you sound just like Bennett. Well, let me think.

"To those on the English side, it is only just for me to hang every Scot I see. And for the Scots, it must be for me to turn every thief I catch back to King James, who will let them go to ride again. Is that what you mean?"

"Well said. But add this. Henry Percy will insist that justice means that neither you nor Jamie will see the half of what he does."

"Then since no one up here can agree on what justice is, I can call it what I will."

Brother Simon pulled at his chin. "That's what most of the wardens have done. They left here richer than they came, lawfully or not. Although for many of them, their next abode was not such as they could take their wealth, however it was acquired."

"Only a jest," Richard said. Then he remembered there was indeed an old and honored precept of service, one to which he subscribed, and he said it out loud. "*Render unto Caesar that which is Caesar's*. I suppose that is what it comes down to."

"Oh, excellent. If you know what is Caesar's. But I'll tell you one thing beyond all doubt: there has been only one misdeed on the border since the days of Adam."

"Another riddle, Brother?"

"I assure you that is truth. One misdeed since the beginning of time. All that has followed since then is reprisal, fair payment for injuries done. Of course, opinions differ on who committed that first offense." He chuckled and rapped a callused hand on Richard's knee. "I'll tell you the proverb you should remember."

"Brother?"

"In the eyes of cats, all things belong to cats."

## Scotland

### 1474.

The bastle house stood on a rocky outcropping above bleak fells laced by cold, swift-running streams. It was built of stone and mortar, three stories tall, the ground floor for the sheep and cattle. The human quarters were reached by an outside stairway on the lee side of the building. If such an arrangement was inconvenient for the householder rising in the middle of the night to tend a birthing ewe, it was decidedly more convenient for defending the house against marauders. The first floor was a primitive living area with shuttered unglazed windows and hearth running nearly the length of one wall. Overhead, footsteps of the household's women and children whispered through the upper floor chambers.

*W*ell, sir, they have me son." Hugh Ridpath was a corpulent man with heavy jowls and a surprisingly small thin voice. "My fair son Davy, who was always a respecter of peace and no common thief."

Richard recalled Davy as a tall young man, not so fat as his father, but no paragon of manhood, either, quick of temper and slow of wit.

"Where, exactly, was your Davy taken?"

"How do I know where the murdering bastards took him? Do you think I would be here talking if I knew where he was?"

"My lord means," Francis said, "where was Davy when he was abducted?"

Ridpath blinked. "How should I know that?"

"Let me simplify it," Francis said. "North of here, or south. He was riding to London, perhaps?"

"North, you fool. What business had my Davy in London?"

"In Scotland, then?" Richard asked.

"Perhaps. What does it matter?"

"Scotland. Then since he was not on English soil, we must determine whether he was truly abducted, or apprehended in a criminal act. He was not stealing cattle when he was taken?"

"My lord! He was in hot trod. The law provides the right to regain stolen goods."

"What goods was he pursuing?"

"Six oxen. Some other kine."

"When were these taken? I have received no reports of cattle stolen from this region in recent weeks."

"Nay, my lord. They were taken in the spring."

Hot trod, indeed, Richard thought. Then I am John the Baptist. "Ridpath, you know the law. You have two days, *days*, mind you, to pursue your goods. After that, you report the loss to me or my agent. When you hunt down thieves later than that, it is considered a new raid, and your Davy is subject to the same terms of punishment as any thief." As if Ridpath didn't know that. As if that made any difference.

"They were his cattle. Last March. Now. What does it matter?"

"Oh come, man. They may have been his cattle once, but now they are no more than skins in a doorway. Count on it. What's to be gained? Do you think he can restore his loss from any stock that strikes his fancy?"

Richard turned from Ridpath to Rob Percy, who stood holding the letter that had caused Ridpath to summon them. "Well, Rob?"

"They want two thousand crowns—in coin, not chattel—to release such a villain. Otherwise, they say they will leave a part of Davy over every league of his murderous trail."

"Whose seal?"

"Ralph Kerr."

Kerr. One of the greatest landowners in Liddesdale. Also one of the greatest plunderers. Why couldn't Davy at least have picked a lesser man to offend?

"Well?" Richard asked Ridpath. "Are you going to pay the ransom?"

"Me?"

"He's your son."

"The duty of the warden is to protect the citizenry." Ridpath's voice managed to sound both pathetic and threatening.

"Sir Hugh. Do you think I can empty the coffers to bring home every man in Scotland who ought never to have been there in the first place?"

"So you won't pay for my son's life."

"I would not pay for any man's son under these circumstances."

"You will let them murder him, then." Ridpath shifted in his chair, rearranging his belligerent bulk.

"I didn't say that. There might be other ways." Richard walked to the hearth and took the letter from Rob's hand. There had better be other ways. If he didn't find a way to retrieve this fool's son, Ridpath would shake loose the border. And that would do no warden's reputation any good.

"Blood of Christ!" Ridpath laid his hand over his heart. "You don't mean the mighty Duke of Gloucester will ride to Scotland and play reiver, himself?"

"Perhaps."

"And these nights as black as a witch's heart. You cannot see your hand in front of your face."

"There'll be moonlight again."

*A* cold gray rain blotted out the sun—and the moon and the stars— for a week. The bastle house, windows shuttered against the weather, hearth burning high against chills and darkness, reeked of peat smoke and too many bodies in too small a space. Deprived of current exploits, the inhabitants amused themselves by telling stories of past deeds and fighting themselves over trifles.

*Eight men you stood off? Bones of God, you lie. It was only six, and if it had not been for me—*

*Say I lie, do you? You, who cheated me out of the best bull I ever bred!*

Children were beaten for nothing, then hit again for crying. The woman who came between two men threatening to settle their dispute with knives got a sliced hand for her efforts, and yelled at for bleeding into one man's bitter cider.

Richard picked up his cloak and hat. Whatever the weather outside, it could not be more disagreeable than this endless sitting and waiting. A blast of cold air came into the room when he opened the door and went out.

He walked down the path that would, if he followed it far enough, wind down from the crag where the house stood to the fells below, or, by its other branch, along the causeway snaking north. He had gone nearly to the fork when he realized someone was behind him. He turned and saw Francis following, head and shoulders bent against the drizzle.

"What are you doing here?" he asked, as Francis caught up to him. "You hate the cold."

"I hate the smoke and stink, too. For a comfort-loving man, there is little to choose between. I thought my company might cheer you."

"Then pray for sun. Good weather would cheer me."

"You don't think the Scots will ride again until the weather changes?"

"Would you, if you were them?" He didn't wait for an answer. "Anyway, we need the moonlight, even if they don't." He thought about crossing all the bogs and mires between the bastle house and Scotland on a black night: there were a hundred ways he'd rather die.

"This place breeds a ghoulish lot, if you ask me," Francis said. "Do you know what one of them told me just before I came out? Davy will die if he's not dead already."

"Oh? Why did he say that?"

"He dreamed last night of a raven. Of course, the mist and clouds could tell us things, too. Shall I read your future?"

"As long as it's amusing."

Francis shook his head. "It's not precisely amusing, but it's true. You can't expect both from a prophecy." He extended his arm and pointed a finger into the mist. The fells below were nearly invisible. "There. That slight parting of the fog. Did you see it?"

"No."

"You must look quickly to catch these things."

"Well, what does it say?"

"The message was clear. After Davy's death, Ridpath makes bloody war on every householder from here to Liddesdale. In the midst of the wailing and crying that follows, Ridpath complains to Henry Percy that when the Percys were the wardens here, such things never happened. In short, he'll make as much trouble for as many people as possible. Especially you," Francis said cheerfully.

"What's eating you?" Richard asked.

"What isn't?" Francis said. "Nothing. I'll be fine once we can move again."

When the rains stopped, they rode west, watching the hills for warnings of raiders—lanterns hung from peel towers, sheets spread out on the hillsides or blowing from trees. But in the end, when the mist cleared for a day, they saw only the wisps of smoke rising in the sky like spirits in a graveyard.

When they reached the site, the stone walls were still standing but fire had gutted the interior. The roof and supporting beams were a rubble of ashes and still-smoldering fragments; the carcass of a sheep lay beneath one end of a fallen timber, and the smell of decaying flesh and wet wool mixed with the odor of burnt wood. At least there were no people dead in their own cottage. Or, worse, half dead.

They left the ruined cottage and led their horses to the stream to drink and graze along its banks. Half the men knelt down to drink, scooping the clear icy water of the stream in their hands, the others holding the horses, watching carefully all about them. There was a light wind in the trees, rising and falling, sighing through the leafless branches. The pebbled brook glinted golden brown in the sunlight; a few bronze leaves skimmed its surface. Rob, his hands cupped before his face, his attention caught upstream, was suddenly very still.

"Richard," he said quietly. Heads whirled in the direction of his glance, and hands straying around the hilts of knives tightened their grips. There was no one, only a patch of color—a dull dark blue— sometimes showing through the dry grass blowing in the distance, a too-solid shape.

James Tyrrell ran downstream, half in the brook, splashing water up in rainbow drops, and Richard followed, the rest staying where they were, watching closely left and right, high and low.

A man lay in the stream, body on the bank, face in the water. Tyrrell pulled the body out and turned it over, and the bloated eyes stared up. An old man, gray-haired and poorly fed, his bony chest showing through the open neck of his shirt.

"What wounds?" Richard asked.

"None." Tyrrell shook his head.

"What killed him? Fright?"

"Drowned, I'd say."

"Drowned? In this?"

"Deep enough if someone held him down."

Householders resisted the raiders, otherwise provoked them, or got in the path of destruction. They were shot down, or burned alive in their houses if they were foolish enough not to abandon everything they had. But this—to hold an old man's face in the water until he drowned. For what? Sport?

"Leave him," Richard said. "Time we were away from here."

*T*he moon was so bright they could see shadows. Rob touched him lightly on the arm. Richard turned, asking the question with his eyes. Rob held out one hand, fingers spread wide. Once, then again, the second time holding down the small finger with his thumb. Eight men: a small party. The second piece of luck. The first had been that they had been able to reach the glade well ahead of the raiders. Richard could hear faintly now the scrabble of hooves, cattle lowing.

They waited in the moonlight behind rocks and trees until the raiding party was in their midst, perhaps twenty cattle with them. The horse of the lead rider tossed its head and the rider turned, watchful, then pricked his horse forward with a jingle of spurs.

A sword rang out, struck loud on rock, and the glade was suddenly full of Richard's men.

"Halt!" John Howard's booming voice. An arrow sang high overhead, followed by another clang of a sword struck on stone. That held their attention. For a moment. Whatever else you might say about the Scots, they were not cowards.

"Stay where you are and listen to me," John Howard shouted. "We don't want your wretched lives. Count yourselves fortunate. We could hang you here and now."

"Who speaks?"

"The warden's man. Put on your prettiest manners and you may live to return to Scotland."

One man did not like Howard's offer, wheeled his horse and spurred, bolting through the ring of horsemen. An archer waited just long enough to give the Scot a little distance from Richard's men.

Moonlight was hardly adequate for a true aim, but the man fell forward and dropped his reins, clutched his horse's neck and held, the arrow in his shoulder.

The other Scots reined in their horses, quieting them, standing still and listening over the grunts and bellowing of the cattle. One man spoke. "How do we know you are the warden's man, and by what right would you hang us? The law lets you take back any goods we have with us; that's the extent of it. If my man dies, you have murdered him."

Dawn was breaking. There was a faint apricot glow above the trees. One of Richard's men retrieved the wounded Scot's horse, the man still holding on, moaning. Richard stepped out into the clearing between two archers. "See for yourself who you are talking to. We found a man dead at the burned cottage. If we are talking of murder, it is you who will hang."

He walked closer to the Scot who had spoken, who appeared to be the chief of the raiders, older and gray, tall on his horse.

"Get down," Richard said. The man looked around, then dismounted. He kept glancing to the wounded man.

"Who is he?" Richard asked.

"My son," the Scot said angrily. "What is that to you?"

"Nothing. Who are you?"

"Why would I tell you?"

"So I can let Ralph Kerr know who he is exchanging for Davy Ridpath. If he cares to make the trade. If not, so I know who I am trying for murder."

"What would it take for you to let us go free?" The man's voice was now serious, thoughtful.

"Two thousand crowns for the ransom, and another five hundred for our trouble."

The man put back his head and laughed. "If I had so much money, do you think I would be riding for cattle?"

"I'm not so rich, either, that I can afford to buy thieves' freedom. So you stay with us. Tell your men to throw down their weapons. You don't want them to dismount; your son needs to get to safety if he is to survive."

When they had on the ground a heap of lances, swords, and knives, Richard said, "Now, sir, you will tell me who you are."

"Christopher Burn."

"Of Dryhope?"

The Scot nodded.

Richard knew the name, decided to keep him and three others as hostages, and let the other man return with Burn's wounded son. Four thieves in exchange for Davy. A good night's work.

"Do you know Lord Kerr?" he asked.

"Yes."

"Ralph Kerr?"

"I know of him."

"Do you know where to find him?"

"Yes."

"Then send your men back with this message. We will meet with him for an exchange of prisoners, of which Davy Ridpath must be one, in a fortnight."

"Where?"

"In this clearing. Noon."

The Scot made a sound of disgust. "In England. You expect him to ride into England."

"You're in England yourself, man."

"At night! We'd have been into Scotland by now."

"Then tell Kerr to ride in daylight like an honest man. He'll be safe enough."

They rode back to the bastle house, heaved the prisoners up the stone stairs and pounded on the door. The inside was as dark and smoky as before. The captives were pushed none too gently into the room. On the floor, in the corner of the dim room, was a child, a boy about eight years, with bound wrists and dark circles under his eyes.

"*What have you done?*"

"Secured my son's life."

"Who is the boy?"

"Oh, this one is a prize, sir. Laird Armstrong's eldest son."

"Ridpath, you fool. We have prisoners to exchange for your son. I don't hold with the kidnapping of children."

"Ah, but you see, sir, I could not be sure who would return with prisoners, let alone any important enough to free my Davy. Now I can rest easy." Ridpath hooked his thumbs over his belt, and stood with his elbows out, his weight thrust forward on the balls of his feet.

"If the child is hurt in this, there will be Hell to pay, and you will pay most of it, I promise you. Armstrong's family will be on yours like hounds onto the kill. You know that, Sir Hugh." Richard ran his hand through his hair, collecting his temper. He'd be lucky if the Armstrongs did not ride before the exchange could be made. "Well, you have him now. We'll take him back with the others. We must get word to Armstrong."

"You'll send a man?"

"No, Sir Hugh. *You* will send a man, and do it quickly."

The Scots lined one side of the clearing, some mounted, some on foot, the English on the other side. Small high clouds moved overhead as the four raiders and the Armstrong child stepped out from the shadow of tall pines into the sunlight of the meadow. Young Ridpath and two other prisoners advanced from the other side. A breeze shifted the grass and dry leaves whispered on the ground. Another sound came as the prisoners advanced, clean and quick, a plucking as distinctive as harpstring. Every man there knew the sound; no one wanted to believe it.

Davy dropped to his knees in the meadow, then pitched forward onto his face. A six-foot lance was in his back, a dark spreading stain on his shirt. There was an instant of silence, a moment's respite from disaster, then Ridpath gave out a roar and ran into the meadow, followed by several of Richard's men. The Armstrong child stood terrified and wailing an arm's length from Davy. Richard spurred his horse and swept the child up onto his saddle as Ridpath reached his son. He glanced at the inert body and headed for the Scots, sword raised. Rob and two other of Richard's men hurled themselves on Davy's father.

Ridpath strained against his captors, his face contorted with rage, the tendons in his neck standing out like cords. "Bastards!" he screamed. "Filth!"

272

The Scots had their weapons raised, hands halted in the very act of hurling spears. Now they all, Scot and English, stood warily watching each other. A second reprieve, there wouldn't be a third. Richard pressed the child closer against his body, his knife against the boy's throat. He could feel the heart pounding in the thin little chest.

"Put up your weapons. Strike, any of you, and the boy dies." The warning was meant for his own men, as well as the Scots.

The Kerr chieftain slid his knife back into its keeper, lifted one hand, palm up. Spears and swords were lowered, and Richard felt it pass, that moment when their lives hovered on a knife's edge. He sheathed his knife and slid from his horse, the child under one arm. He set the boy on the ground and shoved him toward the leader. "For God's sake, get him out of here."

He looked around among the Scots. "Who threw the spear?" The chieftain brushed the boy behind him and took a small step back. The others shifted, almost imperceptibly. One man stood his ground.

Man? Boy, Richard thought. A fair-haired youth with a dusting of freckles across a sunburned face. Richard turned away and walked over to Davy. He pulled the lance from the body and returned to the Scot. "This is yours?"

"Yes."

"Why did you do it?"

A stony-faced silence.

"You murdered an unarmed prisoner at the moment of exchange. I want to know why."

"It's no murder. He killed my uncle."

Richard nodded. "You have a good arm."

"A child could have done it."

The boy's voice was contemptuous, but it was true: what the long-bow was to the English, the lance was to the Scots. A good Scot on horseback could spear a salmon slithering in the stream.

"Yes," Richard said, "except that a child would have known better."

There was no comprehension in the boy's face, only a bewildered rage. How could it be otherwise? He was probably all of fifteen, nursed on tales of revenge and never weaned. Richard wiped the sweat from his face. Damn the boy. It was almost done, the prisoners returned, everyone alive. No new pages in the annals of blood.

"Your aim is admirable, but you were foolish. Foolish because now you must die, too. You have committed a capital offense and the penalty is death." He wanted the boy to understand. *If I don't kill you now, Ridpath will, and many more of your kin, besides. And those deaths will have to be avenged, too, and I won't be able to stop any of it.*

"Bind him." Richard directed two of his men to tie the boy's hands behind his back. Collect the pound of flesh now, and be done.

"Gloucester!" He turned. Ridpath's wrathful face.

"What?"

"I would execute him."

"You would be the hangman, Sir Hugh?"

"Hanging! By the rood, no. I'll kill him inch by inch."

"No." Richard turned away. "Rob, get a rope over that tree."

"Do we have one stout enough for hanging?"

"*Find one!*"

"Gloucester, I beg you!"

"Sir Hugh?"

"It is my right to execute him. I claim that for my Davy."

Richard looked at him. "Very well. You will have your revenge. But your son was one life. You take one life. Do you understand?"

"Christ, yes. What do you take me for?"

The young Scot was led across the meadow. He stumbled as he walked, lurching from one foot to the other. Once his legs gave out entirely, and Rob had to help him to his feet. Finally the boy stood before Ridpath, who waited with sword in hand. The young man positioned himself with his feet apart, knees locked as if to keep his legs from shaking, and a tremor along his jaw, but he lifted his chin, trying to keep the mask of contempt in place.

"Sir Hugh. One last thing." Richard spoke quietly. "One thrust and be done. Play with him, and I will leave you to the Scots. You have my word on it."

Ridpath gave him a look of burning hatred.

Two men held the archer, one on either side. The boy stood calmer now, neither straining against his captors nor supported by them. Ridpath lifted his sword, pressed the point to the Scot's stomach, kept pressing slowly, almost gently, until a circle of blood the size of a coin appeared on the tunic. The boy looked down, as if surprised, then raised his eyes to Ridpath; they stared at each other, neither wavering. All the while Ridpath made the infinitely slow press of his sword. Richard couldn't have said for certain it moved, except that he could see the tendons along the boy's jaw and neck twitch and tighten as the blade invaded his body.

"Sir Hugh!" Richard said sharply.

Ridpath bore the sword home, rammed it in and twisted the weapon savagely upward. Blood gushed from the boy's mouth. He sagged between Rob and the other man holding him. They eased him to the ground, where he writhed a moment then lay still.

There was a great stillness in the meadow, everyone frozen in place. The prisoners, except for the child, stood aside in a little knot, looking shocked and shame-faced, as if they had somehow contributed to the young man's death.

"What do we do now, sir?" One of Richard's men asked.

*Let the dead bury the dead.* He had never understood what that meant. The prisoners were the first to move, slowly, to their own side. Ridpath knelt beside Davy and pressed his son to his breast. Two Scots came for the dead boy and carried him away. "We go home."

Francis brought Richard's horse, his face troubled. *It's not your fault, friend. Your prophecy didn't cause this.* Ridpath's men were wrapping Davy in their cloaks and heaving him over the back of his horse. Richard rested his forearm on his saddle and laid his face against it. Then he gathered his reins and pulled himself up into his saddle. He could not have spared the young Scot. He thought of the Scots behind him and Ridpath's look of hate.

If he got an arrow in the back, he would not even be sure from which side it came.

When he rode in with his men, Anne was in the courtyard, breathless from running down to greet him. Night was falling, snow coming down hard. He dismounted and she walked toward him, and he could see from her face how glad she was to see him. He knew she hoped he would respond in kind, but everything felt strange—the quiet night, the snow-dusted castle, her.

There was snow in her hair. Richard said her name and embraced her. His attempt to return to himself she mistook for an invitation, reached up, and, a hand on either side of his face, wiped the snow from under his eyes with her thumbs, as if she were sculpting clay, then drew his face down to hers. He felt her lips on his cheek, then, astounded, her tongue at the corner of his eye, dissolving a clump on his lashes. Something shifted inside him; he took Anne's hands in his and held them, hard, in his own. She looked startled, then alarmed. He felt the fierceness inside him and knew he must be hurting her. In the moment before he relaxed his grip, he felt safe, knew there was nothing strange here, nothing that could not be met.

# 17  *Unwritten Letters,*
## *Unspoken Words*

*August 29, 1475.*

### Richard, Duke of Gloucester
### to
### Anne of Gloucester

*T*his journey has been a bitter one, but the "war" with France is over, and we will be transported soon.

We have little to show for coming here, although both Will Hastings and Edward tried to explain to me how wrong I am, and what we have profited.

Gold, Will Hastings said.

That is true. Some of us have gold.

Peace, as Edward claims?

Of course. If we can trust the word of Louis of France.

Let's say I trust Louis as much as I would trust a Scot on a dark night.

But shame we have in plenty. We have not even left France, and already the ditties and riddles about English soldiers and meat pasties are flowing. Anywhere we walk, people either start to titter, or else hush what they were saying until we pass. Either way, it is clear that we are the subjects of great scorn.

*All will be well,* Will Hastings said, *we are alive and richer than before.* He said that to me the night before last, while the town was groaning under our soldiers' revelry, just before the mayor begged Edward to remove his men.

I wondered at first why Will, instead of Edward, came to talk to me. My first thought was that my brother was too embarrassed. I think now that I was wrong. I believe Edward sent Will because the matter was not important enough, nor my opinion in it, for my brother to bestir himself. Enough to warrant a small salve to his conscience, nothing more.

The first time I saw Edward, I was a child of seven; he was seventeen and seemed like a god. The next year he was king. For years, whenever I disagreed with his actions, I would ask myself what I overlooked that Edward saw, because the policy of so great a mortal must be right. That opinion changed so slowly over the years that I hardly noticed it and until today I had never taken a public stand against him.

We camped outside Amiens four days ago, and the culmination of this "war" took place some three miles downriver from the town, where the Somme was narrow enough that a structure could be easily built across it. Edward took me yesterday to see the bridge that was being constructed for today's ceremony. We rode in silence, already knowing each other's position on the matter.

This country is beautiful, Anne, nearly as green as England, but the light is different here—warmer and more golden. As we rode, I thought how peaceful the countryside was. Even the birds were quiet, and qualities like honor and disgrace seemed far away. But when we reached the spot and I saw the bridge with its ornate grillwork, the absurd corruption of this affair came back to me and I could not help asking Edward: Why? Why a bridge?

Why, he said, laughing, to have a place to stand, of course. We have to stand somewhere.

Of course. They cannot stand in the river. Nor in the heavens, since neither Edward nor Louis, whatever they may wish, is gifted with the powers of a sorcerer. And they would not stand anywhere else. Edward didn't trust the French enough to stand on French soil, nor would Louis come to our side of the Somme. So this treaty between the two greatest nations in the world was signed by their kings not on earth at all, but over air and flowing water. I pray it proves more substantial than either.

This morning, several hundred of our thousands of knights, archers, and soldiers were lined up along the causeway. The sun was bright after a brief rain, and the silver of the armor and the brilliant colors of our flags and banners were almost blinding in the light.

A splendid sight, you think? Well, it might have been, except that many of our men could hardly sit their horses; they were still reeling from the effects of four days' feasting and drinking. But we brought them all here, and we promised they would put on their armor and the aspect of soldiers. Now we can say that they have.

We can say it, but all the saying in the world does not make it other than it is. Besides the army, we brought with us weavers, gold-smiths, tapestry-makers, and pavilioners, as well as armorers, fletchers, saddlers, carters, bowyers, miners, and God knows who else. May He also know to what use we will put them, as there is now clearly no need to drape the halls of France in English mantles.

I stayed mounted, with my men on the banks of the Somme, as Edward, our brother George, Will Hastings, and two or three other noble lords walked out onto the bridge. All around me, men com-mented on how fine Edward looked, and how he put the French king to shame. I grant he did. Louis is a lumpy, misshapen man with a manner that manages to be both craven and arrogant. They call him the Spider. "Snake" would be more apt—a snake bulging with the remains of his latest prey. He was dressed in sad brown, as if to say, "Look how you English have ruined me," while Edward wore cloth of gold and a jeweled cap. But Edward has grown stout, even if he carries himself well, and his eyes are not as clear as once they were, although he was in much like company today.

My brother and his group approached the center of the bridge, which was divided from Louis' half by a grille, to prevent any would-be assassins of either nation from working mischief, although there were openings in the grille large enough for paper and quill to be exchanged. Edward and Louis faced each other, then Louis reached his hands through, as though he would embrace a long lost brother. Edward ignored the gesture and bowed deeply, once, then again, so Louis' hands were left flaying the air, like a prisoner grasping for a key just beyond his grasp.

I could hear nothing from my position and did not care, but the treaty was negotiated and signed. Later, the jest that traveled the camp was that, after Louis agreed to all of Edward's demands, he offered my brother two additional gifts: dining at court with the fairest of French ladies, and the loan of the Cardinal of Bourbon as confessor, to absolve any sins that might arise from such an occasion, the cardinal being not-ed for finding some particular sins singularly pardonable. Edward, far from being offended, laughed and thanked him for both offers.

Edward has sought war with France for three years. You will have heard all the reasons, and know that many believed they were good. The opportunities for landless lads and younger sons. The numerous misdeeds and treacheries of Louis the Spider. The greater ease for both England and Burgundy in commerce and safety in traveling the seas. Regaining England's ancestral holdings in France.

Whatever one's opinion of the seemliness of the war, one fact remains undeniable: Edward gathered huge numbers of men and great sums of money to fight the French, and did not honor his word. When we were still in London, men were already saying that Edward never intended to fight, but I believed in his word. Even when Parliament first granted the taxes he requested for raising the army, then insulted him by insisting the money be held in safekeeping by the church until the army actually embarked for France, I believed him. I was saying the same to my men a month ago on the shores of France.

Maybe it was true. Edward may have intended to fight, and present circumstances have changed his course. This is what I tell myself, although I don't know that it matters much. Either way, what I told my men proved a lie.

We sailed from England in good enough spirits—setting sail in itself was enough to ease men's doubts—and landed in Calais undeterred except for a hard rain. It was still raining when we marched toward Péronne, one of the Duke of Burgundy's towns, where we expected Charles to provide us with with lodging and provisions. And an army. But there was only Charles's messenger waiting on his horse outside the gate, who announced that Charles could not open the town to us and neither could he let us view his army, he was so embarrassed at its meager size and condition.

Embarrassed, Anne! We had come to make war with France, on Burgundy's behalf as well as on our own, and the summer is nearly over. Winter will be coming on, and our provisions are limited. Some of our men, including myself, were still weakened from seasickness, and we were all cold and wet and hungry. All this, and poor Charles cannot help because he is embarrassed!

Even so, my men's spirits held. They were angry, but anger can serve soldiers well enough. I prayed that the battle would come before the anger dissolved into discouragement and despair.

But then it began to be clear that, whatever his intentions had been at the beginning of the journey, Edward did not mean to wage war now. We had taken a few prisoners on the march, one of whom was a young man who had been a valet in Louis' household. Edward released him and sent him to his master with hands full of gold. A much duller man than Louis would have understood the message: the English could be bought.

So Louis sent food in plenty and wine in more than plenty. Then he opened the gates of Amiens and the doors of all the inns to our soldiers. The cost of goods and services was laid to the account of the King of France.

Our men, weary, restless, and disheartened, ate and drank themselves sodden. The drinking led to fighting, and the fighting to looting and worse. I was sick at what I saw. Shops and houses were destroyed. I saw a child dead in the street, run down by a horse; a man retrieved the small body, but not to claim it, only to place it out of the path of further destruction. Women were raped where they stood. I thank God you are in England, Anne. Had I a wife or family in the town that night, I would have locked them in the cellar and thrown the key in with them.

Finally, at the mayor's plea, Edward agreed to remove our soldiers, and posted guards at the gate. Afterward, Will Hastings said to me, *Take note, Richard. There is a lesson in this: discipline is easier to keep than to restore.*

There is something about Will and me that puts us off each other. We both know it. When he smiles, he looks as though his teeth ache to do it. I don't smile. We are courteous for Edward's sake, as well as our own, since our paths often cross.

To Will's credit, he did not participate in the disorder, although he seemed more amused than distressed by it. When he came to my tent later that night, he was calm and tolerant—but I could feel him condescend to me as a man stoops to a child. He looked pointedly at Francis, who shared my tent.

I would he stayed, I said.

*Very well,* Will said. *As you please.* Then he cleared his throat and went directly to the matter. *You disapprove of your brother's policy with France.*

If you think I have an opinion on that, Will, you have heard it from Edward himself. My views on this matter have not been for any ears but his.

*Ah. But you do not plan to attend your brother in greeting the King of France. You know, Richard, your position in our kingdom is well known, even in France, and your absence would appear very odd. As if the king did not have the support of his own brother, on whom he has bestowed such great riches.*

You have been misinformed, Will. I will not walk with Edward onto that bridge. I will not bow to Louis, and I will not take his gifts or his gold. But of course I will attend the signing of the treaty, and my men will present themselves in full battle array and whatever dignity they are still able to summon for the occasion.

*Which, if they follow the example of their commander, will be more than enough,* Will said, not unkindly. *Come, Richard! Far less blood has been shed—French or English—than if we had fought, and we will return with as much gold, possibly more. Where is the harm? Why must you make a great matter out of a little wine and brawling?*

It is curious how saying nothing is making a great matter, but I did not say that. I said, ill-advised or not, what I believe.

These are soldiers, Will. We brought them here to fight the French, and they came knowing they might equally find their fortune or die in the king's service, but if they died, it would be with honor. Apart from the damage they have done the citizens of Amiens, we have betrayed them. We have made fools and asses of our own men.

*It will be well,* Will said. *Wait and see. They may have come as soldiers, but they will leave with full purses and no broken limbs. I have seen few men's honor that could not be soothed by wealth and health.*

I think that it is not the soldiers whose purses will leave here the heavier.

I feared that I had said too much. But Will was only quiet, as if considering my words, then asked, *You will be there? The king has commanded it.*

Have no fear, Will. I would be there whether Edward commanded it or not. He is my brother.

I had a strange dream that night, so fearful that I woke sweating and shaking, more frightened than I have been since I was a child.

Recounted in daylight, and reduced to mere words, the dream is robbed of much of its power, so I doubt I can convey to you why it troubled me so much, but I will tell it to you.

I was standing on a hillside, and around me the land stretched endlessly, no trees or houses breaking the countryside. I was alone, except for a solitary horseman on the hill directly opposite me.

He rode along the crest of the hill, a dark profile against a white hot sky, from which the sun had drained all color, then turned and started toward me. As he approached, I could see that he was dressed in breeches, shapeless peasant's boots, and a rough hooded cloak. The hood fell forward, hiding his face, and his head was lowered, as if in weariness or great sorrow. The horse, however, moved at a brisk trot, ears pricked forward, and the contrast between the rider's weariness, and the horse's eagerness struck me. Then I thought—although the land was no actual place that I know, and God knows how I came to be there, myself—we are too far from any house or town for the horse to be so fresh. Therefore they are ghosts, but that thought did not alarm me; it seemed natural that they should be so. The rider guided the horse down the slope, on a narrow path through frieze and bracken, and there was something in the lowered head and the set of the shoulders that spoke of both a terrible grief and a relentless acceptance of it.

I stood and watched him approach. Move, some inner voice said. You don't have to wait for him. If you move now, before he knows you, it will be as if you were never here. But I did not move. I waited, at once longing for and dreading a glimpse of the man's face, certain that it was a face I would know, and that whatever he had come to say, he had come to say it only to me.

He rode to where I stood, reined in, and lifted a gloved hand in greeting, lifted his head, too, although his face was still in the shadow of the hood. I remember thinking, shouldn't there be light, at least in the eyes? The hand grasped the edge of the hood and started to pull it back, and it was then I began to be afraid. I thought: don't. I don't want to know you, after all. Go in peace.

But it was too late. The hood was back, and I saw why there was no light from the eyes. There were no eyes, only dark caverns in a gray skull. The skull was smooth and polished. So it is all right, I thought. This man died long ago, whatever killed him cannot hurt. But then, from the eye caverns, and onto his cheekbones came tears, and they lay there glistening like dew on rose petals, as astonishing as jewels.

Talk to me, I think I said, tell me what you want, but there was no sound from him, only the tears, and a feeling of an overwhelming sadness. I don't have to stay here, I remember thinking, but I could not leave, could not move my feet, and then I woke.

I told you, put into words, it does not sound such a terrible or terrifying thing—I never thought the creature wished me harm. But the sadness was so immense, an end-of-the-world grief, and I could not touch it or give comfort.

I don't know what it had to do with Edward, or France, or why I dreamed it. When I return, Sweet, will you tell me that it means nothing, that it is only that I have been too long from home, with too little purpose?

Enough. Soon we will leave France. Please God you and your mother and our son are well. Kiss Ned for me, and know my love is with you.

*Edward, once Earl of March*
*to*
*Edmund, once Earl of Rutland*

*D*amn you, brother, I would you were here. I know, I know. I curse you as if it were your fault you died, just like I cursed everything that went against my will when we were young. When *I* was young. *You* will always be young, of course.

I wonder what you would be like now. You would be, what, thirty-three? Thirty-four. Would you be like me, growing fat, over-indulged with women and food and wine, so sated with the great pleasures of life that they can hardly be called pleasures, but unable to leave them alone? I doubt it. Even young, there was a goodness and wisdom about you. You never minded my cursing, never took it to your heart. You would laugh and say, *The sun is still in the sky, and you still cast a shadow, like any man. Come, then, what can be amiss?*

God, how I miss you. There is no one like you. Richard and George together do not make one of you. George has your laughter and your beauty, but he has no sense. Richard has honor and loyalty, but he has no use for whores, and drinks only to quench his thirst. He sits in judgment on me all the time. Not that he says much. He doesn't have to: I know.

What would you have done here? Whatever Richard thinks about his honor, he must admit we did a pretty piece of work at a small price. The coffers are full, and, believe me, men will notice that, long after they have forgotten that they had not a chance to prove their valor.

Let me tell you what we gained this day.

A truce between England and France for seven years.

Freedom of commerce for both our countries, and the abolition of all tolls, fines, and other fees on any exchange of goods with each other.

The promise that, if either of our nations face armed combat with a third, the other will come to our aid.

The marriage of my daughter Bess to the dauphin of France when she comes of marrying age, and for her, a yearly livelihood of twelve thousand crowns.

And, perhaps best of all. Or most shameful of all, if you take Richard's view--

For England, seventy-five thousand crowns the day we depart from France.

Fifty thousand crowns yearly thereafter, as long as Louis and I both live.

A fine annuity for several of my most faithful lords. Will Hastings and John Howard leave here very rich men. Which Richard could have done, too, had he not been too stubborn. He's rich enough to afford his fine conscience, but I remember when he fought for his share of Warwick's wealth. He put not such a fine edge on his honor, then. I should not be surprised, I suppose; a full belly makes for easy virtue.

Well, what think you? Are the terms not fine? A worthy peace, and trade will prosper. Charles of Burgundy is outraged, of course. Let him sulk. He had his opportunity to stand by us. For seventy-five thousand crowns and a pension, I can bear to be called cowardly and dishonorable.

I *intended* to fight. It was Charles's treachery that made me reconsider. When we reached Péronne, that ass once again forgot the purpose of his marriage to my sister. I met with Will and Richard to debate our course. We could probably have taken France without Charles's help, but a better idea came to me: I could make a magpie lay golden eggs.

Consider. If Parliament pressures me, I can restore some of the tax funds, and need raise no new taxes to the end of my reign—or the end of Louis' life. Charles of Burgundy must speak to me very courteously from now on, if he wishes me to expel one breath to keep Louis from making war on him. Even Louis gains. I pray for him daily: I pray that he dies an old, old man.

Yes, a fine thing, this treaty. But brother, nothing feels as fine as it ought to any more. That's the jest of it, I have everything I wanted, more than I dreamed of, and it brings me little joy. I wouldn't have believed it if some pleasure-spoiler had told me that when I was twenty.

Richard says I drink too much. Too much and too little, it's one and the same; *enough* no longer exists. I used to drink with friends and I could bring it all back, the days when I could feel like a god in battle, and a woman's body was sweeter than wine. Now I drink until

I fall asleep, and nothing happens. Except for once in a while, just for a moment, if the company is fine, and the moment just right. Once in a while everything comes back, but it is as fleeting as the will-o'-the-wisp, and they say that men who chase the will-o'-the-wisp lose their souls.

*Louis, King of France*
*to*
*himself*

*M*y, my, my. The poor deluded English have come to their knees. We have made of them such fools, the continent is laughing. The great heroes of Crécy and Agincourt chased from France with meat pasties and wine.

*William, Lord Hastings*
*to*
*Edward, King of England*

*A*h, Ned, what a profitable journey this has been! Far better than I had hope of. Truthfully, I had no desire for war. Forty is old for soldiering. I have no need to prove my courage in battle. Give me the rewards without the pains. A lot of gold, a little wine, and women. Women, Jesus! To be the king's best friend is to never want for women again. I'm not so sure that is a blessing. I like to know my women, at least a little. Camp followers and wives take the edge off a man's appetite but they leave the deeper hunger unsatisfied; it takes a sweet mistress to fill that. Wives have too much surety to care to please a man, and whores too little.

But enough of women. I want to talk to you about your brothers. You have always worried about George, and you place great faith in Richard. George is a fool, there is no doubt of that. But he is too bid-dable to bring you real harm. I must tell you, my friend, that of your two brothers it is Richard who concerns me. That lad has something so resolute—I should say unbending!—about him that it defies reason. He has some principle or other about this war, and would have had us either fight or ship our men back to England. Actually, he would prefer to fight, I think, now that we are here. And not a penny richer, either, as he would have it. You see, Ned, what the matter is. His "honor," as he calls it, this time overran his loyalty to you.

This morning, after the rain, a dove came to rest on the top of your tent. Some of the soldiers were cheered and remarked that it must be an omen that God favored our enterprise, after all. I called this to Richard's attention. Mark you, I did not expect him to agree, but I thought perhaps it might soften his view a little, at least let him *consider* that our actions might be well-advised. Maybe even cheer him, which I thought he could use. Do you know what he said? He said, and I quote his words precisely: Will, that tent pole is the highest point in camp. Therefore the nearest the sun. The poor bird is drying himself.

As though I were a child, Ned. I would take offense, except that he is young and no doubt did not mean to be malapert. And he has no humor, for which I pity him.

*Francis, Lord Lovell*
*to*
*Richard, Duke of Gloucester*

You dreamed last night. Sat bolt upright in your bed, I could see that much by the moonlight. I wonder what you fear, you who seem to have everything a man could wish for.

Do you remember when we were lads in Warwick's courtyard, and I asked if I could be your man? You agreed, and I was grateful, but I never dreamed it would matter to you—the king's brother. I envied you, but not for that. I envied you because there was so much you loved; you don't know how much I envied you that, even as you were leaving most of it behind.

When I could not have what I loved, I have mocked. Better to mock than weep, I always say. Most of the time, anyway. But a man must love something. Very well. I love you, and yours, and I do not mock when I say that.

When I reached my majority and went home to Minster Lovell I saw only reproach. From the servants, strangers for whom I had been gone too long, although I had no choice in the matter. From the ghost of my father, long dead, because I could not love my inheritance. From my mother, remarried and indifferent—to me, to Minster Lovell, to anything that reminded her of the past. From my wife, for whom

I had come home too soon. For whom the millennium would have been too soon, I suspect. I don't know why. We were commanded to the marriage, it was none of our choice, but what of it? So were many another man and wife who have got on well together, but she misliked me from the beginning.

So I left and sought you in London. Come fight with me for Edward, you said. My God, the things we saw. But that night after Tewkesbury, when I cried—

I have never told anyone, but I cried not only for the horrors of the battle, but because it was over. I never felt so alive as when I might die, and never felt so empty as I did, after, when I had nothing to do but return to Oxfordshire and a wife who loved me not. What a jest—that I, who take no pleasure in watching even a boar die, should mourn the end of battle.

You know what it was like when you came to Minster Lovell on your way back from Parliament.

It was in late winter, the ground cold and bleak, and the horses shaggy in their winter coats. We were standing out by the mews, you and Rob and I.

How is Anne? I asked you.

Very well. With child.

And your Joyce? I said to Rob.

The same, he said, scuffing the toe of his boot in the dust.

The same? What, man? Well, or with child?

Both. He looked up then and grinned.

It must be a strong wind that blows the soldiers home from the wars, I said, all the women's bellies are swelled up like sails!

We were standing there laughing when Anna came up. I saw you and Rob both look and look again, she is that beautiful. Her face is so finely made it might have been sculpted. But she didn't smile, and our laughter stopped, as though we were boys caught at pilfering.

My wife, Anna, I said.

You said, Anne is a good name. It is my wife's also.

It was a pleasantry, you were only trying to bring her into our good humor.

Not Anne, she said. Ann-*uh*.

The harshness of that voice coming from such a beautiful mouth jolted you. I could see it in your face. I know that shock well, I feel it every time she speaks.

So it is, you said. Your pardon, lady.

Francis, the supper is waiting, she spoke curtly, no warmth, nor welcome for you, my guests. We left the mews and went inside, all our laughter subdued.

We ate in poisonous silence. The next day I showed you everything I could possibly be proud of. My horses, my hawks, the history of my estates. Rob, who cannot bear to affront anyone, kindly listened. You were more to the point.

Francis, what is this? Look at who you are talking to. Do you think we are amazed by your fine hawks and halls? What is amiss here, friend?

Nothing. And what else should I speak of? This is my life now.

You offered to be my man, once. I will hold you to that promise.

I doubt you have need of me. The wars are over, the country at peace.

You are sulking, Francis. Like a child.

What if I am?

Nothing. Sulk all you like, I care not. But come and sulk at Middleham, not here.

So I came back, too. Anne greeted me with a smile that would have melted me, had it come from my own wife.

Francis! I have longed to see you again.

I was made reckless with pleasure and relief: How disappointing. I had hoped you would long to kiss me.

Kiss him, quickly, Annie, you said, Lest he leave again.

And she did. With love, I am sure. She is so full of love for you she has it to spare. A quick kiss, all good humor and charity, and then she stepped back beside you. Richard, I would never wish you less than you have. God knows you have deserved all good fortune that comes your way, but sometimes it hurts.

### *Anne, Duchess of Gloucester*
### *to*
### *Alice, Countess of Warwick*

Did you love my father? We have never spoken of these things. You said with a sigh, when this war with France began, Ah, men. They are in love with death, all of them. If they were not, they could not cause so much of it.

Richard, too, do you think? I asked.

You laughed. Well, daughter, is he a man?

You were only chiding me, but other thoughts came to my mind, and I blushed.

Daughter, daughter. So you dream about your husband, you said, and put down your needlework. There was such sadness in your face that a chill came over me.

You said, when I was married to Lancaster, Don't ask for love—to console me, I thought, that I had it not. If you expect love, and do not find it, your heart will break. And if it comes to you, its presence will disguise the more important things.

I remember the day my father told me I was to wed Lancaster. He was sitting at a long table in his chamber in France, his face half in shadow. Then he turned and smiled at me, and his look was warm with approval, even delight. Soon, of course, I knew why the smile was so warm: I was the coin with which he was going to buy England.

Is that what love has been like for you, Mother, that he smiled upon you, and you felt beautiful and good, only for you to discover that what delighted him was the dull gold of profit? Your loss must have been tenfold mine, because he was your husband, not your sire, although I never saw you anything but calm and assured in his presence.

When I was in France, every night, I went to bed praying to dream. I wanted to to see the dales and hear the bells from the abbey in the morning.

And then I discovered I could. I could leave my body and go wherever I would.

One evening, Queen Margaret was talking in that way she had that seemed all courtesy, but hid a world of scorn. There was that girl, Anne, answering in her heavily accented French. I could pity her and hardly feel the scorn, because I, myself, was on the steps of Middleham, watching Mercury run loose through the courtyard, hooves sparking the cobbles while the groom ran panting after him.

Another time, I went not only home, but back in years. I was a child in the huge tithe barn in the summer, before the harvest filled it, looking for the litter of kittens Isabel said she had seen. There was the drowsy heat, the thousands of motes of dust in the sunlight through the open doors, thicker than the stars in the sky, the crooning of the pigeons, and the rich warm smell of hay and grain, as savory as fresh-baked bread. Then I knew I was indeed smelling bread and came back to supper.

That was a very useful talent to have. Once I discovered I could do it, I came home almost all the nights after I had smiled at Lancaster and he found ways to creep into my bed. I did it back in England while I polished the kettles and when Sarah and I huddled together like cats at night, shivering under my green cloak.

When I truly came home again, I still had the habit. But with Richard, I went only far enough to watch him at a little distance, to try to know him. Like all the rest of the world, he had changed.

At the Carters' house, when he found me and said we would marry, for a moment I thought that I, myself, was some portion of the realm he wanted, and then it might be safe to love him. It was such a piercing hope, I could only look at it quickly and then turn aside, as from too blinding a light.

Then he brought his news to me at St. Martin, and I felt like the ground had dissolved beneath my feet. Not that he wanted to delay our marriage—how could I be my father's daughter and not understand his purpose? But that he could tell me no limits to the delay.

It was such a simple surety that I wanted.

I wanted to know that there was some small part of him that would hold constant, whatever the circumstances, a part that could not be bribed, bought, or bartered.

But he put no boundaries around my time there, and every day became a purgatory from which there might be no reprieve. And far crueler than true purgatory, which might at least be shortened by good works and prayers in my name, if I leave behind me people who care enough about my soul to do such things. But the heart of God is easier to move than the hearts of princes, I suppose.

One night after we returned home, Richard asked me, Were you actually *married* to Lancaster? Or just betrothed?

We were married, my lord.

We lay there in silence, and then he said, Did you lie together?

I could not say anything, Mother. The words all fought with each other and tripped on my tongue.

One word: yes or no. Tell me your name: Anne. Tell me the color of your eyes: Hazel. Is it possible for the truth to be so simple?

Very well, I could have said, I came to our marriage a maid.

I suppose that would be truth, for him.

But this is my truth.

I was a maid in name only.

Lancaster knew every inch of my body; I disallowed the ultimate act between a man and woman only by calling up his fear of his mother, should he sire a Neville brat before he reached the throne.

He crept into my bed nearly every night. I pitied and despised him and hated his touch, but I courted it. I lured him to me with smiles and glances because I hated even more a life where no one spoke to me, no one looked at me. Loneliness can make you that desperate.

I wanted to believe that if I spread my truth before Richard like a cloak, he would see the whole cloth and understand. But I did not do it. I feared that, however kindly he might answer, I would see on his face the cast of distaste that is more wounding than words.

Men are such strange creatures. They make a quest for Truth. They willingly give up kingdoms and lay down their lives for it. But *truth*—small, sad, and uncomfortable? I have not yet seen the man yet who wants to embrace it when it walks up to him.

Mother, I think you are mistaken. I don't believe men are in love with death. I think they fear it, even more than women, and pretend not to notice when it walks beside us, as it does, all our lives.

# 18 Unto Caesar

*Middleham*
*December 1476 and early 1477.*

What Richard would remember as one of the worst years of his life began one winter day when he entered the solar. It began simply, with a piece of news that should never have come close to destroying a family and exposing the madness of his brother. Anne was standing in the window, her head bowed, her arms folded, hugging herself. Alice was staring at a piece of parchment she held in her hand. Word had just arrived that Anne's sister, Isabel, had given birth to a son, who died within days, and Isabel herself was gravely ill. Alice had decided to travel to London to be at Isabel's side to see her again, if possible. She hoped that Anne would accompany her. But the winter was harsh. There had been outbreaks of the plague, and fevers had swept through the country, taking mostly the elderly and the very young. Anne feared to leave Ned. The two women had talked and decided the matter in the moments since the message had come.

Early in the new year, Alice returned with grievous news—Isabel had died in December from consumption, a death hastened by her weakened condition after giving birth—along with a tale so strange that Richard at first could scarcely believe it. Duke Charles of Burgundy, his sister Margaret's husband, had died at the siege of Nancy, his head split by an axe.

Edward's court had watched with pity as George wept over Isabel, moaned, grew haggard from lack of sleep and appetite and unkempt from indifference to life itself, until some feared they would soon see him buried, too. Alice had exhorted him to rally for the sake of his two small children, to no avail. His melancholia seemed only to deepen.

But then news of Charles's death reached the court, and the same people who feared for George's life looked on in amazement as, combed, shaved, and cheerful, George went to Edward to proclaim his wish to marry Mary, Margaret's stepdaughter. With her father's death, Mary was heiress of Burgundy.

Perhaps George hoped to become Duke of Burgundy. That was the kindest interpretation of his behavior. But Burgundy had an ancient claim to the English throne. If George married Mary, he could, by a great leap of imagination, claim to be King of England. Edward apparently credited George with more imagination than sense. He forbade the marriage.

Upon the denial of George's desires, rumors rose up in London that Edward was not the son of the late Duke of York, but a bastard, father unspecified, who therefore had no right to rule. No one wondered at the source of the rumors.

The Duchess Cecily faced the rumors with her usual grace and more forbearance than many a woman would have done. Edward was not so tolerant of his brother's folly. He arrested three men: Dr. John Stacy, an Oxford astrologer; Thomas Blake, chaplain of Merton College; and Thomas Burdet, Esquire, on the grounds of plotting Edward's death by magic and witchcraft. All three men were George's close associates.

Vehemently proclaiming their innocence, they were all found guilty. Only the chaplain, Thomas Blake, was released by the intervention of Edward's councilors. Burdet and Stacy were hanged. Whether the two were guilty was not the issue. The lesson was clear: a warning to George to stop his scheming.

George may have been the only person in the kingdom who did not recognize the gravity of Edward's message. Defiant and as unreasoning as a mad dog, George had a former servant of his late wife, one Ankarette Twynyho, dragged from her home. The duke tried, convicted, and then hanged the poor woman for having poisoned his young duchess.

If George believed he had a king's power in staging trials, he was to find out otherwise. Edward had him arrested and thrust into keeping in the Tower, supposedly to await trial for murder.

Not that way. Do not stir it." Anne took the spoon from the girl's hand, and demonstrated. Lately she had a passion for exactness and order. None of the teasing mischief that once lay so close beneath the surface of her seriousness.

"Anne," Richard said.

Anne looked up. "A moment, Richard. Now watch," she said to the girl. "It is a motion like folding bread. After you knead the bread, you fold the dough over on itself. This is the same way of folding, but you do it with the spoon and not your hands. Now, gently." She gave back the spoon.

Something in Anne had changed around the time Isabel died. Richard had thought at first it was grief for Isabel. He had held her when she wept against his chest at night, remembering the two little girls who had been inseparable. In daylight, he was torn between compassion and annoyance, the annoyance directed toward what he usually managed to not notice—that in addition to Anne's refusal to travel with him to London, she had never offered a word of explanation of what had happened that drove her into hiding. And why would she grieve so for the death of a sister she had so steadfastly refused to see?

"Madam, I will try." The girl bit down on her lip and frowned in concentration as she attempted to imitate Anne's movements exactly, but she was hesitant and clumsy, and Anne's scrutiny only increased her ineptness. If any of the kitchen servants knew of Anne's one-time masque as a servant, they must have regretted it; her knowledge left little shelter where any inexperience, any incompetence, however small, could hide. Anne's face was as determined as if the world hung on the success of the brew in the pot before her.

Richard remembered his long-ago self, the little boy who believed he could bring the dead back to life by the way he crept up a flight of stairs. It wouldn't help, whatever she was trying to mend with all this care over the custard.

He laid his hand on her arm. "Leave that for now. Come."

"We will have curds-and-whey instead of blanc-mange."

"I doubt it. Your maid's labors will only improve when you are not watching her."

"Is it so with your men?"

"Of course," Richard lied. He glanced at the girl over Anne's shoulder and was rewarded by a look of deep gratitude.

"Leave it. Her work will improve threefold when you leave her to herself, I promise you."

As she still hesitated, he handed her the linen that lay on the table beside them. She took it and wiped her hands.

$\mathcal{A}$way from the heat of the kitchen, he could feel the chill of the coming winter already entering the castle. Leaves had blown against the windows and huddled there in the corners, like small rain-soaked animals seeking shelter.

"I must leave for London soon." For the Parliament that was to decide George's fate.

"I know."

"My children there are old enough to be fostered. I am going to have them brought here."

They had had this conversation before. Anne welcomed Kate's coming but found the idea of a bastard son joining the household more difficult.

He heard the taut intake of breath and watched her face, the sadness and her struggle to disguise it.

"John, too?"

"He is my son, Anne. He needs a father like any boy."

"Of course he does. Of course he must come, too."

He didn't ask her to come with him. He never did, any more.

$\mathcal{T}$hat night as they lay in bed:

"Richard?"

"Yes?"

"I don't think Ned should be fostered out."

"He's four years old. Of course he should not be fostered."

"I meant, ever."

"Ever is a long time."

"Ever," Anne insisted.

He had married a stubborn woman, Richard remembered for about the one-thousandth time, and was visited by a long-ago memory—watching from a window as his father rode off, never to be seen again.

Why should any child whose father lives have to grow up without him? Or father live without his son?

"Very well, " he said.

"Do you mean it? Are you convinced so easily?" Anne asked him. "You must promise, before I will believe it."

"I *have* promised you, Anne. Just now."

"Never?"

"Never."

How easy. And what a burden she had lifted from him.

*Oh, your son is not fostered yet?*

*I promised my lady wife. You know how women are.*

"Teasel?"

"What is it?"

"I never intended otherwise. It is what I want, too."

*London*
*February 1478.*

"I have been lenient with him for years, and he has repaid me with this," Edward said. "Treason, plots against the kingdom, slander. Our poor good mother. But I suppose I must give him credit for the most inventive attempt to discredit me." He sighed. "Is there more wine, Will?"

Winter's gloom was in the chamber, shadows thick in the corners. Edward sat in the chair with his legs splayed out, his voice not so much angry as infinitely weary. One candle stood on the table; in its light Edward's face shone with an oily glint.

"Thank you." Richard took the cup Hastings had filled. Hastings had been more cordial these past few years than the man Richard had known in his youth. Perhaps Hastings had feared that Richard jeopardized his closeness to Edward, a fear that diminished when Richard had secured a domain of his own.

"The most untrue creature living," Edward continued. "He would destroy me, my kingdom, my peace."

The flatness of his brother's voice chilled Richard. Edward was a living ghost, with no passion for either ruling or life.

"You will execute him," Richard said.

"I will *try* him, brother," Edward corrected him. "The trial will determine whether he dies."

"You make no comment, Richard," Hastings said. "What are you thinking?"

"That King Henry lived in the Tower for a half-dozen years before I ordered his execution," Edward interrupted.

"You would allow George to live, then? You find his crimes pardonable?"

"He is our brother, Will. That is all I am thinking," Richard said "Not whether he is good or evil, guilty or innocent. Just that he is our brother." And about how he or Edward could possibly live with commanding George's death.

George's trial, like that of his friends the previous year, had the feel of an outcome sealed before the evidence was heard, and it was remarkable in that the indictment was brought by the king himself. The due form of the law was observed, however; the king's word, when he has personal knowledge of the event, is, in the ancient and honored words, "the most perfect of records." And what jury would refute, or even question, the most perfect of records?

"I want to see him," Richard said, standing in the antechamber where Edward sat, with, of course, a tankard of wine in his hand. The hearth fire burned with a steady glow, and the room was comfortably warm.

"You saw him at his trial. Arrogant and unrepentant."

"Yes, I saw him. Across the chamber at a distance of twenty feet. I want to see him face to face."

"I do not wish it." Edward's face was ruddy and his clothes slightly rumpled.

"You do not wish it?" Richard had been about to sit down, but Edward's response froze him; he stood with his hand on the back of the chair. "Our brother is about to die, by your order; I am asking to see him for the last time, and you do not *wish* it?" He didn't know which shocked him more—the denial of his request, or the indifference with which it was given.

"Well, I see my meaning is clear enough." Edward barely glanced at him. Again, that flat lifeless voice.

Richard walked over and stood in front of his brother. "Listen to me. I have served you every way you have *wished* for the past ten years—ridden here, to Scotland, sailed to France on your instant command—and still kept the best peace the north has seen in years."

"Don't play the righteous with me. You have been well rewarded for everything you have done."

"Yes. And I had to fight George for every league of my land, every coin of that reward, while I watched you do no more than shrug your shoulders on my behalf. Maybe he does deserve to die. I deserve to see him this last time." Richard despised everything about this—George's foolishness, what he saw Edward becoming, the impotent rage he felt swelling up in his own breast.

"Well, brother. You are very certain of your entitlement, aren't you? You come here every year or two, say a few nice Latin phrases so we can make our laws, and then go back to your dear Yorkshire and loving wife. What do you know of things here?" The question seemed serious. Edward looked up at him and squinted, quizzical.

Richard sat down. The anger had gone out of him like a wind becalmed. The room seemed unnaturally still. "You are nothing like the brother—or king—I once knew."

"Oh, God's teeth! Next, you will be sounding like my good wife. *Don't you think that is wine enough?*" He mimicked a woman's petulant voice.

"Now you mention it, yes. But that isn't what I was going to say."

"Well? Since you have begun your sermon, give it to me whole."

"It grieves me to see you so joyless, with no care for anything you once loved. What has happened?"

"What has happened? I have tried my own brother for a traitor, and you ask me what has happened."

"It is more than that."

Edward sighed. "Who knows what happened? When I was a young man, I felt I had been given King Midas's touch. Now I touch gold and it turns to dust. My wife and I despise each other; the men I loved and fought beside are dead."

"Warwick and Jack died fighting *against* you, if you are thinking of them."

"Well? They're still dead, aren't they?" Edward let his head sink down into his shoulders. "Very well. You want to see George, you shall see him. I will go with you."

"When?"

"Now."

"Now? It's past ten o'clock."

"Do you want to see him, or not?"

"Yes."

"Then now."

George's quarters were no dungeon, but plain and comfortable chambers in the second floor of the Tower. There was a guard without; he unlocked the door and bolted it again after them. A servant dozed in a chair by the fire while George lay, fully dressed, on his bed, one arm over his face.

Edward gripped his arm. "George, Richard is here. Sit up and behave yourself."

"Dickon! My little brother come to see me." George got to his feet and embraced Richard.

He reeked of wine. Richard took a step back. "You're drunk, George."

"I'm drunk, he says." George appeared to be talking to the air. Then suddenly he turned and grasped Richard's shoulder. "I am *waiting* to die. Do you see here any banquets and singers? Perfumed ladies? Even a companion more deserving of the name than that sleeping lout?" He released Richard's shoulder and jerked a thumb toward the servant. "Do you see *anything*, in fact, in this dungeon amazing enough to divert a man from thoughts of death?

"Of course I am drunk! What else is there to do in this hole? Wouldn't you drink, too?"

"I'm sorry, George," Richard said.

"Sorry! What have you to be sorry about? Did you order this?" George staggered away, sat down on the bed, and looked up, his face haggard. "Listen, brother, you must help me. I want another trial—"

"George—" The sight of George so without his old buoyancy was profoundly depressing. Richard wondered if he had made a costly error to the peace of his own spirit in coming here. What, exactly, had been his purpose? A few last words spoken in affection, a reconciliation of a friendship they had never had?

"—a trial by battle," George continued. Edward stood by, silent. "Don't you see, if I am innocent, I will be free by God's will, Edward doesn't have to say a thing. And if I am not, the trial itself takes care of my execution."

"A trial by battle! George, you can't fight. You can barely stand."

"Speak for me, Dickon! That is the only hope I have. A trial by battle." George reached up and seized Richard's coat in both his hands and sobbed. "You cannot abandon me, too."

"George. Don't do this." Richard released his brother's grip from his coat. "I can't help you. Have some dignity, man, you will hate yourself later."

George put back his head and laughed. "How like you—*in the morning you will hate yourself.* Think, Richard! In the morning my head will not know what my heart feels! They will have bid each other adieu. Adieu, goodbye, farewell. Forever. My poor tongue rotting silent in my skull, which is more to the point."

"What are you talking about?"

Edward came between them. "Enough now, George. Say your goodbyes."

The door clanged shut behind them. Richard crossed his arms over his chest, to still a shudder. "You will have him beheaded?" Surely not hanging.

"If he chooses."

"What do you mean?"

"Just what I said. He can choose his method of execution. I promised him that much."

In return for what, Richard wondered.

On the way back to Westminster, Richard asked, "What did he mean by his tongue being silenced?"

The air was damp and cold. Thin spirals of mist rose from the river, and overhead a few stars blinked through shreds of cloud. Edward turned his face and looked up at the few visible stars. "What? I don't know." He was not a convincing liar.

Richard woke feeling oppressed and with a violent headache. He sat up slowly and pressed his fists against his temples.

Oh. This is the day one of my brothers kills the other.

He saw George once more that night. On a litter, everything—his clothes, his fair hair, his skin—drenched, smelling of wine fresh from the cask. Richard knelt down to look closer. This was absurd. Who would waste a cask of wine over a dead man? He looked up at the man-at-arms standing beside the litter.

"What happened to him? He looks as if he bathed in wine."

The man nodded. "He did, sir. Drowned in it."

"Drowned?"

"In a butt of malmsey, sir. It is how he asked to die."

Richard was having trouble taking it in. "He *wanted* to drown? Why?"

"He said he had a thirst for justice, sir, and if that thirst would not be quenched, he would satisfy another."

Join me in a drink, my lord. Sorrows shared are not so piercing."

"No thank you, doctor. I feel no thirst." He was brooding. Edward was on his way to death by drowning, too, albeit more slowly.

"Come, sir. A cup of malmsey will improve your humor."

"My God, doctor! If you think that passes for wit, I want none of it."

"Sir?" Hobbes's face was puzzled. "There was no wit or jest intended. A simple observation."

"Oh. In that case, I beg your pardon. Grief has made my senses leave me, it seems."

Hobbes raised one eyebrow, waiting for him to continue.

"The Duke of Clarence asked to be drowned in a butt of malmsey. I assumed that was common knowledge."

"No. I had not heard that. Well. No wonder you took offense. But I will still take a cup, if that is not too distasteful to you."

"Help yourself. Forgive me if I am not the most gracious of hosts."

"So your heart is heavy tonight." Hobbes moved to the cupboard and poured himself a cup of wine, and sat down, pulling his gown up slightly as he eased into the chair.

"Like a stone," Richard agreed.

"Hardly to be wondered at," Hobbes commented. "I will remember how bitter the dregs of kingship can be when I am unhappy with my own calling."

"And are you?"

"Oh, certainly, sometimes. The abuse people heap on their poor bodies, and then ask the doctor to mend it. They drink too much—" he lifted his cup, "and beg me to ease their livers, eat to bursting and cry for their gout, break their heads in fights and sob for their dwindling wits. No, I have no great regard for the wisdom of man." He took a thoughtful sip of wine. "Why do we say our heart aches, I wonder, when we are grieved? Is that what hurts you now?"

"No, no. It was only a way of speaking. I feel no actual pain."

"You have not been stabbed, suffered the pox or the plague, you mean. But your face tells other than your words. Weep, son, rail at heaven. The death of a brother is a sorry blow, no matter how it comes."

"You are kind, doctor." For all his tart comments, the old doctor was a genuinely kindly soul. A virtue, had Richard welcomed kindness just now. But there was this to be said about anger: the greater the anger he maintained, the less he noticed any pain. "I've no tears left. I stopped weeping over what might have been, long ago."

"I see," Hobbes said. He cleared his throat and settled himself in the chair. "I find your brother a curious man, my lord."

"My brother? Which one?"

"The king." Hobbes spoke softly, like he might to a frightened child.

Of course. You have only one brother, now. Odd how the mind keeps slipping off the path of truth. "In what way?"

"I have never known a man with a greater gift for inspiring love in those around him—or hate for each other among those same people. Does it not seem strange to you that a man who can inspire such love cannot even evoke friendship among those who serve him? For his own sake, if nothing else. I wonder if you have noticed that?"

"I would have had to be a fool not to, being one of the most heartily hated."

"You surprise me. Whose hatred have you inspired, particularly?"

"Elizabeth's. She has misliked me since the day I first came to London, green as salad."

"She seems agreeable enough in your presence now."

"Agreeable? She is positively fawning now, in comparison, believe me."

"Perhaps because now she has Lord Hastings to absorb her mislike."

"Because of Calais, you mean." The post her brother Anthony lost to Will.

"That, of course. Although I was thinking more that she considers him an evil influence on your brother."

"*Hastings?*"

"Ah. You weren't aware. Well, they are great companions in wenching and drinking. Our serious Hastings has another side." The doctor's voice was amused. "As if Edward needed poor Will to lead him anywhere. Listen to me, how I forget whom I am speaking to! Your pardon, sire."

"Truth is truth, Doctor."

Hobbes leaned closer. "In that case, I will tell you something else that must chafe the queen. Her eldest son, Lord Dorset, and Will Hastings are bitter rivals. Not only for Edward's friendship and confidence, but in love. They seem to think it is a matter of the greatest importance which of them has the honor of comforting Edward's discarded mistresses. Think what a corner the poor queen is in! She cannot know whether to be happy because Dorset joins her in hating and wishing to thwart Hastings, or despair that he joins in such a game."

Richard laughed in spite of himself. "Doctor Hobbes, how do you know all this?"

"Why, I have the soul of an old woman, I fear. A very old woman with nothing to do but knit and gossip. But I'll tell you who else knew everything of interest about court. Whatever may be said of the Duke of Clarence, he and I spent some fine moments exchanging malicious tales." Hobbes set down his cup of malmsey. "There, do you see what I have done? I have demonstrated to you the shallowness of my soul. What hope of Heaven do you think there may be for such a man?"

"I suspect the saints would want to keep you near, doctor, for diversion. Your humor has lightened my heart, for which I thank you. But I must say, all the intrigues and hatreds here—so much passion expended for so little gain."

"My son. Never underestimate the power and endurance of stupidity." Hobbes sat back. "Your brother George saw too much of the follies of men, and believed that gave him power. It did not, as you know. But you, sir, if I may be so bold as to say so, err on the side of seeing too little.

"But I may be wrong. There can be wisdom in not seeing, too, sometimes; it keeps you from embroiling yourself in what is best left alone."

$\mathcal{Y}$ou can't seriously believe even a king can match his daughter without a dowry?" Richard had come to Edward's chambers to meet with him and Lord Hastings concerning several marriages of state, including those of Edward's children. Hastings had not yet arrived.

"Why not?" Edward asked.

"In the first place, because the king should have wealth enough to provide a decent dowry." *Because not everyone is so desperate as to think the pinnacle of privilege is to wed the child of a king and therefore leap for a dowerless maid. Because such greed and miserliness are unseemly.* "Because it will appear that you are poor, that the coffers of England are empty."

"Well, brother, they are running low. That is precisely the point of securing a good match."

So even Louis' bribe money did not keep Edward's government solvent. Richard was considering that when Hastings came into the room, smoothing his hair as he closed the door behind him. The door to the inner chamber where Edward slept. Well. Two men in the bedchamber. Don't presume anything. There may have been a dozen reasons Hastings was in the chamber. But right now, Richard could only think of one. One folly even Hobbes had not discovered? Folly? No, perversion.

"Good morning, Richard." Hastings greeted him. Neither he nor Edward showed any discomfiture.

"Will."

"Richard dislikes my suggestions for Bridget's marriage," Edward remarked as Hastings sat down. Bridget was Edward's second oldest daughter. His eldest, Bess, the plum of all Edward's children, would wait for some greater destiny.

"Oh? Did you tell him of Elizabeth's plan for her brother?"

"No. I had not come to that." Edward turned to Richard. "Since George is no longer in the offing, Elizabeth has another match in mind for Mary of Burgundy. She wants the girl for her brother Anthony."

Hastings laughed. "Saint Rivers. Can you imagine that Mary of Burgundy would consider such a match?"

Richard, who had no particular liking for Rivers, still misliked the laughter at an absent man's expense.

There was the creak of a hinge, and a girl slipped through the door from which Hastings had entered. She glanced around in consternation. Her eyes fell on Richard, a stranger, then she tried to scurry past their table.

Edward grabbed her. "What hurry, sweetheart? Would you leave without a kiss?"

Her face and neck flushed deeply. "No, my lord. But I didn't want to disrupt you." She tried to push his hands from her waist.

"It is no disruption." Edward kissed the girl heartily and let her go more quickly than she expected. She lost her balance and stumbled backward to have Hastings catch her on his lap. "And me," Will said.

Richard glanced at the two men and the girl. All three in Edward's chamber? He didn't know whether he was more or less shocked than at his original thought. He felt like the only sober man in a party of drunks.

The girl darted out. There were sounds of voices outside the door and Elizabeth stormed in. She approached the table, cold with fury. "I met your little harlot in the passageway, husband."

"Which was no surprise to you," Edward said. "Don't pretend you lie awake nights wishing for me to grace your bed."

She looked him up and down, letting her eyes linger pointedly at his belly. "Hardly. In fact, I wonder that you find so many who do want to share your bed. But I remember when you swore you could never look at another."

"That was long ago, Bess." Edward's voice was weary.

When she had left, he said, "Be careful what you say to women, friends. They store up your words and fling them back at you like lances. Dipped in poison on their return. Now, where were we?"

*The cottagers in the village repaired the tiles of the roofs. The lambing was done for the season, and the lambs' ears marked. Out on the hills birdsong mixed with the shepherds' pipes and horns, and the sound carried far in the open air of the fells. Fresh garlic was pulled to eat with cheese and boiled bacon, the first of spring's green vegetables.*

It was good to be home. The gardeners were sowing Sweet William and gillyflowers, and dividing the clumps of feverfew to spread throughout the plantings to keep the ants and other insects away. As he sat in the garden, the sun was driving out the last of the cold that seemed always to gather through the winter between Richard's shoulder blades. Alice watched Ned, that he did not go astray in the fishpond.

Anne and Joan had carried out pots of seedlings started indoors to be set in the garden.

"I thought that was servants' work," Francis said.

"And what do you think I am, sir?" Joan retorted. There was something in Francis's manner that inspired women to be bold.

"At the very least, negligent of your mistress," Francis teased. "She will ruin her hands, the servants will fall into disrespect—"

Anne looked up and smiled. "Francis, what the servants think of me after all these years, they will still think tomorrow."

"No, Annie, I am serious. You disturb the order of things. If the mistress will work among the servants, what will be next?"

"The Apocalypse," Anne laughed. "Go away, Francis. Or help us."

"In that case. . . ."

Francis got up and wandered off. Alice gathered up Ned and followed along. As soon as they were gone, some of the gaiety went out of the garden.

"What are you growing there?" Richard asked Anne.

"Basil. A very good plant. It takes away melancholy and makes the heart glad."

She set the pot down on the wall next to where one of the gardeners was tilling. "Do you think Isabel loved George, that she was happy with him?"

Since he had come home, she had asked him one question after another, all somehow connected to George.

"I don't know, Anne. She seemed happy enough, whenever I saw her."

Hobbes' words: You, sir, err on the side of seeing too little.

Some things fell into place should have been clear all along. If he had been willing to look at them.

"Anne?"

"Yes?" She avoided his eyes.

You can know a person for years, and you don't know them at all, what informs their actions, what thoughts they hide behind their careful words. He was tired of seeing too little. "I think it is time you told me what happened in London."

"When?"

"The last time you were there. Before I found you."

Her eyes flicked to his, then around the garden. The castle and grounds were swarming with activity. Where could they find to be alone? For all the ways he knew her incompletely, there were others in which they had perfected understanding. She stepped carefully over the newly planted rows toward him.

*T*he tithe-barn was empty, except for the doves and cats and what mice managed to escape their predators. Anne had turned a bucket upside down to sit on. Richard leaned against the edge of one of the mangers, and watched his wife's unhappy face.

"We had best not linger," Anne said. "Everyone will be wondering what has become of us."

"Everyone will think I have carried off my wife for a moment of lust." As she told him, he wished that was what they were about, rather than this sad business. There was a handful of grain in the corner of the bin. He stirred it with his finger.

"This is why you would never go to London with me?"

She nodded.

"And why you never saw Isabel again."

She had gone very pale. "I never knew—"

"You never knew whether your sister was party to George's plan."

"No." Anne had her elbows on her knees, her head in her hands, staring down at the ground.

"My God, Anne, your own sister. Why did you not talk to her?"

"He was her *husband*. How could I?"

"So you have lived with that all these years." He remembered another piece. "And the Twynyho woman. Did you know her?"

"Yes. She was a kindly soul. If I had told someone about George, she wouldn't have died. And those other men wouldn't have been hanged."

It was unreasonable, Richard thought, that she would take those deaths upon herself. As unreasonable as a frightened fourteen-year-old girl running through the streets of London to escape a murderous kinsman.

"Isabel didn't know, Anne. She was terrified when you were missing. I could at least have spared you wondering that. Why did you never tell me this before?" That stung more than he cared to admit.

"You will not enjoy the answer."

"I have not enjoyed your silence."

"Given the choice between me and your brother, I was not certain you would believe me."

"What else?"

"Else?"

"What else have you not told me?"

"George suggested that you might dispose of me somehow, to keep my inheritance."

"Go on."

"He said that he didn't believe you actually would harm me, but you did not want to marry me. He hinted that there would be men who would do your will."

"And you believed him?"

"I did not believe nor disbelieve. I was never certain of anything."

So this was what lay behind the secrecy, her early ceaseless scrutiny of him. She was trying to decide if she loved a murderer. A would-be murderer, as if that were better.

"Anne, think about it! I would never have harmed you. I *had* to marry you. I needed you, to be accepted here." Well, that did not come out as he intended.

Anne's face drained of its tension, and there was only sadness. "I know. Sometimes I thought I meant nothing to you but the inheritance I brought."

He remembered St. Martin, the clever young man who had seen the way to outwit his brothers, and had not thought of her comfort. "Have I not shown you in all these years what you are to me?"

"I know, Richard. I know you love me. As long as all goes well. But I have never been certain you have loved me enough to defend me against your brothers. Or as much as your property, if it came to that."

The pain a few words could bring. He loved her beyond telling. But then? Had she been no more than part of a world he wanted above else? Perhaps. He had honor enough to not deny it. She had grace enough not to remind him that most of his wealth came to him through her.

*H*igh summer. The gardens were in full bloom. Richard's bastards had joined the household. Kate was beautiful and prim, in awe of Anne as a great lady. Ned and John chased each other up and down the rows of peas. They had some system of make-believe whereby particular plants signified treacherous obstacles. Ned adored John, and shadowed him as Richard once had Edward.

Bennett eyed the boys. "It's time you gave master John more hours with Giles in the tiltyard and less with me over the books."

"Why, does he give you trouble in the schoolroom?"

Bennett grinned. "No trouble, exactly, my lord, but he cannot sit still for an hour straight." Ned could. He had the makings of a scholar, just as John did not.

The boys stopped running, suddenly. Ned had said something, and John stood, gazing intently at his smaller half-brother. Then John strode vigorously over to Richard, who could not help smiling at this child, in coloring so different from himself, but whose face nevertheless held his seal. John had hair the many pale colors of sand, and freckles. He seemed large, his presence was so robust. When he stood still, as now, you noticed that he was only average height, and slender.

"What is a bastard?" John's voice, clear and harsh. Anne started. Bennett cleared his throat.

"Excuse us for a time, please," Richard said. He motioned to John. "Come with me."

He started down the path toward the fishpond and orchards.

"I asked you a question, sire." John's voice came boldly from a pace behind. "Why don't you answer me?"

Richard kept walking. "I will, but this conversation is not for ladies. Or small children, either. And that is not the way to talk to your father." They stopped at the pond. "Now tell me. Who said you are a bastard?"

"Everyone says so."

"Oh? And just now?"

"Ned. Ned did."

"Do you know what that means?"

"I think so. I'm not sure."

"I'll tell you. It means that your father, in your case myself, was not married to your mother."

"Why? Why did you not marry my mother?" There were tears and a furious blinking struggle to keep them back.

"We could never have married. Our estates in life were different."

"Did you love her?"

Richard hesitated. Stay with the truth. "No. I liked her very much, but I didn't love her."

"But you lay with her."

"Yes. I lay with her. You understand what that means?"

"Yes. It's how I was born.

"That's right."

"I hate you." The words were hardly audible.

"What did you say?"

"I hate you."

Richard looked down into his son's face. He saw fear and pain, a bitter confusion, but not hate. This was not a time for chastisement. Nor for ignoring, either. You can't have your children going around saying they hate you. He stooped down, picked up a stone, and skipped it out over the water, thinking.

Finally he answered. "Sometimes I hated my father, too."

"No, you didn't. He died."

"Yes. He died. He died when I was younger than you are now. I hated him for leaving. That's how I thought of his dying. I hated him because I never got to know him."

He glanced at John. Well, something seemed to have hit the mark. The boy was standing attentive, head cocked to one side, listening.

Richard picked up another stone and skipped it, too. He went on. "A man hates who he will. But he must also learn when to behave with civility. You and I, we will have to work together.

"Hate me if you want, if you think I have given you reason. But remember this. You know me. At least I have given you a man to hate. I could have left you with your mother's kin, and you would have had only tales and stories."

He stood up. "I'm going back to the others now. Come with me if you like. Or not."

He started up the path. Before he had reached the garden, he felt, briefly, a child's hand in his, before John ran up ahead of him, calling to Ned.

*A*nd did you tell him how fine a thing it is to be a bastard?" Anne's words jolted him. He had thought that they were done with wounding each other, had inflicted all the hurt they could. Apparently not. After their years together, they had not only their small inventories of injuries, but an armory of weapons, each one shaped exactly to fit a particular tender place.

She had forgotten, apparently, that he was a soldier, and knew something about tactics.

"Tell me about Lancaster," he said. He knew it was cruel.

"Who?"

"Lancaster. Your husband."

"You are my husband."

"The first one."

"What has he to do with anything?"

"You want to know about John's mother. I want to know about your husband. Does that surprise you?"

As a boy, he had believed that when he grew up, he would leave his past behind, all the betrayals, the deaths, and the disappointments shed like the skin a snake sloughs year after year. He believed that we could be born anew if we chose to be, every day. Now he knew he was wrong. The past was not shed. It grew, accumulating in their souls as fallen leaves on the forest floor. Worse, he thought, as layers of leaves lie rotting into leaf mold. And in leaf mold, he knew, there was a heat at the center, a fire that ignites at the merest spark. He could feel the heat that rose from their pasts. He just could not reach its source.

She got up and reached for her shift. "There is nothing about that time I liked, or want to remember."

"Very well. You have memories you would like to forget. I have mine. Let us leave it at that."

"Think of how you came to hold this place before you decide what to speak to me about."

Richard indulged an act of temper that he had not displayed since he had knocked George to the floor after Tewkesbury. There was a short fat candle in a silver holder on the table by the bed. He picked it up and hurled it at the door.

Anne knew something about tactics, herself. She retrieved the candle and brought it to him. She could just as easily have set it in its keeper on the table, but she held it out to him. Let his act not go unacknowledged by either of them. When he did not move to take it, she laid it on the bed between them.

"Sit down," he said.

She did, at the far end of the bed, drawing her feet up between them.

He reached out and grasped her ankle.

"I didn't mean—"

"No, men never *mean*, they just *do*." She leaned her cheek against her hands. He could see tears starting.

"What is it?"

Anne let out a long breath. "I have wanted so much to give you more children." He did not reply, and she wiped angrily at her eyes. "Oh, Richard, I am such a sinner, I can't bear it."

"Such a sinner? You, Annie?" He tried to ignore that fact that his throat was closing.

"When I heard Isabel had given birth, I was so jealous. She was sick, *dying*, and I thought, she has three children, I have one. How could I not have cared for *her?*"

A defeated and repentant enemy always softened his rage.

"Oh, you know what they say. Sons are like wives, three is too many."

"Who says that?"

"Bards and wise men."

"How many do they say is just right?"

"Two, I think."

"Two!"

This time the candle just missed his ear before hitting the carved oak bed behind him. He knew it wasn't meant to hit its mark.

"Peace, Anne! I meant sons, not wives."

He knew that what had happened was an admission between them. No more children. God had blessed them with Ned, but no more. He said it did not matter, but it did. Grief over children only imagined was something he had not expected, and he did not know what to do with it.

# 19  *Lord of the North*

*London*
*Summer 1480.*

For the first time since their marriage, Anne was with Richard in London. They sat with his sister Margaret and the Duchess of York in the garden at Westminster, enjoying relative privacy in the corner of the lawn where the shade of the pear tree provided some respite from the heat.

"It is time and more that my son should bring you here. I have not seen you in a decade, child." Cecily touched Anne's hand. As if in atonement for her sudden aging upon her husband's death, time had treated the duchess very kindly in the twenty years since. Her face was the texture of linen worn soft and old, marked by only the faintest of lines and wrinkles, and she still held herself as erect as a young woman.

"You must not blame Richard," Anne said. "I am not fond of the city."

"Well," Cecily said, after a moment, "it is a mislike you share with my son. I doubt he would leave the north either, had he the choice."

"I remember the earl your father," Margaret remarked. "When I married, he rode in the procession that saw me off to Burgundy. Goodness!" She laid her embroidery down flat in her lap. "That was just before he turned traitor to my brother. Wasn't it, Mother?"

"Meg." Cecily spoke with sudden sharpness, "that was long ago."

"Why, so it was, Mother. No offense meant," Margaret said to Anne. "It just struck me how things have changed."

"Yes. Our fathers' spirits must wonder to see the peace our families have come to once again."

"Well said, my dear," Cecily said.

Meg gave Anne a long assessing look. "Richard, I begin to see why you had no time for anyone else. You broke my poor maid's heart."

"Maid?" Richard asked.

"In Burgundy, Richard. When you and Edward were there seeking aid from Charles."

"Oh. Burgundy. What a memory you have!" But he remembered, too, the pretty young woman with the poignant smile. "Meg, I spoke not a word to her more than good day and good evening."

"Precisely." Margaret leaned toward Anne. "You see how men are. We must teach them everything. Not a word, not a glance, and he wonders why she cried herself to sleep at night."

"Cease, Meg! No more of your tales, please. It was years ago. Am I to be misused thus for allowing myself to be caught here, one man among three women?" He was laughing, but Meg's probing of his affections, past or present, was not a subject he wanted to encourage. He changed tracks.

"Tell me, how goes your case with Edward?"

Margaret had come to London to enlist Edward's support against Louis of France. After Charles's death, the French king had continually threatened his smaller neighbor with war.

Margaret stabbed her needle into her embroidery. "Richard, there was a time, long ago, when if Edward displeased me, I was enough bigger to throw him across my knees and beat him. I long for those days again."

"Meg," Cecily protested faintly.

"Yes, Mother, I do. He has no regard for my country's plight."

"Your country, daughter. I would never have thought to hear you speak so."

"When you live in a place for so long a time, you grow fond."

So, Richard thought, the distant formal marriage Meg had endured with Charles—childless, passionless, but not without a degree of respect—had fostered a surprising depth of devotion. Margaret had made no suggestion of wanting to resume residence in her homeland after Charles had died.

"What did Edward say?" Richard asked.

"Didn't he tell you? He won't help. He says he can't break the treaty he signed in France. I told him that Louis has already broken it; he has been plotting for months to induce the Scots to make war with England."

They had all heard the rumors. Richard was inclined to believe them.

"There is no evidence of Louis' involvement with Scotland, as yet," he said.

"That is just what Edward said." Meg was annoyed. "He has not seen Louis move; therefore we cannot assume he does. I ask you, do we see the sun move around the earth? The fact that we don't hardly keeps it from rising in the east and setting in the west."

Margaret paused to draw breath. "The treaty is five years old; every man with his wits about him knows that Louis can't stay still for so long. And Burgundy has been friend to England for as long as Scotland has been at her throat."

Margaret had apparently forgotten how dearly Edward had had to plead to enlist Charles's assistance when Warwick turned traitor.

She set her needlework down. "Do you understand him," she asked Richard. "Do you see any sense in Edward's reasoning?"

"A treaty's a treaty, Meg. He gave his word. He won't be the first to break it." So Louis' gold was still coming after all these years.

Louis would be thoroughly weary with paying Edward's pension, but if he stopped, Edward would no longer have anything to lose by aligning with Burgundy against France.

Conveniently, there was Scotland. Louis' thinking was perfectly clear. If he could incite the Scots against England, Edward would have his forces and finances committed to his own miserable island. Not even Edward could fight in two places at the same time.

Then Louis could make what trouble he wished for Burgundy, and let Edward's bribe money fade out of sight.

Clever. Richard had to grant that.

*T*hank you," Richard said.

"For?" Anne stood in Richard's grasp as he sat on the side of the bed, a hand on either of her hips. They had brought their northern ways with them, going early to bed while voices raised in oaths and lusty laughter still bounded outside their chambers.

"Not mentioning George. Meg was within a hair's breadth of asking you why after all these years you were here in London."

"I like your sister," Anne said.

Richard pressed his forehead to her waist. His shoulders where she rested her hands were as hard and smooth as polished ivory in the candlelight. She lifted one hand to stroke his dark head. Lightly. Not giving in to her urgent craving to touch him everywhere, to let her hands devour him. She disciplined herself like a traveler who must apportion her water, to drink only enough to survive, never enough to satisfy.

"Do you?" He lifted his head and released her waist. "I wondered if you would. She is very plain-spoken."

"But she has a good heart. Richard?"

"Yes?"

"Who was that lady at supper tonight?" Blast. She had promised herself to do nothing to annoy him. She would be the very model of restraint and seemly behavior, to give him not the smallest reason to pull farther away from her.

"Which lady?"

He was not making it easy. Anne was silent a long moment. "Are you trying to vex me?"

"Certainly not. Who do you mean?"

"The dark lady in the green gown who spoke to you all through the evening and pressed close every time she had a chance." Meg was right, of course. Women must teach men everything. The problem was that they seldom wanted the lesson.

"Oh. Her. Elinor."

"Elinor," Anne said, stepping back from him to blow out the candle. She felt safer in the dark. "Kate's mother? That Elinor?"

"Yes, of course, that Elinor."

Her stomach sank. "Why didn't you tell me? Did you think I would not be interested?"

"There is nothing to tell. That was over and done with years ago. Are you jealous, Anne? You shouldn't be. It is she who has reason to be jealous of you."

"Don't, Richard."

"Don't what?"

"Don't placate me."

He sighed. "You asked me who the woman was. I told you. How is that placating? Never mind. Explain it to me in the morning."

They lay there, separately miserable. She was miserable, anyway. She couldn't help hoping that Richard was, too. A little.

Probably he was as blind to other women and their devices as Meg had implied. But there was small comfort in his abstaining from what he had no interest in pursuing. Since he was not pursuing her, either.

They had been married eight years. If his need of her was less than it once had been, was that not natural? And better? Who would want that delirium to continue, that half-sick, half-joyful madness that swept through you like a gale through an open door and left you depleted, all your resources blown away or so rearranged as to be unrecognizable?

She would.

## London, Middleham & Scotland
### 1481–1482.

Nine months later, in the spring of '81, the Scots were conspicuously violating the treaty, just as Margaret had predicted. Fires erupted all through the marches, and raids had been reported as far south as Dumfries, a good twenty miles into England. The Scots had also seized the English border towns of Berwick and Roxburgh.

And Richard was in London again, planning war.

"I won't have the Scots seizing our towns," Edward said. "James will regret listening to the Spider; he will find himself the fly." Edward's stomach protruded over his belt, and he wheezed when he spoke.

The queen sat quietly in the candlelight a little distance from her husband. Her eyes moved steadily from Edward to Richard.

Edward continued. "In the summer. We will take James to task in the summer. I will lead the army myself. I will gather men and come north. Court has grown stale. I can abide it no longer."

Richard felt Elizabeth watching him, and saw the plea in her eyes: Urge him to go. He wondered whether her motive was bringing Edward to life again, or removing him from his latest mistress. In any case, it was the first time they two had been in partnership.

Richard returned to Middleham. The days grew long, and the hills burst into wine-drenched color. Mist and clouds disappeared, blown back to the sea, and meadow grasses bent to a fragrant warm wind like a woman shaking down her hair to dry.

Edward did not come.

Neither Richard nor Anne spoke of the widening breach between them. Neither understood where it came from, or what to do about it. They were courteous and kind to each other. By some unspoken agreement they read, one aloud to the other, before snuffing out the candles and closing the shutters. It allowed them to talk without talking. Richard took her when he needed her, not roughly, but without longing. Satisfying an appetite. He hoped she didn't know.

Of course she knew. It terrified her.

Solstice passed. Days grew shorter, and the wind sharper. Autumn came, and rain fell for days. The air smelled of the sea, of damp earth, and woodsmoke. The sun came out and reapers went eagerly to the fields. The rain came down again, and grain moldered where it lay. The Scots continued their destruction along the border, which reduced the harvest still more.

In October, Edward finally rode as far as Nottingham to meet with Richard and Northumberland, far too late to begin a full campaign. He wanted to lay siege to Berwick that winter, take it back, and only then decide if anything more should be done about Scotland.

Some directive, at last, Richard thought bitterly. Now that the summer was gone, and the miserable harvest was in, almost everyone, peasant or merchant alike, had more use for grain than for gold.

He dreaded the whole campaign, leading men across a country already starving to starve it still further. What was the gain in that? To see who could live longest on nothing?

He was going through his lists of provisions and of tasks to be sure he mentioned to his steward, Bernard. Francis and John had going a game of fox and geese. Kate was on the floor helping Ned set up some wooden pins that Mark, the master groom, had carved for him. Anne and Alice were both stitching on a large tapestry frame. How he loved them all. What could he possibly find lacking?

Anne stood. "It grows late, children. Go find Agnes and get you off to bed."

Kate smiled and stood. "I'll go, Lady." Kate adored Anne, and Anne, Kate.

Anne came over to the table. She rested her hand on Richard's shoulder. "I hate to see you go into this. What will your men eat?"

"What we buy. Edward has agreed to any price we must pay."

"That won't help if there is no grain to be found."

"Do you think reminding me of it makes anything easier?" His voice was low but curt. As clearly as he'd once seen her face glow at his presence, he now saw the pain in it, before she gained command of it.

He took her hand. "Forgive me, Anne. I mislike it, too. That's all." She would forgive him, of course. Endlessly.

He felt a longing for something he couldn't name, an emptiness he couldn't account for, and something he would never have believed possible—a desire to be away from Middleham.

Richard embarked on war, and didn't like that, either. So he was a man who liked neither peace nor war.

He stayed at Berwick long enough to see camp set up and the siege engines assembled, and to divide the provisions between himself and Thomas Stanley, then left Stanley in command there and struck west with his army. They burned villages, fields, and what stores of grain they could not take with them, and drove off cattle, cutting a swath at least a good ten miles wide.

It was odious work. He didn't know who had the worst of it: himself or Stanley. A siege is never pleasant. The incredible, mind-numbing tedium, the miserable conditions, always some form of camp sickness to deal with. Soldiers down with dysentery, sweats, and fevers. Food almost as stale and sparse in the camp as in the city.

Not that his own work had much to recommend it.

Warfare was never meant to be between any but soldiers. You never truly get used to destroying unarmed peasants. They stand by their ruined huts sometimes with hate in their eyes, but just as often a terrible resignation. You may leave them breathing, but you have destroyed them all the same—burned their peat-roofed huts, and driven off, killed, or eaten their pathetic few and starving swine and kine.

A cycle of hate fuels the destruction. You hate the peasants for making you destroy them when they have done nothing to deserve it. You hate yourself for what you have done to them. Then you hate them for making you hate yourself, and then you are able to destroy them. He had tried to explain that to Roger, his new squire. Something about the lad troubled him. Not that Roger complained. Ever.

They were headed back from Scotland, toward Berwick. The return journey would be quick—the land was burned, the householders scattered, and they had picked up what food they could. If Berwick had not already surrendered to Stanley, their joined forces would make quick work of it, and they could all go home. Richard was beginning to miss Middleham. That was a good sign.

"Did you feed the horses?" Richard asked.

Roger was maybe sixteen, about the age of the Scot Richard had executed a few years back for murdering Davy Ridpath. The boy sat before the fire, staring at it, but not seeing.

Roger nodded. Hardly an excess of respect.

"How is the grain supply?" No answer. "Enough to last until Berwick?"

Roger nodded again, without speaking. He wasn't a churl. Unfortunately. Churlishness was the least troubling explanation of Roger's behavior that Richard could think of. He moved in front of the fire so he could see Roger's face. White and tight-lipped. He didn't like the look.

"Get up." He kicked at his squire's boot.

"What is it, sir? Did I forget something?"

"No. I want to talk to you. Get up."

Roger scrambled to his feet, and they started walking toward the edge of the camp.

"What's wrong?" Richard asked.

"Nothing, sir."

"Nothing. I doubt that. Do you confess your sins, Roger?"

"Sir! Do you take me for a heathen?"

"This is the same thing, you know. It's good for your soul."

They went on a few yards in silence. "Well, speak, or not," Richard said. "It's all one to me. But I remember once, it would have been good had I told someone what troubled me. The heart lies easier."

"I am not fit to be a soldier, my lord."

"No?"

"No, sir."

"Why not?"

"A soldier should not wince and quail at blood like a girl."

"You did that?"

"Yes."

"Everyone does, some time. What you see on the outside is not what we carry in our hearts."

"But sir—"

"Listen. This is ugly work. No man likes it. Burning cottages, killing farmers. Driving them out to starve. Of course you hate it.

"What you must do is tell yourself it is battle. Tell yourself that, because it is."

"Sir, I—"

Richard knew he wasn't going to want to hear what Roger seemed to have decided to tell him, after all. He sighed. "What is it?"

"There was a child. And a horse. The horse had broken its foreleg and kept trying to get up. It didn't seem to understand why it couldn't. I guess animals don't."

"What did you do?"

"The child was dead. I killed the horse."

"Good lad. It was what any man should do." Odd about the animals. Sometimes they grieved a man the worst of all. They feed us, clothe us, carry us into battle. We slaughter them for our needs without hesitation, but it is their deaths more than any human's that are often more than we can bear. Richard didn't know why that should be.

"No, sir." The tears were coming down Roger's face now. "I tried to cut its throat. My aim was off, and it was thrashing about and didn't die right away. So I stabbed it."

"Of course." No, he decidedly did not want to hear this.

"And again. And then I realized I had just gone on stabbing, over and over, after it was dead. Why did I do that, sir?" His eyes were agonized.

Why? Because it's in all of us, that murderous demon. It may be hard to call up, but once called, it's just as hard to banish.

"I don't know."

"You don't know, my lord?" Shock and outrage were in the voice.

"No. But you are not the first. We've all done such things." Welcome to the truth, boy. I know no more than anyone. Command means nothing.

"That's all you have to say, sir?" There was bitterness in his face. What did the boy want, some terrible chastisement to ease his guilt? Probably. Richard hadn't the heart to think of it.

"That's all. I haven't liked everything I have done in battle, either. Go back, get some sleep if you can."

By the time Richard had arrived back at Berwick, there was a new player in the game, one that removed any hope of going home.

Alexander, Duke of Albany, was the brother of King James III of Scotland. Banished from Scotland for scheming to take over the throne, he had fled to France, where he acquired a wife and better grammar, both French. Edward's agents had given Albany some interesting offers to consider and safe conduct to England to consider them at greater length.

Richard joined them at Fotheringhay, the castle where he had spent his earliest years, and of which he had pleasant memories. Memories were all he found pleasant on this occasion.

Edward promised to recognize Albany as lawful king of Scotland. In return, as king, Albany would sever all alliances with France, and marry Edward's daughter Cecily. Assuming he could rid himself of Anne de la Tour.

The Duke of Albany was tall, slender, and pale, with light brown hair, and a short upper lip that perhaps contributed to his seeming perpetually startled, along with an airy way of speaking. He agreed placidly to all Edward's conditions, and expressed a strong conviction that he could invalidate his present marriage, but had no credible plan for doing so. They were well into the third flagon of the expensive sweet malmsey that Edward particularly liked when Richard excused himself from their company, the malmsey being only Edward's final offense in a litany of offenses.

*E*dward was seated in comfort with a great cup still in hand when Richard rejoined him much later. Albany had gone to his own quarters.

"Wine?" Edward asked, raising his cup. He did not seem drunk. He did seem angry.

"No," Richard said. "I prefer water if it's all the same to you." A servant saw to it, then left.

"So. You ask my leave to choose your drink. Very courteous." Edward set down his tankard. "But when did you decide you didn't need my leave to exit a council of which you were a central part? Sit down. I don't like having to look up at you."

"Oh, I don't know." Richard compromised on sitting—he leaned against the table behind him. "Some time after you started believing you could crown the King of Scotland. When was that?"

"That's idiocy. Albany will win the crown for himself."

"You sent for him. You promised the English army behind him. You pledged Cecily to him. How old is she now? Ten? Eleven?"

Edward shook his head. "Thereabouts. Why?"

"She's young. Why worry about dissolving the French marriage? In three or four years, the Frenchwoman may have died, anyway. Having your way will be easy."

"So here we are with your conscience, again. Must we go over this one more time?"

"Not at all," Richard said. "I'm just commissioned to make war on the Scots. My conscience and I can keep our debate private."

"That's just the trouble. You keep nothing private. You get up and walk out of our council with affront written all over you. Tell your conscience not to show its face, if you're so bent on keeping it. Don't you understand yet that acts earn their own justice?"

"High-sounding words," Richard said, "if they are true. I suppose, for example, that George was as deserving of the crown as you. Assuming he had succeeded, of course. His only sin was that he failed. And Warwick's. Do I have it right now?"

Edward looked at him blearily, his face blank, as if Richard's words were too difficult to follow. Richard had rarely been angrier, but saw no use in continuing the discussion. As he himself had said, he was hired to make war, not to have opinions. But he didn't need them; he could talk about horses and supplies perfectly calmly.

Richard returned to Scotland by way of Berwick. He was able to muster a small supply of provisions, again to share with the Berwick contingent. He found Stanley still in good state, his men bored, but so far not dangerously so.

Richard took his own army north to Edinburgh. By the time he arrived, King James had been captured by Albany's supporters and held at Edinburgh castle, and a goodly number of his nobles had been hanged.

James was out; Albany was in.

The one thing that could be predicted absolutely was the unpredictability of the Scot nobility—rich as lords, which they were, and lawless as brigands, which they also were. They came forth in force to reverse the most recent turn of Fate, freed James and restored him to the throne.

Albany surrendered, happy to keep his life and permission to remain in Scotland. He renounced his marriage to Edward's daughter Cecily and all pretensions to the throne. Negotiating with James later, in Edinburgh, Richard demanded only the return of Cecily's dowry and the ceding of Berwick back to the English. He had no interest in who Albany married or did not marry.

Richard and Edward implemented a courier system of a change of horses and riders every twenty miles. It allowed news to pass at the rate of a hundred miles a day. The much-esteemed communication system between himself and Edward brought no further instructions while Richard was in Edinburgh. He released the greatest share of his men, and returned to Berwick.

Thomas Lord Stanley, punctilious as ever, had awaited Richard's return before lifting the siege. The city had surrendered; only the castle still held out. Provisions were running low. Stanley had resituated himself and his immediate retainers in rooms at a comfortable inn after the Scots had vacated the city and opened their doors to the English. The inn had no food other than what Stanley brought, but it did have a roof and beds.

Stanley had a strip of dried meat in one hand. "Would you like to eat? They still have ale here. Innkeeper!"

Richard motioned him away. "Thank you, no. I'll eat with my men."

"I must say that your return here so quickly after taking Edinburgh was quite a surprise. Although your courier system was quite effective."

"Why the surprise?" Richard asked.

"You had the Scots under your thumb. When you had Edinburgh, you could have brought King Jamie to his knees. Maybe squeeze him like Edward squeezed Louis. If you don't mind my saying so, that is." Stanley washed down the meat with a long draft from the tankard. "Does it not seem irregular that Edward would not press for further advantage with Scotland before you left?"

"Such as?" Richard idly took a piece of cheese from the platter before them. "We've Berwick and Roxburgh back. Cecily's dowry is on its way back. James is on the throne again. Everything as it was."

"Everything as it was," Stanley agreed, wiping his mouth with the back of his hand, then his hand on a napkin. "Everything, that is, except for the fortune spent and the loans Edward must pay back. An expensive sojourn, I would say."

"Yes, Thomas, I would say so, too. Pity Edward didn't make his wishes known, if he wanted more from me. Pity he hadn't any idea how to feed an army for a few more months in the field."

Richard left Stanley enjoying his meal, and rode back to where the remainder of his army had pitched camp.

One of nine surgeons with the army, William Hobbes had come by to make his report.

"A few wounded, sir. The wounds are mostly minor. Two men died some time back of burns sustained from the defenders. Some with broken bones, all mending. We've some men ill, however. From flux, unstable diet, bad water. I've never understood what makes some men fall ill to the conditions that don't affect others."

Richard nodded. Hobbes thought he seemed distracted. "Nor I, doctor. Once you understand that, I suspect you will have made your fortune. What are you about, now?"

"Just seeing to my patients."

"You might think how best to transport those too wounded or ill to ride."

"So it's true, then. We are returning to England." Hobbes had heard that rumor, and disbelieved it. Surely Edward would expect Richard's army to conquer Scotland, now they were so close.

"My captains know," Richard said. "I will be dismissing the rest of the soldiers in the morning."

Hobbes had always suspected there was something slightly different about the nature of soldiers, that they could kill with impunity. Looking at Richard, he saw the lines deepened and lengthened around his mouth, and thought, perhaps not so much impunity.

"May I walk with you, doctor?"

Hobbes assented, a little puzzled to be appointed what he suspected was to be Richard's confidante, then thought, maybe there are things that must be confided out of reach of one's peers.

He was glad of Richard's company. He found the duke's conversation refreshing—not the endless preoccupation of most nobles with their wealth and might.

Richard watched as Hobbes changed a dressing and lent a third hand.

"You might have been good at that," Hobbes said.

Richard smiled. "Had things been only a little different, this might have been my life's work."

"Oh?"

"If my father had not made the bid for the crown, that is. I was the last of four sons. Did you know there were four of us?"

"Yes."

"Edmund died first, when I was very young. I spent little time with him. Edward said he might have been the finest of the lot of us, had he lived."

"Easy enough to say that about the dead."

"Yes. I'd have gone to the abbey to learn, then it's anyone's guess whether I'd have tried to save men's lives or their souls.

"And you, doctor? How did you come by this particular task? I remember you were at Amiens, too, though we had few battle wounds there." Said with a downward twist of the mouth.

Richard was a seeker, Hobbes thought—of something. Probably of more than the world would offer up to him. Seekers were often disappointed people.

"Oh, I was trained as a battle surgeon," Hobbes said. "It was my first calling."

"You were a barber?"

"No, I was trained at Oxford. Surgeons there were taught as physicians. More, in fact. The lessons in surgery were in addition to the rest."

"I'm appalled not to have known that. Forgive the blunder, please."

"Oh, no need for that. Few people out of the profession know the difference or care."

They walked a while in silence. The stars were thick in the night sky. Richard looked up.

"No wonder we fix our natures on the stars. The further from ourselves we can attach blame, the better we like it," he said.

Hobbes was struck, not for the first time, by what seemed to him Richard's odd combination of being locked in the old ways and beliefs, and looking beyond the horizon for some dawn not yet come.

"We live in strange times," Hobbes reflected. There were some ideas in the air, voiced mainly by heretics, ridiculed and laughed nearly into nonexistence. But not quite. "I have heard men say that the earth is not the center around which the rest of the firmament turns."

"Why, how can that be, doctor?" Richard's voice was bitter. "If the earth is not the center, than neither is man. And we know we are. Why else has God made the world?"

Hobbes could not quite give credence to the idea. Could not dismiss it, either. "If that should prove to be true, it would be a blow to our pride," he conceded.

"Well," Richard said. "Perhaps man could do with a reduction in arrogance."

Hobbes smiled. "Most of the great ideas of man were first voiced by heretics."

"Truly? I had not thought that."

"Consider. If a thought is in line with the doctrine, how does it change us?"

"So we leave it to the heretics. We hang them and burn them. Long after they turn to dust, we listen to them. Another sad thing in this sad old world. It has done nothing but grow in corruption since the Fall of man."

*I*n late August, Richard finally left Scotland. A cold rain came down, and the wet rocks were slippery beneath the horses' hooves. On a steep rocky path near the border, Francis's horse stumbled and fell. Richard heard the crack of breaking bone almost before he saw what happened, and called for Dr. Hobbes.

He watched Hobbes' knowing hands feel along Francis's shin. Francis lay back with his hand clamped down over his mouth.

Hobbes rose abruptly. "Get him in a wagon and keep him dry, then let us get off this hill and find a place we can talk."

They made room for Francis in one of the larger wagons and found a spot at the base of the hill where a few trees partially offered shelter. They stood under the trees dripping rain.

"Your femur is broken, Lord Lovell, but it is a clean break. Whether it will still be so after you are jolted all the way to Middleham, I can't say."

Francis rose up on his elbows. "Christ have mercy, you are not going to leave me here!"

"Not precisely here, sir. But Alnwick is nearby."

"No! I won't stay here." He lay back and threw his arm over his face.

"Easy, Francis. Can it be done, Doctor? Can he be taken home?"

"If it were me, I wouldn't go so far with an injury like that. More agony than I would choose to bear." He glanced over at Francis. "But who can blame a man for wanting to be home, when he is sick? Well, we can try it. If the weather improves and his lungs stay clear, I doubt it will kill him. We can always stop if there is trouble. We must set his leg and bind it well here, though."

"Now?" Francis was attentive again.

"Yes, my lord, just so. Sir," to Richard, "if you would get him some wine, and for me, some splints—spears will do—and strips of cloth."

A soldier brought three wineskins. "No, no," Hobbes said. "Just one. Too much wine, and he will go down with the chill. We only want enough to mute the pain." He folded one of the rags and handed it to Francis when the wineskin was empty.

Francis looked at it. "What is that for?"

"For you to set between your teeth, and clamp down. You are not so drunk this won't hurt." "I don't want that in my mouth."

*329*

"You don't want a hole in your tongue, either."

"A hole in my tongue?"

"Take it. Common men—and most women—have sense enough to scream, instead of trying to bite back their pain. Lie down, now, and do as I say. There's a good lad."

Hobbes arranged a half dozen men around Francis. "Very well. Now, hold firm when I pull on his leg." He ran his hands down the broken thigh again, then, satisfied, grasped Francis just above around the knee and yanked. At the second grinding crunch of his bones, Francis did not cry out. Neither did he avail himself of Dr. Hobbes' tongue-saver; he fainted.

*A*t Middleham, they carried Francis into the keep on a makeshift sling of folded blankets. Anne came running, and Richard saw on her face a look of pure dread that changed to relief when she turned from the litter and saw him standing there.

*A*nd now?" Anne asked.

"Now I must go to London for Parliament, and to meet with Edward about the Scots."

"Is that finished?"

"I hope so."

"When will you be back?"

"I don't know. When Parliament ends. Perhaps by late fall, perhaps in the spring."

"I hardly know you, Richard. I have seen so little of you this year."

"Come with me, if you like."

"No. To be in London with you is not being with you at all. Besides, Francis should have someone near him."

"As you wish."

He was not disappointed by her refusal.

He was starting to understand. When he was gone from Middleham, he missed her. When he was home, he missed wanting her as much as he once had.

He told himself that the lack of continued childbearing had left Anne's body more fair than that of most women her age. It was true; it didn't help. What he resented was that her body did not accept his seed. He never could bear having no affect on those he loved.

He wanted to again want something so badly he thought he would die without it.

What he longed for was longing itself.

# London
## 1482.

Edward's health seemed worse, but his spirits better. Elizabeth was actually cordial, almost flirtatious, which would have been offensive except there was a wry, knowing air about her, as if she were acknowledging that her manner was the only way she knew of making amends.

Richard pitied her. She had aged, and no doubt Edward had his usual young and beautiful mistresses.

Then he discovered there was one mistress in particular, a certain Elizabeth Shore, but "I call her Jane," Edward said. "Just Jane. There could be a certain confusion, else."

When Richard made no comment, Edward added, "You disapprove, of course. As usual."

"It is not my place to approve or disapprove. You must choose your own."

"About Jane Shore," Richard said later to Hobbes. He had cut short Edward's own description of the woman because the pleasure and poignancy in Edward's voice reminded him of a lovesick youth, and he could not bear to see his brother so craven. "Who is she?"

"A merchant's wife. You have not seen her?"

"No, I've not had that pleasure."

"My, my. A shade bitter, sir, are you not? My advice is to hold your opinion, until you have met the woman."

"You have?"

"Of course."

"Well?"

"Well, she's not one of your brother's usual light ladies. Neither particularly young nor especially beautiful. Intelligent, though—comes to me for advice. Far more than Elizabeth does. She's one of those women who make a man think more of comfort than of love." He smiled, clasping his hands across his belly. "Unless I'm just getting old, and comfort is all I ever think about."

It was true, what Hobbes had said. Richard liked her. A woman who liked men, rather than lusted for them, or coyly tried to please, one who seemed to invite men's confidence.

*I*t is time I added to your holdings, brother. Such service as you have given me should not go unrewarded."

Such service? A bitter, tedious siege. Victory over an enemy that had already defeated itself. Edward's extreme gratitude was pathetic; Richard would have preferred the old arrogance.

He waited, and listened.

Permanent possession, for himself and his heirs, of the wardenship of the marches.

All the king's lands, manors, fees, and profits of Cumberland County.

The right to select and appoint the sheriff of said county.

The castle and city of Carlisle.

Possession of any land of the West Marches subdued and won from the Scots.

He was the richest man in England, outside of Edward himself, with, certainly, more than enough power not to concern himself with Henry Percy's discontent. Truly, Lord of the North. There was no one in the northern counties, no one in fact in all of England, who could touch him. Nor Ned, when he inherited his father's estate.

"What have you to say?"

"I thank you for the honor." It was all he could find words for. The gift had the same bitter aftertaste as Warwick's offering Mercury too late in the day. He walked to the window. "I remember when there were men that others thought over-mighty. You had to break them to make them understand who was king. Have you no fears regarding me?"

"Should I?"

"No. I am your servant, and the crown's. But why now?"

"Brother, it is in your nature to be loyal. A man does not change his nature."

## *Middleham*
### *Late 1482.*

Richard rode across Middleham's drawbridge remembering the night he arrived home once from Scotland in a snowstorm to find Anne waiting for him, breathless, in the courtyard. There was no one there tonight but the grooms. What did he expect? That was six years ago. Things had changed since then. He walked on into the great hall, where the butler greeted him.

"Welcome home, my lord. May we bring you some supper?"

"Not now. Ask my men if they want to eat, though."

On up the stairs and into his own chamber, also empty, but a page followed him in. He handed the boy his cloak and hat. "Ask the servants to fill the bath." Perhaps Anne had gone early to bed. He debated whether he should walk across to the lady chamber, or wait until morning. Once, he wouldn't have had to think about it.

*F*ootsteps down the passageway. His sons, followed by Kate and the countess, Ned and John running like thieves, Kate almost a woman, above all that, dignified.

"Mother." He kissed Alice's cheek. "Where is Anne? Has she gone to bed already?"

"No, she is in the solar." Alice returned the kiss.

"With Lord Lovell." Kate spoke knowingly. She was aglow with self-importance.

*A*nne held out her hand to him, and Francis started to stand.

"No, stay seated," Richard said. "How is the leg healing?"

"Very well." Francis was thin, and pale from the weeks indoors, but indeed looked well—rested and content. Richard drew up a chair and sat down between them. They broke off their talk, and drew him into their circle, welcoming him, but still he felt odd, as if for them he had only left the room a few minutes before, and then returned, instead having been gone for months. No eager embraces, no pleading with him for tales of the journey. Why should he mind? What tales were there worth the telling, anyway? He wanted their attention, that was all, and because that want seemed so childish, he withdrew into silence to keep from showing it.

*H*e could imagine what happened while he was gone, had done so far too many times. A foolish thing, to torment one's self, as though life did not of its own accord bring torment enough.

Anne brought Francis many of the trays of his meals, because it pleased her to serve those she loved. And she loved Francis, Richard knew. Loved him as her husband's dearest friend, and the household's most welcome guest. And maybe because he was what Richard suspected all women secretly want—a captive man. A man wounded in body, who could not just stand up and walk away when she sat down beside him. Wounded in spirit, too, perhaps, needing amusements and comfort that would be trifles at any other time. But certainly not so wounded that he could not talk, look, and listen.

After a while Francis was well enough to sit up, to swing his feet over the edge of the bed, and gradually, day by day, ease a little more of his weight onto his injured leg. Soon it bore his full weight, and he walked haltingly to the window to stand in the sun trembling with the effort, and marveled at how rapidly a bedfast man became feeble, before limping back to bed, exhausted.

Anne often sat beside him, first in silence, when he was feverish; later, as he recovered, amusing him by talking and reading. Now, bound by relief—the leg was healing straight and true, and he would not be crippled—they talked easily and laughed together often. Once or twice, in the laughter, their eyes met, and held. Finally Anne grew bold. Or else she was merely comfortable, and innocent enough to indulge her curiosity.

"Francis, don't you ever miss loving someone?"

"Sweetheart, you wound my pride! I had thought my fame greater than that." Francis lay fully clothed on the coverlet, propped against a stack of cushions. He leaned forward toward Anne. "I would tell you how much I have loved, Annie, except that is considered discourteous."

Anne did not even blush. She was so used to Francis by now, it was like hearing a brother boast. "Oh, your ladies. I meant truly love. One person."

"As you love Richard, you mean?" Francis was suddenly serious.

"Yes." Anne answered quickly, no faltering. Almost too quickly. Something had altered. Change was in the air between them like smoke, stinging their eyes and parching their mouths.

"What, so I could see on some poor woman's face the fear that was in yours before you realized it was me that was hurt, and not Richard?" Francis' voice was bitter.

"Francis, I—" Anne was aghast, not having known so much showed in her face.

"Don't apologize. Of course you should be happy Richard was not hurt. He is your husband. But that is the point of love, isn't it? The kind you speak of, anyway—that you are always inflicting pain, or bearing it? Why should I wish that on any woman? Or myself."

The dismay on Anne's face was sharp.

"Forgive me," Francis said very quietly. "Sometimes I can be clumsy. That was unkind when you have done so much to make these miserable weeks bearable."

"You didn't hurt me."

"Well, something has. I can see that. What's amiss?" Francis put his hand on hers. He hadn't far to reach; over the weeks her chair had crept closer to the bed. "Come here. Come sit beside me, and tell me."

She did, and was besieged. By sadness, that it had been so long since she and her husband had truly touched each other's hearts; by how handsome Francis was. How could she not have noticed before the blue of his eyes and the slant of his cheekbones? But most of all, she was undone by his noticing her, the changes in her face, when for Richard she had been invisible for months. Berwick was surrounded by no weapons as powerful as those that assaulted the fortifications of Anne's heart.

"Come," Francis said again, "tell me." He stroked her cheek with the backs of his fingers, and in his eyes was all the time in the world.

"Oh, Francis," she said, and her stomach dropped within her like a stone down a well. Their faces moved toward each other, slowly, but as certainly as her chair had edged closer toward the bed. As they kissed, he felt her cheek wet with tears.

Scotland

Middleham

Yorkshire ✧Sheriff Hutton
✧York
Pontefract
Wakefield ✧✧ Castle
Sandal
Castle
England
Nottingham ✧
Castle
Market Bosworth✧ ✧Leicester
Ludlow✧
Stony Cambridge
Stratford ✧
✧
Milford Haven✧
Epping Forest
London✧✧
Wales

Burgundy

France

# Book Four
# The King

*1483–1485*

# 20 *The Protector*

King Edward died just after sunset, while a salmon sky still shone through the window in his chamber. Lying in his great carved bed, he had ordered the curtains left open and stopped Lord Hastings from closing the shutters. With three pillows beneath his head, Edward could see the Thames bend out of sight as lanterns along the river's edge were lit. He intended to keep the view in front of him for as long as he could. What did it matter if he caught his death of cold now?

As the light faded, his wits grew dim, and he forgot who was with him and who was not. He called for his wife Elizabeth and his mistress Jane and his brothers Richard and George. *Keep my peace, all of you,* was what he wanted to say, but Jane could not be admitted into Elizabeth's presence, George was dead, and Richard was in the north.

Elizabeth sat beside the bed, her hand lying on the coverlet near her husband's. But she didn't touch him. Edward's skin was slimy with the sweat of sickness, and she doubted he cared whether she were there or not. Their daughter Bess sat at Edward's other side in the chair Hastings had drawn close for her. She did not touch Edward either, but she was quick to feel his eyes on her and smile in answer to his groping gaze.

A servant renewed the fire as the priest administered last rites. Elizabeth rose, shook the folds from her skirt where long sitting had creased it, and walked over to the window. She leaned against the casement and closed her eyes. She felt old. For the past twenty years, men had marveled at her beauty, scarcely able to believe that she was older than her husband. She knew their praise was no exaggeration. Then. Now she sensed her face, with the cold air striking it, not as a part of herself but as a crumbling shield floating before her. Her hands yearned to creep up to touch the shield, but she willed them to stay calmly clasped before her.

"Madam?" Hastings's hand slid down her arm, as he turned her gently from the window. The death of this man, whom they, each in their own way, had loved above any other, had temporarily halted the enmity between them.

"It is over, madam. He is gone."

At the bedside, Dr. Hobbes, black-robed, felt the pulse one more time, pronounced the king dead, and folded Edward's arms across his chest. In spite of his tart warnings to Edward, Hobbes had truly expected the king to live at least a decade more.

As the chamber filled with courtiers come to look their last on the king, Elizabeth began to cry, shoulders heaving with helpless rage at being left alone and aging. Her children came to her and began to soak her velvet bodice with their sobbing, and while she didn't gather them to her, neither did she repel them.

The queen's sobs were as subdued now as earlier they had been clamorous. When Edward first hovered at death's door, sentient but increasingly indifferent to the demands of the living, she had flung herself at the foot of the bed, had actually grasped his feet and shaken them, screaming at him not to die. "Ned, don't you dare to leave me now!" Even knowing Elizabeth's famous reluctance to take leave of anything she badly wanted, Dr. Hobbes and Will Hastings were appalled.

Bess, Edward's favorite daughter and the child who most resembled him, felt no rage, only sadness. He was her father, and she had loved him. She rose, leaned down to kiss his forehead, and sat on the bench by the door, away from the throng of courtiers. Outside the door, Caesar, Edward's wolfhound, sensed the changes in the chamber. His tail ceased its hopeful beating against the floor, and he began a low whimpering whine.

## Middleham Castle
### April 1483.

April was piercingly cold. Gales came in hard, battering Middleham like ocean waves crashing on shore, hurling dirt like needles in the faces of any man or beast unfortunate enough to be at large.

Richard stood in the wind that roared around the castle ramparts, watching the distant object in the dusk. For a moment it appeared stationary. It could have been anything—a tree, a cart broken down and abandoned where it faltered. Soon, however, the object could be seen to move; it assumed the shape of a horse and rider, in a tearing hurry.

When the horse swerved toward the gatehouse, making its destination undeniable, Richard left the wall and crossed the arcade into the keep. Trouble, of course. Why was there never such haste to bring good news?

He hurried down the stairs and almost collided with Francis, on his way.

"There's. . . ." Francis began.

"I know. Send for food and hot wine, and bring the man to the solar."

*R*ichard stood at the hearth, prodding a fire that didn't need prodding. Oh, God, his brother dead. The nightmare paraded before his eyes. Elizabeth and her family seizing control of the kingdom—the treasury, the best navy in decades, young Edward. Edward was what, now—twelve? Thirteen? Old enough to have opinions, loyalties, hatreds. Oh yes, hatreds most of all. Elizabeth would have summoned Lord Rivers to bring his royal charge to London, crown him, and appoint his advisors with as much speed as could be summoned.

Less certain was how Edward's death would affect Richard's own life. Legally, Elizabeth could not touch any of the offices or holdings Edward had bestowed on his brother. But with enough power, anything could be done. The years of working the peace with Scotland. Restoring the northern estates. The new floor he had added to Middleham, making of it a true home, not merely an ancient bulwark. His protection of the City of York. Maybe other men could have done what he had done; no one could have loved his domain more than he had.

He roused himself from his thoughts and turned to face the boy. "Pardon my ill manners. I have not even asked your name."

"It's Nicholas, sir. Nicholas Grey."

The messenger was a lanky youth with black hair cut square at the neck and across the forehead, a thin face that couldn't possibly be as young as it looked, and eyes reddened from dirt and wind. He huddled over his steaming cup, looking, if anything, more exhausted than when he had first entered.

"Then tell me, Nicholas Grey, when did my brother die?"

"A fortnight come next Monday, sir. Do you mean this is the first you have heard?"

"Nothing."

The boy nodded. "My Lord Hastings thought as much. He said it was for shame that he should have to be the one to summon my lord to his office."

Richard stared at Grey. "You're *Hastings's* man?"

"Yes, sir."

Well, of course. If the lad had been one of the royal couriers, he would have worn Edward's colors. How like Elizabeth to neglect even the minimum courtesy of sending word herself.

He was so embroiled in Elizabeth's slight, that he missed the most important fact.

Francis caught it. "A moment," he said. "You said *office*."

"Why, Protector of the Realm." Grey turned his face toward Richard, his eyes wide and startled. "Did you not know, sir? The king's will stated so. I—we assumed you knew the content of the will."

Richard shook his head and put down the poker. "No. Official word seems to stop at the River Trent. You had best tell me."

The boy took a breath and proceeded heavily. "The king's will stated thus: in the event he were to die before his son came of age, your grace was to serve as protector until the prince reached his majority. The will has been read; Hastings has seen it. There is no doubt, sir."

The fire crackled as a log split. Richard watched the sparks go out, one after another. Protector? That was a shock greater than Edward's death. It shouldn't have been. Any king might be wise to name one, precaution against the nightmare of a child ruler. And himself to fill that office? Reasonable, too, as Edward's only surviving brother. But the prince had not been raised by his father's family. The queen and her kin—for that matter, probably young Edward himself—would not find the choice agreeable.

"Where are my nephews, now?" he asked.

"The Prince of Wales is still at Ludlow. The young Duke of York is with the queen his mother in London. Sir?"

"Yes?"

"My lord Hastings said to tell you to secure the king and get to London with all possible haste."

*R*ichard sat before the dying fire, watching the embers glow and fade, long after Nicholas and Francis left. Protector. He hoped Edward had seen the irony of that. The office that could give him enough power to hold what was his would be the very thing that would take him away from it, perhaps forever. Something he could not quite grasp hovered in his mind, a thought that would not emerge. Finally, he slept fitfully for a time in his chair, waking when the night was still dark. He walked out to the stables to have Orion saddled, shaking the stable boy out of a sound sleep, in so ill a humor he actually enjoyed the boy's misery.

The night was cold and still windy, and he rode not for pleasure but to out-race his thoughts. All the men of his family dying young. Stupidly. He could find no purpose in any of their deaths. Warwick's ambition and Jack's loyalty. His father and Edmund cut down as they trustingly observed a truce. George lying drunken and drowned on a crude litter. Edward bloated and old before his time, dead at forty. To what purpose was any of it? To what purpose were his own efforts to secure a domain here, to seek surety for his family and this country he loved?

The ride changed nothing. He returned in as poor a humor as he had left. He went up to the solar, where, in their usual custom, Anne, and Alice, Francis, and the children were taking breakfast. One of his hounds came up and barked in greeting, and he smacked it on the nose with his glove. Francis's hat was on a chair, and he picked it up and threw it across the room.

"Good morning to you, too." Francis said, without rancor.

Alice rose at once and shepherded the children out of the room. Richard caught the look that flashed between Francis and Anne, a look of instant understanding, like the one that had passed between them when he returned from London, after leaving the injured Francis to recover at Middleham. A look he could not put words to, but which had in it longing, sorrow, and great tenderness. What that amounted to, he supposed, was love. What form the love had taken, he didn't know, and realized with great shame that he probably could never bear to ask.

Francis stood. "I have letters to post. I will be in the schoolroom if you want me."

"I don't have the plague," Richard said. "There's no need for you to leave."

"Truly, I've finished." Francis laid down his napkin. "I will leave you with your lady."

"Richard," Anne said. "Francis told me."

There was bread on the table, and a wheel of cheese. A servant started to pour his wine. Richard reached for the flask and waved him away. "Thank you. We will serve ourselves now."

Anne waited until the servant had closed the door behind him. "I'm so sorry. I saw the rider come in last night. I knew something had happened. Why did you not come to me?"

He saw that her face was tired and pale, the skin shadowed beneath her eyes. She must have slept no more than he had. "It was late. I didn't want to wake you."

"You know I sleep little when you are not beside me."

It was a reproach. Gentle, but a reproach just the same. He didn't answer.

In a moment, she said, "What will happen now?"

"I must go to London to see to the young king." The bread in his mouth was dry like paper.

"When will you leave?"

"As soon as I can raise men for the journey."

"Men-at-arms?"

"Of course. What did you think, men-at-books, men-at-music?" He was instantly sorry; she didn't deserve his bitterness.

"You expect danger from the queen?" Anne's face was expressionless, her voice low and cool and even. By now, he knew well the careful voice, the still face: the greater her control, the greater the fear or pain it masked.

"I *expect* the queen to honor Edward's will. I *expect* it will be easier for her to do so if I come with more than a handful of household knights. That is all."

"You make a small matter of this."

"It is a small matter. A journey I have made a hundred times."

"Never in these circumstances." She laid her hand on his. "I am afraid for you."

And now the shadowed thought teasing his mind on his cold and unpleasant ride came clear: Elizabeth did not simply neglect to send him word. His knowledge of Edward's death was what she most wanted to prevent.

*R*ichard settled his cloak around him and let his head fill with the clean cold smell of the night. A light wind stirred in the trees below, and a skiff of snow had fallen. His lonely and often cold sanctuary on the rampart brought a bit of solace, as it had done so long ago, when he had first come here.

Hastings had sent word a second time, informing him that Anthony Rivers was making haste to London with the young king, accompanied by two thousand men-at-arms. Harry Stafford, Duke of Buckingham, had offered Richard his support and an equal number of men. Richard had requested Stafford cut the number to three hundred.

He smiled to himself, a little bleakly. Hastings would not be pleased. Will wanted to meet power with power. But numbers were not always power. Sometimes, like words, they were parable. Sometimes ruse. Rivers's show of strength was meant to daunt. A warning for him to abandon Edward's charge. Or to incite him to rash actions that would justify retaliation. Rivers could have ten thousand men, Richard thought, and he would not use them save in defense.

So he would not offend. He would do nothing that was not in strict accord with both the law and Edward's will; he was not fool enough to give anyone cause to say he had violated either.

It was *afterward* that worried him, after the country settled again, after the funeral, after the coronation. *Brother, if you knew how little I want to go to London and untangle your knot.*

If Edward had married another woman. If he had eaten and drunk more moderately, had picked his advisors more prudently. . . .

If, if, if.

If-the-rope-had-been-weaker had never saved a man from hanging.

"Richard?"

Anne paused in the archway, flanked on either side by the torches, then walked over to stand beside him. "All is ready for your journey?"

"Yes."

"Then come to bed, my lord. The night is already short."

"Soon, Anne." He kissed her cheek. "Go and keep warm. I will join you soon."

"I think you will not, Richard." She stepped a little apart from him. "You will stay here late with your thoughts, and then go to the lord's chamber, and say in the morning that you would not wake me."

God save him from her insistence on small truths. "You know me too well, Annie."

For a moment, neither of them spoke. The castle was almost eerily quiet, the sound of the wind no more than a breath in their ears.

"You plan to meet Lord Rivers on the road to London?"

"Yes."

"And he rides with two thousand men."

"Yes, Anne. As I've told you."

"Buckingham has three hundred men, as do you. Six hundred to Rivers's two thousand." She often did that in preparation for argument, line up every point of indisputable agreement, as though he would not notice when she departed into the matter of contention.

"I see you mocked me," he said, "when you said you had no skill for numbers."

"As you mock me now, and my fears for you."

He could think of nothing useful to say to that, and so was silent.

"Richard, I would you do not go to London tomorrow."

"Waiting won't help," he said, deliberately patient. "The longer I stay, the harder this journey will be."

"No. I meant, don't go at all. Stay here and rule the north. Let Hastings meet Rivers and take Edward to London."

Plans made, troops mustered, arms gathered. His word given. "My brother appointed me protector. I can't ignore that."

"Of course you can."

"Anne, what are you saying? There is no other choice I can make."

"Of course you can. Men have always a choice. They say they do not and then do exactly as they please. You fight to take the throne, and you think it better to die than to see another there, your pride is so great."

Presumably "you" referred to all men, not only him.

She was twining and untwining the tail of her braid around one finger. "Tell me this, Richard. If you knew beyond doubt that you would fail, that Rivers would make war on you, even that you would die and the protectorate end in disaster, would you go anyway?"

"Yes." The question had no meaning. You never knew when an effort is fruitless until you had given everything.

"You would throw away everything for your brother." She looked around the rampart as if expecting someone to help her plead her case. "Even from the grave he controls you."

"What do you mean?" He stepped closer to her until she backed up to the wall.

"You know it's true. Edward says, go to France. You go. Go to Scotland, you go. And now he says go to London, and you go. You will go to a place you hate, and leave us and everything you love behind, even if it means losing your life for a man who never loved you as you love him. Did you *ever* tell him no?"

"That would trouble you, of course, since you *always* told me no."

"What do you mean?"

"Of all the times I asked you to go to London with me, you went *once*, because you had not the courage to either go and face your sister, or to tell me why you were so afraid. I had to bear the jibes about my marriage, my loving wife. And the lies I told—my lady this, my lady that."

She was staring at him. "I didn't know it mattered so much. I didn't know *I* mattered so much. If I had—"

"Go to Francis," Richard said. "He'll listen to you. No one commands him from the grave." Thoughts flashed through his mind. If his words confused her, he would know he was wrong. But she knew exactly what he meant. He heard her gasp, the small halting sigh after.

"You are cruel. I didn't know how cruel you could be."

He stepped back from her. "I have done talking about this. If you have more to say, look for me in London." He could tell how angry he was by how calm he had become, the words measured, dispassionate. Not even an edge in his voice.

She recoiled as though he had struck her. "Any words I have to say to you in London, I will have to sing over your bones."

They stared at each other a moment over the wreckage their words had made, then Anne let out a staggering breath. "I didn't mean that. Forgive me." She pressed her hand to her mouth, turned, and fled.

## Northampton
## April 29, 1483.

They rode into Northampton in a steady drizzling rain—three hundred men, with meat on the hoof, baggage, and supply wagons. The lane, already muddy, was turning into a mire that dragged at the cart wheels and enveloped the horses' hooves, releasing them with a vulgar sucking sound.

Snow at Middleham, rain at Northampton. The weather matched Richard's mood—dreary, chill, and gloomy. He could hardly wait to see what conditions London would summon to greet them—sleet, a total eclipse?

He was exhausted. Having slept not at all the night before he departed, he had to make the succeeding nights virtually sleepless, as well, simply by telling himself how important it was for him to be well-rested, in order to have his wits as clear and acute as possible.

They passed the fallow fields that lay between them and the town, and then the lane narrowed again. In the distance Richard could see the peaked shapes of tents and a mass of bulky shapes—horses in huddles, tails flattened with wind and rain. Not enough to be Rivers' horde—unless Hastings had exaggerated the numbers. More probably Buckingham's three hundred. Which meant that either Rivers had not arrived or was riding hard for London.

The town was quiet as they approached. A few men-at-arms walked the streets, shoulders hunched under dripping capes. They watched Richard's party with an air of appraisal, but no visible alarm.

"Richard." Francis shouted in the rain. "What do you know of him? Rivers?"

"I was just thinking about him." Richard pulled in his horse, letting Francis ride closer. "He writes verse. And he's said to be the finest swordsman in England. Mostly I tried to avoid him. He always made me uncomfortable."

"Is he a coward?"

"Just the reverse. He was uncommonly skilled at anything he put his hand to. Why?"

"Well, look. The courts are full of his family, no man could have an easier rise to whatever dukedom or earldom he wanted. No marriage dripping properties and titles. Yet in all Edward's reign, Rivers never held a position of power. People said that your brother had tried to appoint Rivers to an office, and he declined in order to go on pilgrimage. Rumor was Rivers hadn't the guts for a captaincy."

"That's one version of what happened. I doubt it's Rivers's. What's your point?"

"I wonder if he'll be here at all. Or if we should expect some deception at the inn."

"Why brother, you forget," Richard grinned. "Lord Rivers is a holy man."

Francis laughed. "Let's hear it for the holy men!"

*A*fter turning their horses over to be stabled, they entered the inn to find themselves in a large common room. Four or five tables were clustered around the hearth, and several travelers ate a supper that smelled of pork and apples. They seemed to be a happy group. No faces he knew—a few men in monks' habits, tradesmen, even a couple of families, one including a dark-haired child about Ned's age. How long would he have to wait to see his son again? Surely not more than a few months. Once Edward was crowned and his advisors settled, the protector could resume his own life.

The innkeeper, a tall man with a bulging stomach and a handsome florid face behind gold-wired spectacles, looked them over.

"We are expected," Richard said. Looking like a fine pair of drowned mice, but don't smile, friend, my patience is short.

The innkeeper continued his indifferent appraisal. "It may be that your lord is expected. I can't say I was waiting for you in particular."

Richard took a handful of coins from Francis along with a requisition for billeting his men, and laid them on the innkeeper's account table. When he looked up, the proprietor had realized his error and surprised him with a genial smile.

"You're Gloucester. Indeed, you are expected. There are fine chambers at the rear of the tavern for you and your household knights, upwind of the stable. Will that suffice?"

"Excellent." He could sleep *in* the stables tonight, and never notice.

The host unlocked a drawer in the desk. Francis laid a hand over the coins before the man could sweep them away. "Now," Francis said, "who else are you expecting to arrive tonight?"

"There is a gentleman already here. In the parlor." The innkeeper waited for Francis to lift his hand, dropped the coins into the drawer, closed, and locked it.

*T*he man at the window was tall and thin, his angularity visible even under his black cloak. He stood with his back to them, as though he had not heard them enter, with their clatter of spurs and swords. He was not Buckingham.

Richard spoke to the black-draped back. "Rivers."

The man turned and calmly extended his hand. "Gloucester. I trust you had a pleasant journey."

"Uneventful, at any rate. The next best thing to pleasant." Richard grasped the proffered hand. He wondered if it was true about the hair shirt. Rivers's outer wear was rich enough. A black velvet doublet under the cloak, clearly fine silk, lush and thick, heavily embroidered with silver and gilt thread. The man was pale as well as thin, but it was a pallor that emitted an inner light.

Rivers inclined his head. "I grieve our recent loss. Edward's death is a blow to all England."

"Thank you." He didn't want to talk about Edward.

"My sister also sends her regards." Rivers's face shone with its austere saintly glow.

"Your sister, Anthony, thinks I'm the antichrist. I doubt she sheds a tear for my sorrow."

"Oh?" Rivers appeared mildly surprised. He moved quickly to a table set nearby. "Wine, gentlemen? You must be ready for refreshment." He lifted the flagon.

"Your thoughtfulness is appreciated," Richard said, "and we are almost as hungry as we are dirty. But if you would be so kind as to let us make ourselves more presentable before we share a cup with you?" He meant to have more than bread and cheese, and a little time to think. He saw no sign of the king, and where in heaven was Buckingham?

"Of course," Rivers said. "I will await you here. Pray do not hurry yourselves." He smiled. The man had charm. Richard didn't trust charm.

By the time Richard and Francis returned to the parlor, Buckingham had arrived. Harry Stafford, Duke of Buckingham, was a well-knit man of medium height, with a lion's mane of waving golden hair and a sensual, almost insolent face, with its full lips and heavy-lidded blue eyes.

"My lord," Richard said pleasantly to Rivers, after they had all seated themselves, "I cannot pretend your presence here is anything other than a surprise." Francis and Harry both had the sense to keep quiet.

"My lord confuses me. We agreed to meet here."

Richard bit into a slab of the pork. The meat was well-cooked, crisp outside but moist within, fresh, and gloriously seasoned. A basin of water, a few minutes before a fire, and a well-prepared dish. He marveled at how a few comforts could restore a man, body and spirit. "I'll be plain, then," he said. "Are you alone?"

Rivers blinked. "Of course. I have only a handful of men. I came in trust."

"Is the king with you?"

"King Edward sleeps at Stony Stratford, and will wait for our arrival."

Richard leaned back. "Then, Anthony, what have you come for?" Both Francis and Harry looked up at the blunt question. No doubt neither of them would have handled the meeting this way. Well, he'd never had a talent for dissembling. He recognized wryly, and with a trace of sadness, that he still feared being found credulous over almost anything else. Rather be hanged and quartered than laughed at for a fool. He went on. "If you came in peace, it seems you'd have the lad with you, as we agreed. On the other hand, if you planned to block the protectorate, the reasonable thing to do was to make haste for London and not honor our appointment at all. But you have done neither. Your presence here, alone, is neither fish nor fowl, and I must ask why."

"Ah, Richard. May I call you Richard?

"Yes, please." Since we are all such hail-fellows-well-met.

"You make this too complicated. I am a simple man. I have come because you and I have a common goal—to protect the good of the realm and the safety of your brother's young sons." Rivers's eyes, that cool steel blue, shone with what Richard suspected was one of the greatest intellects in England.

"There is one *simple* explanation—the king *is* making haste with your army, and you are only delaying to give them time to reach London. In which case, your efforts are wasted. I don't plan to talk all night, and I would have stopped here with or without your presence. I'm no good at all without a night's sleep."

"Anthony, that's all very well, but who are you protecting the boys from?" This from Buckingham.

Rivers shrugged. "Well, Harry, maybe you, now that you mention it." He continued, "My lord, we both loved your late brother, as did my sister. Neither Elizabeth nor I intend to defy any terms of the late king's will. But young Edward knows me, and he has seen you—what, twice?—in the last ten years. It seemed a courtesy for me to meet you first. All, save the king's presence, is as we arranged. I am here, and we will advance to Stony Stratford and then to London tomorrow."

Richard poured some of the hot wine and felt its heat through the tankard. "Anthony, it eases my mind to know your purpose before we meet Edward tomorrow." Rivers inclined his head, as if accepting a tribute.

Richard continued. "I want to be sure you understand, however, that I intend to honor my brother's wish for the protectorate. No more, no less. I expect to see the boy at Stony Stratford and not be looking at a row of archers when I arrive. I also expect to accompany him to London without incident.

"Further, I do not intend to act as king while Edward reaches his majority, but neither will I tolerate anyone else standing in that part. I mean to keep a clear field so that Edward can learn and grow to maturity in a stable realm."

"Well said, Richard. It is what all of us wish."

$T$aking Rivers was easier than it should have been. He chose to sleep in relative privacy, one man guarding the door, who was easily overcome, his squire on the pallet bed in his room. Rivers may have been the finest swordsman in England and a paragon of courage in battle, but he knew nothing of vigilance. He had far too much confidence in his ability to beguile.

The earl raised up on one elbow at the sight of the three men who had burst through his door. "Gloucester, are you mad? It's far too early to rise."

"Go back to sleep for as long as you like. All day, if you wish. I start for Stony Stratford now."

Rivers reared up, groped for his sword and called out for his men.

Buckingham sat down on the bed. "Don't trouble yourself. The inn is surrounded. Under siege, you might say."

"Really, Rivers," Francis added, taking the duke's sword out of reach, "we insist you stay here."

"By God, Richard, I'll—"

"Anthony, let's wait to discuss reparations until we see on whose side they are due."

*Stony Stratford, England*
*April 30, 1483.*

$R$ichard and a handful of his men reached Stony Stratford as dawn was breaking and stopped just outside the courtyard of the inn. Richard rode over to Tyrrell. "Captain, hold the men here. I'm riding in with Lovell and Buckingham now."

Tyrrell shook his head. "The courtyard's full of men, sir."

"So it is, James. But Grey's a fool if he would cut us down here."

"Well, sir, men have done foolish things before. If it were *my* life, I wouldn't wager it on Grey's brains."

"No. Well, thank you for your concern. If you hear anything that even *sounds* like fighting, you have my permission to slit Rivers's throat." Tyrrell grinned. "That's all, James. If this fails, dismiss the men and ride for safety as best you can. Understood?"

"Sir." Tyrrell nodded.

Richard turned to Francis and Buckingham. "Gentlemen. Now we find out whether Lord Grey is the fair and honorable knight he claims to be."

Tyrrell hawked and spat. Since the ground was already soggy, it didn't leave a mark.

Richard eased the reins. Slowly now. For Grey to cut him down in front of his nephew was too blatant a disregard of Edward's wishes, and Edward was too much loved and too recently dead to risk offending the whole country. If he was wrong, the fight would be bloody quick. Later, perhaps, slow poison in his eggs.

Only a few men in the yard were mounted; most were afoot, waiting for the squires to bring their mounts. The boy should be easy to spot. Damn. Richard ran his eyes over the crowd, wishing he had Rob's long vision. He rode very slowly toward a knot of men waiting for their horses—Grey would be among the first to be so served—and picked out a tall fair-haired man as a possibility. Suddenly a youth darted out from a side door of the inn, a tall, wiry boy, thinner than Richard expected, but unmistakable—golden-haired, with a gold sun emblazoned on a blue tunic.

Richard pressed his knees into his horse; it took a couple of slow steps forward. The boy saw him and stopped in his tracks, his face blank with amazement. Pure shock, not dismay or anger, just disbelief. Finally a puzzled smile of recognition. "Uncle Richard?" Then a cough and a stammer, as though he had been discourteous or undignified. "My lord Gloucester?" The boy's surprise alone was enough to tell Richard what Rivers's plan had been.

The fair-haired man turned. Not Grey, then. Just then another man pushed through. Ah. No doubt about this one. The man had a hand on the hilt of the sword, the other worked into a fist. All his knuckles were white.

"Gloucester!" Anger issued from the man like steam on a hot rock. A vast stillness, like a collective indrawn breath, filled the courtyard. For a moment the silence was so complete that a horse's sudden pawing filled his ears like the rumble of a rockslide. Edward's eyes flicked from Grey to Richard and back again.

"Lord Grey," Richard said. "Since my nephew did not arrive with Earl Rivers, we came to him." He spoke quietly and felt young Edward's eyes on him as acute as a hawk's. "I hope you'll leave that thing in its sheath. I would like to dismount and greet my nephew properly, but I don't want to feel the point of your sword in my back. My friends and I have come in peace. If we end up in pieces, I promise you so will your Uncle Anthony. Now, may I dismount?"

Grey stepped back and one hand dropped to his side. A little of the tension went out of the air. Richard let out his breath, which he seemed to have been holding, and dismounted. When Grey pulled at his sword Richard lifted his hands, palms up. "You've nothing to fear, Grey. Look around you. Myself and two other men." He walked the three paces over to Edward and dropped to one knee. Francis and Buckingham followed suit.

Richard lifted the boy's hand and kissed it, the time-honored gesture of fealty. "God grant you a long and happy reign, sire." He stood and put a hand on Edward's shoulder. Again that quick dance of the boy's eyes from him to Grey and back again. The slim shoulder tensed under Richard's grasp.

Richard removed his hand and looked into Edward's eyes. "You did not expect me."

"No, sir, I—" Edward stopped. "No, I did not," he said. This time he didn't look at Grey.

Good. Perhaps the boy would be man enough to try to find his own ground. "Then, sir, since it is clear that we have surprised you, it would be good, I think, for us to try to put an end to your confusion."

So I am your prisoner," Edward said, surveying his keeper.

"Under guard," Richard corrected. He had dismissed the earl's men, promising to pay them for their time, and sent word back to Northampton to have Rivers conveyed to guarded quarters at Pontefract along with Lord Grey and two other of Edward's advisors.

"The same thing."

"Guard works both ways, you know. I keep you in here, but I also keep out others who might harm you."

"Keep others from me that you don't want near me, you mean. What will you do with my tutor, uncle? And should I call you *uncle*, now that you are my captor?"

"Lord Rivers will be kept under guard until his trial," Richard said.

"Trial?"

What words did you use to tell a boy that the man who taught him Aristotle and the rules of arms, schooled him in virtue and knightly honor, was guilty of treason? "As I told you, your father appointed me as your governor, effective upon his death. Since Lord Rivers no longer held that office, his attempt to keep it was a violation of your father's will."

"Why would neither my father nor Lord Rivers make mention of your office, if that is so?"

"I imagine neither Lord Rivers nor your father himself expected he would die before you were grown. This was not an appointment they ever thought or hoped to have to act upon."

"Then, uncle, if my father never hoped to have you serve in that office, why did he appoint you at all? Why not keep Sir Anthony, if he was fine enough for me once?"

The ultimate question. Because Edward did not, finally, trust his own wife or her kin. Because he feared Rivers would do just what he had tried to do, put the kingdom into his sister's hands.

"I know this is not easy to understand. The education of princes is not the same as the wardship of kings. Perhaps your father thought that while Sir Anthony was expert in matters of philosophy and knightly skills, he had no experience in governing."

"You have not ruled England, either."

"No. Only a part of it."

"I see. But is there any reason a king may not have both governor and tutor?"

"Think, boy!" Buckingham's voice was sharp. "If your uncle had intended to cooperate with us, wouldn't he have told you that you were to meet with Gloucester? Why did he stay at Northampton alone and let you ride here without a word of his plans, if he did not intend to betray your father's will? Your Uncle Anthony is a traitor."

Buckingham was not the most tactful man in the world, but better, perhaps, Richard thought, that those particular words come from someone else's mouth than from his own, if he was ever to make peace with his nephew.

# 21  *Voices of London*

Charlotte Alleyn was Queen Elizabeth's tirewoman. Together, the queen and the difficult day had twice compelled Charlotte into unprecedented behavior. First, Elizabeth had suddenly told Charlotte to gather the queen's gowns and jewels and pack them for travel.

"Pack them?" Charlotte asked, she was that stunned.

"Pack them," was all Elizabeth said. She did not strike or even chastise Charlotte. In fact, she seemed hardly to notice the lapse of propriety, which struck far more worry into Charlotte's heart than if the queen had raged.

Charlotte recovered her placid exterior and asked no more question, not even where they were bound. She threw the queen's favorite gowns into a trunk while other servants ran back and forth carrying things for all the queen's daughters and her son Dickon. By evening, the queen, princesses, and little Duke Dickon, along with a dozen servants, had moved only from the palace at Westminster to the abbey. As workmen brought in chest after trunk, piling them in corners, stacking some up as high as the men were tall, Charlotte realized her second failing of the day: she had been so rattled that she had packed not a single gown for herself.

She sat with Bess on one of the coffers and struggled with her problem. The gown she wore would soon become soiled and wilted, and then Elizabeth would rail at her. She glanced at Bess. They were near the same size—tall and large-boned. And Bess was as different from her mother as a child could be, sensible of mind and mild of disposition. Yes. She would ask Bess for the loan of an old gown or two.

*May 4, 1483. Afternoon.*

Daniel Hindley ran the Rose, a tavern on the Strand, with his wife Nell and his eldest son, Christopher. People were all out from behind their doors, running in the streets, shouting that the young king was riding in. Daniel was about to tell Christopher to mind the inn when Nell came up and told both of them to be on their way.

"Go," she said. "Take yourselves away! There will be no more than dregs of trade until the king's procession passes through. If I cannot manage alone till then, I do not deserve to be counted an alewife."

Daniel was a tall man, but even so he had trouble seeing, the people were that thick in the streets, calling, waving, jostling each other for a better view. Finally, there he was, young Edward, a slender boy at the head of the troop of men, followed by baggage carts piled with arms and armor. The dark man at his side would be the Duke of Gloucester.

And the fair one? Daniel guessed him to be the boy-king's tutor, Earl Rivers. There were rumors of a skirmish at Northampton. Daniel pushed forward and craned his neck to get a closer look. Young Edward seemed frozen and unhappy, not at all as you would imagine a king, taking over his city.

Daniel refused to let his spirits be dampened. London had a king again, and if ever there was a city that loved her kings, it was London. It might be that the boy did not care for crowds; there were grown men too private to enjoy such things. And twelve was close enough to manhood; you could hardly call him a child. Now that he was with men who, unlike Rivers, could teach him more than poetry and a knight's pretty manners, he would mature quickly. Give him time. The boy would do right well. By God, it was good to have the king in the city!

*May 4, 1483. Evening.*

"Sanctuary!" Buckingham exclaimed, when they reached Westminster.

Will Hastings lifted a hand. "Those are the queen's words, not mine." He laughed.

"Thieves' cache would be nearer the mark," Richard said, not laughing. All around the denuded room were dust-free circles on tabletops where silver bowls and gold candlesticks had vanished, and blocks of pristine wall where tapestries had hung.

"You speak true, sir." Hastings said. "but we always knew she was a rapacious wench, didn't we?"

"Good God, Will, what was everyone doing here," Richard asked, "sleeping?"

"Hardly, Richard. Some of us were doing all that could be done until you arrived. Some of us," Hastings continued, unruffled, "were hard-pressed to try to see that you did, in fact, arrive. Alive."

"Yes, Will. I know. I'm grateful. Go on."

"That's all. You already know Edward Woodville seized control of the navy."

"Yes. And now I know what funds he has for buying more ships."

"As you say. Dorset was quite brazen about it. He said at the last council meeting that he could make any decisions he wished, without waiting for the king."

Or the protector, Richard thought. "When was this?"

"Immediately following Edward's death."

Richard traced a dustless circle. "Why did you not tell me this sooner?"

Hastings hesitated. "What could you have done if you had known earlier?"

Will—Edward's old friend Will Hastings—playing cat and mouse with him? *Stop it. You can't mistrust everybody.* "What's the mood of London, would you say?"

"Mostly with you."

"The rest, where?"

"That's difficult to say. Everyone wants to see Edward's son crowned." Hastings shrugged. "At the same time, everyone fears a child-king. No one wants the succession wars back. I think we would all breathe easier if Rivers had ridden in with you, brought to heel, so to speak."

"Bringing Anthony to heel was not a possibility, Will. I would have had to bring him and Grey here in chains, and what would *that* have said about the unity of the kingdom?"

"I know, I know. Everything considered, it was very neatly done. But I tell you this: even with no love lost between London and the queen, she is the king's mother. If you would end the curse of child-kings, win her support. A smooth succession is all you need to have the city in your hands."

### May 5, 1483. Late morning.

"Can she do that?" Richard asked Will Catesby, the prominent young lawyer Hastings had sent him.

"As you see, sir, she has already done it."

"What does she think they need sanctuary from?"

"Perhaps you." Catesby shrugged. "Perhaps nothing. But consider, sir, if she wishes to embarrass you, what could she do that would be more effective? She is in sanctuary, therefore it follows that she must stand in danger of some cruelty at your hands."

"I can hardly demonstrate otherwise unless she comes out."

"Precisely, sir."

"What do you suggest I do? Can I demand she come forth?"

"You can, indeed. And she can refuse."

"What then?"

"Why, then you can batter down the doors and drag her and her innocent children from sanctuary by force, like the tyrant she says you are." Catesby had a narrow, clever face, and a cool voice that betrayed nothing.

"That is the best advice you have to offer me?"

"That is not advice, sir."

## May 5, 1483. Evening.

Ralph Darnton wrapped the cheese wheel back in its linen, put it in the sideboard and closed the door. Ralph had been one of Edward's retainers when the king had lived, and the councilmen trusted him. Or perhaps, like many privileged men, they thought servants had neither eyes nor ears.

But Darnton had both, and he was an astute observer. Everything had been done most courteously. In person, the protector seemed other than his war-like reputation, rather quiet and restrained.

The council had smiled and bade him welcome.

The protector had smiled and thanked them for their service to his brother. He requested that the council arraign Earl Rivers and Lord Grey for treason, based on their actions at Northampton.

To a man, the council deplored Rivers' actions.

To a man, they refused Gloucester's request.

At their denial, he thanked them again, this time for their courtesy in meeting with him. He spoke pleasantly, with no sign of wrath at the denial.

Now Ralph wondered what the Duke of Gloucester would do, wondered what he *could* do. Who, in the end, would be safer to offend? He doubted that anyone in London knew the answer to that question.

### May 6, 1483. Morning.

The windows of the chamber at Westminster opened onto the garden below and the warm May day, onto grass the bright green of spring and pear trees in full fragrant bloom. One of the men below wore a pair of absurd piked shoes with toes so long they tied to the knee with satin bands.

*The man must think he's in Burgundy.* Richard turned from the window as Francis laid a stack of papers and letters on the table amid the pile already lying there.

"Tell them all," Richard said to his clerk, John Kendall, "that I will consider redistributing the wealth of London as soon as I have retrieved it.

"I *jest*, John," he said in response to Kendall's blank face, "I jest." The serious Kendall made him look like the soul of levity. Richard rather liked that, not being the most grave person in the room. "Tell them that matters will stand as they are until the king is crowned. Then we will consider all requests."

He left the window and crossed to the table, leaning there, palms down. "Tell me, Catesby," he said, "how will it appear if we crown the boy while his entire family are still behind sanctuary walls?"

"Hmm. No worse than the truth—that the queen defies your appointment as protector. However, you have a greater worry than that, sir, that being what will happen to your office after the boy is crowned."

"I am protector until Edward reaches his majority. Three years. Perhaps four."

"Hmm, yes." Catesby drummed his fingers on the arms of his chair. "So states the late king's will."

Richard sighed and straightened. "Catesby, will you please stop humming and insinuating and *say* something?"

"Very well. As I am sure you know, Richard, there have been several instances of minority kings in England, most of which involved a protectorate government. The most recent was that of Henry VI, who preceded your late brother.

"As soon as Henry became king, at nine months of age, a new king's council was formed. One must assume that it formed itself; that being, that certain men who had access to the king, who was after all only a child, appointed themselves. We know that the protector, who should have been the kingdom's major voice, could not have had a hand in the selection, because the first official action of the council was to dissolve the protectorate.

"May I remind you, sir, that the protector—also a Duke of Gloucester, by the way—was later murdered. Presumably by some of the king's advisors, who wished to be certain Duke Humphrey would not try to regain the power he had lost.

"You are correct about the terms of the will, however. For what that is worth." Catesby's eyebrow lifted. "Words of a dead man. Dead men's words are often ignored."

### *May 7, 1483. Just past midnight.*

*Words of a dead man.* Of course, a will was precisely that. For that matter, much of the law, too. Richard had not considered it in quite such blunt terms before.

He had started reading the stacks of petitions. The candle burned low, and he sat in its guttering light considering his brother's reign. A personal rule, dependent upon the king's familiarity, his hand and his memory, the force of his will. Nothing new in that, of course. What he had not seen was the degree to which Edward's own presence, not the office of king, was the hub that held in place the spokes of the wheel of government. And when the hub is gone, the spokes shatter into chaos and disorder.

### *May 10, 1483. Evening.*

Council of King Edward V: Appointees and Offices

Richard Duke of Gloucester. Protector of the realm.

William Lord Hastings. Captain of Calais and Lord Chamberlain of England.

William Catesby, Esquire. Chancellor of the Earldom of March.

Bishop John Russell of Lincoln. Council member. Succeeded Archbishop Thomas Rotterham of York, who was indiscreet enough to slip the Great Seal of England through the walls of sanctuary into the hands of Elizabeth.

John Howard, Duke of Norfolk. Master of the Game of all the king's forests, chases, and parks south of the River Trent.

Francis Viscount Lovell. Appointed Chief Butler of England, the office formerly held by Anthony Lord Rivers.

John de la Pole, Earl of Lincoln. Council member.

Henry Stafford, Duke of Buckingham. Chief Justice and Chamberlain of both north and south Wales, Constable of the royal castles and forests and chases therein.

John de la Pole, Earl of Lincoln, son of Richard's sister Elizabeth, considered with great interest the list of Richard's appointments to the new king's council. In such seemingly ordinary matters, lines of battle were drawn. The talk was that since the old council had not honored Richard's requests, the protector would purge the lot of them. But he had displayed an admirable moderation in his selection, Lincoln thought, a reasonable and seemly balance between his own friends, men he knew and trusted, and former retainers of his brother, who had served faithfully and deserved to have their loyalty recognized.

People were so foolish, fretting over out whether Richard would try to take control of the country. Well, he had already taken control over the young king and the Palace of Westminster, in case no one had noticed.

And it appeared that what he was going to do with that control was try to reconcile the country. London could be very interesting the next few months, Lincoln thought. He was glad he was going to be a part of it.

## *May 14, 1483. Afternoon.*

Today young Edward would make his formal entrance into the city. The lord mayor was waiting, along with several hundred of the city's officials and citizens. The mayor and city fathers were dressed in scarlet, plain citizens in violet, and the king himself in blue velvet.

The Duke of Gloucester and his Yorkshire men all wore mourning black. When Harry Stafford, Duke of Buckingham, rode his horse out into Hornsby meadow, from whence the procession would begin, Richard and his men, the city fathers, and the citizens were all gathered and waiting.

So one could not help but notice Stafford's arrival, a handsome fair man on a black horse. And, like Richard himself, dressed all in starkest mourning, not a gilt collar or jewel on him. Buckingham's statement of allegiance could not have been more clear. For a moment, the duke's resemblance to the late king was so striking it was as though Richard rode once more beside his brother.

The likeness must have occurred to Richard, too, for he glanced at Buckingham, then bowed his head as if in prayer or some deep private thought, before gathering his reins. "Harry," he said finally, and spurred his horse to the young king's side, Buckingham and Francis falling in behind them.

The mayor also noted that neither Richard nor his nephew seemed particularly joyful, nor warm with each other, and that the queen was not among the crowds that cheered and tossed hats, flowers, and coins into the air as her royal son made his way down the Strand. The lord mayor would have been happier had she been there.

## *May 18, 1483. Midnight.*

Richard lay in the great oak bed in Edward's chamber. Out of long habit, he stretched one arm across the bed, the other side of which was empty, of course. He stared up into the shadows, listening to the sounds around him. A stifled cough, footsteps padding in the passageway. Someone up to tend a sick child, or slipping away to a tryst.

Night sounds; night thoughts.

How much of a Woodville was young Edward?

Say that, as protector, he pursued his office with moderation, acting only as Edward's advisor, which had been his original intention, he could be sure that Elizabeth and Rivers would try to mold the king to their desires. What boy of twelve was capable of resisting that kind of influence? The prince had been with his mother and Rivers all his life, while his uncle Gloucester was little better than a stranger; moreover, a stranger who had publicly disgraced his advisors.

Or he could fulfill his office by force, use it to keep the boy virtually captive, limit access to him, particularly by his mother. The king would become the puppet of the protector and the council. If the boy's spirit were not destroyed altogether, he would resent the man who thus controlled him, and exact payment for his years of subordination at the first opportunity of his majority.

One last possibility. Suppose he laid down his power now, became protector in name only, returned north tomorrow. Except for two things, he would do so as quickly as he could pack his belongings.

First, his brother had entrusted this responsibility to him and had feared for the kingdom under the Woodvilles' hands. Second, what attitude would Elizabeth take regarding the offices and estates of the Duke of Gloucester, whom she had disliked for as long as he could remember, and who was now the primary threat to her power?

Grants had been revoked, laws overturned before. Richard had no faith that the young king, left to his mother's guidance, would feel obligated to honor those bequests. *Words of a dead man.*

One other practical issue. What to do with Rivers and Grey?

Every condition, every danger here, seemed Hydra-headed, every evil he might eliminate capable of spouting multiples more. His decision had within it the seeds for destroying a kingdom.

One small blow now might save rivers of blood later.

Blood of Rivers; rivers of blood.

A knot drew together in his back, winding tight between his shoulder blades. He shifted onto his side, missed Anne, and tried to sleep.

### June 6, 1483. Nightfall.

All Anne's things were strewn around her—boxes, trunks, bags. Her cloak, her fine wool cloak that had the richness of emeralds in its dye, lay in a dusty heap at her feet. After the morning warmed, she had removed it and tied it behind her. Now it lay under its veil of dirt and mud as dull and drab as a garden toad. She sat down on the edge of the bed, prodded its folds with her toe, and looked about the room.

The walnut bed, polished to a deep sheen and carved with wreaths of flowers and thorns, was hung with blue curtains embroidered in stars and suns. The light was dimming in the mullioned windows over the courtyard, with its fountain and rose gardens. A pretty room, but she could not enjoy it. She felt like a child overcome by the strangeness of everything around her, on the verge of tears.

Today was the first time she and Richard had seen each other since the morning he had left Middleham. She was embarrassed to remember the last night he had spent there, and had feared she would see anger, resentment of their bitter parting.

What she found was almost worse. They had greeted each other formally and awkwardly. No embrace. He had called servants to take her things, and directed them to her chambers, and then had disappeared.

She had had more than enough time to bathe and dress before supper, and had hoped for a chance to talk with him, but saw no more of him until he came to her chamber barely in time to walk with her down to the hall. All through the meal, she tried to understand what her husband had ridden into, tried to understand *him*. He laughed and talked more heartily than she remembered him doing at any time in the past, but seemed at the same time abstracted, watching with a keen vigilance for something just out of his vision. When the entertainment began, she excused herself, pleading fatigue, hoping Richard would follow. He hadn't.

On her return to her chamber, the servants had not finished unpacking, but she sent them away. She was in the depths of self-pity when someone knocked at her door. At last.

She answered the knock quickly, expecting Richard. It was Francis.

He looked around the room and made a sweeping gesture with his arm. "Ah, so the maid has neglected her mistress. Garments in their boxes, trunks still strapped. Why, not even your cloak taken to be brushed! It's enough to try a lady's patience." He picked up the cloak and folded it over a trunk; even that much handling caused puffs of dust to rise. Francis sneezed.

Anne smiled. "You mock me, Francis."

"Yes, but with affection."

"I know."

Francis said, "You left the hall early."

"Yes. I was lonely there."

"I see. Feeling lonely and unattended, so you leave the gathering and send all your servants away."

She laughed in spite of herself. "Yes, Francis. Women's reasoning. I don't expect you to understand."

"Perhaps you would be surprised at what I understand, Annie." He gently tapped a knuckle against her forehead. Anne held still until his touch had entirely faded from her skin. Francis' understanding could be too heady a comfort, as she had reason to know.

He sat down on one of the trunks. "Where is Richard?"

"Why do you ask me? I haven't seen him since I left the banquet and you were with him then."

"Oh. Well, he must be about."

A servant came in to close the shutters and light the torches. Anne waited until he had gone again. "Francis, what is happening here?"

"What do you mean?"

"Please don't act as if nothing is wrong. I can't bear it. I can feel it all around me." She glanced around the room. "Everyone acts as though they were expecting something to happen, but pretending not to. What is it?"

"Well, Annie, where shall I start?"

"It is that bad, then?"

"I'll let you judge. When we first arrived here, I think everyone was relieved: someone was in control again. Then soon it became clear that all the factions were horribly divided. The queen's family was keeping all the wealth and power in their own hands. Edward is said to have left a fortune. If that's true, we haven't seen any of it. The coffers are meager."

Anne nodded. "You said *factions*. Who else?"

"I'm not completely certain, actually. But everyone hates everyone else, and Richard doesn't know who to trust."

"Trust?"

"Since the king is a child, everyone wants to be the man—or wom-an—behind the throne. Richard is that man, for the moment at least, so everyone is lining up behind him. The question is, who stands there to support him and who to stab him in the back?"

"Francis. No."

"Symbolically speaking, of course. I didn't mean it in fact." He stood and walked over to her. "I'm sorry. You wanted comfort and I have only added to your fears."

"No, they were thriving very well on their own. You only gave them names. Even the most unruly children need names, don't they?" She looked up at him and made herself smile. "Stay close to him, Francis. And to me."

He took her hand and held it in a firm grasp. "I intend to."

*June 6, 1483. Midnight.*

When Richard came to her chamber much later, Anne was waiting in the window, tired, but too taut to sleep. She had a book in her lap. The candles in the room provided barely enough light to read. It didn't matter. She was too taut too read, too.

Richard paused just inside the door and kept his hand on the latch. "Your chamber is agreeable?"

"Excellent." It was all she could do to keep her voice level, his tone was so polite, so distant. If they were going to talk about hearths and bed curtains, she would go mad.

"Please come in." And if he said it was too late, and he would dis-turb her, she would throw her book at him.

He walked into the room, pulled up a chair and sat down near the door. "Why did Ned not come with you?"

"It's a long ride for him." Anne watched him. The abstracted man-ner still; he wasn't really there.

"One I made at just his age. I want him with us."

"Perhaps. We can talk about it later. Francis says your situation here is dangerous."

"Francis says too much."

Richard's face was drawn and tired, no trace of the forced joviality she had seen earlier. Anne felt a new surge of fear for him and stilled it. Nothing would be gained by that. It was the wrong place and the wrong time to try to mend the breach between them, but it was the only time and place she had.

Well, not everything need be said with words. "Richard, bring your chair and sit before me."

"Why? What is wrong with where I am?"

"I can't reach you. Come, and I will knead your shoulders."

He made an attempt at laughter. "You sound just like your mother."

"Oh? Then you may as well take the part of a son, and do as I tell you, as you have not been remarkably pleasant as husband. Now come."

Peremptory words and soft voice, and he took them more kindly than if she had been all softness.

"Witch," he said. "I accept your challenge. Now let us see if your hands are as potent as your words."

A little later, when Anne finally closed her eyes, with Richard asleep beside her, his hand on her hip, her last conscious thought was of gratitude, for a marriage suffused with pain but still enduring.

## *June 7, 1483. Evening.*

Nell counted the money, locked and closed the coffer. It was her pleasure every evening to feel the hard cold coins, solid in her hands, and reassure herself that she and her family would never see the poverty she had known as a child. But the really good days were past.

The day that Edward the boy-king rode into town and a few days after brought such crowds of men into the Rose, and in such a generous humor, that Nell thought she had never seen such wealth as she and Daniel took in. But now business was back to normal. Actually, a little less. The men frequenting the tavern now were thoughtful, brooding men, and Nell knew from experience that it did not take much to change a brooding drunk into a violent one.

No one knew what was happening, that was the trouble. The coronation had been postponed. The young king was rarely seen, and those who saw him said his demeanor was so sad as to break men's hearts.

Nell herself thought the key to the truth lay in whatever had occurred at Northampton when the king's advisors were seized, and she
suspected more happened than any common soul was able to guess.
All those carts of weapons and armor following the king's entourage,
confiscated, it was said, from Earl Rivers' men.

No one really knew the protector, either, for all the years he had
been in and out of London, but he seemed to have acted with peremptory speed—which is exactly what you would expect from a northerner.

Nell set the coffer down, pushing it with her foot under the bed.
She hoped young Edward was crowned soon, but she had a premoni-
tion that he would never sit on the throne of England, a feeling like a
clammy breath on the back of her neck. She shuddered to shake it off,
left the room, and closed the door.

*June 8, 1483. Morning.*
A stooped old man dressed in a white bishop's cope requested audience
with the protector. When granted his wish, the old man insisted on
seeing Richard alone, with no clerk to record or even hear his words.

When the door opened more than an hour later, Richard stepped
out only long enough to send for Catesby, the lawyer, then stepped
back inside.

"Please sit," Richard said. "be comfortable. No harm will come to
you. My lawyer is here only to advise me how best to proceed with
this news. You will not be harmed."

The old man sat, lowered his eyes, and began his story.

"Sir, as I told my lord Gloucester, I have been burdened with a
heavy secret these past twenty years. The late King Edward was
troth-plight to a young woman. I say *young*, but she was in fact a
few years older than the king. I was the priest who witnessed their
vows." He seemed to think this sufficient information, for he stopped
abruptly.

Catesby was impatient. "Well, Bishop, that was common enough
practice. Still is. Some man wants to bed a woman; she refuses. The
troth-plight is close enough to marriage that she will bend her virtue,
but far easier to dissolve than marriage. I think we can assume that
Edward did not intend to keep the lady as his wife."

The bishop cleared his throat. "No, sir. But if you will pardon me,
that is not the point. The lady, whose name was Eleanor Butler, bore

Edward a child, stillborn, and the troth was never annulled. It was still valid when Edward married Elizabeth Woodville two years later."

Catesby nodded. "What you are saying is that the troth-plight was conspicuously consummated, and the woman was not some peasant girl to be sent home with a coin and a new comb."

"Precisely." The bishop seemed noticeably easier.

"Was the lady still living when Edward married the present queen?"

"She was, sir, although she is long dead now."

"Well, well," Catesby said. "So Edward left no legitimate heirs: his sons are bastards. Strong words, Bishop. Can you support them?"

The man spread his hands. "No. No records exist to prove my word. There was the church register, but I no longer have it in my possession. I suspect it no longer exists."

Catesby leaned back, folded his arms across his chest. "I see. You kept the secret for a score of years, more or less, and now, without a shred of evidence for this tale, you felt compelled to tell it. Why?"

"Consider, sir. As long as Edward was alive, the rightful ruler held the throne. No one was wronged by the king's early actions. Besides, until quite recently, if Edward's issue were known to be illegitimate, the Duke of Clarence would have been heir to the throne. Now. . . ." He left the thought unfinished.

"Ah, yes," Catesby said. "Now it is my lord Gloucester."

"Yes, sir."

Catesby spoke, smiling. "Well, Richard, this is a convenient piece of information for you, isn't it? Assuming you want to be king, of course. And doesn't everyone, these days?"

"That's offensive, Catesby."

"You had better not be so easily offended, my friend, because I am not the only person who will say that. Please note that I have made no assessment concerning the accuracy of the information. I only want you to be aware what men will say, should you decide to use it."

A point occurred to Richard. "Will—the princes were not born until after the Lady Butler's death. Perhaps we concern ourselves with nothing."

Catesby shook his head. "No. The boys are bastards. Only if Edward had renewed his vows to the queen after the death of his first wife, and before the children's births, would they be legitimate. As long as the second marriage was invalid when the princes were born, they would be bastards and remain bastards, no matter how long after

Eleanor Butler's death they came into the world. However, you must realize that I speak only of strict legality. Many would say a troth-plight was of little practical importance."

Richard rubbed his forehead. "All the struggle to gain possession of the king, and he's only a bastard. Is there precedent?"

Catesby frowned. "For bastard kings? Of course. The conqueror was a bastard. But for what you are thinking, no. A bastard may fight to claim a throne when the true heir is weak or otherwise unsuited. But to bar a man already designated as king when bastardy is later discovered, no, I know of no precedent. None at all for this particular circumstance."

For a moment Richard had forgotten the old man. Now he turned to him. "Bishop, how is it that you are still alive? I would have thought Elizabeth would have had your head."

"I came very near to losing my life. The queen would have had me hanged on the spot, but Edward intervened. After all, I had kept the secret for a number of years, and had nothing to gain from disclosing it. And," he said ruefully, "the power of the queen to cause me great trouble should I ever speak of the matter was made very clear to me. I was forced to surrender the church register, so that the troth-plight could never be proved to be anything but the raving of a silly old man. And I never again held a position of true authority in the church."

He continued. "It is a strange tale, I know. And one piece of it has always eluded me. What can have prevented the royal couple from making a second marriage upon the death of Lady Butler? To have done so would have eliminated the question of bastardy of all children born after that date."

Richard laughed. "Why, Bishop, there is no mystery in that. To marry Elizabeth again, Edward would have had to tell her the purpose of such vows. I'm not sure I would have courage to do that, and I know Edward had not." His laughter died. "But how did Elizabeth know of it, if neither you nor Edward told her? Did anyone else know?"

"Yes, my lord. The Duke of Clarence knew."

"You *told* him?"

"Please, my lord. There are limits to even my follies. I had met the duke when he was a boy, about the time the king took vows with Lady Butler. He recognized me once not long before his death, when we happened to meet on the street in London, an entirely chance occurrence, and he questioned me. He was a little older than you, sir, and he had some memory of the early marriage, which seeing me jogged. I did not give him the information he sought, but I have been told I am a poor liar."

Richard sat very still, and the man continued. "The duke thrived on intrigue, as my lord knows. I don't know whether he actually intended to use the knowledge to set himself or his son up as heirs, which they would be, of course, when Edward died, or whether he only wanted to have power for favors and to needle the Woodvilles. I think probably the latter, but of course the plan turned backward on him."

"So Elizabeth wrote George's death warrant," Richard said. And Edward had not been strong enough to prevent it. Or perhaps not. Perhaps George's death was Edward's wish. God.

*June 8, 1843. Afternoon.*
"What choice do you have?" Buckingham's lazy, slightly amused voice expressed amazement that they should consider even a pretense of a discussion.

Francis was more cautious. "It's not that simple, Harry."

"*How* it's done may not be simple. But this much is: Richard holds no real power as protector, not to mention the risk to his life. He may as well flee to Burgundy now and be done with it."

"There is truth in what he says, sir." Catesby spoke to Richard. "But you must consider this, also."

"Yes, Catesby, what is it?"

"If you take the crown, it is a death sentence for the boys." He lifted a hand forestalling denial. "You also need to hear that I do not say that as a deterrent to your doing so. As things now stand, I consider it an impossibility that both you and the lads will live to enjoy old age. It is in the nature of an irregular succession that only one contender should survive."

"Oh, come," Harry said, impatient laughter in his voice, "it's not so grim as that. There is one other path, Richard. Make the boys love you."

Catesby lifted his head, and there was neither pleasantry nor humor in his face. "Yes, and in the morning, my lord Gloucester will wake to discover he can walk on water, too."

*W*hat do you need to convince you?" Buckingham asked after Hastings and Catesby had left. "The bishop's word is a godsend. It is all you need in order to keep that surly child from the throne and restore order to this country. How can you fail?"

Richard rubbed the back of his neck. An ache had been hovering there for days. Now it was winding around his skull to flower into a heavy throbbing at his temples. "Oh, there are always more ways of failing, Harry, than there are of succeeding."

"And you, Lovell?" Buckingham looked over at Francis. "Do you not agree with me?"

"Hmm," Francis said. "Hmm."

"Please, Francis," Richard said. "Not you, too. I have enough of that from Catesby."

*June 9, 1483. Dawn.*

Will Hastings flung his arm over Jane's lovely white shoulder. She laughed. "You want me to carry a message to Elizabeth?" She reached out and tousled Will's hair. "You dream, love. The queen will tear it to shreds. And me with it."

"No, pretty Jane. Elizabeth will listen. And she will kiss your feet, after."

Hastings could hardly believe his ill fortune. Just when he thought his life was shaping with the utmost sweetness, his old friend Edward had betrayed him from the grave. Perhaps it was Edward's revenge on him for loving Jane. For Jane did love him; perhaps long had. Jane was a loyal little thing. She would not turn away from Edward in his last days, though he would hardly have known if she had, fevered out of his mind as he had been.

Jane Shore, his. The office of chamberlain, still his. But with a difference. The new king was a stripling that could be bent. Hastings could have had power and influence he would never have dreamed of holding while he served Edward. And now there was this meddling bishop, teasing Richard into thinking of taking the crown himself.

King? You are to be king?" Anne's voice was puzzled, and Richard watched as disbelief registered and then slipped from her eyes. "Oh, my dear," she said, after a moment. "May God have mercy on us both."

*June 10, 1483. Noon.*

"Elizabeth and Jane Shore? In league with each other? And with Hastings? Please, Harry, that surpasses belief." Jane Shore, Edward's once-favorite mistress, was once again slipping through the halls of Westminster, this time on her way to and from Hastings' chambers.

Only a day or two ago, Richard had become aware of their relationship and remembered with a kind of amused chagrin how shocked he had been to discover Edward and Hastings sharing a girl a few years past. Now here was Buckingham saying that Jane had been discovered slipping letters through the sanctuary door to Elizabeth. From Hastings. To destroy the protector—office and man.

*June 13, 1483. Morning.*

Richard stepped into the chamber. A partial council, selected from his larger staff, meeting to discuss his coronation: Francis; Buckingham; John Morton, Bishop of Ely; Thomas Lord Stanley; Thomas Rotherham, Archbishop of York; and William Lord Hastings. All of them laughing and jovial this morning. And why not? Summer was in the air and a new king about to be crowned.

"Gentlemen, your pardon; I am late." He turned to Morton as he sat down. "Did I hear you speaking of strawberries as I came in?"

A mild wet June. Apple blossoms a white blur misted by a fine spray of rain. And John Morton's garden walls were said to shelter the best strawberries in the city.

"To answer you, my lord," Bishop Morton said, "yes, my strawberry crop is like none other this year."

"Indeed. I have heard your skills at gardening are unequaled. Perhaps this year they yield other fruit, as well."

"Why, yes, my lord. Apples, pears, and cherries, all in their season. But now is the peak for strawberries. I will send for some, and it please you."

Richard slammed his fist on the table. His ring cut into his finger. "Morton, do you take me for a fool? I am speaking of treason."

"Treason?"

"Treason. Shall I spell it for you?"

The door opened and a dozen armed men poured into the room. Neither Hastings nor Stanley tried to brazen it out with protestations of innocence. They leapt to their feet and drew knives. Hastings dropped his weapon almost as soon as it was drawn, and Stanley had his forced from him. The two bishops, unarmed, were still.

Richard looked at the four men. Guards held Hastings and Stanley at knifepoint, arms pinned behind their backs. Morton and Rotherham sat still and watchful under the alert eyes or more guards. "Bishop, Archbishop, to your feet, please. You are in this, too."

"In what, my lord?" Morton raised his face, bland and urbane, and touched his fingertips together in a steeple. "What could you possibly be speaking of?" He was better able to dissemble than Rotherham, who sat looking dazed, and trembling, his control clearly faltering.

Stanley's control was breaking, too. He was nervously blinking back tears with an odd twitching movement, and biting down on his shaking lower lip. Hastings, however, met Richard's glance levelly, his gray, slightly protuberant eyes betraying neither fear nor supplication.

"You will have the charges explained to you. Take them out. All but Lord Hastings. I would speak with him alone."

On his way out of the room, Francis set upright a chair that had been kicked over in the fray.

"Just outside the door," Richard said to one of the guards. "Close it behind you. Sit down, Will."

*R*ichard pulled over the chair Francis had righted and straddled it backward, his arms resting on its slatted back. "Well, Will, what have you to say?"

"Well, Richard, what would you have me say?"

Richard ignored the insolence. "Why you did it, for a start."

"Ah, Richard. You will be having me tell that at my trial soon enough. Do you really want me to say it twice?"

"As you wish." Richard started to stand. Nothing could come of this save losing his temper, which would not improve the matter.

Hastings stopped him. "I have one question for you, if I might." "Yes?"

"How you did you discover it?"

"How do you imagine, Will? Through your lady, of course. What's her name? Jane?"

"Jane? Is she well?" Hastings showed the first tremor of fear.

"Of course she's well. Do you think I have the appetite to torture women? But then, she talked easily enough without torture. It may have helped that Harry Buckingham is young and handsome. Your Jane was very easily persuaded. Is that not your experience with her?"

"That is revolting, Richard."

"Really? More revolting than inheriting Edward's mistress and using her for conspiracy? I wonder that the great love you say you bore my brother allowed you to do that."

After a silence, Hastings made a sound of derision. "Your brother is dead, Richard. And if you have your way, it is not his son who will reign. Don't talk to me about loving Edward.

"Anyway, who designed this tale about Eleanor Butler that you are putting about?" Hastings' tone managed to combine anger and amusement. "How much did you have to pay that old fool?"

Richard almost answered in heat, then caught himself, and spoke in a tone of deliberate forbearance. "I think you knew Edward well enough, Will, to suppose that the tale is true. You may even have had knowledge of it, yourself."

Hastings made no reply.

"Will, you poor fool. It would never have profited you for the boy to reign. Elizabeth hates you almost as much as she hates me. You would have been expendable the moment young Edward took the crown."

"Ah. And you, Richard? You love England so much? You expect me to believe you are taking the crown for England's sake?"

"Yes. I believe England will fare better under me than under that child and his mother." Only then had he realized that he had known what he would do from the moment he had called Catesby in to hear the old man's tale: he would have had to let the secret be between only himself and the old bishop to have refused the crown.

Richard stood and moved the chair toward the table. "It seems we have underestimated each other, doesn't it? I had no idea of the treachery you were capable of. And you thought I'd never know. What were you planning to do, stab me in my bed? Oh, I see. You hadn't worked it out that far. Further intrigue still to be decided.

"But," he struggled to get hold of the thing that most troubled him. "You say you loved Edward. This was *his* kingdom." He had clenched one fist. Now he knocked it against the chair. "Why would you do that which tears it in half?"

Hastings could have said a number of things, some of which might have saved his life. But he did the thing least likely to gain Richard's forgiveness. He laughed.

"You are not your brother," he said.

Richard walked to the door and summoned the guard into the room. "Prepare to take him out to the green." He spoke so quietly and calmly that Hastings' first thought was that the whole incident would be dismissed as a brief difference of opinion. Then Richard was standing in front of him, saying things which didn't match at all the subdued voice.

"Lord Hastings, hear your sentence. You stand convicted of high treason. You will be taken to the block and executed."

"You can't do that, Richard. I have had no trial."

"High treason is a capital offense. Plotting against the king's life. The king may pass judgment on all such offenses, if he has personal knowledge, of which you have given me plenty. You know that much law yourself, Will."

"I am not shriven!"

"I will send a priest down to you. And I want you to know this: had you shown the least remorse, I would have pardoned you for Edward's sake."

"Richard. Have mercy!"

"You have it already, Will. You are spared the ignominy of a public trial, and you will die quickly."

"A traitor's death."

"A noble traitor's death. You die by the blade; say it is a warrior's death, Will, if it helps you."

*M*orton and Rotherham were taken, briefly, to prison quarters and then granted clemency.

Thomas Stanley was, also briefly, guarded within his own quarters and later released.

William Lord Hastings died with the hour, beheaded on a block of timber that was intended for construction.

*R*ichard sequestered himself behind a closed door, leaving instructions he was not to be disturbed. It was nearly dark when Francis violated the injunction.

"My friend, you should not have done that."

"What? Execute Hastings?"

"*Execute.*" Francis blew out a heavy breath and turned his head aside. "So that is what you call it. I seem to remember when executions were sanctioned by trial."

"He was a traitor," Richard said.

"Yes, he was. A traitor and a great fool." From somewhere in the castle, sounds of singing and a pipe drifted about the edges of the chamber. Nearer, a cricket chirped.

"And you wonder why he had to die."

"That he was a traitor was all the more reason to have sent him to trial. You could afford to let the courts, and the country, see him for what he was."

"I try enemies. Hastings was a friend. Anyway, you know the law. I was justified in what I did."

"Oh, maybe you were. The north might understand, even applaud you. London won't."

"Save your breath, Francis. The thing is done." Richard rested his head in one hand, as though shielding his eyes from the sun, although the light was rapidly dimming.

Francis put a hand on Richard's shoulder. "I don't care whether you were right or not. But I do value your life and reputation, and I doubt London gives a tinker's oath for either."

*June 25, 1483.*
Parliament named Richard III King of England; London was bitterly divided in opinion as to whether the decision was the mercy of God to be spared a child-king, or a violation of the divine order.

Anthony Lord Rivers, Lord Richard Grey, and two other advisors of Edward, former Prince of Wales, were executed at Pontefract for treason, and Elizabeth surrendered the young Duke of York to the king.

*June 26, 1483. Afternoon.*
"How do you lads fare? Are you comfortable?"

Edward was reading in the window while Dickon played at skittles on the floor. Dickon looked up uncertainly, and Edward flashed a smoldering look at Richard, then returned to the book. Richard drew up a chair.

Edward kept his eyes on the book; Dickon answered readily. "Mother wouldn't let me go outside when we were with her, and Edward says you won't let us, either. Can we?"

"That's what I came to talk to you about, in part. It isn't safe for you to be outside just now."

"Uncle." Edward's sarcastic voice. "I know what you have come to tell us. Why don't you say it? It isn't safe for *you* to have us outside. You think we are stupid and deaf. Well, I'm not stupid and gossip goes everywhere, even in here. You are going to make yourself king, and you have murdered my uncle Rivers and my advisors. Are you going to kill us, too?" He delivered the whole speech without raising his eyes from his book.

The young fool ought to have a care for his brother. No nine-year-old should be subjected to such fears as Edward's comments must raise.

"Edward," Richard said. Hate-filled eyes deliberately turned toward him when he spoke, then away again with a great show of indifference. "No one is going to kill you. But you are correct in part of what you say. The issue of your father's marriage to your mother—"

"Which is us."

"Which is you, yes, is not legitimate. You—"

"Are bastards."

"Yes. You may hold nearly any other position in the kingdom, but you may not be king."

"How dare you impugn my mother?"

Richard rose and stood over the boy and took the book out of his hands. "Stand up. Now." As Edward remained stationary, Richard took him by the shirt and hauled him out of the seat.

"That's better. Now, look at me. Keep looking while I talk to you. Listen well, you little fool. No one impugns your mother. She had no knowledge of your father's prior marriage. No blame lies on her. Your father deceived her. Probably you don't believe that, but it is true. Men must learn to live with the truth, no matter how little they like it.

"I don't expect you to like any of this. What I do expect is that you refrain from insolence, toward me, toward any of my men. And that you think of your brother when you speak. Do you understand?"

"Yes." The eyes steadily on him. "I understand I must do your bidding, uncle, that my life is at your command in small as well as large matters. Therefore I will look at you when you speak."

"What a disagreeable little speech, Edward. You don't understand a thing I said to you."

"I understand everything. Now, may I have my book back?" Edward's voice may have been a trace more civil.

"What? Oh, damn, yes."

"My lord?" A very small, frightened voice. "If we are good, may we go outside?"

"Yes, Dickon, I hope so. Soon." The little boy's eyes were full of tears.

"Come here," Richard said. There was no reason the boy should find him a comfort, but Dickon came to him, and Richard leaned down. "Your brother is very angry. He has reason to be, but it makes him say things that are not true, that are foolish. You won't believe everything he says and let him frighten you, will you?"

"No, sir."

Richard could hardly bear how touched he was by the little boy's trust. He felt like crying, himself.

*Westminster Cathedral*
*July 6, 1483.*

Multicolored light from the bank of windows behind them illuminated the faces in the choir. The archbishop's hands and gown were covered with circles and squares of light, and apparently the pages of his missal, too: the old man was finding it hard to read the text in the dancing array. He blinked, shifted the book a little to the right, and finally tossed his head like a horse trying to escape flies.

What a press of people! The air was heavy with the smell of incense, and the animal smell of the hundreds of people each with their own scent and sweat, packed into the cathedral. The nave, with its lofty vaulted ceiling reaching almost to Heaven, the walls of windows astonishingly beautiful in the blinding sun that changed their images to pulsing color, and the masses below the podium made Richard think: Heaven and Hell are waiting in this abbey, all humanity gathered for Judgment Day. What would God do with such a crowd? Hear their stories one by one? Would God himself have that much patience?

The archbishop was nervous. His face was flushed and stumbled over the words. He stopped, held the missal a little farther from his eyes, and tried again. Richard breathed in deeply, held his lungs full for a moment, then slowly let out his breath. *Keep going, Bouchier, just keep going. No one out there can hear a word. You could speak in Arabic with a mouth full of marbles, and no one would know the difference.*

But Bouchier was an old man. He would not perform many more state rituals, certainly not another coronation, and he wanted it right.

He had crowned Edward, Richard remembered.

How could any man want to indulge his follies as casually as Edward had done? There was no end to the people affected by his actions. Himself. George, who died because he knew. His own dear Ned, named for the uncle who had changed his future. Most of all,

Edward's own sons, who would always regard their uncle with hate and bitterness.

Oh, yes, they would always hate him. Even Dickon would come to do so, in time. Any office he tried to give them, any lands, any power, would seem a sop, a bone thrown to dogs after the marrow was sucked out.

Richard flexed his toes and straightened his back. His shoulders were beginning to ache. Twelve feet of the finest Belgian velvet hanging from them, *and* trimmed with fur. Whoever devised that ritual was not a man who had been crowned.

Buckingham laid down the massive purple cloth, and Richard felt its full weight. Attendants stepped forward and loosened his garments and Anne's, exposing their shoulders and back for the holy oil.

The crowns were placed on their heads. Anne's lady put hers a little too far back. It started to slide, and with an embarrassed little gasp, Anne grabbed and straightened it. Crowns in place, shoulders redraped, they moved to hear the holy mass, walking hand in hand the few steps to the high altar.

Kneeling carefully, Richard relinquished Anne's hand. He moved his head and could just see her profile, an arm's length away. Her back and neck were erect and graceful, and her expression would have seemed appropriate carved in marble.

He rocked forward and back a little trying to ease the ache in his back. There was a dragon here waiting to be slain, but where was its head? The executed traitors, in which case the dragon was already rendered powerless? He wished he could believe that.

Perhaps the church, obviously disapproving that he had not submitted Edward's errant action to them first. Let the bishops haggle about the legality of marriage while the country simmered in insecurity.

Perhaps Elizabeth and her surviving kinsmen, with their plots and counterplots to grab the throne.

Edward's sons. Boys now, but they would be men all too soon.

Or his subjects, that huge mass surrounding him, their faces blank as empty plates.

Ah, yes, it was Judgment Day. But the people were the judges. Even as Bouchier proclaimed Richard God's anointed, the people were deciding whether they and God were of like mind. Richard felt a cold lump like uncooked gruel somewhere between his throat and stomach, and tasted it. It was fear.

# 22 Sons of Kings

For the first month of Richard's reign there was a tense peace like the calm before a thunderstorm. Then the uprisings began—plots to restore Edward V to the throne, royal property burned and pillaged, scurrilous handbills posted on tavern doors. Richard was not surprised. Disorder had followed every time a king came to the throne by other than traditional means, and the strangeness of his succession surely surpassed any before him.

Now he considered the present trouble. "It appears," he said, "that the rebellions are mostly here in the south and a few in the midlands. Not a ripple north of the fens."

"What do you make of that?" Francis asked.

Buckingham answered. "I would have thought that was obvious. The men of the north know Gloucester's governance and trust him too well to want to rebel." Ever since Hastings' death, Buckingham had conducted himself as though he were the perfect courtier, every statement designed to ingratiate.

"I know." Francis did not appear to have taken offense. "What I meant was, not all the southern counties are disaffected. I was wondering what distinguishes those that are from those that are not."

"Here is one clue." John Kendall ran a finger down the list of names he had drawn up. "Look at the names of these men known to be instigators." The clerk was tall and wiry, with fair, fine-textured hair and a quiet voice. Richard was beginning to know him not as humorless, but as a moderate man who could be counted on to supply a voice of reason when passions threatened to throw others off course.

Francis peered over Kendall's shoulder. "They are almost entirely former servants and retainers of Edward's, for one thing."

"Precisely," Kendall said "Men who loved and served the late king." He glanced up at Francis and back to Richard. "So if you will pardon my saying so, sir, they dispute the validity of the pre-contract, either for its own sake or out of loyalty to your brother." He frowned. "Either way, they would appear to see you as a common usurper who has deprived their friend's son of his legacy."

Or they believed the pre-contract and found it trivial. Catesby had warned him. *Strict legality may be of little practical importance.* "Usurper," Richard mused. "Half the kings of this century have had that accusation flung at them, including Edward, and they weren't necessarily the worst rulers."

"Whether or not there is justice in their claim, sir, it is a dangerous opinion and one that could be difficult to revise."

"I don't know." Francis was reading down the list. "Usurpation may have nothing to do with it."

"Meaning?" Buckingham asked.

"The legality of the succession is a fine argument to throw about. But it may be only personal concerns—the position of these men at court, that sort of thing. Richard's taste in friends and supporters is very different from his brother's. Some of these men stand to lose a good deal of what they have presumed for years was theirs."

"No, no. There I must disagree with you." Buckingham spoke passionately. "The real source of trouble is the bastard princes. They have become the magnet for all dissatisfaction."

The boys were undoubtedly a difficulty. Young Edward was alternately sickly and imperious. He continued to resent his keepers and released his resentment not only onto them but to his brother, as well. And once he had caused a disturbance at the archery butts, where Richard had allowed them, under Tyrrell's eye, some outside activity. Edward had called out to a passerby: "God's mercy, sir! You see what becomes of princes of the realm, when impostors reign."

That in itself could have started a small riot, except that this passerby had been Catesby.

"Imagine the power the revolts would gain if any of their leaders managed to apprehend one of the bastards," Buckingham was saying.

"Well, Harry, they are no longer at large, so I doubt they can be apprehended." Richard had stopped their excursions after the incident with Catesby and moved the boys to more interior apartments where they would not be in constant view from the windows.

It was not an adequate solution, however. By all rights, prince or bastard, the boys ought to be at hawks and horses with other youths learning their way in the world. Confinement to any quarters, however luxurious, was indeed a prison. He would count it so, himself, and hate it.

The bells had begun to peal for vespers, first from St. Paul's, then around the city. Today they sounded like a consort of warnings, a choir of reprimand.

"You know what I would do with them?" Buckingham asked.

"Tell us, Harry," Francis said amiably. "We await your solution to the unsolvable."

"Why, I'd kill the bastards," Harry said, smiling.

When his eyes met Richard's the smile faded. There was no attempt to flatter in Buckingham's face then, only something cold and stark.

The silence seemed to stretch on forever.

"Harry, your humor goes awry," Richard said, finally.

"Humor? Believe me, I do not jest. We have surely lost by now the good opinion of those to whom the boys' lives matter, and we would gain the surety that they will never rise against us. Ghosts may walk the night, but I've never heard of them leading rebellions."

"Harry," John Kendall said, "be careful. You will make Richard a passport to Hell with talk like that."

"Come, gentlemen. It's never murder. You know how it's done. What was poor Henry said to die from? *Pure displeasure*—a most threadbare fabrication. We could any of us imagine a better explanation than that." Buckingham glanced around the room, a benign tutor explaining what should be an obvious lesson to students who have not seen the light, but surely will.

"But then," he laughed, breaking the spell, "that is what *I* would do, but I am not their keeper. And, of course, I have no need to kill them, so their lives rest secure."

Richard twisted his ring on his finger. A gloom descended on him. When, in all England's history, had a deposed king died a natural death? And when had he crossed that borderland from the arrogance that had let him believe that he, unlike any king before him, could defy the consequences of taking the throne to the despair that he likened to the clamor of the bells? Quiet at intervals, he knew it would return, setting off with appalling regularity a rumbling chaos in his head, the certain knowledge that he had no good answer to the disposition of his nephews.

385

*York*
*1483.*

With his rule marred by rumor and unrest, Richard set out to know his country in its entirety, as he had once set out to know the north. On one of his last days at York, he took his sons to the autumn fair, the largest in the country. John was twelve now, Ned nine, and Richard thought it a good opportunity both to pass some pleasant time with them, and to give them a view of a wider world than what they could see at Middleham.

There were merchant stalls of Venetian glass, both water-clear and jewel-colored, Saracen carpets, as well as the familiar Yorkshire sheep and horses, and acrobats and musicians performing for the crowd. Also a few things Richard was in no hurry to have his sons view. A girl who could have been no more than fourteen, with a pretty face and a short leg which gave her an ungainly limp, whom he saw haggling with an unkempt, rather blank-looking man. A mounted sergeant suddenly spurred his horse and a man at the far end of the row of pavilions darted around a corner into an alley.

"Why is he chasing that man?" Ned wanted to know.

"Most likely he is a cutpurse." Richard could more comfortably explain market thieves than lame young girls selling themselves.

"What will he do if he catches him?"

John explained. "Put him in stocks. Isn't that right? He looked to his father for confirmation of his knowledge, but then was distracted from hearing the answer. "Oh, look! There's a dancing bear. Let's go see it."

Richard saw an old bear, or an unwell one, with patches of bare skin, the hair worn thin on the neck where the collar rested. A piper struck up a tune, and the bear rose up on its hind legs and shuffled a few half-hearted steps before dropping back down to all fours. Its keeper pulled at the chain on its collar and prodded it in the ribs with a cane. The "dance" alternated between a few weary steps, a return to its natural posture, and the persuasion of the cane.

Laughter rippled through the crowd, sometimes when the bear frustrated its owner, and sometimes at the animal's misfortune.

"Let's go," John repeated.

Ned spoke, quiet and serious. "I don't want to go over there," he said, his face troubled.

"Go, John." Richard caught his son's sleeve before the boy spun off. "Stay there. Do not stray until we come, do you understand?

Don't move." It was not that he feared John could not handle himself in most circumstances he would encounter; he just did not want to spend half the afternoon looking for his son.

"Yes, sire!"

"So," Richard said to Ned, "you don't want to see the bear."

"It doesn't want to dance. The man has to poke it with a stick. Why does he do that?"

Richard sighed. "It's how the owner lives, Ned—by what the crowd gives him when they watch."

How do you explain to children, prepare them for the follies of the world without inflicting on them some of your own darkness? Ned's question called up too much of the fear and pain he had felt as a child, himself, a child's helpless rage.

"I don't know. I don't always understand the things men laugh at, either." Richard glanced over to the bear, looking for John. The boy had moved a little distance away and was talking to two older lads holding bows. One of the boys handed John his bow and John was stroking it.

His sons broke his heart. There was John, his bastard, laughing, talking, already at ease with men, while Ned was too tender by half. Each should have been born in the station that fell to the other.

$\mathcal{T}$he weather had turned by the time they left York, keeping up a steady rain through the next three days. When Richard arrived in Lincoln, there was a letter from John Howard waiting for him, apprising him of the state of the revolts.

Harry Buckingham, perfect courtier, had joined forces with an uprising in the east, and was attempting to reach Henry Tudor in Wales. The rivers were swollen with rain, the Severn too deep and rapid to ford. Finding no route into Wales, Buckingham had sought refuge with a former servant, who delivered him to Richard's men.

$\mathcal{N}$o, he won't see you," Francis said. "I told you he wouldn't."

"Did you ask him?"

"Yes."

"But did you plead my case for me?"

The room was small and square, a narrow cot at one end, on which Buckingham sat, hands bound. There were a table and two chairs, and the guard sitting at the table stood and joined another guard at the door when Francis entered.

Francis sat down on one of the chairs. "I gave him your words, just as you said them to me. You can't expect more."

"I thought you might urge him to mercy. If any man could persuade him, it is you."

"Christ, Harry! Why would I want to?" Francis turned his head aside, then went on. "There are things you might want to know. There's a headsman in the village; there will be no drawing and quartering. It will be quick."

Harry turned startled eyes to Francis. "He's really going to do it, isn't he?"

"Why, yes, Harry, he's really going to do it. What did you think?"

Buckingham lowered his head onto fists clenched above the bound wrists. Every decision he had made, he had made suddenly, without knowing the consequences, guided by an instinct he trusted more than his brain, which was clever, nonetheless. When he had declared himself Richard's man instead of casting his lot with his own wife's family; when he had the good fortune of discovering Hastings' plot and decided to share the knowledge. There were other choices both times. Then Tudor appeared in the arena, and that path seemed inviting. It was clear by then that Richard had his own ways, his own ideas, friends, and opinions, and was not amenable to abandoning any of them. Tudor, on the other hand, would be a stranger to London, to England, and would have cause to be grateful for guidance.

And Tudor, Buckingham had no doubt, would have no foolish qualms about the little bastards. It was then he began to see how, if Richard and the boys were gone, he, Henry Stafford, Duke of Buckingham, could be heir to the throne. He could always decide later whether to support Tudor, or be rid of him, too.

Once, a very long time ago, when Buckingham was a little boy with no thoughts of kings or courts in his mind, was only a child fascinated by the mystery of the workings of the world, one of his teachers had been an old monk.

"You see," the monk had said, trying to help the boy expand some too-rigid position, "we watch the sun rise and set in its path around the earth. But for all we can be sure of, the earth may move around the sun. From where we stand, it would look the same."

The earth around the sun; the sun around the earth. Himself serving Richard; Richard serving him. He could not tell from where he stood. He began to laugh, and his laughter was a gasp from deep in his chest.

Finally, having neither handkerchief nor free hands, Buckingham snorted back the congestion that had come with the tears. "Tell Richard he does not know how great a favor I have done him. But he will. Tell him to light a candle for me, then."

## Tower of London
### 1483.

Sir Robert Brackenbury was Constable of the Tower at that time, a short squat man with crisply curling brown hair, a soft-spoken, even reticent, man. He and James Tyrrell had become good friends, and Richard was struck afresh by how the voluble Tyrrell seemed drawn to friendships with people unlike himself.

Richard didn't call at the Tower immediately upon his return to London, being reluctant to see Edward's hate-filled face, or even Dickon's trusting but increasingly reproachful one. He ran into Tyrrell the first day he was back, who rather pointedly commented that he and Brackenbury would confer with the king whenever he wished.

"Thank you, James." Richard nodded, much of his attention still on the events of the past few weeks, and was surprised to note that Tyrrell seemed offended, even angry.

That evening, both Tyrrell and Brackenbury came to his chamber, insisting on an immediate audience with him. Tyrrell's air of irritation had not lessened. "As you seemed in no hurry to give us the news, we thought perhaps it would help if we came to you."

"I doubt there is much you nave not heard already, and the council will meet in two days' time. What is it you want to know?"

"Oh, begging my lord's pardon. This old soldier's wits are not as quick as you seem to think." Tyrrell could wax as eloquent as any man when he chose. The bluff, dull soldier's stance was in fact his most ponderous sarcasm.

Brackenbury cast a glance at Tyrrell and said directly, as courteous as always, "What we have come to inquire, sir, is whether the lads reached Sheriff Hutton."

"Lads? Sheriff Hutton? What are you men talking about?"

Brackenbury fumbled behind him like a blind man for a chair. Once seated, he thumped with one fist over his heart, as though the organ might cease to beat without his assistance.

"There were three men, Richard," Tyrrell said, "who came bearing a letter from you."

"I wrote no letter."

"No, sir, I see that now. But it could have been your hand, it was like enough, and it bore the Great Seal."

The lamp must have been badly trimmed; the shadows it cast lurched and wavered. "Gentlemen," Richard said, "It seems that you are the bearers of news, here, not I."

*I*t was simple enough. Three men had come to the Tower with a writ obtaining the release of the lord bastards, for conveyance to Sheriff Hutton. It bore the stamp of the Great Seal, which in Richard's absence was in the keeping of his Lord Chamberlain, the Duke of Buckingham. One of the men was a trusted household servant; all three had been in service in the Tower. And Brackenbury recalled that Richard had spoken on more than one occasion of removing the boys from London.

"Does anyone else know about this?" Richard asked.

"No, sir," Brackenbury said. "Only myself and Sir James."

"How did you come to know of it, James?" Richard asked.

"I was there the night it happened. We were playing at cards together."

Richard stood and walked to the window. He held up a hand for silence, for the moment unable to speak, riding out the sensations that wracked his body. He felt light-headed, half sick, half giddy. He had to think very deliberately, a word at a time. While he thought, he looked at all the ordinary things around him, the window, the rings on his hand.

*Why, I'd kill the bastards.*

How does a man become a child-killer? How does he murder his nephews? He only looks into another man's eyes, into the mind behind the eyes, and to the thoughts that lie there. He looks a fraction too long, and the deed is done, as surely as if he had commanded it.

"What do we do, sir?" Brackenbury's voice was despondent.

"Nothing," Richard said finally, turning away from the window. "What is there to do?" He perhaps could be certain that Buckingham had ordered to have the boys killed. He could not be certain the deed had been accomplished; they could be turning to dust, in hiding, or even lying in wait to take their revenge. He resolved to say nothing, to admit to or deny nothing. From this day on, it would be as if the sons of Edward IV had never lived, for all he would have to say on the subject. It was the only integrity left to him in the matter.

But now he must address what would be unforgivable to neglect.

"Sir Robert. James. You're not to reproach yourselves. The purpose of the Seal is to verify the king's word. To allow the king's will to be executed in his absence. You can hardly be blamed for doing exactly that."

𝒯wo weeks after the boys' disappearance, a hunter found a body at the edge of the forest. The man was about the size of Richard's servant, but could have been anyone, the clothes torn, the flesh ravaged by animals.

After receiving the news, Richard had gotten quietly and methodically drunk. Not so drunk as to lose control of himself, nor so drunk as not to notice that his condition seemed to frighten his men, most of whom had not seen him overindulge himself in anything.

In the morning, he rose early even though hammers were beating behind his eyeballs and went into the solar for breakfast. Anne watched him curiously, as though he were a stone that had arisen and walked.

"Well," he said, sitting down. "What do you want to say?"

"Nothing."

"Nothing? No reproaches, no I-told-you-thus?"

Anne's voice was quiet. "Will it help? If it will, I will say it."

"No, Anne, it won't help."

"Then I will not say it."

## Cambridge
### 1484.

In the spring, Richard made another procession of his country. The quick suppression of Buckingham's revolt had strengthened his reign, as well as his reputation abroad.

Anne accompanied him. By unspoken consent, and the kind of understanding that sometimes existed between them, they did not speak about any affairs of the kingdom. An unexpected peace fell on them, almost such as Richard remembered from the first years of their marriage. In Cambridge one afternoon they walked along the pathways of the colleges, through old court, where the students passed with their bright cloaks and fine knives hanging from embroidered girdles, the knives and the colors of the colleges giving them almost the aspect of soldiers in procession. They saw the new chapel, built of limestone carted all the way from Yorkshire, with its fine timber roof, complete now except for the tower.

Even this place, which should be a sanctum of knowledge and wisdom, had seen its share of violence, Richard knew. Around the turn of the century, grievances between town and college had led to riots, the seizing and destruction of muniments, walls broken down, and men hanged.

But today the peace could not have been more profound. The sky was a bright clear blue, and, between two fine stone houses, a garden of daffodils gleamed like gold. Richard felt hopeful, almost unsullied as he stood there, feeling the breeze, watching the flowers sway on their slender stalks. The wheel could turn again. Things could come right in a way no one could foresee.

*A*fter leaving Cambridge, they planned to stop a few days at Nottingham, Richard's favorite castle next to Middleham. The room was the freshest he had been in for months. New rushes covered the floor, and the windows were thrown wide to the clean spring air and the sound of shepherds' pipes fading down the hillside. Another month and the breeze would carry the smell of hay and clover up from the fields below.

Two of Anne's ladies sat at the table in the corner playing chess. Pretending to play, Richard thought. Mostly they were laughing and gossiping—about men, no doubt. Madge, the pretty yellow-haired one, slid her eyes toward Francis. He seemed to feel the glance and looked her way, but she anticipated him and he was left staring at her profile. *Francis, you must be quicker, flirting maids are sly as snakes.* Francis and Rob were making plans for the next day's hunt, but Richard doubted it would materialize. They were all pretending. Not one of them had an ambition more worthy than finishing their wine and waiting for spring to come in the window.

Except Anne. No pretense there. She sat in her chair, her head leaned back, eyes half-closed, her hands hanging limply over the chair arms while Joan brushed her hair. Anne looked asleep, but he knew better: she might go trance-like with the pleasure of having her hair brushed, but she wouldn't doze and miss a stroke. Her head bobbed a little with each pull of the brush, and the dark curtain of hair gleamed as it spilled over Joan's hands. He watched a while as Anne sank deeper into her body, the beautiful shining hair rippling and catching the light, a small half-smile on her face, as blissful as a cat.

Any moment now he would stop pretending, too. He would send everyone out of the room and do what he had been thinking of for an hour now. Do it lazily, dreamily, with the bed curtains open to let that gentle breeze touch their bodies. He glanced toward the window. Streaks of red and purple colored the clouds. It was late enough.

Afterward, he would think the cruelest thing of that evening was that the news came in a moment of such peace and pleasure. Boots and spurs clattered in the hallway, the sound of stomping feet, voices, and then the door opened. A young man stood blinking in the torchlight. Whoever he was, he had ridden hard. Grime was thick on his face; his boots and cloak were splattered with mud. He pulled off his cap and looked around, his gaze stumbling from face to face. He appeared confused, as though he were not sure he was in the right place, or as though, now he was here, he couldn't remember the reason that had brought him. Perhaps the lad had been directed to the wrong part of the castle. Someone would take care of it.

No one did. The strange young man waited, looking less confused, but tense, almost frightened. Richard was sure now that he had seen the face before, the square chin, the short broad nose. It made him uneasy not to be able to place him. He stood and touched Francis on the arm. "Go see what that lad needs, will you?"

"A bath, most of all," Francis laughed. "Sorry, we were deep in the hunt."

Richard watched Francis cross the room and bend his head to listen while the boy began, very earnestly, to explain something. The lad kept turning his hat in his hands, as Francis shook his head slowly, and once hugged his arms tightly to his body the way a man will do if he is cold or trying not to show hurt.

Richard could not hear the words, but the room had grown very quiet, and he felt a sudden sense of alarm. He tried to push it away, but all that happened was a heaviness pressing on his chest, and he found it hard to breathe. Faces seemed to loom and float in front of him. He turned to look at Anne, wondering if she understood.

Then he saw the livery on the boy's sleeve, his own and Middleham's colors, when he saw the anguish in the face he knew the message, and the knowledge took him to his knees. He put out his hand. Francis took it, and he was almost as quickly back on his feet. "Richard, sit down. Please."

Francis eased him into the chair. A memory came, a child's longing to change what is to come with a simple charm. If I turn my back, if I can get Anne and go to bed, this boy will not be standing in front of me with his awful knowledge, and Francis with pity in his eyes.

"Sire," the boy said, "forgive me." He was trembling.

Francis stepped forward and put his hands on Richard's shoulders. "My friend," he spoke in the most gentle, quiet voice. "Your son is dead."

"Ned?" But he didn't need to ask which son. All the servants were crying. Anne sat on the bed leaning against Rob, sobbing into his shoulder.

Small things suddenly seemed incredibly urgent. He had to do something.

"Francis. Get this man some food and a bath. See that he has a bed—a bed, mind you—not some corner of the floor, and a fresh horse tomorrow."

He turned to the boy. "I know your face. I should remember you."

"Yes, sire. Mark Harrington. The smith's son. I was my lord Ned's squire this past year." He began fiddling with his hat again.

"How was it you came to this task?" Men used to be killed who brought such news.

"My lord, it was the last thing I could do for him."

"Yes. Well. You have stretched some since I last saw you. Get some food now, lad. I'll talk to you before you sleep. Not now."

Francis led the boy off.

"Rob, get these people out of here. No." He shook his head at Joan as she started to rise. "Stay here, please, with her." With all the crying ladies out the door, he hunched forward and put his head in his hands. In a few moments he would go find Mark and ask him all the useless questions.

*A*lice watched Richard and Anne carefully. Richard held Anne's horse while she dismounted and steadied her descent with a hand on her elbow. "Thank you," she said, but did not look at him, only leaned her forehead a moment against the horse's withers. Richard kept his hand on her until she straightened and pulled away, then released her with no change of expression in his face. The poor children, Alice thought. They cannot comfort each other.

Without an heir, Richard's kingdom was at great hazard. Only a monarch of immense wealth and a claim on the heart of every lord in the country could hope to keep his throne without a blood heir. Please God, this had not occurred to them yet. Let them heal a little before they understand how dangerous their loss is.

Alice embraced Anne, pulling her daughter's face into the hollow of her neck and stroking the dark hair, as she had not done for years.

"Countess," Richard said. She looked across Anne into his face and saw, as she often was able to, the thought he would prefer to hide. He knew very well the danger he was in. But there was more, she would swear. What, in their grief, had they done to each other?

Anne got up from the table and kissed her mother. "I'm very tired."

"Of course, dear. Rest well. We shall see you in the morning."

Silence hung after her for a moment. Finally Francis wiped his mouth and laid down his napkin. "I must bid you goodnight also. Pray, do not think me rude. The meal was excellent, countess."

"Of course you are not rude, Francis. You are the soul of courtesy, as always. Goodnight."

After Francis left, Alice looked at Richard. "Would you join me by the fire? My thoughts are poor companions these nights."

At the hearth, the steward served them steaming cups of spiced wine. "I find it takes away the cutting edge of pain," Alice said, "without making me besotted."

"Thank you." Richard sat without drinking, holding his cup between his hands.

No one thinks to outlive their children, Alice thought. No matter how often we see others suffer that loss, we believe we will be spared. "How is it with you and Anne?"

"We grieve, Alice. What else is there to say?"

"Then let us talk of something else."

Richard gave a harsh laugh. "What should we find happier to talk about? The state of my kingdom?"

"Whatever comforts you, dear." Alice waited, thinking he might like to talk to someone who would not advise or suggest, who would only listen.

"Well, Alice, as you know, Hastings is dead. He seems to have been plotting almost as soon as Edward died, but he was well-liked in London, so his death didn't endear me to the city." Richard glanced down at his cup of wine. "Henry Tudor, of all people, has decided he has the best claim on the throne. He's in Wales trying to raise men, while the Scots are still playing tag across the border."

Alice noticed he made no reference to his nephews and found she did not want to ask. "But you did have a good Parliament. We heard about it, even up here."

"Oh, yes. We passed a lot of fine laws. Bookbinders, felons, and wives of dead traitors love me. If any of them had troops or money, I'd be well set up," Richard said. "Do you want to know the jest of all this, countess?" He didn't wait for her answer. "The first is that, when I considered that Edward's son should not be king, I wasn't thinking that I should rule; I was thinking of Ned." His voice broke on his son's name, but he recovered himself. "I thought no one should cheat him of the crown: I actually thought he'd want it. And the second is, of course, now he's dead."

*T*he hot wine and the hours before the fire became a nightly ritual with them. Alice watched the sparks fly up as a charred log broke into pieces. "It is good to have you here again, no matter how much I grieve the circumstance that has brought you," she said.

"Ah yes. My soul in Hell, myself at home. Hades and Middleham both have their tenants, God be praised." Richard's voice was savage.

"So much bitterness, Richard. I hate to hear it. It rots the soul."

"Well, since I have just said that I and mine have parted company, it hardly matters, does it?"

She stared at him. "I have never heard you speak so. What do you mean?"

He set down his goblet. "Nothing, Alice. Pardon my ill humor."

"No pardon is necessary. I know what it is to sorrow. Sometimes it seems that the pain goes on forever." Alice struggled to find words that offered comfort without mocking what could not be changed. "When we lose loved ones, it seems we must never mend. But we do. The patch always shows, but we survive."

Now it was her turn to fall silent with her memories. Then she heard Richard's pleasant voice, the bitterness gone, "Yes. A husband and a daughter you have lost."

She waited a long time before answering. What did it matter now? Perhaps it would ease her to speak of it. "I wasn't thinking of Isabel just then. Nor of Warwick. He was my husband, but Jack had my heart." She looked quickly at Richard. "I have never told anyone else of that. Even Jack. He knew, I think, but we never spoke of it. I was always a true wife to my husband."

Richard said nothing, seemed only waiting for her to go on.

"Jack loved you dearly, you know," she said finally. "Like a son."

"Yes, I know."

"He told me once about a time he carried you off to bed, at Ludlow. I marveled that such a thing would matter to him, to remember it and find it worth speaking of."

"What did you say?"

"Oh, it is no great matter. You were a little child, and sick, and he took you off to bed. There is no reason you should remember."

"I have remembered it for years. I always thought it was my father."

"And now I have robbed you of a memory of a father." She had inflicted a small boy's pain on a grown man and wondered how he would take it, grown men being, in her experience, more brittle than small boys.

"Jack. So it was he who cared more for a sick child than for the succession. Well, he was a kind man, one of the kindest I've known."

*R*ichard's little hawk released the dove, and he held the soft limp body in the gloved palm of his hand. The beak was slightly parted, and there were beads of blood on the gray breast.

"Uncle?"

John de la Pole, Earl of Lincoln and the son of Richard's sister Elizabeth, was a tall young man, fair like most of the Plantagenets, with a wide smiling mouth, and green eyes that seemed to shine with an inner restlessness, as though he knew there were wonders to be seen all about him, but had not yet located them.

"Yes, John." Richard kept his eyes averted as he dropped the dove into the leather pouch hanging over his saddle.

"You wanted to speak with me, I thought."

"Just so." Richard fastened the pouch, slid the hood over his hawk's head, and finally looked up. "The matter is this. As you know, since the death of the Prince of Wales, the only heirs of my body are my bastards, and bastard slip does not rule. I intend to name you my successor." They passed from a shoal of deep shadow into the dancing pattern of sunlight and dark beneath a canopy of oak leaves moving in the breeze. The forest floor was a carpet of ivy sprinkled with violet and oxlip. "I don't know what the future holds for either of us, but God willing, you will have years before the realization of this office."

Lincoln nodded. "I am honored you would have me, sir."

They turned their horses out of the speckled forest light onto a leafy lane. "Don't be a fool, John. It may well be a curse I am placing upon you. Give me at least the comfort of knowing that you realize the burden."

"Curse, sir?"

"If we defeat Tudor, we may have a long and peaceful reign. Who else is there, after all, to try for the crown? We have all killed each rather effectively, don't you think?" A phrase came back to him, from one of the old Romans, who would have had plenty of cause to know about the terrible emptiness of conquest: *They have made a desolation and they call it peace.*

"Sir?"

"But you are not my son," Richard said. "No matter how long or well I may rule, when I die there will be other grandsons and great-grand-sons of kings who will think their claim superior to yours. You are a paper heir, nothing more, unless when the time comes, you are strong enough to defend what I have so effortlessly bestowed on you."

*R*ichard worked late into the night. His hours had a feverish gray quality, the distinction between days and nights barely discernible. He sometimes read the same petition five times before he got the gist of it, and when he did, the stupidity of the complaint weighed against the death of one small boy awed him. But he stayed doggedly with the documents, reading, weighing requests and making judgments. Imposing fines and slapping the wrists of poachers had no meaning for him, but the things that had meaning he could do nothing about.

Tonight he took stock of his realm.

He had ruled for one year and four months, and had held one Parliament.

His brother's sons, whom he had sworn to protect, he must assume were dead. He had no idea of the manner of their death, nor where their bodies lay. No matter how much he might regret that, there was a part of him that was relieved at not having to face them for the rest of his life. The relief, too, was a part of his guilt.

He and Anne were as strangers. They ate in silence and went to bed without speaking, each to their separate rooms. For this, he knew himself entirely to blame, and could not manage a single gesture that might heal the breach between them.

Men whom he raised to power were mostly humbly born and often resented—Catesby, his lawyer, and John Kendall, his clerk, the son of a former servant of Edward's.

Nevertheless, he had accomplished some good. He had created the Council of the North to accommodate his absences, but the council's value would far out live him: never again would justice in the north depend solely on the wisdom or folly of a single man.

And he had loved the law of the land, which he saw not as a series of edicts, but the manifestation of the country's spirit, the breath of England.

Perhaps the law encouraged him particularly because its life ran in a direction contrary to the lives of men. Men flourish in flesh and substance on the earth for a time, then pass, leaving first the dust of their bodies, then only memory in the minds of others. Finally, with the turning of generations, even memory fades.

Law, on the other hand, exists first as thought and unformed longings in the hearts and minds of men, then as words spoken in courts and taverns, and finding, at last, incarnation in ink and parchment, sealed and stored in the stone chambers of Westminster, enduring forever. Now some of his own thoughts and longings were a part of the body of law. Whether they proved to be the vital organs or long bones of that body, or of as little consequence as one of the thousands of hairs on a man's head, remained to be seen. Either way, they were good laws, redress to some of England's longstanding injustices, the fruit of his reign as surely as his children were the fruit of his body.

*H*e put his head down on his arms and closed his eyes, waking much later to a dim, cold room. The fire in the hearth was nearly out; a red glow came from the charred remains of a log. Every few seconds a piece of the wood fell away from the rest and sent a little shower of sparks upward into the black mouth of the chimney. The wall torches burned low, and the candle on his desk had melted into a pool of yellow wax. Outside, the wind sent a small clatter of twigs and leaves spinning against the window, dropped them, and whistled around the cold stone of the turret.

He stood, restored the fire, exchanged the butt in the candlestick for a new fresh candle, and reordered his papers. Perhaps he should go to bed, although he seemed to sleep best unintentionally.

He rubbed his eyes. The fire blazed up, and a glow of light spread about the room. Among the curtain's shadowed folds, in the window seat a form took shape. Anne. She should not be up in the night chill. And her being there would mean she wanted something, or worse, wanted to give him something. He wanted nothing. Not comfort. Nor love.

He walked over to her. "Why are you here, Anne? It must be nearly morning."

"Sit beside me, Richard." She slid her hand from the folds of her robe and laid it on the window seat.

He made no attempt to accept her invitation, and after a moment she spoke again. "I talked with your mother today. I told her how your sorrow is so great, it appears that I have lost you as well as Ned."

Richard heard none of the blame in Anne's voice that her words might imply, and listened.

"I was so full of pity for myself." Anne shook her head slightly. "She has had so many losses, your mother, I thought she would comfort me for mine.

"But she only said, 'My child, the way to be close to those you love is to take steps toward them. Had you shown so little courage as a babe, you would not be walking upright today.'"

"Anne, no one could accuse you of having no courage. You are as brave a woman—"

"Hush." She laid her palm whole across his lips. "I did not come to talk about that." She moved her hands to his shoulders and drew him closer to her, and he was forced to put his arms around her to avoid toppling into her lap. He felt ridiculous, and worse, saw the encounter moving in the direction he had feared.

Anne slid her body down from the window seat to the floor, managing somehow to keep herself in the circle of his arms, and pulled him to the floor beside her.

"No," Richard said, but felt robbed of strength, Samson with his hair shorn, too weak to stop her from doing to him anything she wanted.

She kept one arm under his neck while the other hand reached through his robe, smooth and cool on his skin.

What was she thinking, that she could slake grief in desire? "Don't, Anne. There will be no more children for us."

Her hand stopped its caressing movement, but didn't pull away from him, and after a moment, she spoke. "No. No more children. Do what you must for yourself and the kingdom. Seek an annulment."

"No."

"Divorce me. I will blame you not."

"You know I won't divorce you."

"You may as well, Richard. As you have put me from you in fact, you may as well do it in law." Again the calm voice, without recrimination.

"I love you," he protested.

"As I love you, but I think that love that cannot share sorrow is nothing."

"Anne—"

"Put down your grief, my lord. It is no shame to still find joy in life." She turned his face to hers, and he was startled to see, in the soft glow of firelight, not a plea for his affection, but compassion, the wisdom of one who has known the depth of loss and had the strength to find life good. And find *him* good, Richard thought, stunned.

It was as though she had reached through the folds and darkness of a monk's hood, and lifted his face to the sun. For a moment, he did not hate himself, and found he could believe again in forgiveness. Was it possible that she could know his spotted soul and still look at him with love in her face?

He allowed himself the luxury of believing. The last illusion he would knowingly harbor. He swore it to himself.

"Come," he said, rising, and pulled Anne to her feet. "What do we here on the hard floor?"

# 23 *A Place to Stand*

*Kings are most contrary creatures.* This thought came yesterday as I was walking through the gallery where hang the portraits of our king and his late brother.

Item: Kings surely have greater temptation to fall into vanity than ordinary men. So why, in the one circumstance when their vanity might be said to serve them, do they abandon it altogether?

Why should not a king request, nay demand, the painter to look on his subject with a forgiving eye? Better, garnish him like a good cook improves an over-ripe goose?

Our late King Edward was a handsome young man whose presence and vigor were obvious the moment he walked into the room. His portrait compels no memory of his former beauty, however, only of the days when I urged him to change his habits for the sake of his health, as the deterioration of a once splendid constitution was slowly made visible on his person. I failed in persuading him, and now I must pass daily the reminder of that failure.

Richard is a handsome man, too, in his way, but the face in the portrait shows every worry and care that has crossed his mind in the past two years.

He asked my opinion of it. When my opinion is asked, I do not withhold it, albeit I try to steer a reasonable course between truth and tact. I said that it did not represent his grace in the most sanguine of humors. He laughed his singular laugh, the short, sharp laugh that has less to do with amusement or merriment than with his happening upon a surprising truth.

"What you are trying to say, doctor," he said, "is that it looks like me." He gestured toward the painting as though it were a slightly disreputable kin. "And it does not please you."

So cornered, I answered honestly. "I wear my thoughts too plainly. I was considering that the best stage players are those who make their actions seem effortless; perhaps that is a skill no less useful for kings than *for mimes and players. It is an excellent likeness, sire, and you do appear worried."*

*"Well," he said, "if that's the case, don't add my worries to your own." With that rather obscure remark he left the room, touching my arm in passing, as though to remove any offense from his words.*

*A few weeks past, Richard appointed his sister Elizabeth's son, the young Earl of Lincoln, as his heir, since he has no legitimate son. This is generally conceded to be an intelligent choice. But who else is there? The heir apparent must be old enough not to resurrect the fears of child-kings, must be of the house of York, since to be otherwise would negate Richard's own claim, and must not have a better claim than Richard himself, as would Edward, son of the late Duke of Clarence.*

*Now has arisen a circumstance likely to render any appointment of an heir useless and unnecessary. On a recent night, I attended the king, who had complained of aches and stiffness in the joints upon his rising. He brought me this complaint as a father might drag an unruly son by the ear to be chastised. The man has little tolerance for any weakness in himself, however ordinary and human. In another humor, I might have said all manner of things to him—an overabundance of bile, to be corrected by bright and sanguine foods, or, closer to the truth, too many hours over his writing table, but finally I said what I believe to be more truthful yet: the king is victim to that disease for which there is no cure but death, the beginning, however slight, of the body's yielding to age.*

$\mathcal{A}$ge! Doctor, I'm thirty-two."

Hobbes raised his eyebrows and peered over his spectacles. "Your brother was only forty when he died."

"I'm not my brother. I am neither glutton nor drunkard, nor do I hunch my back over a stable of mistresses."

Hobbes had never heard Richard speak with such anger or crudity of his brother. "And you think your virtue buys you health and long life?"

Richard gave a short and mirthless laugh. "Ah, no. That is not what I meant to say."

"Well, sire, however unfair you think it, thirty is not too young to feel some of the less pleasant effects of age."

Richard laughed again, less bitterly. "So I'm an old man already. An odd kind of comfort you dispense, doctor."

Hobbes relented, uncertain why he had felt compelled to provocation. Perhaps just growing old himself, bearing an old man's infirmities and resenting the young. "Young man—which, indeed, you are—it may be that your moderation does buy you a measure of health. I would all my patients chose a path of such sanity. It would work wonders for my reputation. But your moderation is not complete. Spare yourself some of your late hours. Your body is not a horse that can be replaced for another when it is ridden to exhaustion."

"I thank you, doctor. Now I must beg your leave."

My best advice in one ear and out the other, Hobbes thought.

*I gave Richard such common precautions as seemed appropriate and noted to myself to speak with the queen before the day's end. Anne's cough has been with her for some weeks now, raising fears I am unable to dismiss.*

*A*nne broke off a piece of bread, dipped it in the bowl of stew and crumbled it on her plate. She looked lovely, Hobbes thought. Too thin, but with a higher color in her cheeks than he had seen in some time. Indeed, it was precisely that color which worried him.

He walked around to her side of the table and laid a hand on her shoulder. "Madam?" He spoke softly, not wanting to alarm her. "I would like a word with you when you have finished your meal."

She turned a startled face toward him, and one hand went to her throat. Not a good sign. He knew how often patients betrayed their fears, laying their hands on the part of their bodies that pained them, as if to protect and heal themselves.

In her antechamber, Hobbes thought with near certainty that he knew what ailed her. Besides the high color, there were the bright eyes that heralded the body's consumption by its own fires, a cruel and mocking disease that could briefly seem to add luster to its victims. He laid a hand against her forehead. "Lady, you are feverish. And the cough has come back."

"Sometimes."

Hobbes sat her down on the bench, himself next to her. "Here, child, cough for me."

She looked at him as if bemused.

He smiled. "Can you not do that on command? Come, a child could do as much."

She smiled back and shook her head, tolerant, maybe even grateful for his small attempt at levity, took a breath, and coughed. He bent his head and listened.

It was that moment that Richard entered the room, as though for once he intended to take his doctor's advice seriously. He apparently didn't catch at once the sadness in the room, for he said, with broad, if misdirected, humor, "Well, doctor, do you reproach my wife for too many years, also?"

*Upon examining the queen, I was forced with great reluctance to conclude that she was afflicted with lung fever, which, as I already knew, had killed her sister. Richard came into the room at that moment, and made a remark which, unintentionally and unknowingly, made light of Anne's illness.*

*The effects of players are like those of doctors, miraculous when they succeed. But no players I have seen could have conveyed what passed between the king and his queen then. Anne's face showed shock and sharp pain at his remark, as though he had wished her ill. Then she seemed to grasp that he meant no slight, and her countenance changed—dismay, sadness, and pity, whether for him or herself, all playing there.*

*Richard made none of the signs by which people usually show they have apprehended ill tidings. His posture didn't change, no sagging of the shoulders, nor an obvious dismay in his aspect, just an intense attending, as if he were watching a pageant of great mystery and could not afford to miss a single word or note of music. Yet his face held all knowledge of what was to come.*

*Anne stood and went to him, then, as though he were the one condemned. She took one of his hands in each of hers, and leaned her forehead against his shoulder. He freed one hand and put his arm around her, as if to shelter her from my eyes. It was then I had the sense to take myself out of the room.*

*All this must have taken only seconds, and I had been prepared to speak to Richard for Anne, to answer any questions he might have, but it was not knowledge they wanted, or answers. It was comfort, and I had none to give. As I passed them, they took no note of me, but stood there thus embraced, swaying slightly on their feet, each cradling and rocking the other.*

*It surely has occurred to Richard that, cruel truth though it is, if Anne is to die, for his sake it were best she do it quickly. He is young enough to*

*marry again and sire children, and the country will expect it of him, now*
*he has the choice.*

*Kings have many privileges which ordinary men do not, but choosing*
*which trials Fortune will send is not one of them.*

*London*
*January 1485.*

Anne and Francis and Richard sat in Anne's chamber. Servants cleared
away the meal while Anne and Francis played at chess. Never one for
games, Richard read.

The kingdom was divided over Edward's sons. Anne knew the
rumors: Herod, slayer of infants. She glanced at Richard's face, sober,
contained, marked by weariness and sorrow. And by a kind of acceptance. She knew he hadn't murdered his nephews, just as she knew
that, in some other way, he had caused their deaths. Was that what
dying did, let you believe one thing and its opposite at the same time?

She knew he was a good man, and that was enough.

Snow was falling, heavy and slow and mysterious. Beautiful. Her
illness was mysterious, too. There were nights like tonight when she
felt nearly well, was able to breathe easily.

"Check," Francis said. "You are dreaming, Annie."

"Yes, dear friend." She smiled at him, and Richard looked up from
his book. A look of pain. Francis rose, lightly kissed her forehead.
Richard rose, too, laid down the book and saw Francis to the door.
Then walked over to the window and stood with his back to Anne
while Joan helped her prepare for bed.

Anne lifted her hands over her head, like a child, as Joan eased her
out of her gown and into her nightdress. She would not sleep naked
now, saying she needed the warmth of a gown, which was true, but
more blankets could be piled on. It was her own body she wished
not to see. No mirrors in her chamber. She didn't deceive herself, but
what she did not see, she could think about less often.

She sat for Joan to brush her hair. That was still a pleasure, the
gentle pull from the nape of her neck, making her scalp tingle. Richard brushed it once in a while. More to please him than for her own
need, she let him; he was almost too gentle with her.

Joan put down the brush and lit the candle.

"Are there extras?" She wanted enough light to last through the night.

"Yes, lady. Will you sleep now?"

"Not yet. I would sit a while." She let Joan wrap her warmly in a fur robe, and sat watching the snow and the shadows cast by the candle.

When Joan had left the room, Richard turned from the window and stood uncertainly by her side. "Do you feel able to talk?"

"Yes. What is it? More trouble."

"No." He broke off and looked away. "There is something I would know?"

*Before I die.* She understood his hesitation. Whatever it was, because she was dying, he was ashamed for needing to know. And because she was dying and there would be no more time, he must ask.

He sat and looked down at his hands. "Swear to me you will tell the truth."

"A liar will lie with an oath, you know," she said.

"Ah, there you have me. Nevertheless. . . ."

She stopped him. "You will have the truth, Richard. In any case. Any question."

"You remember when Francis was hurt and stayed at Middleham while I went to Scotland?"

"Of course."

"When I came back, something had changed between you."

"Yes."

"Yes? You loved him?"

Trust a man to ask a question in so unanswerable a way. She looked up at him. "I have always loved Francis."

"But that time was different."

"Yes."

"What happened?"

"I was lonely and sad, because of how things were between us—between you and me, I mean. We kissed."

"And then?"

"Nothing. I cried." And Francis had mocked himself. *Kiss a girl and make her cry.*

"Why 'nothing?'"

"We loved you more. Both of us. Husband, you are a very great fool." She meant it tenderly. He had carried such a useless fear alone. As she had once done.

The love in his face made her uncomfortable. Why, when once she thought she couldn't live without it? Because, the answer came clearly, love asked to be received, and she was preparing to have no more need of all things earthly.

## London
## February 1485.

Richard came into the room late. The candle burned by her bedside as always, a light against demons, devils, and nighttime terrors. She slept, her breath shallow and rasping. *I'd give you some of mine, if I could, Annie.* Or of some others he could think of. Others who wasted enough wind. He stood a moment watching her, then pulled up a chair and sat down.

February. The bleakest month. The feasts of Christmas, Epiphany, and now Candlemas were past. It was as though, with the passing of festivities and the joyousness that lightened the Holy Days, even the candles burned a little lower, the hearths a little less warm. All that was fancy, he knew, although the month was grim and harsh enough. Cold sharp winds blowing in gusts, the roads becoming more muddy and rutted with each successive thawing and freezing. But this year he had no reason to be eager for spring. He believed completely Hobbes' warning that Anne would not see another flowering of spring into summer.

*Sire, this disease is contagious. It is not safe for you to share you wife's chamber.* Blunt, ironic old Hobbes for once groping for words.

So. He didn't lie with Anne. That was no sacrifice, her body too ruined to feel the stirrings of mortal love or to inspire his.

But he spent long evenings here, his chair by the bed, a stool to prop his feet. He lifted Anne's hand, holding it lightly in his, her bones like twigs wrapped in skin as fragile as old silk. *Think of that, all we are in the end, a body like a bag of sticks.*

Once she had had as radiant a beauty as any woman was granted. But she never saw it, measuring herself against some Venus or Helen that had never lived, save in men's imaginations. The vanity of women baffled him. What more could they want, than fair smooth skin and shining eyes?

He laid down her hand on his thigh and felt, not a movement, but a quickening under the skin, like a brook's current beneath a skim of ice. He leaned back and stretched out his legs. The memory of wanting her was often fierce, like the ghost pain in severed limbs he had heard men speak of.

When it was good, there was no dance better than that dance of flesh with spirit that men called love. They had been blessed with their portion of those bright dances. Other times, almost too sharp for memory to hold, there was a mystery he could not explain, that in their coupling they were not alone, but brought others, angels or demons, into their bed, not to dance, but to wrestle, to battle with until they yielded up their names.

*When I came back from Scotland that time, you waited in the court-yard, snow in your hair. You ran to meet me, joyfully, as though you had waited forever just for that moment. Your hands, warm and hungry, wiped the snow from my face, my cheeks. Your lips were even hungrier when you kissed my nearly frozen face, drew down my head, kissed my eyes and then, boldly, as though there were no one in the courtyard but the two of us, licked the ice from my lashes. I could have died then and there.*

*From wanting you. From fear that my men might laugh, however quiet-ly, at me, or, worse, make something lewd of your love. Most of all because you called up more tenderness than I knew what to do with, so much as ill-becomes a man.*

*I was so young. That is the only plea I have, Annie; I didn't know what to do with so much love. It might ask something of me I didn't know how to give. Remember. . . .*

*How I took your hands as you would have slid them under my cloak, and you tried to free them, but I held you fast, like stilling the light of a small bird. You looked up at me, wondering perhaps, if you had been unseemly, if I was angry. The fear that was mine, before, now there in your eyes.*

*How seeing your fear gave rise to sharper wanting, and I was startled by it, made almost ruthless. I would have you then, no matter, and felt safe again, the too-great tenderness replaced by something fiercer and more familiar. I said goodnight to my soldiers, turned Orion over to the stable boy without so much as a slap on the rump.*

*And truly, that night was sweet. We played that fierce and almost ruthless game well. I took the knife from my belt and cut your ribbons. But carefully, not to rip your gown, always too much caution for true ruthless-ness. Or true ravishing. You bent to my will and we danced that particu-lar dance to the music of groans and sighs, carried on rivers of sweat with lip and chin-bruising kisses.*

*Still, with all that sweet pleasure, I fell asleep with sadness creeping in like the bitter aftertaste of spoiling wine. Something was lost, that night and for a time to come. Perhaps you feared me, after all. Perhaps it was that you had tried to make me a gift, and I was graceless enough to insist on always being the giver.*

And then another night, a night so wounding that he could, after all this time, hardly quiet his mind to think of it. But he had delayed the reckoning long enough. Now he would take that memory out of the shadows, stake it spread-eagled before him, strip, and search it.

He had come into the chamber they shared at Nottingham, sat, pulled off his boots and threw them on the floor, growling at the page who would have helped him undress. He had talked to Mark, asked all the terrible, useless questions. *How? How long? Who was there? Why?* As though by finding the right question he could somehow bring forth a different answer to the only one that mattered. *Did you say my son is dead?*

Mark, nodding in his chair, answering patiently, kindly, over and over, even though he was so tired his eyelids were twitching. Francis finally saying, *Come, there is no more here to find out.* Offering to sit up the night sharing a cup and the long cold hours until morning.

And himself, a madman that night. *No, my friend, that is kind of you, but I must to my wife.*

Francis' nod of understanding, of compassion. Of admiration, perhaps. None of which were deserved, for in that instant when his boots hit the floor, any thought of ordinary comforting left his mind, and something much grander took its place. For he had seen, finally, after all that time questioning poor Mark, what surely he should have seen sooner—that which would make the evening not only bearable, but right. Better than before. Even perfect.

*He and Anne will conceive another son this night. In this castle where they heard the news of Ned's death, they will, from their great sorrow, bring forth new life. And this child, as yet unformed, will be not only as beautiful in person and spirit as Ned, but hale and hearty, too, full of health and long life. The kingdom will have an heir, and perhaps more children to come.*

*For here is the point: with this great loss, the curse of their long childlessness has come to an end. They have paid the price and bought their redemption—if he has the courage to seize this instant, this crucial and magical instant when their fates can be turned around.*

He was crazed, for certain, for those were the thoughts that filled his head. Also a need for secrecy, but not from doubting himself. Just the opposite. It was the secrecy required by magic, a vaulting belief that he and he alone understood what action was needed that night. If that was not lunacy, what was?

*He slides naked between the sheets, where Anne lies, surely still awake, for she is flat on her back, arms at her side, not curled around herself like a kitten. Half dazed with the drugged wine her ladies have given her, she responds thickly, as from a fog, not protesting, but baffled, as he parts her knees and enters her.*

*She finally understands what must have seemed a monstrous dream, and pushes at his chest, turning her head from side to side, weeping. No, Richard. No.*

*Of course she doesn't understand why he must do this, is doing it with passion, but a brutal, madness-glazed passion, no tenderness in it. He takes those slender wrists from his chest, holds one in each of his own soldier-strong fists, pinned about her head. Finally she says in a hoarse whisper, more disbelief than horror, though there is plenty of that, too, in her voice, Richard! Stop! What are you doing?*

*He can hardly keep from laughing, knowing what he knows, what he is bringing to her—to them—anticipating the joy that will follow when she understands. He says without irony, Why, I am loving you, Anne.*

*Abruptly she stops resisting and says clearly, no wine or drug fog about it: You are mad.*

*He can feel the sobs shaking her wherever he touches her, thighs, belly, hands. Sanity comes crashing back, and with it, shame and grief like has never felt. He finally and absolutely understands that he has lost his son and any children that, in another future, they might have had, and knows the excruciating folly of believing he had the power to mitigate such a fate.*

*Falling from her, he moves away, leaving a measure of empty bed between them. There are not words in the world for explaining to her how he thought he was enchanted, when he was, in fact, possessed. He puts one arm over his eyes, shudders, Oh God, Anne, and reaches with his other hand for her. But she has pulled from him as far as she can and still stay on the bed, has drawn herself up into a knot, blankets tight around her face to muffle the sounds of her sobbing.*

*He regards himself with contempt, the position of his body on the bed the emblem of his life: one hand extended toward Anne, but not touching her, his body turned away. Could he never put himself wholly in one direction?*

*He cannot even weep then, can only feel the loss like a cold void in his own body, where he should have heart and brain.*

That was a night of demons, certainly. But they wrestled angels, too. One night in particular.

The least likely night he could imagine for a blessing to appear in any form. Working late, mostly to avoid the failure of not being able to sleep. Wanting never to dream or love again, both of which Anne drew him into. The tears he had so long denied, he released. He wept the whole time he loved her and afterward, while they held each other falling asleep. He wept not only for Ned, but for his nephews. For the long-ago girl he saw ravaged, the man burned alive. For the child he had been, who had lost a part of his soul that day and didn't even know it. He had slept much later than he would have believed possible, waking in full daylight, astonished to remember what it was to wake feeling rested and good.

Like the world was good. Like he had had enough of everything, both sleep and pleasure, but not so sated that he would not, if he could, lie there just a little longer, warm and content, letting the sun take the chill out of the morning. And why not? The cares of the world would wait for his rising. Even the king's cares could some-times wait.

Feeling also peace and acceptance like a benediction, sorrow and joy so mingled that he saw a celebration in the brief life of his son.

Poised on the knife's edge of joy and sorrow, tears starting in his eyes, he laughed. Out loud, but not loudly. Anne woke and smiled. "Oh, Richard, it is so good to hear you laugh again." Then hid her mouth with her hand as she coughed, a small tight cough that, when it was over, left her breathless but still smiling.

Richard?"

"Go back to sleep. I didn't mean to wake you."

"I'm glad you did. I don't want to sleep, now you are here."

"Shall I read to you?" Always the doubts. Other men's words the meeting place when his did not come easily.

"No. Just stay a while."

"Shall I tell you tales of court?"

"Richard—" she paused. "Do not feign a merry heart. You have no skill at it."

"Very well. But be warned. If you do not wish feigned merriment, you may suffer real tears."

"Let them fall. You have suffered God's plenty of mine. But listen. I must tell you something."

"I am here."

"I'm so afraid for you. Because I gave you no heirs."

"Hush. I know. Do not trouble yourself. That is resolved."

"Lincoln, you mean. But no longer. Now you must marry again."

"Yes. I will."

"Who?"

" I don't know." Without releasing her hand, he drew back in his chair. "You will admit I have at least a little time to think on it, that the decision need not be made tonight?"

"Don't be angry."

"I'm not, sweet, I'm not."

"I know the kingdom goes ill. And you blame yourself."

"Hush, now."

"It is true. Let me go on. And you have feared you caused me grief."

"I have known so."

"But you were always enough. I would have you know that. You have brought me more joy than sorrow."

"Anne—"

"Wait. If I had given you more sons, you would face less danger now. There is nothing I can do to change that. Except pray for you. And bless your marriage. I would have you love your wife, whoever she may be. Truly."

"If I can, I will."

"But, forgive me, Richard, I cannot help wishing—" a faint smile, a hint of her old mischief.

"What?"

"That you would love her less than you have loved me. A little less."

"Very well. A little less, I swear it." It was the easiest favor she had ever begged of him.

And this too, could be borne, he thought. Some day he will be old and the passions in his blood long since run cold. He will have married again and made another son, and his wife and he will be at ease with whatever affection or indifference has grown up between them. He would sit by the fire and warm his bones, content, and it would not even hurt when he closed his eyes and remembered her.

*But my God,* he thought, *who will ever touch my face again?*

# 24 *My Brother's Daughter*

*London*
*March 16, 1485.*

Richard had watched the astounding eclipse, had seen time as it might appear to God, passing from morning to darkness, and darkness to light in only heartbeats. He had watched the crowds out in the street stand fascinated and silent, some gawking directly at the hidden sun, although the astronomers had warned them not to. Now, through the window, the roofline of London stood dark against the evening sky, lamps shining from windows not yet shuttered while the city breathed the soft sweet air of spring.

He was with Anne when she died, not long before the sun vanished. He had never before held any of his loved ones dying, had not comforted them as they left the world. Not John Parr. Nor Jeremy, Jack, or Edward. Not even his own son. Since he had not felt their weight, he was burdened forever with carrying their ghosts.

Perhaps he would not carry Anne's. He prayed not. It was as hard a death as he had seen, and he had seen many hard deaths. Her eyes like a frightened animal's.

*What is it?* he had asked Hobbes.

*She is drowning.*

*Drowning?*

*Her lungs are filling with the fluids of her body. It is like drowning.*

*That is terrible. Can you not ease her?*

*No, sire, but it will pass quickly now.*

The humblest he had ever seen old Hobbes. And the saddest.

He leaned back against the sheepskin padding on his chair, kicked a smaller chair closer and propped his feet there, rested his head against the wall, and closed his eyes. After a while he heard the door open, then creak shut, and footsteps in the chamber. Someone had decided he had been alone long enough.

Francis was standing by the hearth, his eyes not quite fixing as they became accustomed to the dim light. "There's chill in here."

"Is there? I hadn't noticed."

"No. I suppose not. Still, I think I'll tend the fire." Francis stooped and stirred the dying embers into flame, took a stick and began to light the wall torches.

Quills, paper, and a penknife were laid out on the table by Richard's side. As was a little wooden horse of Ned's, brought back from Middleham. Who carved it? Giles' large rough hands? Perhaps. Possibly Mark. Richard could imagine Mark and Ned sitting out by the stables with the warm dusty smell of grain and the coo of pigeons in the rafters. Or in Ned's chamber when he was too ill to go outside, the horse carved to bring a little of the world to him, in imagination if not in fact.

"Tell me something, Francis."

"My lord?" Francis' voice was cautious.

"Please Francis. Don't 'my-lord' me. I'm not speaking as your sovereign." Neither was he mad, to be humored with a too-great deference. "I ask you, what do you know of grief?"

"I'm afraid I don't follow you."

"I used to think it would cut sharp, like a sword. But it's more like a great weariness, the worst tedium on earth." Dull and heavy, as if nothing would have purpose or savor again. Richard picked up the little knife. "No one ever told me that."

The knife lay in his hand, small and silver, engraved with his initials. *RG, Richard Gloucester.* Also brought from Middleham, where Anne had given it to him.

Small as it was, the knife was sharp enough to make a wound that would cure him of the sorest pain—and worst tedium—he felt. He would not do that, as he very well knew, but he ran his thumb along the blade, testing its edge. Oh, very sharp. He felt the streak of pain where the flesh opened and stared as the blood welled from the cut and dropped onto the papers on his desk.

Francis turned, letting fall with a thud the log he had been about to add to the fire. "My God, what have you done?"

"How red it is."

"Of course it's red! It's your blood."

"Lend me your handkerchief, Francis. And stop gaping. This will hardly kill me. Thank you." Richard wrapped the cloth around the wound. He would not have been shocked to see his blood gray, sorrow starting in his heart and coursing through his body. How could so much grief leave no traces?

"Richard, I worry for you."

"Don't. It was only an accident. But sorrow brings strange thoughts."

Richard. It is as you expected." Francis leaned forward, his elbows on the table. Catesby and John Kendall were silent. Sober faces all around. "Tudor has a fleet, men, and money. He surely intends to strike by summer's end. Perhaps you would rather I call the spy in and let him give you his report himself?"

"Not yet. But make certain he stays close by. I may want to speak with him later. Continue."

"Very well. First, there appears to be little value in your pursuing negotiations with France. Since Louis' death, his grandson's councilors have been happy to let the peace die with him. If France had a man instead of a child on the throne. . . ." Francis let his words hang in the air, then went on. "Well, no doubt, it would depend on the man. With some, it might be worth your trying to persuade them to refuse aid to Tudor. But this infant is under the sway of his advisors, who see in the situation an opportunity to redress old grievances."

"The same dance, different music."

Francis eyebrows raised. "I beg your pardon?"

"I was thinking of when Edward was struggling to hold his crown, and Louis supported Warwick."

Francis tidied the stack of papers he held. "Oh. Yes. I suppose it is much the same. Anyway, France has given Tudor both ships and men. A goodly number of ships—fifteen at the spy's count. Not much can be said for the men, however. They are from the gaols and prisons, men whose lives are not of much account, to themselves or anyone else."

"What of that?" Richard asked. "They are bodies, fighting arms. We had better look to our numbers."

"Yes."

"Well, tell me the worst of it, Francis."

"The worst?"

"What English? What of our countrymen are with him?"

"We think no more than five hundred altogether. The remains of Buckingham's movement. Some few men who fought for Lancaster during your brother's reign."

"Ten years ago."

Francis shrugged. "Old bitterness dies hard."

"Perhaps it never dies, only sleeps. Very well. What else?"

"Richard, if I might speak?"

"Of course, Catesby."

"There is something closer to home which could cost you the loyalty of more men, but which you can prevent."

"Go on."

"Find a husband for the Princess Elizabeth. Men say that Tudor seeks to marry her."

"Of course he seeks to marry her! He seeks to conquer England. Marry the queen, or the princess royal. That is what conquerors have always done. But he will have to kill me first. The Earl of Lincoln, as well."

"Henry's intentions toward Bess are not the main fear as I understand it. There are people who say you would marry Bess yourself."

"Catesby, she's my niece."

"Precisely. Edward's daughter. The point of such a union would be to restore Edward's blood to the throne, and the purpose would be the same as for Tudor. Rumor has it that, since her marriage to Tudor would cause you ill, and you could easily thwart that by marrying her to another, the reason you do not must mean that you want her for yourself."

"God help me. Do the people who say such things ever listen to their own words? How would marrying Bess help my cause, even if she weren't my niece? I declared her brothers bastards. Since she was born of the same union as her brothers, that makes her a bastard, also. At least by my understanding of procreation. Am I missing something? If so, please enlighten me."

"Richard, Richard. You want reason, but when was public opinion ever guided by reason? This particular serpent is easy to slay, however. Find the girl a husband. Presently."

"What kind of husband could be found for her before the crown is secure? A makeshift match to stop idle tongues? No. I won't do that. I will issue a statement if you think that will help."

"A statement? Well, better than nothing, I suppose. Perhaps a statement will suffice. Particularly if you were to add more words, words about her brothers. The royal bastards."

"I have nothing more to say about Edward's sons."

"Nothing *more* to say? Richard, you have said naught, ever. All London is saying they have have disappeared from this earth, and you say naught."

"Old news, Will. They have been saying that for months now."

"Then I mislike being the one to tell you this, but if you don't know, it is time you did. What they are saying is that you killed them. And they do not like it. Executions—even without a trial—are one thing, but the murder of children is quite another."

"I did not murder them. I will say that now, *once*, here. And I will say it to any man who has the courage to ask me to my face, and there's an end to it."

"Then bring them out, Richard. Show them and stifle the rumors. End this evil speculation." Catesby waited for a response. "You don't answer. Then perhaps the rumor is true."

Catesby's eyes swept the room. "Am I the only man here who knows not where they are? Do you know, Lovell? Ah, you turn your eyes aside. What about you, Kendall? Have you seen them?"

"No, Will. I do not know where they are, nor do I need to see them to trust Richard that he has done nothing dishonorable."

"Oh, very good. You're a good man, John." Catesby clapped his hands together. "Be careful. The good die young, it is said."

"Catesby, that's enough!"

"Forgive me, Richard. I have never been accused of trying to act as the royal conscience, but sometimes I must be a spur to your sense. Do you think I care where the bastards are? Kings must look to their own. They were dead when you took the crown; I told you that in the beginning.

"If you didn't kill them, someone else would have. But if they are dead, for God's sake display them properly. Mourn and beat your breast. Then bury them."

"I suffer your clever tongue for the knowledge of the law, Will, but you abuse my patience."

"No, Richard. You retain me for my tongue to tell you the truth. And I will give it to you, even when it is not pretty to hear."

*W*hen the Duchess Cecily was told that Richard had arrived, she went out to the garden to await him in the April morning rather than remain inside and have the servants see how very awkward she feared she would be. She waited on the flagged path as her son approached,

Benediction

pale and somber in his mourning black, and she felt stifled, as if the garden were too close a place in which to breathe, although in fact the air was fresh and cool and fragrant. Where a month ago only crocus and snowdrops stood bright in the grass amid splotches of melting snow, there were now speedwell, celandine, and comfrey, and the orchard behind the garden wall was a cloud of pink and white bloom.

Richard lifted her hand lightly to his lips. "Mother." She was thankful for the gesture; it allowed her not to have to decide whether or not to embrace him.

"Tudor has come, then." Cecily found her voice.

"No," Richard said. "He's still in Normandy if reports are to be believed. Can a man not pay a visit to his mother without a disaster to report?" He took her elbow, easing her along the path, as she seemed to have taken root where she stood. "But I'll be leaving London within the month. I want to be in Nottingham well before he lands."

"Why Nottingham?" Why the castle he had called his Castle of Care after learning there of Ned's death? Penance? A reminder of his sins? Child-killer though he might be, she knew him to feel his own son's death as sorely as any man.

"Well, the ends of the kingdom are well fortified. Francis has the navy at the southern coast, and Northumberland is strong in the north. Tudor will almost certainly land in Wales, then try to penetrate the midlands."

Cecily knew what Richard was not saying. The north was his own country. Only a fool would try to invade there. London and the southern counties had given him their grudging admiration after his rapid crushing of the rebellion of '83. But the midlands remained unsettled in their loyalty. The less of central England Tudor marched through, the fewer men disaffected with the present reign would have a chance to join him.

Odd, she thought, how London could denounce him for killing Edward's sons and still cast their lot with him. Was there no end to the sins men could reason away?

She had stopped asking herself if Richard could have killed his nephews. Of course he could have, just as George could plot to destroy Edward, just as Edward could execute George. The only question was: *had* he?

"And how will you pay for an army," Cecily asked, disguising her grief with mock chiding, "now that you have done away with benevolences? I know the state in which Edward left the royal treasury."

"Then you must also know," Richard said, "that kings may do as they will. We have new names for old practices. I must still entreat the people for money, but now we call it loans. If I defeat Tudor and his army is rich enough, I may actually have spoken the truth." His voice was quietly mocking.

They had come to the end of the garden. On the corner pillar of the wall a little stone gargoyle sat, pointed ears like a bat, web-fingered hand crossed over its mouth, guarding its words. Richard stooped and pinched a sprig from one of the plants blossoming at his feet. "Speedwell," he said, spinning it between his fingers. "For god-speed and prospering, Anne used to say. It blooms earlier here than in the north. A good omen for a soldier, don't you think?" He smiled, which only made the strain in his face more apparent.

Cecily felt a coldness in her heart like she had not know since that long-ago day when she learned that her husband, a son, and a brother had all died in the snow by Sandal Castle in Wakefield. God had betrayed her. Not because of what she had loved that He had taken from her, but because after all these years of praying, of striving to detach herself from the love of earthly things, this last, troubled son, whatever he had or had not done, was dearer to her than any promise of immortality.

"Please be careful," she said uselessly. The little gargoyle, sad-eyed, silently rebuked her. "I don't think I could bear to lose you, too."

Richard let the tiny cluster of white flowers fall from his hand. "Why, Mother," he said, very quiet. "Tears already, and I have not even gone from here? Tudor has only a ragtag army, cutpurses and gaolbirds, one man to every three of mine. What's to fear?"

"Oh, my dear." Cecily reached out to touch his cheek and was startled to find her wrist held hard in Richard's grip, to see him flinch as though she had been about to strike him.

*R*ichard walked beside the woman. She smiled and he felt a twinge of longing, thin and sharp, painful in its sweetness and as quick as a bee sting. His first thought was that it was good, because it meant he could still feel. Then he remembered who the woman was. *Oh, no. Not you. Not you, my brother's daughter.*

Bess stopped and put back a strand of hair that the wind had blown across her mouth. "No one has seen my brothers for months now. The whole city is remarking on it."

"I know."

"Some people think you put them to death."

"I know that, also."

"Did you kill them?"

How odd it was to hear someone ask that so directly. "No." And what relief to refute it equally directly.

Bess stopped to look at him, the question plain in her eyes.

"I know what you are wondering, Bess, but I am not sparring words with you. I didn't kill them; neither did I order their deaths."

"But you know they are dead."

"No." A lie. In his heart he knew. It could hardly be otherwise. "That is, I have no proof, but they almost certainly were killed."

"Who? Who murdered them?"

"It matters not. The man is dead now, too."

"Then I know. It was the Duke of Buckingham. People say he meant to be king. Why do you not make this knowledge public?"

"Think about it, Bess. Do I know how it was done? No. Do I know where their bodies lie? No. Can I produce the man who did it or at least a confession? No. I don't know how you would greet such a tale, but I would laugh to hear it."

"But people who say you killed them would be happy to think otherwise if only you would give them something else, *anything* else, to believe. Why do you not speak?"

"Because Bess, besides the fact that I have no credible tale to tell, your brothers were in my care. I should have been the one to keep them safe. I failed. But you seem to believe me."

"Yes."

"Why? Why are you so certain of my innocence?"

"I don't know. I would say, because I can judge a man's nature fairly. But probably you think I am too young for wisdom in such matters."

"Oh no, Bess. Being the beneficiary of your judgment, how could I disparage it?"

"Then I will tell you something else that may surprise you. My mother also says you are innocent."

"What?" Bess was either daft or she was an outright liar—neither of which he believed.

"Actually," Bess said, looking at him closely as if to determine whether she could safely go on, "what Mother said was that it was a sorry pass this country had come to when, of all the fools she must deal with, the man she trusted most was her worst enemy."

Startled, Richard put back his head and laughed. "Now you put it like that, I must believe it."

*F*rancis had seen them walking about the gardens, along the wharf, their heads bowed in thought. Seen them stop and look out over the Thames, seen Richard's hand on his niece's shoulder, even—rare occasion these days—seen him laugh. It might be that Bess fed a hunger in Richard, but Francis doubted it was the kind Catesby spoke of. He had seen that often enough to know the look of it. He imagined briefly that it was his duty to remind his friend of what people were saying, but Richard had already heard the warning, so if he continued to keep in Bess's company, it was because he chose to, not because he didn't know. *Then leave it. Leave it.*

So it was not Francis who approached Richard one of the last nights before his departure for Nottingham. Late one evening while he worked, alone, she surprised him by knocking at his chamber. She stood outside the door, tall and fair, with that high color which made her seem like a country girl, awkward and uncertain, and he was reminded that her height made her seem more mature than she was. Twenty was so young, although he hadn't thought so when he was that age, and she wouldn't think it now.

"Sire, I would speak with you."

"The door is open, Bess. Come in." He gestured to a chair along the wall. "Sit down."

She stepped a few feet into the room and remained standing. He guessed what she had come about. Damn the gossip, he thought wearily, and braced himself.

"You are sending me away." She avoided looking at him.

"Only to Sheriff Hutton, Bess. I'll send one of your sisters with you if you like."

"Because of what people are saying about you." Bess coughed primly. "About us. You do know what they are saying?"

"That I would marry you? Yes, I know."

"Have you thought of it?" Her voice not quite accusing, but with a sharpness, challenging.

Would he marry her? No. Even if the idea were not abhorrent to her, which he could not imagine, he was neither such a fool nor such an exploiter of children. But that was not her question. Had he thought of it? *No, child, it never crossed my mind.* God's teeth, that was

423

a lie. The truth was that when he looks at her, he longs to shake his
sorrows on her fair bones. Sometimes. For a moment. Only a moment,
knowing how it would end, in bitterness and remorse, their souls
damned to Hell. Knowing that these days he could no more trust the
sense of his desires than he could embrace a dream.

But knowing that he must marry, and soon, who would he wed
if one sanction were levied and another removed? *You, Sir King, have
a fortnight to choose a bride, and all the stain of blood is removed.* What
then? Would it be Bess? In a heartbeat. He did not have to search his
soul for the answer to that question, and the tongues that wagged
over his incestuous passions would be struck dumb to know so plain
a motive as his: the thought of sharing his life and bed with a stranger
sickened him. Bess was her father reborn. She had his sunny smile and
his calm belief that the world would treat her kindly, that life was a
banquet spread for her pleasure, although she appeared to have not
nearly so insatiable an appetite for it. She was, in a word, familiar. But
none of these things could be said; neither to her nor to anyone else.

"No, Bess. I wouldn't marry you." He could say no more. She would
either believe him or she would not.

She met his eyes at last. "Why not?"

He couldn't believe he had heard her correctly and hoped the
shock didn't show as strongly as he felt it. Her face was as naked as a
child and he had no wish to hurt her.

"Child," he said, refusing her as gently as he could, "you are my
brother's daughter. And I am half again your age."

"No. You are more than that. You are twelve years older, sire, not
ten. As if that had anything to do with it. You could be old enough to
be my grandfather, and if it suited the purposes of peace and policy, I
would be wed to you faster than the banns could be posted. That is
true, is it not?"

Richard winced. There was no anger, no sting in her tone, just
that solemn young face, child enough to ask for truth and believe she
would hear it. But he was stung, nonetheless. Of course, he would
marry her himself or to the man in the moon if it would stop the inva-
sions and secure his kingdom. Fortunately for her, he had no discourse
with any being with so great a power.

"Bess, come here and sit down." He got up, pulled the other chair
closer to his own and guided her to it. "This is not a thing to be
talked about standing." She sat and seemed to relax a little. "Should I

understand from your question," he asked, "that the thought of marrying me does not displease you?"

She nodded, looking down at her hands clasped in her lap. A surfeit of modesty, now that she has been so bold? Well, if truth she wants, truth she must tell. "Why?" His voice sounded harsh and hoarse. So much for gentleness.

"Oh, uncle." Bess looked up with tears in her eyes, and wiped them away awkwardly, like a kitten cleaning its face. Then laughed. "*Oh, uncle,*" she repeated, mocking herself. "That is not what a maid would commonly say to the man she would marry, is it?"

"No, Bess, it is not."

She shook her head, slowly in command of herself again. "Sire, I have known you since I was little. You were always kind to me. I don't want to go to a foreign country and marry some arrogant prince I have never seen who will look down on me because I have not the fine manners of the ladies of his court, and because I can't love his poor country, whatever it may be. Lady Anne told me—" she broke off, and looked away. "I'm sorry."

Richard shook his head. "No matter. Go on."

"I don't want that." She closed her eyes. "My father is dead, my brothers are lost. What will become of us now?" Her eyes opened and she looked squarely at him. "You are my liege lord and I will take whatever husband you deem fit. But you are the last man in my entire family still alive. Could we not be kinder to each other than strangers?" Bess pressed the last point for her case. "You need an heir. I am strong and never sick. Once there was a son, you would never need seek my bed again."

Heaven help him, now what? But she had more. She said earnestly, "I would mean to be your wife in every way, but I would not have you believe I say this out of any improper longing for you." Even with her high color, a violent blush spread to her hairline.

"God forbid," Richard said solemnly, then laughed at the two of them, so serious and so foolish. "Well, it's not so horrible an idea as all that." He took her hand between his own. "No doubt we could be kind to each other. But that is not the way of the world or seemly in the eyes of God. And you are a fair young woman, one no man should find reason to look down upon." Although, princes being what they were, still might do so. *Don't try to appease her.* "Bess, I would I had the power to make things other than they are. While I am king, I will not marry you to any man you despise. That is all I can promise."

# 25 *Let It Fall*

*Nottingham Castle*
*August 1485.*

The August sun hung motionless in a white, hot sky. The road to Nottingham Castle wound through wrinkled fields, ridges of cut grain alternating with stubbed hollows where the reapers walked, swinging their scythes. In the swirling heat-haze, magpies sat drowsily on the harvest. In planting time, there would be a bird-chaser with a bow and arrow to drive them away, but now a reaper half-heartedly shouted and waved his arms at them. A horseman galloped for the cooler forest beyond, the horse's chestnut tail lifting as the hooves raised clouds of dust.

By late afternoon, the castle's stone still held the day's heat, but a breeze had come up. Richard stood in the window and watched a shepherd boy on the road below. The same breeze rippled the hem of the boy's brown cloak and brought up warm summer smells of hay and clover from the fields. The boy and eight or ten ewes and their lambs passed the first large stone outcropping, then crossed into the long shadow of the side of the hill.

Richard was dressed, as always these days, at once austerely and richly. Velvet doublet of a deep wine-red. Black hose and black velvet cap with a simple unjeweled silver medallion pinning the brim, and on his feet, black leather riding boots so worn that the folds at the cuffs were rough and suede-like. Those boots, so dust-free and immaculate as to seem contemptuous of travel, of weariness, and the summer's heat. Of grief.

He knew his own appearance and designed it with so great a pride as to be sinful.

He had come back to this castle he once had loved, but which now seared with the pain of his memories, and had implemented the old northern system of sending news by lighting beacons from hill to hill. For two months he had waited, watching the hills for fire.

Now John Kendall stood beside the door he had just pulled shut behind him, keeping his hand on the latch. He was dressed in black, a satin doublet with silver embroidery at the collar. "What shall I tell my lord Stanley?" Kendall asked.

Richard imagined Sir Thomas waiting outside the door. "I don't want to see him now. Tell him I'll talk with him in the morning."

Kendall gave the door an uncertain glance, as though Stanley might have his ear to the keyhole, then let go of the latch and brushed the palms of his hands together as if ridding them of some unpleasant dust, and crossed over to the window. He stood close enough to speak softly. "He plans to take his men and return home tomorrow."

"Let him."

Kendall stood still for a moment, perhaps trying to decide whether the answer came from simple weariness or something harder to deal with. "I would have you understand what he is truly about, lest he catch you by surprise. Richard, listen to me. That man will turn traitor."

"If he is determined to turn traitor, do you think I can stop him?" Could he have stopped Hastings? Or Buckingham? "What would you have me do? Shall I summon spirits to fetch his loyalty? Lure him to my side with promises of eternal life, or my eternal gratitude?" Richard sighed. "Very well, John. Send him in."

*I* would not trouble Your Grace," Stanley began.

*There is your first lie,* Richard thought, but looked up as a sign for Stanley to continue. It would have been easier to ignore the man, because he already knew what Stanley would say and how easily and unimaginatively he would say it.

"Sire, I have served you well these last two years." Stanley showed no irony or embarrassment as he spoke, "and will continue to do so, of course, but I begin to be uneasy. The summer is nearly gone, and I have not yet been home to my own estates."

"No," Richard said. "None of us have had the ease to do so."

Stanley nodded. "I know that, Richard. You are ever watchful for the good of the realm. May I point out, however, that my own lands are not so well-staffed as yours, and at the same time lie nearer to Nottingham, so that I could be at hand easily, when need be."

No lies there. The request was to the point, and the conditions made it seem reasonable. Indeed, Stanley's great talent was to seem reasonable; he had survived more changes of allegiance than Richard would have thought possible, and in each isolated situation the man's behavior was well-justified. It was only when the events were strung together that their true ugly colors clashed and revolted against reason.

"You will notice the fields," Stanley continued. "The grain stands as high as I've ever seen it. My tenants will have to bend their backs to get it all in. I suppose you have a trusted steward to act in your absence, but with myself and Lord Strange both here. . . ." He left the thought unfinished.

"Shall we drop the pretenses, Thomas?" Richard said. "Being able to come is not the same as being willing, and I doubt you would bestir yourself for me any more quickly than you would for the Prince of Egypt. Or for your tenants, for that matter."

"You offend me, Richard. I dislike having my intentions disputed."

"You have my leave to go, Thomas. God forbid I should have on my head the ruin of your estates." Stanley smiled. "But you will leave your son here in my custody. As a token of your noble intentions."

"Sire!"

"Lord Strange will be treated as a guest, of course. Since you are, as you say, my loyal subject, he has nothing to fear." Stanley opened his mouth to speak, but no words came out. "That is what I heard you say, is it not?"

After Stanley left, clearly dissatisfied but unable to protest further without damning himself, Richard stood and went over to the window again. The shepherd and his little flock had entered the meadow below, irregular specks amid the other specks that were the field workers.

What lay close to him was still clear. He did not need the reading spectacles of gray-bearded men, but the leaves on trees now had a soft-edged blur, as did the rocks below him. He narrowed his eyes, and for a moment the rocks resolved into a sharper outline. Why did narrowing the eyes have that effect? He would have to ask Hobbes.

Hobbes was right that in men's strongest years of life they were already leaving it, growing older with every heartbeat. Was what was true of men true also of kingdoms? he wondered. England during the years of Edward's reign so apparently thriving, years of prosperity, even glory. But all the time coming to chaos from within. Did his own reign have the seeds of death planted from the minute he took the crown? What he wanted to believe, of course, was that it was

Edward's rule, not the brief years of his own reign, that brought the crumbling.

$\mathcal{A}$ week after Stanley left, the beacon fires flared, and a messenger arrived at Nottingham: Tudor had landed at Milford Haven. The rebel army was small; Tudor had not picked up the numbers moving through Wales that he had hoped for. Nevertheless, the mayor had opened the city gates without resistance. Taking his army south, Richard estimated that his path would converge with Tudor's somewhere near Leicester. He began to consider where they might pitch battle.

He entered Leicester on the evening of August 20 to find Francis, John Howard, and Robert Brackenbury waiting for him. Thomas Stanley's men were approaching, John Howard said. Richard nodded. Good. So far Stanley had been true to his word. Of Henry Percy, Earl of Northumberland, there was nothing to be seen.

Northumberland had been responsible for mustering the York men, but something had gone awry. Richard had received from the lord mayor of York a puzzled and slightly injured query: after all the king had done for the city, did he not want the assistance of its citizenry now, in this, his time of greatest need?

The following morning, Richard led his forces out of Leicester to set up camp and prepare for battle in the rolling hill country south of Market Bosworth. Even without the Yorkshire contingent, Richard's army was of formidable size, but Tudor's army, camped along White Moors, appeared to be a good deal larger than earlier reports had indicated.

Some time after camp was struck that afternoon, John Howard came to Richard distressed, bearing with him a scrap of paper torn from a map, a jagged slit in the center.

"A lad had pinned it to the ground just outside my tent." Howard jabbed his finger at it.

Richard took the paper and smoothed it against his thigh, then looked at the fragments of roads and rivers.

"The other side," Howard said.

Richard turned it over. Heavy dark writing trailed away at the ends of words smaller than the beginnings, as though the writer had backed away as he wrote, sly and secret.

*Jocky of Norfolk, be not too bold*
*For Dickon your master has been bought and sold*

Invocation of names. Names had power. *Ask it in my name and it shall be granted to you.* "Who wrote this?"

John Howard shook his head. "We nabbed the lad, but he knows nothing. Someone gave him a coin to do it. A knave in a cloak. It could have been anyone."

Richard crumpled the paper and gave it back to Howard. "Take it. I don't want it near me." The older man's eyebrows raised. *Easy now,* Richard told himself. The message was not necessarily menacing; it could have been written by someone who wished him well, someone who wanted him to be aware of potential traitors in his midst.

No. People who wanted to help would put a name to their voice.

"I wouldn't have troubled you, sir," Howard said, gruff and awkward, "but I thought you should see it."

"You did well, John. But it's nothing. Not worth your thought. There are two sides to every battle and ill-wishers for both. Put it from your mind."

Richard excused himself, went into his tent and tried to distract himself from thoughts that wouldn't help by mapping out the formation for the morning. He had slept poorly at Leicester the night before, haunted by dreams of his dead son, his betrayed nephews, and of the spectral horseman that had so appalled him as a young man at Picquigny. The visitations seemed in themselves ill omens. With the menacing verse, he was finding his composure harder to maintain than he liked.

$\mathcal{N}$ow night had fallen, his men were settled, and Richard sat at his narrow camp table, the map he had drawn spread out before him, as he listened to the soft rhythmic brush of Roger's cloth on his armor. The boy was fiercely proud of his work. Richard had suggested a little earlier that Roger might want to rest, and the only response he had received was to see Roger frown and bend closer over the shield. He wished the boy would desist and sleep; he was aware of a slightly heightened effort to appear untroubled in the presence of another person.

The lantern hanging from the tent pole cast a shadow like that of a looming gargoyle, and Richard looked up to see Francis bend his tall frame to enter the tent.

Francis took the remaining chair. "Northumberland's here at last."

"You talked with him?"

"No. I spoke with his runner. He asks your pardon for Percy's late arrival."

"How late?"

"He's here now. Just rode in."

"And?"

"His company's around three thousand. Mostly infantry—archers and foot. Maybe three hundred horse. No more."

A cannon boomed in the distance. Richard turned in the direction of the roar, half expecting to see the tent walls shake. There was a second boom, a silence, then a volley of cannonfire. Poor Market Bosworth. He waited for the rumble to subside. "Three thousand. That is only Percy's own muster."

"I know."

"Any word of the men of York?"

"No. The runner said troops had been dispatched, but he didn't know when."

Richard saw his hand fingering the map start to tremble, and laid his palm flat on the table to still it. After a moment, he tossed the charcoal back into its pewter box and worked the tremor out of his hand by rolling up the map. "Roger?"

"Sire?"

"Put that up. It's good enough. I want you to find Northumberland. Tell him I want to see him here immediately."

*R*ichard heard the booming voice when Northumberland was still yards away from the tent. Francis offered him the chair and perched on the armor chest.

"Good to see you, Henry," Richard said. "I was beginning to doubt I would."

"It was a hot day, Richard. Every man who died on the march was one less to fight for you."

"How many died?"

"None."

"I commend you. You managed that duty well. I wish I could say the same for my charge to you."

"Sire?"

"You were to have summoned the men of York."

"I did, Richard. I can hardly help it if they are slow to move."

"On the contrary, Percy. Either you didn't send word in time, or you failed to communicate to them the urgency of the situation."

Henry Percy inflated his large chest. His expression changed from indifference to petulance. "You can't blame me for other men's faults."

"Henry," Richard said. "I am your king and your commander. I can blame you for whatever I see fit. But you're right in one thing. I never found blame to be of much use when things go wrong. I wonder if you happened to notice our positions?"

Percy nodded. "Good ground." Something changed in his face; it became less dull, even gained a semblance of respectful intelligence.

"Fair enough," Richard agreed, "as far as it goes." The entire royal force—his cavalry and Norfolk's foot—covered a long knoll that ran west, culminating in a broad flat-topped mound girded by a marsh on the south. The royal army had the high terrain, and the marsh was impassible. "Thomas Stanley's position, however, is ambiguous." Percy's face was blank. "I mean," Richard explained, "that Stanley's position can suit his loyalty, which is always less than certain. I want you to help him be sure both are with me."

"Yes."

"I have his son, Lord Strange, in my custody. It will go ill with him if his father equivocates." *Equivocates.* Another wrong word. He could see Percy's face cloud with distrust, always afraid someone was laughing at him for what he didn't understand. "I want you to help Stanley keep his course true and his son alive."

"Yes, sir."

After Percy left the tent, Richard stood and walked out into the night, not realizing for a moment that Francis was beside him. They walked in silence to the row of chain-linked cannon that divided Richard's infantry from Norfolk's archers. It was a beautiful clear night, the black moonless sky pierced with stars. The armies spread over the hills were like small walled cities: officers' tents in the centers, common soldiers sprawled on cloaks and blankets on the ground, horseparks barricaded by baggage carts and weapon wagons.

Francis stopped and leaned his elbows on a cart, probably about to say something. Richard wished he wouldn't.

"What will you do, after?" Francis asked.

"I suppose I must go courting. Assuming we win, of course." Richard's voice sounded hideously bright and false to his own ears.

"God, Richard." Francis turned and made an awkward gesture, like pushing something distasteful away. "I didn't mean that."

"I must make some order of the ruins. Where else should I start? I can't bring the dead back to life."

Francis was silent a long moment. Finally, "God is merciful," he said quietly.

Richard gave his sudden short laugh. "Think, Francis. God is *just*. Even God may find it difficult to be both just and merciful."

Francis lifted his head sharply and turned from the cart to face Richard. "That's right. Laugh. Refuse my attempt to comfort you. Refuse God, too. You're right, of course. I don't know how He manages to put justice and mercy together, either, fools that we all are. Comfort yourself with being right because I've done trying."

*R*ichard stared at Francis' retreating back. *I'm sorry.* The words formed silently in his mind. But why should he be sorry for what was only the truth? Why should he regret insisting upon this one last piece of integrity—acknowledging the gravity of his failings?

The campfires around him were dying, the flames melting down into red and black ash. The guns had quieted, and, for all its activity, his camp had an odd dream-like peace. He could hear the ring of a smith's anvil, men laughing and talking. A horse came over to him, extending its head across the cart and blowing its snuffling breath on his hand as he reached out to stroke its velvet nose. When the horse turned aside, Richard held his hands up to his face and stared at them: fingers, knuckles, bones, and skin, perfectly formed tools that would do whatever his mind commanded. His mind, however, he seemed unable to rule.

He knew the mind's pre-battle demons so well they were almost boon companions. Fear as sharp and sour as spoiled gruel, rising up in his throat. Then in the morning just before he marched, the killer fear that threatened to turn a man around and send him running, the Devil take honor, courage, and purpose.

There was power in fear. It could push men toward what they dreaded, instead of away, but it needed a lever to turn it. It was not arrogance to say that he knew how to do that, turn men's fears for their own use. And in serving his soldiers' courage he had always found his own.

What he felt tonight, however, was not fear, but something harder to name, an emptiness, an eerie hollowness like a blown-out eggshell.

Whatever it was, he had better understand it and do something with it before daybreak, or he would do them all a disservice. It must be well after midnight. He turned and picked his way back toward his tent.

Roger was walking toward him, breathless and distressed. "Sire!"

"What's amiss?"

"I wanted to pray before I slept, but when I asked Lord Howard which was the chaplain's tent, he said we had none."

"Did he? I suppose he knows."

"Why, sire?"

"An oversight." Richard went into his tent, Roger following. "Pray if it helps you. You don't need a chaplain."

"But who will bless our cause?"

"God knows if our cause is just."

"Yes, sire, but. . . ."

"And if it's not, to ask his blessing is a sacrilege. Rest now, morning will come soon enough." His response was entirely inadequate. Pretending alarm would have comforted Roger more.

Richard lay back and laid a forearm over his eyes against the last of the lantern light. In spite of his words to Roger and to his own great surprise, he found himself wanting to pray. Talking to Francis, he had believed he had lost the right to petition for anything. But now, in the midst of despair, a little hope crept in; even he would not make an imperfect creature, then condemn it for its imperfections. *Truth or longing? Perhaps, pushed to our limits, we will most readily believe what most comforts us. Perhaps what we call God is only this: the alchemical union of our longings and our suffering.* As he silently prayed where he lay, Richard feared he was praying into a vast emptiness, but hoped against all reason that Francis' merciful God might be there and listen.

*D*awn, and the sky was hanging fire. Richard's lines were arrayed on the hill, archers and gunners firing down onto Tudor's ranks below. "Well?" Richard was listening to Roger stammer through his report from Stanley.

"As I told you, sire. He said he would not dissuade you. He is best able to help where he is, and if you must vent your fears on his son, he is powerless to stop you."

"What else?" Something had unnerved the boy. Eyes that wouldn't meet his own, a distaste in the set of the mouth.

"Else? Why naught? Stanley would not be pressed to more of an answer."

"Roger. Must I make threats you know I won't keep? Tell me everything he said." About to pitch battle, and he had to coax the traitorous Stanley's words from his delicate squire. "God's blood, Roger, how can I read the man if you amend his words?"

Roger looked away, then shrugged. "It won't help, sire. It's nothing. He said, "Kill him if it pleases you.""

"There is more. *Tell* me."

"He said," Roger coughed. "He said *he* has other sons."

Richard blinked. Red pinwheels of light danced behind his eyelids. The petty cruelty of the man amazed him. Not an intelligent man, Stanley. If he had a knife he had to use it, even if he cut his own fingers.

"I'm sorry, sire. I told you it was nothing."

Richard felt himself go cold with the depth of his anger. "Send for Lord Strange."

"Yes, sire."

Roger returned from the captive's tent with Strange following between two guards. Strange looked as if he hadn't slept, and clearly he had wept during the night; shining pink tracks ran down his cheeks where tears had cleared the dust.

"My father said to kill me, didn't he? He doesn't care. I told you that."

Strange had said that yesterday, not with the bristling defiance Richard might have expected from a helpless man trying to give the illusion of power. Just a toneless statement of fact. *I won't do you any good.* Lord Strange. An apt name for an odd young man, one who had learned to wear indifference. Something, though, a quick widening of the eyes betrayed a flicker of hope. He wasn't ready to die.

"Sire," Strange was saying, "I know whatever I say may seem a pitiful attempt to prolong my life, but you do know he is equivocating? He hasn't decided to go to the other side, either, I should think. He may still come to your assistance."

"Henry Tudor is his stepson," Richard said quietly.

"Could be his mother, it's all the same to him."

"You say that of your own father?"

The quick indifference again. "I know him. I meant no particular disrespect. Killing me won't stop him from going to Tudor." He shrugged. "On the other hand, killing me wouldn't stop him from helping you, either, if he decides the battle is going your way. He'd not hold my death against you later, either."

Of course. It was what he had expected all along. Stanley would try to hold out until the battle was decided, then go with the victor. "Take him back to his tent," he said to the guards.

The sun was ascending rapidly now, the orange-red of sunrise fading to saffron and rose and blue sky. The ground still shone wet with dew, and the flowers that had closed for the night were beginning to open. As John Howard brought his men into formation for the first assault, Richard walked up and down the lines talking, smiling, saying whatever came to his mind, a word of cheer, a query of home. The men seemed to respond, giving abashed half smiles in return. Edward would have done that sort of thing effortlessly, would have had them laughing, as if it were a privilege to march away to die. The gunners hammered away. Smoke and the smell of sulphur. Nasty weapons, nearly as dangerous on the firing side as on the receiving. John Howard had told of seeing a man blow his face off, just loading the thing. One archer kept plucking at his bowstring and cursing; he had let it get wet during the night.

John Howard and his captains stepped forward to kneel and kiss the ground they defended. Twelve years ago, Richard remembered, Howard had insisted he never again wanted to command a battle. "God go with you, John." He smiled. The old man didn't mind being back in the front line. Cries and cheers ran along the lines slowly at first, then swelled into a great roar, like a fire catching hold of its tinder. The standards hung limp in the still, warm morning.

Richard called for White Surrey and mounted, pacing the crest of the hill. The enemy's formation caught his attention, a line of men broken at intervals by dense wedges of pikemen standing tight around Tudor's red dragon standards. From a distance, the unit looked like the jagged edge of a saw, a deadly formation if they could hold it. Beside him, Rob Percy said, "Oxford?"

"None other." Few men besides Oxford would attempt that maneuver, fewer still could succeed.

The armies met with a great clash of metal on metal. The first screams of the dying came, piercing in spite of the din. Surrey fidgeted and pawed, tossing his head. "Easy, old man. Soon enough." Richard patted Surrey's withers and kept the reins taut. Below, Oxford's wedges were proving surprisingly resilient. Howard's assault had not the strong first impact Richard had hoped for. The earl had the greater numbers, but the marsh and the hill kept him from using his men as effectively as he might have. Many of his troops were massed at the backs of their fellow soldiers, more or less waiting for someone in front of them to die and clear a space. Oxford's men, mostly mercenaries, were fierce fighters and held their ground, undiscouraged by the odds.

It was the first time Richard had watched his battle from a distance. He didn't like it. He noted with some surprise how clearly he could see the spread of blood, an occasional flash of red, quickly turning black; it was by that, more than anything, that he could judge Howard's progress. The assault was so densely fought that it appeared almost as a single creature, an unholy beast writhing, the line of battle like the edges of a gaping wound, bleeding more and more as it crawled toward death. Howard was pushing Tudor's men back, but painfully slowly. A few men on the peripheries of both battalions were fleeing, small as ants.

The fighting had gone on for perhaps half an hour, Howard still slowly pressing Oxford's men back, when it happened. The beast below was dealt a death blow, somewhere along the ever-widening wound. Richard could feel it like the heart missing a beat, then a rise in the ocean roar of noise, men screaming, running out of formation. Richard spurred Surrey over to Rob. "Get a runner down there. Find out what happened."

But a messenger was already scrambling up the hill, and Richard knew. "Howard's dead, sir."

A great wave of sorrow. For Howard, for the hope of a short, clean battle.

Richard could gauge the temper of the men behind him, a growing restlessness, an urge for revenge that he needed to harness. The momentary confusion, then the renewed passion, borne of grief and rage over a leader's death. Put rage to use before it turned to sorrow.

Time to move the center. Time to take his thousands of men down to Tudor's thousands. He knew what kind of battle that would be, the scope of that destruction. A battle like England had not seen. The best blood of England soaking these hills.

Well, what was he going to do? Wait for Tudor to come up the hill and shake hands with him? Run? Throw himself on poor Meg's mercy once again? Edward ran and came back to win. It was possible.

No. No exile, no gathering of new armies and pleading his cause. He had never had faith in his power of persuasion, only in what he could do himself.

*God grant me light.*

Well. Now he saw it, it was simple.

This one was all his. Not a thing you asked anyone else to do for you. Jesus' bloody wounds.

Afraid now? Oh, yes. Fear crawling on his skin like a thousand ants, his heart like a butterfly trapped in his chest, guts sliding like eels. His body a veritable Noah's ark of fear. Didn't know he could be so afraid. Or care so much about living. All the sorrow and tears, all the dread of what lay ahead, he still wanted to die old, in his bed. *Don't think about that. Don't think.*

He dismounted, thrust Surrey's reins at Roger and took Francis aside. Only the glance between them acknowledged the night before—and that it had passed. "In a moment, I am going to redirect this battle. You will not participate in what follows." Francis started to say something, then changed his mind, his rebellion showing only in the tense rope of muscle along his jaw.

"Neither you, nor the Earl of Lincoln."

Francis nodded.

*If I die, get Lincoln out of here.* That did not have to be said. Francis would know.

*And if I die, friend, it pleases me to hope that you will live.*

Richard heard his voice calm and steady, *must be someone else talking,* explaining what he was going to do. He saw Francis shaking his head, Roger stunned, his face drop-jawed, like a flounder. *Don't speak, Francis. Spare me the tender crushing weight of your love. For now. Afterward, we will fill our cups and make stories of this. Tell how with one bold effort we saved England.*

Wasn't that what men had always told themselves, in order to bear the unbearable? Say it was for God and England.

Richard laughed. Francis slid him a quick look, alarm in his eyes, then fading into relief, God knew at what.

"Bring me the crown, Roger." The narrow battle crown that fixed to the helmet.

*If we are to make a story of this, let us a make it a good one. All our lives are anyway, a story within a story.*

Roger's eyes lit, and his boy's body expanded, his king now behaving as one ought, but Francis was appalled.

"Richard, for God's sake, if you must do this, don't wear the crown. You'll be obvious a mile away."

Another time, he would have attempted some battle speech to raise confidence and rouse the blood, but these men would not be deceived by such words. He looked at them all for a moment, wondering what thoughts lay behind their eyes, then said what was the only battle cry this fight could have. "I will live or die King of England."

*We all move toward death. It is only the sun in a white August sky.*

The meadows were brilliant green. A stand of elm and ash edged the skyline above where Henry Tudor and a small body of knights clustered at a vantage point apart from the main army. *The easiest thing in the world. Just kill one man. One man, and it would all be over.*

Richard mounted, the best of his men beside him. He breathed in deeply, exhaled, and was aware of the confinement of the helmet, the warmth and closeness of his own breath. He lifted his hand. Touched spurs to White Surrey's flanks, a forward leap, the chilling cry along the lines, pounding hooves carrying him down the hill. The charge happened in dream-time, at once quicker than the blink of an eye and infinitely slow. Fear transformed into passion. The rest would take care of itself.

Richard's first thrust took Tudor's standard bearer, banner of the red dragon falling into the press of men. He thought he saw Francis from the corner of his eye, doubled over and clinging to the horse's neck. Curse him. Rob's big roan ran loose, wild-eyed in riderless terror, girth cut partway through, saddle hanging upside down. There was only one man now between him and Henry Tudor, the huge John Cheney, and then White Surrey screamed and pitched to his knees.

Richard kicked his feet from the stirrups and half jumped, half fell to the ground. A great horse, he'd never find another like him. A hand reached out. He took it and pulled to his feet, dropped his shield and took the sword two-handed.

An axe came down on his left. He felt the pressure of the armor bruise his arm even before the bite of the blade. *Should have missed that, lad. Not the boy you used to be. Thirty isn't nineteen. Thirty-two. Tell the truth. Even now. Tell the truth and watch your work. Don't think. Thinking will kill you.* He threw his whole body into the swing of the sword. The blade went in, went through.

A blow from behind. Oh, God, cut somewhere, back's on fire. Blood down his spine, eyes blinded with sweat. Richard blinked. Bind the wound and wipe the sweat, but he had no time. No time and no strength. His legs were falling under him.

*H*e dreamed of home and cool air fragrant with the sea. Opened his eyes and saw through narrow windows a white hot sky. He must have slept a long time, for he had the heaviness in his limbs and eyelids that came with oversleeping. What had he been doing that he should wake looking at the sky? *Lazy the man who sleeps at midday.* But the sweetness of the dream lingered with him, and he was in no haste to rouse faster than his body seemed inclined to do. He tried to reach for Anne, but his arm was too heavy and he gave it up.

The sun was very hot. He blinked his eyes to clear the sweat, which was running like blood, and tried to change positions to make himself more comfortable, but couldn't remember how to do it. A dull ache banded his back below his shoulder blades and his temples throbbed. Something unpleasant was waiting to be done. He closed his eyes and slept again.

When he next woke he remembered where he was. What had seemed like hours could only have been an instant. He was afraid for a moment, trying to understand what he should do. John Howard, John Kendall dead. Rob down, too. Where was Francis? *My friends. I can't get up. Can't help you.* Then the fear left. Nothing left to do. *We are finished. Didn't reach Tudor. Tried. Close, but it's over.* His body felt light and hollow. Not sweat, but blood running out the joints of his armor; he was melting into the earth.

His senses were clear and sharp, almost overwhelming. Bright patches of blue shone through the slit of his visor. He closed his eyes and the slit remained, but it had turned a pulsing red. His ears were filled with the sounds of shouting men and galloping horses, a great roar like being under a waterfall. There was no pain. Thank God. Not so terrible to die. He sighed and seemed to float on the earth.

Voices drew near. A shadow crossed his vision and hand snapped open the visor.

"Is it him?" A voice from his right.

"Can't tell. Never looked into his eyes before." A Welsh voice, lilting and amused.

"Well, blast it, find out!"

More fumbling with the helmet. *Easy, man, easy.*

The helmet slid off. Richard's head dropped back down; pain came in rolling waves from the base of his skull to his temples. Air, warm and gentle, touched his cheek. Richard blinked, his eyelids sticky and heavy. A circle of men stood around him. He wished they would leave. He wanted to watch the sky, see the leaves move on the tree at the edge of his vision, feel the air on his face.

"Well?" The first voice, impatient.

"Come see for yourself."

A face bent over him, then quickly back. "Yes, that's him." A silence. "Finish him. What's stopping you?"

A leg crossed his chest and a man stood straddling him. *Don't. Please.* Something he had never done, break a man's face. *Anne would cry. Poor Teasel.* Slowly the knight raised his arms, both hands grasping the hilt of the sword, the blade pointing downward. Leaves flickered above the man's shoulder, sun flashing bright on the sword. *Let me look a little longer.* But he had not strength to stay the hand, or voice to give to words. Nor wish, either. Would not beg, if he could. Let it fall, then. The dream was over, or just begun.

The sword descended, its point centered between his eyes, over the bridge of his nose. Richard saw the man's face and their eyes held. The blade moved a fraction off center before it struck. Light flooded his eyes, a fiery sphere of pain spun into starbursts of dazzling lights, red and blue and gold, all the gorgeous colors of the universe.

# Afterwards

London
October 1485.

Octor Hobbes took a last look around the room. The east wall showed two large rectangles of pale color where the portraits of Richard and Edward had hung; he didn't know what had become of them. The windows with their panes of blue, gold, and scarlet stood open, and he moved into the sun. Every year winter entered his bones a little earlier, and every spring drove it out later. It was time he left London.

"I hate it that you must leave," Bess said, her face drawn and tired. "I am losing everyone I have loved."

"I know. But it is not unexpected, my dear, that Henry should rid himself of his predecessor's household. Your husband is only following in the steps of many before him."

"Don't call him my husband. We are not yet wed."

"Forgive me, Bess. I know you do not welcome this marriage."

"I will survive it, I am sure. He doesn't seem a cruel man, just so . . . so *cold*. But perhaps that is a blessing. He will leave me to myself. Do I shock you, doctor?"

"Hardly, child. You are not the first maid married against her will who wishes her husband to have a weak appetite."

A bee lighted on Bess's sleeve. She didn't notice until Hobbes called her attention to it. "Come over to the window. Move slowly."

"Get it off me! Kill it!"

Hobbes was surprised at her passion. "Easy, child. A bee in October, I doubt he has the vigor to sting." He led her to the window. "Here. That's it. We will just let him go free." He flicked the insect off her sleeve onto the sill, where it stayed, sluggish, until he brushed it gently into the autumn air.

"Why did you do that? The summer's over. The thing has no life left." Bess looked both hurt and angry, a child bewildered by an adult's strange actions.

"Why, Bess, how unlike you to begrudge any creature its life."

She started to cry. "How can you care about a stupid bee, when everyone is dead?"

Hardly everyone. But of what use was that truth just now? "Oh, daughter." Hobbes' heart ached for her, for Richard, for all the men he would never see again. He put his arm around her. "Let him die in the sun, child. Let him die in the sun."

## Acknowledgments

The family of Virginia (Ginny) Cross is profoundly grateful to the following people, without whom our mother's manuscript never would have found its way to final form.

Deborah Robson, for her relentless dedication to making sure the finished novel lived up to Ginny's vision. Deb did the work normally done by countless others, taking files, notebooks, and author's notes and turning them into a completed manuscript. We are deeply grateful for her labor of love, knowledge of the publishing industry, and dedication to the smallest details.

Heidi Yoder for creating the illustration that graces the cover and appears as the frontispiece. Stephanie Barr for the cover design and maps. Meg Weglarz for her proofreading and general enthusiasm for the project.

This book was helped along by Ginny's many friends and writing group members who read countless drafts, encouraged her to complete the book, and supported her vision that the book could not be shortened, as publishing agents requested. We especially wish to thank everyone who took a chance and supported the first print run for this book. And finally, you dear reader, we thank you for sharing this book with others who might find delight in its pages.

—*Beth Rosen and Jeni Cross*

# About the Author

Virginia Cross was a Colorado native, raised on cattle ranches in the foothills of the Rocky Mountains. Being an exceptionally bright child, she advanced two grades ahead of her peers by the time she reached fourth grade. Even then, she was easily bored and preferred to be experiencing the world on one of her beloved horses. She graduated from the University of Wyoming with a bachelor's degree in English and later earned a master's degree in human development and a doctorate in counseling psychology. She spent her adult life in Fort Collins, Colorado, where she raised her two daughters as a single parent. Her home was always occupied by a cat or two and many plants. In addition to writing, she found fulfillment and joy in other creative outlets from designing doll clothes to playing the piano and gardening. She was an avid reader and student of medieval English history. She held a lifelong fascination with Richard III, convinced that history had gotten him wrong.

Lightning Source UK Ltd.
Milton Keynes UK
UKHW04f2302170918
329055UK00001B/287/P